THE LAST BATTLESHIP 3

GATES TO HELL

JOSHUA T. CALVERT

D1715739

PROLOGUE

"Jump successful," Chief Petty Officer Fang reported from power control. The young NCO was surrounded by several displays at the center of the semicircle formed by the bridge crew arrayed in front of Captain Anchalla Kruznik. "Power matrices at twenty percent. Pattern cells depleted, recharging. Containment chamber integrity at one hundred percent."

"Very good. So, can we make it back with our antimatter supply?" Anchalla asked.

"I think so, sir. But, as expected, this system will be the last, I'm afraid."

"Hmm."

Anchalla leaned back in his command chair and looked at the system through the large panoramic window after the massive beam shields had slid open like a mighty portal. To the right loomed a partial silhouette of the local gas giant. Nearby was the gravitational conjunction zone that had functioned as their exit from hyperspace. Ahead lay only the twinkle of stars in infinite space. One shone a little brighter, and a few colorful specks were just visible. He gave the order for a complete system scan and acceleration away from the jump point.

The TFS *Vasco da Gama* was one of the oldest research vessels in the Terran Fleet, a one-hundred-meter-long cylinder with water tanks attached to it like cartridges in a six-shooter's cylinder. Only a negligible fraction of the stored water was used for the ship's life support, including drinking water. Instead, it primarily served as propellant for the ship's extended prospecting voyages. Inside the thicker rear third of the ship was the retrofitted Valkyrie II anti-matter reactor with its impressive array of magnetic coils, and behind it the propulsion nacelle. Around the long hull, surmounted by the bridge, which resembled a cyclops' eye, was a mighty 80-meter-radius ring that contained the quarters and laboratories of the thirty-one science officers and the forty-four crew members who ensured the researchers could get from system to system and do their work. As with most prospector ships, their families traveled with the crew. Some voyages lasted several years, which was highly unusual for Fleet ships. The *Vasco da Gama*, therefore, contained several unique features: childcare facilities, noisy mess halls, sports programs, and frequent movie nights.

Anchalla had had to listen to a lot of jokes from his comrades on Eden before starting the trip: "bus driver," "nanny," and "field trip teacher" were just some of the monikers they had jokingly hung around his neck. He didn't mind. The Fleet was a rather tedious place for a commanding officer. Duties typically consisted of endless underpaid patrols along the trade routes to hunt down pirates or maintain order at the jump points. The Federation forces were plagued by what had always plagued the military in peacetime: inactivity, lack of recognition among the civilian population, constantly shrinking budgets, and aging hardware. The second expansion phase was over. The first fringe worlds were now core worlds, and everything was subordinated to hyper-capitalism. All this made the Federation rich. Two centuries of peace were enough to drive the transformation of the defense fleet into a research fleet. Anchalla knew this, which was why he was here. He was a man who preferred to be the first to show up at the party so he could choose the dance music. Expeditionary ventures were the future for skippers like him, not endless maneuvers and patrols.

If heading for the stars and exploring the Federation's frontiers meant flying families through space instead of soldiers, then he was happy to hear his comrades deride his voyage as a field trip knowing they were probably jealous that he had an exciting job.

Well, at least in theory. The last thirty systems they had approached in the past forty-one months had all been disappointing, populated only by gas giants and either frozen or ultra-hot planets that could not even serve as industrial outposts because their jump points were so small that the big freighters could not rip open a sufficiently large terminus. Anchalla had long since said goodbye to his actual dream of finally discovering intelligent life. Simple microbes and sometimes more complex fungal structures had been collected and analyzed in endless series, but this was not something new. The universe seemed to be not actually *dead*, but rather *stupid*.

"Initial scans show the jump point is stable. The *Sao*

Vicente is just coming out of the event horizon," Lieutenant Karagh reported from the sensor station. "She is undamaged."

"Very good."

The *Sao Vicente* and her sister ship *Garibaldi* were the two corvettes that served as escorts for the *Vasco da Gama* since they had joined the voyage as replacements a year ago. They were slender arrows forty meters in length with no habitat ring and thus no gravity. That made daily life on board much more unpleasant than on Anchalla's ship. He had very quickly become accustomed to sports in normal gravity, as well as sleeping, playing cards, and showering in it. Being a teacher on a field trip had its advantages.

He called to his first officer, "Peter, go check on our civilian crew. I want to know if everyone's come through hyper in good shape."

"Already on the way."

"And prepare them for the fact that we'll have to sterilize the habitat. It may take up to twelve hours before we can fire it up again."

"Sure."

His XO floated out of the bridge. They had already waited two days longer than planned to perform the habitat's monthly basic cleaning so as not to delay the schedule any further after the unforeseen repairs they had to make in the last system. With over one hundred breathing people on board, the ever-present humidity made mold and microbial infestations a serious problem. Life support fought it, but the microscopic beasts always found a home somewhere, so once every four weeks every square nanometer was disinfected. In a few generations, this could cost them dearly.

Longer non-exposure to germs would cause passenger immune systems to degenerate. He was counting on the geneticists to get a handle on it. After all, they were able to grow people red hair, new kidneys, and six-fingered hands.

"Very well. Karagh, what do you have for us?" he asked his sensor specialist after a half an hour, more bored than interested.

"Two gas giants, hydrogen-helium—the outermost planets in the system. The last one could be an ice giant, five times Earth's mass. The penultimate one, the one we dropped out of the jump point next to, has two Jupiter masses and a fair percentage of methane in its outer atmosphere. There's a sterile rocky planet this side of the asteroid belt and beyond it, a single ice planet, just outside the habitable zone. The innermost planet is also terrestrial, carbon dioxide atmosphere, half Earth mass."

"The ice planet. What else do you have there?"

"Eighty percent Earth mass, large semi-major axis of 1.76 astronomical units, sidereal orbital period of 843 standard days, synodic orbital period of 911 standard days. Its mean orbital velocity is 28.8 kilometers per second. Gravitational acceleration of 6.99 meters per second squared. All sounds promising if it wasn't for the frozen oceans. The ice sheet is probably dozens of kilometers thick, and the atmosphere is very thin and rich in sulfur dioxide."

"Volcanic activity?" Anchalla wondered. "Then I'm sure our smock wearers will want to go fishing again."

The bridge crew chuckled.

"Quite possibly. And it has two very small moons that... hmm."

"What is it?"

"I'm picking up electromagnetic radiation from the satellites," Karagh said thoughtfully.

"Just now?"

"No, it was there before, but due to our current position, some of the asteroids in the ring interfered with it. The signals are getting clearer now."

"Signals?"

"The radiation indicates high energy profiles that don't match a rocky body."

"Comets, perhaps?" Anchalla felt stupid as he asked.

"No. They are in a captured orbit around the planet."

"Then what? Any evidence of technology on the surface?"

"No, just ice, except for a large hole near the equator where there are some lights. That could be a subcrustal volcano erupting. The only signals are coming from the satellites."

"Don't tell me we've run into aliens. If we allow ourselves another premature victory like we did at Tracitus V, which turned out to be radiation anomalies, we'll have to hide our faces in shame," Anchalla grumbled. A slight flutter stirred in his stomach, but he refused to let it grow to a real itch of curiosity... yet.

"I... I have to wait for some more scans."

Anchalla turned to his navigation officer, "Scott, bring us in closer, full speed."

"That means two Gs for several hours," the junior lieutenant objected. "The civilians..."

"... will be able to take it. And cleaning the habitat ring can wait until later. Sound the acceleration alert. Have everyone get to their gel beds. This one could be important."

"Roger that."

Shortly thereafter, an ascending alarm tone resounded through the corridors and quarters. Anything that could possibly come loose during the jump was strapped down or stowed, and children were placed on their acceleration couches in the habitat ring and sedated.

Anchalla waited impatiently as messages from the individual sections gradually appeared on his command display confirming they could finally get underway. The *Sao Vicente* stayed behind at the jump point as instructed, while the *Garibaldi* took up position at the *Vasco da Gama*'s side with weapon systems activated as prescribed by the protocols for a possible first contact.

After what felt like an eternity, his ship's propulsion nacelle finally flared up, accelerating her at a gentle two Gs. It wasn't much, but enough over an extended period to bring her to an appreciable fraction of the speed of light and bring her rapidly to her targets of investigation.

Tension reigned on the bridge for the ensuing twelve hours. Anchalla did not need to read the minds of his crew to know what was going on inside them. Evidence was mounting that the two moons were using technology that tapped artificial energy sources. This could only mean that they were dealing with some form of intelligence. No one wanted to say it, lest others regard them as overzealous or even unprofessional, but they were all thinking it: *First contact!*

When they passed the asteroid belt, they debated

whether the power could be the relic of some long-dead alien culture, or a machine intelligence, which frightened them all. The possibility of encountering intelligences that turned out to be non-organic, either as remnants of a vanished organic civilization or as its weapon, was a frequently debated topic in the Federation. The results of these discussions were always that the latter case would represent a disaster, since machine beings would probably evolve much faster and weren't constrained by the same physical and mental limits imposed on human space travel by factors like radiation and acceleration forces. He envied the civilians in the habitat ring who were strapped on their couches and killing time with VR programs without worrying about any of the things that were bothering the crew.

Discussion died as they left the last asteroids behind, and Lieutenant Karagh gave a shrill shout: "Radar contacts!"

"Lidar sweep!" Anchalla's order was as automatic as it was unnecessary.

"Confirmed. Three bogeys approaching from the larger of the satellites."

"On screen!"

The twinkling stars and the bluish glow of the small, blue dot they were heading for were superimposed on a holodisplay showing three exhaust flares. The bow tele-scopes zoomed in several magnification factors and showed three chunky drops of dark material approaching them at a rather gentle 2.5 Gs.

"They're ships," he noted. "No doubt about it. This is a first contact, ladies and gentlemen!"

Cheers erupted on the bridge, though it resonated with

a detectable undertone of fear. They were now flying blind into the unknown, into a situation that the Federation's brightest minds had imagined for centuries without ever reaching any clear conclusions about what to expect from such an event. But the Fleet wouldn't be the Fleet if it didn't have a protocol for such situations.

"All right, open a channel, radio only, no directional beam!" he said, breaking through the excited chatter on the bridge.

"Channel open," Karagh replied.

"This is Captain Anchalla Kruznik of the Terran Federation Ship *Vasco da Gama*. We send peaceful greetings on behalf of the Federation and its worlds as emissaries of all human civilization," Anchalla announced in a clear baritone. He felt like he was in a science fiction VR. The situation was so surreal that he wanted to bite his lip just to make sure he wasn't dreaming.

His address was followed by tense silence as the message crossed the one and a half light minute distance to the alien ships. The regular *blip* of the radar and the hiss of the lidar scan filled the silence. Only the crinkling foil sounds of computers, all too loud and intrusive, disturbed the pregnant anticipation.

After three minutes, Lieutenant Karagh visibly tensed.

"What's going on, Lieutenant?"

"I'm picking up something from the ships, but it's very strange."

"Why?"

"The frequency band is one I would expect but the audio equivalent doesn't sound like a response on waves we can hear."

"Turn it up."

A moment later, clicking sounds filled the bridge as if Edward Scissorhands was playing the piano.

"Interference?" he asked.

"Possible. The cosmic background radiation here is higher than expected, but not high enough to interfere with the radio."

"Turn the ship around, initiate braking maneuvers. I don't want our flight path to be interpreted as an attack. But take it easy, please."

"Roger that."

The *Vasco da Gama* rotated along its transverse axis, like a giant cigar in the middle of a ring, until the massive drive nacelle pointed "forward" and began spewing blue plasma again. Gravity instantly returned to the ship and pressed them into their gimbaled seats.

"Bogeys are turning and braking as well."

Okay, they use space technology similar to ours, Anchalla thought. *Acceleration, drift, brake. Their speed shows they're not prone to breakneck maneuvers. Could they be like us?*

Images of every alien face he'd ever seen in VRs rattled through his mind, until he squeezed his eyes shut and shook his head to dispel them.

"I don't think we're getting anywhere with this. Send the first five of the prepared mathematical equations," he ordered.

The Fleet science corps had prepared some simple mathematical equations for first contact that could be represented pictorially and without numbers, since aliens probably knew nothing about human character sets. But quantities could easily be expressed in general symbols like dashes and combined with a few arithmetic symbols that could be derived from the quantities when the result was provided. Again, it was a matter of waiting.

An answer came after two minutes.

"They sent back the equations with supplements," Karagh noted.

"What kind of supplements?"

"Um, that's not so easy to say. I'll play it for you."

On the holoscreen, the first equation appeared: $I + I = II$, followed by a short whistle, a bass note, the same short whistle again, then a click and a long-pitched whistle.

"Are you streaming this to the labs in the ring yet?" Anchalla asked and gave an impatient wave when Karagh shook his head. "Tell them to get right on it! What could that be? The aural equivalent of our equation?"

"Maybe they don't have a visual typeface, just sound sequences," Scott suggested. "But how are we supposed to answer in sound sequences?"

"Let our smock wearers worry about that. Karagh, continue transmitting the images. Again, the first five from the first contact file."

The following hours were much more monotonous than expected. They slowed down, just as the alien ships did, until they hovered in the vacuum of space twenty kilometers from each other. Captain Sartosa of the *Garibaldi* proved to be a rather nervous fellow, remarking several times that he would only deactivate his weapon systems under logged protest, but he dutifully kept his feet still. The scientists in the labs at the back of the ring seemed to spend forever conferring and endlessly analyzing the transmissions sent by the aliens, who were quickly dubbed "Clicks" by the crew because of the strange clicking signals they constantly emitted. Then they suddenly came up with an idea and tried audio-based messages as well. The response was mostly the same, which they interpreted as "I don't know what this is supposed to be." They sent geometric forms, and the aliens responded with supplemental symbols that the researchers argued over for hours. Some said these were clever additions to the complexity of the shape, others that it only meant they had not understood, while still others proposed the aliens were trying to tell them something completely different and that they were merely trapped in their own human interpretation framework.

Anchalla was a diplomaed social scientist. It had earned him a lot of ridicule in the Fleet, but at least he knew what symbolic interactionism was. A symbol could mean alpha to him, and omega to a civilization with a completely different reference system. Without any common intersection, misunderstandings were bound to occur. The only thing to do was exercise patience and forbearance and continually remind oneself that no interpretation could stand unchallenged. Even the transmission of an image, like that of an axe, could start a war, even among humans. Did the message senders intend the axe as a tool for cutting down trees and fighting fires or for splitting skulls? Something as simple as a nail could be understood as a symbol for connecting two unrelated things or as the instrument of chastisement in a crucifixion or as the point of an arrow. The list was long, and even in earthly civilization the symbol did not have a clear meaning without context. Therefore, he understood why first contact was turning out to be much more protracted and boring than most of his crew members had probably imagined. It was entirely human for a spectacle to become a part of a ship's daily routine surprisingly fast. All one could do was wait.

At twenty hours after the first exchange of messages, the intercom in his cabin rang and jolted him out of a restless half-sleep.

"What?" he croaked in a thick voice once his finger found the intercom button above his bunk.

"Doctor Octavius and his team have an idea they'd like to discuss with you," he heard Scott say.

"I'm on my way." Anchalla withdrew his finger, ran it through his hair with a sigh, and then tidied himself before leaving his cabin and shuffling down the central corridor to the bridge. There, Scott and Karagh were already waiting at their seats.

"Anything new?"

"No, Captain. Nothing significant. Doc thinks they're machine creatures."

"I see. Why?"

"Because their answers suggest binary perception, and they haven't responded to the emotion queries—music, abstract and impressionist imagery, and so on. Math, on the other hand, seems to be what they enjoy dealing with."

"Well, if that's not jumping the gun..." Anchalla dropped into his seat and turned on his armrest display. With two quick gestures, he opened a link to the conference room. The habitat ring was still stationary and undergoing disinfection while the scientists worked.

"Ah, Captain!" Doctor Octavius's mass of gray hair, correspondingly small face, and bulbous nose appeared on the tiny display in front of his hand. "We have come up with an idea that could enable direct communication after all."

"I heard. So, what do you have in mind?"

"We'd like to use the habitat ring as a light organ."

"Uh... *excuse me?*"

"Astraglossa."

"Again, I beg your pardon?"

"The plan is this," the physicist explained with childlike enthusiasm, "the ring has sixty high-powered spotlights on flexible arms. They were designed to point forward, to allow for maintenance work."

Anchalla waved impatiently. "I'm aware of that."

"If we set a reference point—for example, at one of the spotlights—which we mark with a color or by blinking a primary sequence of signals, we can then create complex sequences of long and short pulses by rotating the ring. This is the simplest form of mathematical communication. We already know that they know math over there and they seem to be patient, too. So, we'll try it with Astraglossa. If that works, we can go one level higher, to Lincos. That's a mathematical language with more complex logical symbols that we can use to lay a broader foundation for communication. We'll have the solar foil we use for solar observations deployed and spread between the ring to act as a sensitive pickup mirror for the answers."

"That should be feasible. What if the Clicks don't have any spotlights to respond with?"

"We'll find out soon enough. But with the help of light signals, we can work up a simple Morse code. At worst, the absence of a light response would confirm what some of us already suspect: that our cosmic friends out here may not be visual beings at all, that is, they have no eyes, and..."

"I get that, Doc. I'm putting you in charge of rotation control. But don't forget to strap in first. And you'd best get the kids down to the crew mess. All of you might get sick if gravity is constantly changing direction," he warned, and the physicist nodded eagerly.

"Thank you, Captain. We'll get right on it."

Anchalla disconnected and waited. The aliens' three clunky teardrop ships were still twenty kilometers in front of them in a simple triangular formation, large black shadows not quite as dark as the universe beyond. In the background was the faint blue glow of the ice planet, and he imagined he could see two glittering dots in front of its silhouette though he knew it was impossible to make out the supposed space stations without zooming in.

"I wonder what they're doing there?" Chief Petty Officer Fang said to no one in particular.

"On the planet?" Scott shrugged. "I guess they're research stations."

"Then those are research ships?"

"Maybe. Or the local navy to protect the scientists on site."

"Nah," Fang said, shaking his head. "I still think they're robots. If they weren't, they would have agreed to a picture link by now."

"This isn't *Star Trek*," Scott countered. "Aliens aren't just people with wrinkled foreheads or big ears."

"No? What are they then?" Fang wanted to know.

"We'll figure that out when smarter people than you have thought about it." Anchalla interrupted the discussion by pointing to the power node specialist and asking. "How's the energy redistribution?"

"It's about to peak. The ring will need sixty percent of the power available for about forty seconds to deploy the solar foil inward and bring the nanoassemblers up to full power. Unless we take more time, which would only require a fraction of that."

"No, I want to keep it that way."

Two minutes later, everything was ready. The habitat ring's superconductor systems were filled to bursting with energy and spreading the pitch-black foil that reflected no light whatsoever before reversing polarity. All the lights flickered several times in succession as part of a systems test. Then the ring began to spin.

"Oh shit!" Lieutenant Kharag cursed.

"What is it?" Anchalla asked, alarmed by his sensor specialist's sudden change in tone.

"Significant power surge in the bogeys!" Kharag almost choked.

"They're transmitting on all frequencies!" Scott shouted from his station on the left as he frantically input instructions.

A staccato of eerie clicking filled the bridge, and then several objects that resembled fireflies detached themselves from the dark, toroidal alien ships. They quickly increased in size and grew into tiny suns before a hailstorm of much smaller dots rained upon them. Two explosions lit the darkness of vacuum, then another, and three more in quick succession. The defensive fire from the *Garibaldi*'s short-range defenses wasn't enough, despite Captain Sartosa's speed. Four torpedoes slammed into the habitat ring, ripping out entire pieces. One spoke was hit and disintegrated in a shower of charged particles and glowing debris. Some of the wreckage hit the water tanks on the *Vasco da Gama*'s hull, sending the contents shooting away in fountains of ice crystals. The solar foil dissolved in a tornado of fine shrapnel invisible to the human eye, as if the sinfully expensive material had never existed.

Paralyzed, Anchalla watched the habitat ring break up, taking the fifty-eight souls inside with it. Their bodies, torn into space, flailed through the void in brief agony. Then their limbs stiffened as they froze.

The *Garibaldi* fired a volley of its own torpedoes followed by sustained fire from its two Gauss cannons, but it was destroyed shortly thereafter, perishing in a short-lived white flash when one of the antimatter coils was hit and the entire antimatter supply collided with the nearest molecules, obliterating everything around it... including the TFS *Vasco da Gama* and its crew.

1

Fidel Soares let the swaying motion of the donkey cart lull him into a fitful half-sleep that summoned more memories than dreams. The last three days had been hectic as Fleet Headquarters burst with activity. The tens of thousands of employees manning the Federation's most important military facility flowed ceaselessly through the countless corridors and caverns under the peaks of the Himalayas like termites in a broken mound.

Reports from all over the globe converged here, and they painted a rather depressing picture. The Clicks had swept all orbital resistance aside after the human defenders had exhausted their last reserves battling the sinister aliens that had emerged from the hyperspace gate to Sol. The fact that *Artemis* and *Unity* halos had survived was probably due to Fleet Admiral von Solheim. He had ordered defenders to use their last ammunition reserves to obliterate the shattered remnants of the *Novigrad* halo that had been descending toward Earth for 36 hours before they could become a serious threat. By the time the Clicks passed

Luna, there was little to oppose them except the sixty shot-up survivors of Strike Group 12 that the admiral had ordered into the outer system. It had been decided that what could still fly should not be sacrificed in a futile attempt to protect something that could no longer be protected.

Terra was lost. Every member of the Fleet and every human with access to a news feed were painfully aware of that. The last civilian ships to jump out of the system via S1 were truly fortunate. When the Clicks had arrived in orbit, every analyst at Headquarters and in the media had expected them to bomb the orbital defense platforms next, then the zero-G industrial facilities followed by Luna.

But they didn't.

The final strategy executed by von Solheim had been a highly controversial one: no resistance. Anger over this had burned so brightly in the corridors under the Himalayas that Fidel had imagined dark smoke billowing from the ventilation shafts in the ice above them, giving away their position. But either the fleet admiral knew something they didn't at Headquarters, or he could have taken up a career as a professional gambler.

That didn't mean that the aliens had been passive, on the contrary. First, they had blasted the four equatorial orbital elevators, then destroyed the one that connected the ground-based and orbital sections of the Fleet Headquarters. This included the communications panels at both bases, making them effectively unable to talk to each other. Since then, Earth had been cut off from orbit because radio or laser signals were completely useless. The Clicks' massive jamming barrage overwhelmed transmissions with white noise. In addition, they had dumped vast amounts of microcellulose into the upper atmosphere, creating a hazy glow. It would take days, if not weeks, for the ultra-light particles to settle to the ground.

But they didn't have that much time. Earth was dependent on supplies from the hydroponic farms on Ganymede and Europa. Although it produced enough protein mass for the planet's synthesizers, the moons located at the edge of the inner system were a vital source. With their huge orbital mirrors, they could produce the masses of vitamins and minerals pressed from natural sources needed to enrich the food packs on Terra with vital nutrients. Supplies had not reached Earth for days. It was not something that would kill people in the short term, but the population did not have weeks, let alone months, before famine set in—and the dying would begin.

But there was a reason why Fidel Soares, clad in a nanonic spacesuit overlaid with wool rags against the cold, was driving the rumbling donkey cart over the bumpy gravel roads the Sherpas normally used. He knew the reason as he struggled through the heavy snow drifts as he tried to make out the pale line that distinguished Mount Everest from the night sky, its moon and stars obscured by the microcellulose fog.

There was a chance—a slim one, but a chance, nonetheless. The fact that it rested entirely on his narrow shoulders did not worry him. He knew why he, a test pilot for atmospheric hunters, had been chosen for this mission. He knew what was coming and what was at stake, but he did not let that plunge him into irrational thought. He knew he could succeed, so he remained calm and focused on the job ahead while blocking out the desperate need that drove him.

A day ago, his superiors tried to shoot an improvised sled along one of the main elevator cables to establish contact with the sky fortress, and with Solheim. But the Clicks had immediately vaporized the two-meter-long device with a laser. In the process, they had nearly severed the cable, which would have been an absolute disaster. If that happened, the entire elevator would shoot into space and no force in the universe would be able to stop it. They were lucky that the aliens had not aimed for maximum destruction, which they could have easily achieved. They merely had to blast *Unity* or *Artemis* apart and watch the debris turn the Earth into a radioactive hell. Those who didn't die from the massive impacts would be driven back into the Stone Age. A very grim and very slow death would then ensue in the weeks and months afterward.

But just because the end of the world had been delayed for the moment was no reason to pop champagne corks. In fact, this unexpected development posed another problem: the enemy was not behaving as predicted, and that was bad news. In war, being able to predict the enemy's next moves was worth more than surprise.

The Clicks had made it clear that they were not here for fun. Their targeted bombardment of all ground-based communications facilities and the EMP bombs they detonated over planetary defense centers were ample proof of that. They had also blasted any ship that tried to reach orbit. The result was, in effect, a blockade. They remained strangely passive aside from the shuttles they sent into the Pacific and Antarctic oceans. Reconnaissance data was sketchy at best without satellite imagery, but analysts were certain that dozens of shuttles had disappeared into the ocean. Some remained submerged for hours at a time, others never reappeared at all. Fidel had no idea what that could mean—and it wasn't his job to worry about it—but many of his colleagues were only too eager to engage in conjuring fantastic scenarios: The Clicks wanted to enslave them and gradually ship them off to their industrial moons where they would be worked to death in some sort of gulag. The Clicks wanted to harvest humans as nutritious raw material for their own protein synthesizers yet keep the total number of humans stable and manage them like herds of cattle. The Clicks wanted to install a puppet human government and make them a vassal race in their empire. The Clicks had established a blockade until they could finally decode human language, then locate and abduct Earth's best scientists to exploit human know-how to upgrade their technology. The Clicks had added a toxin to the oceans that would slowly mutate humans once it mixed with the atmosphere.

The list of theories was long, but Fidel had not engaged in such speculation because he was busy preparing for his mission. The Admiral's Council at Fleet Headquarters had been very clear that their one chance was a slim one, but not impossible. Should he succeed and von Solheim agree, they could at least give it a try. Fidel looked forward to a challenge that would go down in the history books, just as any other test pilot would. Still, under the present circumstances, he would have been happy if they hadn't needed help from orbit and could have just pressed a red button.

An hour later, his cart reached the end of the trail. He

dismounted, shouldered a backpack containing eighteen oxygen dispensers, and began climbing the rest of the way. As he went, he was preoccupied by the fact that thousands of people had completed this very ascent hundreds of years ago, without an oxygen supply and without his completely insulated nanonic spacesuit. Just a glance at his heads-up display that measured oxygen content in the ambient air made him grimace at the thought. Then there was the bitter cold and icy wind. It wasn't exactly a stroll in the park, but it was not much more than a strenuous hike either. His intelligent suit kept his body temperature stable. He breathed recycled yet fresh air that, with his spare oxygen packs, would last for two days. His visor display precisely marked the route that would take him to his destination as quickly and safely as possible.

The orbital elevator ended—or began—in a hole fifty meters in diameter at the top of Mount Everest. The hole ran down to a station that housed a total of six elevators on the six cables. It had been quite busy in its heyday, transporting officers and adjutants to and from orbit. When Fidel reached the edge, however, he saw no one, and when he looked up, he could not see the tattered remnants of the elevator cars hanging from their cables somewhere along the 35,000 kilometers between his location and the sky fortress. There was only the hull, as thick as a man, wrapped in six arm-length cables. That something so fragile looking could hold such a massive space station at one end exceeded even Fidel's imagination as a trained aeronautical engineer.

He retrieved the magnetic hook gun with its coiled monofilament rope from his backpack and clipped it to his magnetized tool belt. He then activated his magnetized gloves. The ruined elevator cabins had used magnets to move up and down the cables, which was exactly what he was going to do now. It sounded crazy, even to him, a man who had flown through the stratosphere at fifteen times the speed of sound in tiny streamjets that some ambitious tinkerer had rigged up.

"Crazy times require crazy measures," he muttered inside his helmet. It was weird standing there in complete silence while the wind whistled around him and blowing snow pounded his body in the -30°C air, but if he hadn't turned off his acoustic receiver, the hostile sound of the gusting wind would have distracted him.

Fidel held his hands out in front of him and waited until his HUD signaled that his palms were magnetized, then he crouched and leaped. Eight meters was a long jump, even for him, so as he arced forward, he descended several meters before he reached the cable he was aiming for, and his magnetic gloves took firm hold. It was no thicker than a forearm, and he was able to get a good grip on it.

He allowed himself a minute to calm his breathing and almost turned on his helmet lights before remembering that was exactly what he shouldn't do. Carefully, he released one hand, drew his knees up to wrap his legs around the cable, then freed both hands. He swayed like a chimpanzee on a tree branch as he removed the backpack and carefully extracted the small boxes of programmed silicon that quickly self-assembled into a sled before his eyes. This product of the engineers' workshop looked like a slightly larger tube, a cone half a meter long and thirty centimeters in diameter. Zero-T energy storage units inside lay tightly next to the magnetic sleds and would hopefully provide enough juice for his crazy scheme. Their capacity was kept as low as possible to allow a maximum amount of space for the Carbin wool that would serve as shielding. Either it would be enough, or the admirals would see him again very soon—as a briefly flashing red dot before he hit the ground.

When he was done, he shouldered the backpack, grabbed the two tiny indentations on the cone—magnetic induction fields—and placed his feet on the even tinier catches on the bottom.

"Roccat ready," he spoke into his helmet. He knew no one could hear him, not on this mission. Still, he felt better maintaining as much normalcy as he could in such exceptional circumstances. Otherwise, he might have just turned around and walked away. "Launch in three, two, one..."

Fidel activated the sled and within three seconds he was accelerated to one hundred kilometers per hour. He felt like a fly about to be swept from a windshield, but he didn't slide off. He steadily ascended the lonely stalk of the space elevator into the hazy night. The firmament shimmered, unreal through the glitter of microcellulose that diffused moonlight from above, as if some ancient deity had poured milk over the sky. Below him, Mount Everest lay in complete darkness, except for a few red position lights at the edges. Since Terran Fleet Command had switched off all active signals to avoid betraying possible targets to the enemy, Fidel could almost imagine what the Himalayas had looked like before mankind had hollowed them out to house its most important planetary military installation—even if it was mostly for the unpopular training and bureaucratic sector.

After half an hour, he pierced the cellulose barrier

without any significant effect other than briefly thinking his visor was fogged up before he saw the stars again. The moon floated off to the right, shining between the elevator's stalk and the cable, which disappeared in the shimmer below. It continued above him until it was lost somewhere in the darkness. Proceeding in complete silence, with no light source but his passive systems, his ascent felt like a revelation. Fidel was one with his surroundings, literally merging with the darkness without any sense of resistance or heaviness.

Another half hour later, air resistance had ended and the sled accelerated to ten times its normal speed until it reached one thousand kilometers per hour. Fidel would not have noticed if his HUD had not informed him. The sky fortress was still over 35,000 kilometers away, somewhere in the darkness among the stars. He could not see it, neither with the naked eye nor with his visor's highest zoom level. The elevator cable seemed to disappear into nothingness. After twenty-four hours, he was halfway there, and at kilometer 19,800 he reached the remains of the elevator the Clicks had melted into a molten wreck. It looked like a shattered railroad car with only the floor remaining. Its deformed edges looked like melted plastic, and it appeared to be hanging loosely from the cable. It looked like a corpse's ribcage, colored red by the victims who had been inside when the lasers had wrought their brief but thorough destruction.

Fidel dismantled the sled and stowed the silicon packs in his backpack before climbing hand over hand over the wreckage with deliberate care to avoid falling. Since the sky fortress was in geostationary orbit and not freefall, gravity at this altitude was virtually the same as on the planet's surface. One wrong move meant a long descent and a quick end as a short-lived shooting star burning up in atmospheric friction. Since he was on the night side again, he at least had the advantage of working in the moonlight. The sunlight had been so glaring that he hadn't been able to make out his hand before his eyes and his darkened visor had hardly let any light through. If he had been equipped with an energy pack, he would have had access to sensors and active software.

Fidel patiently felt his way forward until he found a piece of jagged wreckage that could support him and slid a foot upward until he found purchase. He repeated the procedure with the next hand and the next foot. He blocked out any thought of the nearly 20,000 kilometers that stretched below him, where Terra lay beneath the pale, obscuring glimmer. He consciously ignored the fact that no rope secured him and that the cabin was not metallic, which rendered his magnetic gloves useless. Instead, his attention was dedicated solely to the next ten meters along the wreckage.

Just like a climbing wall, he assured himself in his mind, and continued to carefully choose each hold. It was an exhausting exercise and his suit had trouble adjusting its temperature quickly enough to prevent perspiration. But even that didn't faze him. Finally, after twenty minutes, he reached the top and sat on the magnetic track of the cabin's remains to reassemble the electric sled. As soon as he was done, he jammed himself back into position and activated it.

Fortunately, the engineers had remembered not to let

the improvised vehicle accelerate too fast after it was assembled the second time, so ten patience-testing minutes passed until he was again speeding along at one thousand kilometers per hour.

The sun came around the terminator line, first as a soft glow, then, within seconds, as a gigantic flood light that turned Fidel's surroundings into a glistening white expanse. Now he could see the blockading Click vessels. Although the distances above the planet were enormous, he only needed to turn his head away from the sun to see hundreds of white dots that, although they appeared tiny, were far too close to be stars. They were the alien ships that enveloped Terra like a blanket of pinpoints, vigilantly doing whatever they were doing.

Fidel wondered what was going on in the robots' minds. Until now, he had always thought of them as machines that thought like the old humanoid 'bots before they were outlawed and banned in the Federation, cold and algorithmic, lacking empathy, simulating reactions that would be perceived as empathy. He wondered if their programming wasn't more different than the Fleet believed. Fidel, at any rate, thought that cold logic would have dictated turning the planet of their human archenemies into a radioactive hell if given the opportunity. After all, that's exactly what the Fleet admirals had intended to do to the Clicks' world with Operation Iron Hammer, and they weren't robots. Perhaps empathy was no protection against committing atrocities or following cold military logic, and machines free of such biochemical ballast could keep a cooler head.

They would surely find out soon unless he succeeded in

his mission and the Admiralty was able to end the blockade, even if Fidel shivered as he thought about what that "solution" would look like in practical terms.

Twenty hours later, his supply display showed four and a half hours of oxygen after he had connected the last two packs. He could finally see the sky fortress as a tiny star at the end of the cable. If he thought of it as a continuation of the short stretch, he could just see in front of him.

"I think I can do this," he muttered into his helmet as the sled tapped into the last percent of its zero-T energy reserves. If the Clicks didn't blast him away, this suicide mission might actually succeed. What could he do after this ride?

Nothing, because he would not be returning to Earth for the foreseeable future. He was sure of that.

2

Nicholas lifted his eyes and stared at the face looking back at him from the bespeckled mirror. It was a face that should have looked young and toned but was instead wrinkled and sunken. The cheeks seemed to have fallen inward, and bags threatened to bulge under the eyes where the skin had taken on an unhealthy, dark tone. Even the short hair looked brittle and lackluster. The entire area between the nose and forehead betrayed a dull ache, as if something was pressing against it from within. Nicholas knew exactly what this pressure presaged, and it had to eventually find a release or it would destroy him. And yet there was no way to relieve it, no valve he could open. Since their jump, they had gone into normal shift work, which meant every crew member, including him, got eight hours of sleep—if he could find it.

He usually lay awake in his bunk, refusing to do what his body wanted to do—scream and howl and punch anything in his cabin that wasn't made of steel or composite. This denial had a very simple reason. If he gave way to the mixture of crushing grief and paralyzing impotence that the sight of his father's execution had caused in him, he would simply disintegrate like a bursting balloon. At least, that's how it felt. Laura's brutal murder had hit him hard and only the anxiety, stress, and tension of imminent battle had kept him from sinking into shock and grief. Seeing his battered father executed like a lamb on the slaughter block was simply too much. That he still functioned during his shifts at all was only because he knew Jason was still on Earth.

Voices in the dark corners of his mind tried to whisper that his brother could not possibly have survived. He refused to listen.

"I'm coming for you," he whispered to his reflection, seeing Jason's face in his imagination. "I promise."

Before he turned away, the imaginary countenance before him turned into the ugly, sunken grimace of Pyrgorates, his bloodless lips parted into a spiteful smile. Unbridled hatred rose within him.

"I'm coming for you," he repeated, this time snarling like a wolf. Pain flared up in his right hand. He looked down at his hand and the burst knuckles. Thin threads of blood formed small reliefs on his skin. He looked up again and noticed a crater of dense shards had formed in the center of the mirror. Bloody streaks filled the cracks in the safety glass.

His chronometer beeped, alerting him that his shift was about to begin. He cried inwardly and clenched his hands into fists before silently getting dressed. He disinfected and dried his wound, then stood motionless in front of the cabin door for five minutes. Once he was sure he could control his face, he stepped into the corridor and made his way to the bridge. The crew members he encountered along the way raised their joined thumb and forefinger to their berets in a Harbinger salute. He returned the courtesy but avoided looking at their faces. In the last few days, he had seen enough of what he himself felt—or repressed—in them. The pain they expressed could only worsen his and rob him of the last bit of self-control that kept him on his feet and on duty. Now more than ever, in their shock, the crew needed strong leadership to continue to function.

It wasn't over yet, after all. Not until they retrieved Jason and had taken care of the refugee fleet from Lagunia.

The mood on board since their jump brought them near S1's sun could be described as subdued at best, abysmally defeatist at worst. There was almost no talk in the corridors and stations. Elevator rides with other crew members were funereal, and at every shift change, the observation deck and both hangars were packed with crew members holding vigils.

The *Oberon*'s officers had printed huge banners with Konrad Bradley's likeness and hung them, and the entire crew accepted the image as an opportunity to mourn. Nicholas knew there would be talk because he hadn't shown up at any of the vigils yet, but he couldn't bring himself to do it. He knew he was expected to be there, and certainly many of the men and women on board were hoping to see him, the next-ranking Bradley on the *Oberon*, sharing their pain. Nicholas would have liked to give them what they were hoping for, a silver lining, the feeling that their entire world had not ended along with a captain —*admiral*—they had almost fanatically revered, and the hope that somehow they would be able to carry on in his name.

But he just couldn't do it. He felt like an over sensitive depth charge that would burst at the slightest prick. Just the thought of looking into a thousand or more faces reflecting his pain crushed him.

A similar graveyard atmosphere prevailed on the bridge. There was little of the usual hushed conversation between specialists at workstations on the various tiers. Instead, the noise of computer systems overlayed the latent hum of the engines that could be heard and felt in every corner of the *Oberon*. As expected, he encountered only Daussel and Meyer on this shift. They stood on the command deck at the far end of the bridge, where a holo-representation of the Sol system slowly rotated around the sun.

They didn't notice him until he stepped onto the pedestal and into the holo's reflective glow. They looked up and, as always, there was a brief flash of tension that they quickly masked. As always, he pretended not to notice and nodded at them with a neutral expression.

"XO," they greeted him one by one.

"Colonel, Lieutenant Commander." Nicholas tilted his head slightly and folded his arms behind his back. "Any reports from the last shift?"

"Nothing major," Daussel said, pointing to a few points in the outer solar system. "There are survivors on Saturn's moons. Some stations and settlements on Jupiter's moons are also sending distress signals. It looks like they can sustain themselves for a few more weeks, but the ice supplies from the belt are drying up. Many of the ice haulers were used for evacuations. Now, ironically, the only ones still available are owned either by smugglers and other criminals or those who refused to evacuate civilians from the system."

"Not the best means for maintaining supply routes."

"No," the lieutenant commander agreed with him. "But it looks like they're all doing their part as best they can. So are the pirates who seem to have come out of their holes. They're patrolling near the remaining stations and habitats, according to the sparse reports we're getting from the remaining listening posts and our limited sensor arrays."

"Either that or they're guarding their stolen booty," Meyer said grimly.

"What about Earth?"

"Terra?" Daussel sighed, then shook his head. "No change. The Clicks are maintaining their blockade. Anything that takes off from the surface—including aircraft or salvage drones—is mercilessly destroyed by laser fire even before it reaches a hundred meters altitude. In effect, all air traffic has ceased. The already problematic supplies are being maintained by ships at sea and land transport."

"Still no opposition?" Nicholas asked.

"No. Most of our ships are wrecks or seem to be dead in space. Our telescopes have sighted the *Concordia*; it looks like a ghost ship. Empty launch bays seems to indicate that she shot off all her predator drones. It's a shame to see that mighty carrier intact and ready for action but with no ammunition. The sky fortress is also silent. They haven't uttered a word since the beginning of the short battle against the Clicks. We still don't know why and can only speculate."

"That damned old man has his tail between its legs," Meyer said.

"Or, their communications equipment was damaged," Daussel said in a much more measured voice.

"I thought the remaining Earth defenses had unilaterally ceased firing after the first few skirmishes."

"It seems so, yes. The enemy hasn't launched any attacks since then, either. As far as we can tell, they are merely maintaining a blockade."

"And what about the bombardments?" Meyer asked, glaring at the bridge officer from the corners of his eyes.

"The initial bombardments with precision lasers appear to have been aimed at military research facilities."

"For the most part," Nicholas said.

"Yes. Several fusion power plants, two civilian research facilities, and some industrial facilities were also destroyed. But we have to assume that we won't be able to deduce what their true purpose is from the targets destroyed."

"They probably based their tactics on reconnaissance they've gathered," Nicholas speculated. "So, they have a plan, but we have no idea what it might look like."

Neither Daussel nor Meyer answered.

"What about the *Carcassonne*?" he asked. The *Oberon* had jumped to the inner emergence point near the sun after Silly's insane atmospheric transit that had nearly torn them apart in the process. Although the repairs had been in full swing for four days, supported by more than 2,000 mechanics from the space fortress and just as many war drones, it would take a very long time for the old lady to recover from the stresses she had undergone. The commander of the *Carcassonne*, Admiral Rosenberg, was anything but pleased about their sudden appearance, but at the same time faced a dilemma. The fleet admiral's last communication had reported that the *Oberon* had mutinied and was therefore to be considered an enemy. However, it was the only large warship in the system, and in the end, it had not inflicted any damage on Earth except for a valley north of Shanghai that had been completely devastated by the impact of debris of the *Novigrad* when the halo was obliterated by ground defenses. But since word had spread that subversive elements of the Federation had been on it, no one was likely to shed a tear over it.

So, Rosenberg had met them with a mixture of reluctance and a grudging cooperation born of need. For the moment, which was probably more than they could have hoped for.

"The admiral is still demanding a personal meeting with the captain," Daussel said stiffly.

"Is she..." Nicholas began to ask, but the lieutenant commander was already shaking his head.

"The problem is that Rosenberg is getting impatient," he said.

"If he withdraws his personnel and drones, we won't be able to repair even the most serious holes in a week. According to the Chief Engie we only have enough raw materials on board in the first place because the old man"— Meyer faltered briefly and looked apologetic—"because the old man sold our shipment of hyperspace torpedoes in Lagunia and crammed our storage bays full of composite ingots and Carbin tanks in return. But without the *Carcassonne*, we can't make use of it fast enough."

Nicholas nodded silently. The *Oberon* had taken a beating. The descent through Earth's dense atmosphere, something her builders had not designed her for, had not only compromised the ship's internal stability, but the hot plasma created by atmospheric friction had severely worsened the hull breaches the ship had sustained during the battle. Added to this were the ground defense missile and laser strikes she had absorbed during the last few meters after Silly had to lower the flak screen to avoid killing their own fighters in the air and their Marines on the ground.

"This meeting is expected to take place," Daussel stated needlessly. "And judging from my last conversation with the admiral, it has to take place sooner rather than later. He seems to be losing his patience, and I don't know how else to explain why our commander isn't available."

"I'll take care of it," Nicholas said, carefully hiding his reluctance. If there was one place in the ship he didn't want to be right now, it was Silvea Thurnau's quarters. But it was his duty as XO. *And as Konrad's son,* he thought and swallowed.

"However, that means your shift—"

"No problem," Daussel said immediately. "I'll stay as long as I'm needed."

Nicholas nodded and left the bridge. He felt Daussel and Meyer's sympathetic thoughts follow him. Kindly intended as they were, they bored into him like laser strikes. His burden lifted slightly once he was in the corridor and only had to endure the blank stares of the crew, who were more focused on their own pain than on him. But that did not last long. The path to Silly's quarters led right past his father's. Nicholas struggled to ignore it and collected himself with a few deep breaths before pressing the announcement button on the panel next to the access door that bore the inscription "Executive Officer."

He waited a minute, then another. He pressed the button again, and again, and again. When the door did not open after five minutes, he unlocked it with his priority code as XO and entered the quarters. Before his eyes could adjust to the sparse twilight, the stench hit him like a hammer. It was a mixture of sweat, greasy hair, and unwashed skin, along with the acrid odor of spoiled food.

When his pupils adjusted, he saw chaos everywhere he looked. The place was strewn with items of clothing and ripped-open protein bags whose contents formed small piles on the honeycomb pattern of the floor. Wrecked picture frames hung splintered on the wall or laid among the debris.

He could not locate Silly at first and went to her bunk, which was rumpled but empty. He finally spied her, crouched under her desk. Dressed only in briefs and a tight tank top, her knees were drawn up and her arms wrapped around them. Her hair seemed to have grown longer, but that was probably because it hadn't seen a clipper in weeks. She had rested her face on her knees and did not move.

"Captain?" Nicholas asked cautiously but got no response.

"Silly?" he tried again, this time with as much warmth in his voice as he was able to muster.

It wasn't much.

"L-l-leave me alone," she said, her voice slurred. The fragility in her voice startled Nicholas. There was none of the hawkish toughness for which she was so notorious.

He looked at the empty bottles strewn about the floor

between her and the bunk. Puddles of high-proof liquor had formed around them.

"It's me, Nicholas," he said after he recovered from the shock of his commander's miserable state. Silly was not only his superior, but the closest thing he had to an aunt. She had never been warm or even cordial, but she had rocked him on her knees as a toddler, given him toys on his birthdays. Brief snatches of memory surfaced in his mind of her smiling as she looked down on him. How old they were, he didn't know, but they existed and caused a wave of compassion to stream out of him.

"Silly. It's me, Nicholas."

She raised her eyes and looked at him with watery eyes. If he hadn't known better, he would have thought she was a drug addict from a Lagunian flog.

"K-Konrad?" she whispered thinly.

"No. Nicholas." He went to her and squatted in front of her. The stench emanating from her was repulsive, and yet he moved automatically and did not back away. A volcano was boiling inside him, building to an eruption, but he could not afford to give in to it now.

"You've been in here for four days."

"Nicholas." Silly wiped her hands over her eyes and sniffled. "Is he still dead? Is it true?"

He swallowed and nodded slowly. Of course, she couldn't see it.

"He's dead," he said, and the volcano threatened to explode. Instead of letting it happen, he fought down his surging emotions with all his might. He had to function now. For Silly, for the crew. For Jason. Something inside him knew that if he gave in to his grief, it would destroy him on the spot. If he succumbed, he would fail not only his brother, but his entire family and his people. "But I'm still here, and the crew is still here. Harbingen is still here, but they need you. You're the commander now, Silly."

"*No!*" she screamed so abruptly that he flinched. Saliva dripped from the corners of her mouth as she stared at him, her body quivering in a fury. "*I am not! I am not a commander!*" Her scream died into a whisper, punctuated by deep sniffles. "I never wanted to be. I only wanted to serve alongside him. It was he who was meant to, after all."

Silly began to sob so hard that her body shuddered. Unsure of what to do, he moved toward her on all fours and tried to pull her out from under the desk, but she fought him off with halfhearted shoves.

He hesitated. He knew that this ruin of a woman was his superior, and he realized she was doing exactly what he longed to do and had barely avoided. Finally, he squeezed himself next to her under the desk and wrapped her in his arms. Silly struggled, tried to break free, and hissed inarticulate curses, but he withstood her attack and ignored the stench emanating from her.

Eventually, her resistance gave way, and she cried some more, this time even unrestrainedly. Her entire body seemed to collapse into his arms. her emotional outburst was an ethereal wave that washed over him and almost carried him away. Everything in him longed to let go and let his body do what it needed to do to free itself from its emotional pain.

"I failed him," she whimpered. "I couldn't save him."

"*We* couldn't save him," he corrected her in a whisper.

"He was the best of us. *The best.* How could I ever fill

his shoes? It's impossible! Just impossible! I want him back. I *must* have him back."

"My father's not coming back. He's gone, Silly. But the one who killed him is still alive." His voice had become a low growl as he pictured the conniving commander's face. "We have to change that. And Jason is still on Earth."

"I can't save them. I couldn't save him."

"You moved heaven and hell to save me and our Marines," he countered with honest indignation. "You were the first to ever make a jump from an atmosphere. The calculations for that were either ingenious or insane—probably both. The crew is calling it the Silly Maneuver. I don't think there's a more apt name for it. I wouldn't have thought the *Oberon* was capable of it. But *you* did because you know the old girl better than any of us. My father was the heart of *Oberon*, but only one of her two heart chambers. *You* are the other, Silvea Thurnau. If there were any doubts about you, there are none left, at least since your maneuver rescued me and our Marines. You acted like a real commander. Under time pressure and at maximum risk, you acted and made calculations faster than anyone else could."

"We could have died."

"But we didn't."

"*He* did."

"I know," he breathed. "He was my father, Silly. I know what I've lost. But I refuse to let Pyrgorates win by destroying myself. I refuse to leave Jason behind and accept that humanity is lost. I will not stand by while other Harbingers destroy the Federation."

She did not reply.

"The crew believes in you, Silly. They're devastated about my father, but they haven't given up hope. I wouldn't have thought it possible after the crew had half its heart ripped out. The reason they're still working and patching up the *Oberon* for the coming fights is because of you."

"I can never be *him*."

"You don't have to be. You can say all you want about not being a commander, but I and all of us here on board saw what you were in the Battle for Terra. *We* saw a commander," he insisted, adding in a firm voice, "a commander my father would have been proud of. You've shown all the doubters why he chose you as his XO. Now it's time for you to step forward and take responsibility. Don't take away their hope. Don't let them see you like this. Accept your pain. But remember your duty. It is—"

"... heavier than a stone," she whispered the rest of one of the Harbinger fleet's guiding phrases. "And death is lighter than a feather."

"Yes. We have unfinished business here, Silly, and I need you to do it. We all need you."

3

Sirion had been walking along Seattle's rainy, canyon-like streets for two hours. His hood was pulled low over his face. The acid rain beaded and ran off his coated jacket like mercury and merged with the streams that flowed around his boots like tiny whitewater rivers. He had only been to Terra a few times. He hated the crowded arks as much as the people in them. There were so many crowded in such a small space that part of him was glad the aliens in orbit were creating an almost tangible atmosphere of tension and sheer panic among the civilian population. It kept most of them home.

There were, however, some drawbacks. Local traffic was restricted, and overland travel was not even a possibility. Ninety percent of the traffic between the arks and the industrial plants around the world had used vectored push machines and drones. The road infrastructure between cities had gone unmaintained for over a hundred years, and what was left of the old interstates didn't exactly allow for safe driving. But if he believed the few news feeds that still got a signal from orbit, the Clicks weren't allowing air travel and answered every launch attempt with laser fire, and their vigilance had increased after they started sending shuttles to the oceans. But they didn't stop there.

Two days ago, Sirion had stocked up on much-needed provisions at an army depot downtown. On his way back, a lance of red light ten or more meters wide had been shot from space, vaporizing the clouds as it turned a skyscraper into a mound of slag. The orbital bombardment had lasted less than five seconds, splitting the sky with a column of light, yet the effects had been devastating. The building was gone except for an ugly composite pile atop the foundation, and nearby structures had been singed and pockmarked by debris. Hundreds of passersby had either been vaporized into gas molecules or, if they had been less fortunate, burned so badly they were barely recognizable as human beings. For more than 24 hours, firefighters and rescue workers struggled to extinguish secondary fires and recover the dead and injured.

Sirion didn't know what the aliens were targeting, and he wasn't interested in the speculations dominating the news feeds—they were almost always unreliable because they weren't based on solid fact. In any case, there had been no further bombardments and the rest of the city was relatively quiet. Most of the inhabitants gradually seemed to realize that if the Clicks were going to do what the media feared most, they would have been dead long ago.

He was personally not interested in any plans the aliens might have since they were not his target. His was all too human, just like his pursuers.

In front of a Chinese fast-food restaurant that crouched

unobtrusively in the continuous facade facing 5th Avenue, he looked over his shoulder and quickly scanned the street. The two lanes were clear, except for a few autonomous-drive vehicles delivering to restaurants and supermarkets, advertising their corporations with obtrusive holo-advertisements. On the sidewalk behind him, he saw two groups of pedestrians walking in the same direction. The acoustic amplifiers in his ears had trouble filtering out their conversations from the noise of the rain, but he understood enough to know they were complaining about the weather.

Normal in Seattle.

Across the street, there were a few people shielding themselves with wide umbrellas, shoulders hunched against the damp creeping cold. Nothing conspicuous.

No amateurs, he thought. *Good.*

He opened the restaurant door and slipped into the excessive warmth of infrared heaters and the glare of fluorescent lights. One of the cooks behind the counter, fiddling with deep fryers and stirring in large woks, threw him a routine "Welcome to Au-Hey-Yan, what can I get you?" without lifting his eyes.

The dining area was jampacked and noisy. Over the din of conversations, mostly in Chinese, he sensed a different kind of tension than that which reigned outside. It was louder and more intrusive but reeked just as much of fear.

"Number three," he said without looking at the neon sign displaying the various dishes above the counter, and then slipped unseen through a group of waiting people.

"With or without..." he heard the cook start to ask before his voice was lost in the confusion of the crowd. Sirion had his sights set on the kitchen. As in most fast-food restaurants of this type, there was a rack of trays that a constant stream of kitchen helpers retrieved, brought into the kitchen through a swinging door, and fed into the vacuum dish cleaner.

He paused next to the door, pushed it open with one hand, and glanced at a dozen or so workers busy sorting soyfood into their several varieties, noodles, rice, "vegetables," meat, and fish, into large molds for the display. He waited until someone noticed the open door then let it close before he moved next to a group of very animated guests. From the corner of his eye, he saw two figures moving simultaneously in the direction of the tray rack— or the kitchen door. Others might not have noticed the connection, but Sirion had been in the business too long to disregard tiny discrepancies such as the suspiciously identical timing of movement in the same direction. Nothing in life happened synchronously or was perfectly timed, and sometimes it was only a few fractions of a second that separated a deliberate simultaneity from a coincidence.

While his pursuers continued moving forward, believing he had fled through the kitchen to the back, he kept his head down and moved in the opposite direction, back to the entrance. There he waited briefly until three women pulled on their hoods and retrieved their coated umbrellas from a basket to leave the restaurant. He joined them and followed them to the right along the sidewalk as he watched the street. A delivery truck that hadn't been there a moment ago was parked not ten yards away. Its windows were dark and covered with advertisements for what claimed to be the most vitamin-rich protein synthetic in town. Sirion switched to infrared vision, but it didn't show any signature.

As with most autonomous vehicles, there was no windshield. The car was basically a closed box on four wheels and covered with tiny sensors arranged around the body. Only a cargo door on the side indicated there was anything to interact with.

Sirion grabbed the handle and, using the induction fields in his palm, slipped an aggressive codebreaker into the vehicle's system. In less than two breaths the lock released. He pulled the sliding door aside and used its momentum to spin like a dancer, so his body remained protected by the steel. A silenced gun coughed twice and the facade behind him sprayed some shattered plaster.

He let go of the door, ducked under the field of fire, and glided to one side in a single fluid motion. Driven by his reflex booster, which accelerated nerve impulse conduction threefold, he saw a muzzle flash and had already grabbed the weapon when the projectile whizzed just past his ear.

Amazing, he thought as he broke a forearm and slammed his free hand sideways against the groaning defender's ear. He closed the door behind him and locked it with his induction implants before quickly searching the stunned man for weapons and grabbed his face.

"Let's go. I'm only going to say this once."

His pursuer seemed to grasp the gravity of the situation and sent a signal to the vehicle control software. The car began to move. Sirion wondered if the two in the restaurant had yet realized that he had hoodwinked them. He turned on his white-noise generator and injected his victim with an aggressive paralytic that immediately made him go limp. Then he looked around and spotted some thick insulation wool and two open military crates containing weapons and nanokits.

Augmented, he thought. *Not high-end, but well-funded and trained. My clients' arms have a long reach if they are still operating with such forces here on Earth now. Or there is another reason.*

Sirion placed a diaphragm on the larynx of the paralyzed man, a young man with straw-blond hair, and searched one of the crates for a painkiller injector.

"I'm going to ask you some questions," he said coolly. "Your first answer will determine how things will go. Either"—he wiggled the injector—"I free you from the pain of your broken arm or I break the other one. You're a Harbinger. Stubborn. I get that. You should know that I'm one, too. Do you understand?"

"I understand," sounded the computer-generated voice from the diaphragm. The young man lay there like a corpse, not even able to blink.

"Are you working directly for Pyrogorates? Or for the exiles?"

"The exiles." The androgynous voice of the small device, which translated brainwaves into words using simple AI, conveyed no emotion. Sirion liked that.

"How many of you are left on Terra?"

"Twenty."

Sirion thought about it. If the situation was what he suspected, then the exiles had known what was coming toward the Federation. So, almost all of them had evacuated long ago. Only a few had remained—by mistake or for safety's sake. He pressed the injector into the young man's thigh.

"There's no air traffic. How did you get here?"

"Vector thruster near the ground."

"What's your mission? Dead or alive?"

"Alive. No brain death."

They want what I have. So, Pyrgorates is behind it, but they don't know him.

"Does the control software memory know your drop-off point?"

"Yes."

"Is that where I'll find the vector thruster?"

"Yes."

"You exiles... What is your objective?"

This time the diaphragm was silent. Sirion had expected it. His opponent had weighed his options, to either suffer the pain made several powers worse by the helplessness of paralysis or betray information limited to items that he thought would not make much difference.

The last question had apparently exceeded that limit.

Sirion nodded and killed the Harbinger by breaking his neck. Then he set about reading out the car's navigation memory and found, as one of the last five stops, a pier in the cargo port where route planning had commenced yesterday shortly before sunrise. He considered and saw the sense behind it. A vectored thruster had to fly extremely low to avoid being identified as an aircraft. That was nearly impossible over terrain that took them between mountains, over trees and the ruins of abandoned towns and villages.

He instructed the car to take him back to where its journey had begun. Using a data cable, he connected directly to the sensors and inspected the rainy roads on the camera feeds. Traffic remained sparse considering the ark normally overflowed with commuters, and the rain dominated the bleak picture Seattle presented in the gloom. Even the lights of the monolithic skyscrapers looked colorless and pale. Sirion had no particular interest in sensory impressions that served no purpose, so he stuck to observing his surroundings, analyzing the driving behavior of the vehicles in his vicinity, and looking for discrepancies.

He found none and two hours later reached the south cargo port. It encompassed a vast area cordoned off by monofilament fences and was patrolled by Doberman drones and security personnel. Sirion had expected to find an above-average number of them, since shipping had suddenly become more important for securing supplies and conducting what little trade was still possible once air traffic had been abandoned. The presence of security was, however, sparse, perhaps because many employees did not bother coming to work given the impending end of the world that hung over Earth like the Sword of Damocles.

Nevertheless, he took no chances. He downloaded the navigation data into his data cortex and left the car near one of the access roads. Once he was far enough away, he anonymously sent a bomb threat to the security network and waited for armed personnel to emerge from the gate and surround the abandoned car. He had no trouble grabbing one of them from the shadows, overpowering him, and slipping into the port area amid the commotion caused by the weapons found inside the vehicle.

He walked past the massive piers between huge, automated cranes and swarming loading drones until he reached one of the smaller ones, a pier operated not by large corporations but by local logistics companies.

Sirion took his time finding the vector thruster and observed the pier for a while. He saw no one there at this hour. About a dozen ships were magnetically anchored to the designated bollards. The hydrogen-powered vessels were flat designs with narrow superstructures and low displacement, unlike the big freighters with their towering Flettner rotors docked at the main quays.

At the very end of the pier was a vessel built a little taller and that did not match the shapes of the others. Sirion had to approach and hide behind one of the many containers before he could see why. The Harbingers' vector thrust machine was covered with a structural mesh. The hardened fibers that made up the programmable mesh created the impression of solid structure, which could be dissipated by the right signals. The mesh's profile was not enough to be noticed on satellite images and camera shots, but just different enough for the human eye to perceive that something did not seem right. He scanned the craft with his eyes but could find no signature onboard or under the net.

He waited a quarter of an hour, then half an hour, until two dark figures appeared at the end of the pier. Sirion changed his position and hid behind a cargo pallet loaded with barrels, opposite the hidden vector thrust machine.

When the two men arrived, the structural mesh lifted from inside and a third figure climbed out into the rain.

"What are you doing here?" he hissed over the pattering sound that was amplified by the toxic waters of the Pacific.

"He hijacked the car and drove here. Looks like security

either caught him or ran him off," one of the new arrivals replied.

"What about Peter?"

A shake of the head.

"Damn."

"We need new orders. The trail is cold. I can't shake the impression that this son of a bitch wanted us to find him."

"Not a chance." The one from the vector thruster shook his head under his hood. "We can't get a signal out. The few terrestrial radio stations still available have been confiscated by the military and we can't get into any of them. And the satellites... well, you already know what's wrong with them."

"We can't just stay here and wait until he strikes!"

"I heard from a contact in the army that the planetary defense network has a plan that could clear away the Clicks, but they need help from the sky fortress for some reason."

"Great."

"My contact also said they sent someone up the elevator in Nepal. Must be the Fleet equivalent of a tin can phone."

"Bullshit!"

"Maybe. Anyway, we have two options. We go ahead and search or we wait to see if the plan is real and works, and then ask for new orders."

Sirion continued waiting in cover to see if they would split up again, but it looked like they were staying together.

He crouched and sprang from the shadows like a predator. The two newcomers had their backs to him and had barely turned when he landed on them. He stepped toward the man on the right and broke his shin bone. The man fell to his knees with a strangled yelp. Sirion jabbed an elbow into the side of the one on the left, fluidly twisted his torso forward to avoid a blow, which swept ineffectually across the top of his head. He kicked the one in front of him in the abdomen. The man was not exactly slow pulling a pistol from his jacket, and the kick bought Sirion two precious seconds. He contracted his fingers and the monofilament blades snapped out of his forearms as he swung and sliced the ones on his right and left open from hip to armpit.

Before they hit the ground like wet sacks and their blood mixed with the rain, the man in front of him fired. It would have hit Sirion in the forehead if his reflex booster hadn't sent him sideways. He cut the pistol in two with one blow of his monofilament blade and turned it into scrap metal.

His right arm was across his chest for the blink of an eye, so his opponent was able to take advantage. He slung the useless weapon at Sirion's face and aimed a kick at his ribs with a lightning-fast spin. Sirion ignored his defensive reflex and dropped with his fingers spread, forcing the blades back into his forearms so he wouldn't hurt himself.

The leg whirled over him, and the Harbinger lost his balance from the lack of resistance. That was enough for Sirion to grab his foot and yank him forward.

Before the stranger hit the ground, Sirion broke both his wrists and rolled him under the structure's mesh. After a quick search he discovered a vibroblade and a data connector. He threw the blade overboard and took the connector.

"Are you the pilot?" he asked the dazed man after turning on his white-noise generator to block out unwanted eavesdroppers.

"Yes," the Harbinger growled reluctantly.

"Your mission is over. The leadership is gone."

"You don't know anything."

"I know where I want to go."

"That's hardly going to do you any good." His opponent smiled weakly through bloody teeth. "I'd guess you can't fly, or I'd be dead by now."

"That assessment is correct," Sirion admitted. "But I am capable of learning."

"Empty threats. Kill me if you must, traitor!"

"You will fly me."

"No. But even if I did, you have nowhere to go. Terra's on lockdown, in case you haven't noticed. Doesn't matter, though."

"I think there may be a way. You're going to pilot this machine just the way you came in. I know where I'm going. You told me."

His counterpart frowned.

Sirion deployed his forearm blades again and gave him a cold look. "You will take me there. Now."

It took him another half hour to convince the pilot. The vector thruster lifted a few meters with whirring turbines and sped out over the powerful swells of the northern Pacific into the open sea and darkness.

4

Jason raised the electronic binoculars to his eyes and turned the small wheel above the right lens to maximum zoom. The Clicks' shuttle looked like a dark blue drop plunging from Olympus into the gray waters of the Pacific. The pilot had turned off the brake engines 500 meters above the surface, so its dive into the waves resembled a meteorite impact. Why he had not maintained braking was a mystery to Jason. Water was extremely hard if you hit its surface at speed. Any child who had belly flopped off a five-meter board knew that.

"That one looked bigger than the others," he said without taking the binoculars from his eyes. The sight of the Pacific's wildly tossing waves made him shudder. He had grown up on Harbingen and New California and was used to turquoise water, and later green on Lagunia. The Terran oceans seemed filthy, colorless and sick in contrast. It wasn't hard to believe there was little life worth talking about in that hot, sour broth for centuries.

"Impressive shuttle," Baker agreed with him. "Told you my eyes didn't deceive me."

Jason didn't know how to respond. His electronic binoculars could reach magnification factors of several dozens and had made the 200 kilometers distance to the shuttle appear like a stone's throw. Yet he had still been unable to see it in the upper layers of the atmosphere. Baker's chrome eyeballs obviously had no such difficulty. A couple decades of cannibalizing augmented victims had apparently made the mutant a walking hardware store of the highest price range.

He lowered the binoculars and handed them back to Baker. They were standing on a long sand dune on China's Pacific coast. The beach was littered with dead seaweed and stank horribly. Twenty kilometers south of them, the silhouette of Shanghai's mega-arcology loomed out of the morning haze. Skyscrapers like columns of light emerged, densely packed and connected by so many bridges and corridors that he was reminded of a spider's web. Even at that great distance, the huge walls were clearly visible, hiding the lower city where the less privileged never saw daylight and lived mostly trapped in poverty and violence. Did those people even care whether the Clicks were now in charge or the rich and powerful, under whom they had been forced to vegetate for decades?

"I wonder," he said over the crashing waves, "if the Clicks have something like that."

"What, arks?"

"Ghettos. An underprivileged class of wage slaves you talk about pityingly at cocktail parties and then, undisturbed by pangs of conscience, fly home in a sinfully expensive tricopter, and get rejuvenation injections that cost millions of credits."

"I don't know," Baker admitted in a flat voice around a cigar tucked firmly in the corner of his mouth. Jason wondered, not for the first time, where the seemingly endless supply of rolled tobacco leaves might come from. "But if there's one thing I've learned is that evolution is not fair, nor does it comply with any of our other fine narratives like 'inalienable human rights' and 'the pursuit of happiness.' Nature is interested in survival and advancement and does not discriminate. It simply rewards those who withstand evolutionary pressures and persist."

"You don't think we're fundamentally flawed as a species?"

"Nope. I look like you, although I'm not the dimwit you are. Still, you could argue that I'm just as much an alien to you as the Clicks are. Our bodies are almost identical, the genetic differences are less than two percent, just like between us and domestic pigs. However, the differences are still huge. After all, we were labeled 'errors' because of our differences. The Clicks may have some other form of political organization, but in the end it all boils down to the same thing: evolutionary success."

"The world's lost a real philosopher in you," Jason said laconically. If he were honest, he didn't expect to hear such semi-profound reflections coming from Baker's mouth. After the *Oberon*'s jump had left them heavily scarred, the mutants had gone berserk in the valley's underground tunnels. They had stormed a cavern where injured and completely disoriented Harbingers, clad in their black uniforms, had sought refuge and they had hacked everything and everyone to pieces. Jason hadn't felt much sympathy for his father's killers at the time, yet the naked brutality Baker's comrades had shown as they turned people into mincemeat—people who had been just as scared and shocked as they were—had felt like a slap in the face. Later he had found out why: the butchers had needed blood, which they fed through valves on their bodies to heal themselves. Their augments and clone organs had a much higher metabolism than normal humans and were specialized in making up for energy loss quickly. They were obviously not choosy about the source.

"So, what are you thinking?" Baker mumbled around his cigar as he blew out a steady cloud of smoke that was carried away by the persistently strong wind.

"I think the plan is completely insane."

"Of course, it is. But we can't get into the ark where we would actually feel comfortable. Everything is on lockdown."

"Except for the fact that the Clicks might decide at any time to drop a few nukes after all."

"Exactly. If there's any way to get off this pile of manure, it's that." Baker pulled the cigar from the corner of his mouth and pointed out at the gray waves.

"That is dangerous. And we don't know how long they'll even be there," Jason said. "We're low on supplies, besides."

"Out here, we'll starve or die of thirst someday, too."

"Hm." Jason looked at the outer slopes of the valley, where huge boulders along the ridge bore witness to the wrecked and fled space shuttles he had seen on the screens as his escape pod had approached. He tried not to think about the lone cross at the head of a grave mound where the battle had taken place. A grave they had dug with their bare hands.

"Got a fair amount of ballast in your head, huh?" Baker asked, who had caught his gaze and was squinting at the hillside through cigar fumes.

"I hated him," Jason admitted softly, ashamed of the words, although they were as familiar to him as breathing.

"He didn't hate you."

Jason eyed his companion and stared up into his large face.

"I had a father, too. He bred me in a test tube, but before he hanged himself to take the easy way out, we had a long talk."

"You killed your father?"

"No, he killed himself, I told you."

"You *wanted* to kill him, though."

Baker shrugged. "I was young once, too."

"Excuse me?"

"He made me into a bulky giant of a man, doomed to take on the nastiest jobs in the pits until he was dead. I've always been good at solving problems quickly, and at nine years old I was bigger and stronger than he was." The mutant eyed him. "The thought had occurred to you, after all."

"That's true," Jason admitted with a sigh. "But now that he's dead... I don't know what to feel."

"Of course, you don't. You can't cut his head off anymore, but you can't reconcile with him either. As long as a relationship with someone is defined, by hate or love, it makes you what you are. If the relationship doesn't end naturally, if it's suddenly interrupted, you lose something without ever resolving things one way or the other. It will ruin your life, just wait and see."

"Very encouraging."

"What did he do to you anyway?"

"He killed my mother."

"Uh-huh. Should have shot him."

"I never asked him about it."

"About what?"

"How he felt about it; the order he gave," Jason said thoughtfully. "I knew my pain and I blamed him for it, but I didn't know his because I only cared for mine."

"Anyway, now he's dead and six feet under. It's useless to worry about that." Baker pointed a thumb over his powerful shoulder. "The boys should be done soon."

"You've already ordered them to build a flog?"

"Sure. Did you think I was waiting for your permission?" The butcher pulled his cigar stub out of the corner of his mouth and laughed. "You're a loyal son of a bitch, kid. That's really impressed some of my boys. But we make our own decisions."

"Do you even know how to do that?"

"You explained it to us, didn't you? Hardened algae is just like wood and there's enough stuff lying around in the valley that we could probably pile enough together to make a damned spaceship." Baker tugged at Jason's crude suit. "We got you this in time, too, so your little bones won't be eaten away by the acid rain. It will float all right, don't worry."

"Your word in God's ear."

"I'm going now. Tonight, we leave."

"Agreed. I'll join you later," Jason said and remained by himself on the beach and explored his feelings.

He was stranded on Terra in the middle of a blockade by the worst enemy humanity had ever faced. Beings with his homeworld and nearly all its inhabitants on their consciences, if they had any. His father had been executed by a Fleet officer he himself had supported when he was still in Augustus's service. When he thought about how he had come aboard the *Caesar* less than two weeks ago to spite his father and humiliate him in front of the Fleet, he felt sick.

"How could this happen, Dad," he whispered into the wind.

∼

He spent most of the evening trying to fall into a fitful sleep. The butchers had converted one of the caverns in the mountain into a workshop and, with their typical racket, were tinkering with the vehicles they would carry across the Pacific up to the last minute. Jason dreamed of how the exiled Harbingers here had spent twenty years or more building these secret passages and caverns and camouflaging their shuttle launch pads with monolithic stone formations. They could only have managed it with connections in higher places, and that was not good news for the Federation.

His father had repeatedly insisted that not all of Omega's opponents had left Terran-controlled territory behind and that they had scattered to every corner of space under human control. But, apparently, even Konrad Bradley had underestimated what the exiles had built in the shadows. The only question was what was their goal? What were they after? What was it all for? Anyone who would spend so much money to work toward such a distant day had to have a vision strong enough to motivate every one of their members to the utmost effort.

Baker woke him from his dream stupor and troubled thoughts.

"We're starting, kid."

He merely nodded and screwed up his face at the sickening taste in his mouth. The poisoned Terran atmosphere might seem normal to its inhabitants who were used to walking out the door with breathing masks over their mouths and drugs in their bloodstream. But for him, who had spent his life breathing the clean air of Harbingen, Lagunia, and, later, various spaceships, recycled though it was, it was an experience he would gladly have done without.

The "flogs" that Baker's mutants had built looked like ugly pancakes of stinky algae that had lain along the dunes for decades and dried into woody skeletons. Welded together with thin pieces of metal, they made rafts five to ten meters long. Each could carry four of them without sinking. They launched a total of twenty. The water did not appear to affect their dermal armor. Jason, on the other hand, was glad to be in a closed suit and not to have to touch the filthy broth.

I wonder what the recruits are doing, he wondered, as he climbed onto the first raft with Baker. In the darkness, the ocean ahead of them looked like an expanse of black mercury. Sending the young people away had been both a relief and a loss to him. He knew they would be admitted to the arcology and did not belong out here. At the same time, he worried that something might happen to them without him having any control over it. Despite the short time they had been his responsibility, he blamed himself for the fact that only a fifth of them had survived.

At any rate, they were safer now, despite the Clicks, than they were with him and these butchers. His conviction only grew more certain with each kilometer they put behind them. At first, he did not believe that they could ever make the 200 kilometers without engines, but the mutants soon convinced him otherwise. They lived up to their reputation as enduring and indestructible work machines as they paddled for all they were worth with improvised oars that Jason could not even lift. The flogs were repeatedly caught by waves and looked incredibly frag-ile, especially since their crews were not exactly lightweights. The constant splashes of spray didn't seem to bother them. They still cracked jokes and yelled against the roar of the wind, which must have shifted during the night, he noted. It was now blowing from offshore and was at their backs.

"Are you sure it's the right spot?" he called out to Baker. Morning had already dawned as a pale silver streak on the horizon, bathing the sky in a dirty gray. Still, the never-ending wind whipped at them with undiminished ferocity, constantly spraying them with the ocean's soup.

"Nope, but we didn't have any better idea, if I remember correctly," the giant roared back, laughing heartily. The few patches of skin on the mutant's face that weren't made of artificial dermal armor were red and had obviously become inflamed under by the ubiquitous toxins in the air and especially in the water.

"Once we get there we can't go back!" Jason warned.

"Not with this following wind."

"And it's always blowing. Although this is more like a lukewarm breeze, if my comrades from Terra at the academy were correct."

"Then we should hope all the more that we find what we're looking for." Baker laughed again. Since his cigar would not stay lit, he had taken to chewing the stub bit by bit, periodically spitting out black tobacco saliva.

"Sounds like the worst operational tactic I've ever heard," Jason grumbled.

"What?"

He waved it off. *I am a logistics officer, after all, and that part seems to be working out miraculously.*

The day drew to a close. He had spent most of his time looking through Baker's binoculars for the center of the carpet of trash where the Clicks' ferry had struck. The floating carpet of plastic and other debris was about the size of what used to be the United States and was dense enough that ships with screws had trouble passing through it. He had read that the structure reached fifty meters below the surface and was riddled with dead biomass and algae that had managed to either digest plastic or use it as a hiding place.

By nightfall, they were paddling through the foothills of the carpet that gave the waves an unreal texture. It stank even more than before, a sweet-sour aroma that caused him a persistent feeling of nausea. They reached the midpoint two days later in the middle of the night. They had long since stopped moving as quickly as when they had started out. The swaths of plastic made a gruesome effort only crueler for the butchers, and even the usually loquacious mutants became increasingly monosyllabic as they visibly perspired despite the cool wind.

"Holy shit." Baker's sigh sounded like a landslide. The mutant had put down his oversized paddle and dangled his legs in the water as if it wasn't the plastic-strewn, polluted scum it really was. A wave lifted them up and lowered them down. "That was unpleasant."

"True, and I didn't even do anything," Jason agreed with him.

"Anyway, this is the spot. I'll go down with some guys later and see what's going on."

"How is that even going to work? Not only is the ocean water toxic, but it's pretty deep out here." He looked around and saw only gray swells flecked with mismatched colors, as far as the eye could see, stretching to the horizon. It was easy to feel lost and small, as if solid land were only a distant promise. Fitting, he thought, since they would not be able to return. The nearest land were the peaks of Hawaii with its flooded city ruins. But not even the butchers could paddle that far before they died of thirst and starvation. Or capsized. So, they had only one chance: this one.

"Some of us have built-in air filters with high-performance lungs and balancing pumps. They're actually designed to work in zero G, but it will work quite well underwater, I think."

"So, what's the plan?"

"The plan?" Baker grinned. "We brought some toys."

The mutant pulled out a fission cutter the size of a toddler that was usually mounted on drones.

There was a loud splash behind them, and when they turned around they saw a small fountain of spray.

"Ah. Diagev's stuck his little toe in first." Baker laughed, coughing, and shrugged his mighty shoulders. "Don't make that face, kid. Either we make it, or we die here. Life ends in death either way, remember."

"I'm coming with you," Jason decided.

"Is that a good idea?"

"I don't know, but life ends in death either way, and at least then I'll know what this suit and breathing apparatus you've assembled for me are really good for." He gestured at himself and struggled to put on a carefree look.

"Baker," someone boomed. It was Diagev, his angular giant face peering out of the waves, a faded plastic bag perched on his head. "Found the shuttle."

"The shuttle?" Jason gasped, jumping up before he had even said "shuttle."

"Yep. Not ten meters below us. Must be lucky they really thought we were flotsam, what without motors and all."

Baker stood as well. Their flog swayed menacingly.

"All right, men. Get your cutters ready, then. Time for a little robot ballet," the mutant called to his men, pulling his helmet over his head. "That'll make for some decent booty."

Or a cold grave, Jason thought.

5

"Transit in sixty seconds," Aura reported. Her voice lacked emotion, yet Dev could almost physically feel her tension. They had spent the past five days limping from one jump point to another, repairing as much as they could along the way. It had helped that, during his recovery, Aura had ordered the crew to collect whatever debris they could find after their first jump. With a half-destroyed Starvan and a disassembled corvette that had materialized in the wreckage of the passenger liner, there was plenty available.

Despite that, the number of usable components was manageable at best, and many just didn't fit in size or shape. Thus, they had only managed to patch the largest, or rather the "very largest," holes in the hull and had restored their radar. Willy had been able to salvage the Starvan's plant, and only an hour ago, and after an almost endless stream of curses, had finally been able to connect it to their system.

They had, in effect, rescued a dying patient and put it into a comalike state where it was occasionally able to respond to stimulation with a fluttering eyelid. The ship could do no more, but at least no less.

One serious problem remained. Since the hull had been imperfectly sealed, life support was only partially able to maintain temperature, a problem made even more difficult by the unregulated reactor waste heat. The oxygen they had recovered from the Starvan had been used to refill their breathing apparatus. But if they didn't find a replacement in the Lagunia system, then they only succeeded in altering the time and place of their demise, but not much else.

"Willy?" he radioed to his flight engineer. "Are you inside?"

"Yeah, just climbed in, boss," the Dunkelheimer replied breathlessly. The fact that he'd been clambering around on the hull until just before transit said a lot about the *Quantum Bitch*'s condition, something Dev hated to admit. "If that piece of shit doesn't work now then fuck it!"

"Let's hope for the best. Thanks."

"Better make sure we don't materialize in a fucking debris field."

Dev grimaced. He certainly did not need the reminder. They had made the last ten jumps practically blind and deaf, relying only on the jump data in their onboard computer. It had been fed with all the Starvan's recorded navigational data while they were attached to its underside like some sort of parasite. That they were still in one piece so far bordered on a miracle and proved his wisdom in keeping the AI up to date with the latest technology. What they had achieved so far resembled a blind man walking from one golf hole to another, relying solely on the fact that he had counted his steps and was able to calculate distances the last time. And they had done it five times.

"Jump!" Aura announced. The universe expanded into infinity for a fraction of a heartbeat before shrinking to a tiny dot. "Transit successful."

"All systems operating normally," Jezzy confirmed behind him. The breathing mask she wore muffled her voice. "At least, no worse than before."

"The cripples are back!" Aura shouted in wry exultation. "Back in the shittiest place in the whole Federation."

"Yay," Jezzy joined in.

"At least it isn't Harbingen, and we're not surrounded by trigger-happy spastics," Dev said, trying some positive remarks to counter his crewmates' defeatism. "Besides, there's plenty of junk to salvage here that could save our asses."

"I like it when you deny reality," Jezzy said with a half-smile.

"You know, we could have let you out in one of those dead systems between Harbingen and here, but you didn't go for that, did you?"

"At least there aren't any aliens there shooting at everything they see. So much for trigger-happy spastics."

"I swear we'll turn around and drop you off. I can't take this shit anymore..." Dev turned angrily but was interrupted by Aura.

"Shut up, both of you. Willy's radar system seems to be working. At least it does for about two minutes before going offline for ten seconds because the system insists on initiating its diagnostic routine."

"What about the bow telescope?"

"Still junk. We simply don't have the components for it. The lenses are screwed up and all the relays are burned out."

"Too much to hope for." He sighed and stared at his navigation screen. It was gradually filling up with contact signals that the onboard computer was assembling into a visual simulation. They had come out as planned at S2 near the gas giant Artros, in the center of the wreckage what was once a hyperspace gate. The debris field created by the massive battle with the alien invaders was so gigantic and cosmically dense that the automatic security routines flooded displays with warning messages and collision alerts.

"Is anything moving differently than it should?" Jezzy said.

"Doesn't look like it," Dev replied slowly. The numerous contacts displayed were all moving, but they only reflected the constant collisions that sent debris off in other vectors and toward more collisions. Chaos reigned in a spherical area over 200,000 kilometers across. A few emergency transponders with Fleet signatures were still transmitting. The rest glittered in absolute silence in the pale light of the central star.

"No exhaust flares or significant energy signatures," Aura said.

"So many people," Jezzy whispered.

Dev saw it, too, thousands of radars contact reports that could be clearly identified as human bodies, figures frozen into lumps of ice in their brief death throes as they were sucked from their spaceships. In their last seconds they had seen their capillaries expand and burst in the vacuum and then died as the blood froze in their veins. Their sheer volume made Dev catch his breath. He was no softy or else he could never have earned a living as a smuggler and pirate, yet flying through this enormous graveyard made it impossible not to imagine the boundless suffering these bodies experienced. Every single radar contact was a person with family and friends, a human who had loved and hated and felt as close to others as he did to his crew. They had all been wiped out in a single battle—and one that had been fought for no reason.

The war against the Clicks, a war that broke out after first contact had gone wrong, was a matter of naked survival. Attacks and retaliations had been exchanged so rapidly that the whole conflict had come down to a matter of bringing one or the other to its knees. It seemed the only way to secure peace. The invaders who had appeared here in Lagunia, however, had not even tried to communicate with them as the Clicks had. They had immediately fired at them without transmitting a single signal.

He cleared his throat after a few minutes of awkward silence. "All right. We're not going to get the *Bitch* back on her feet by staring out there. Priority is life support, then resource containers so we can replenish our printers."

"And how are we supposed to do that? This debris field is so huge it would take an entire junk collector fleet months to even map it," Jezzy objected. "Not to mention you can already see the gravity of that ugly gas giant slowly but surely pulling all this stuff into orbit. Then we'll be dealing with a ring that stretches so far around Artros that it'll take even longer."

"We don't have that much time anyway. The oxygen for our breathing apparatus will last another thirty hours, maximum." Aura met Dev's gaze as he turned to her and shrugged. "It's true."

Thank you, we didn't need that now. Aloud he said, "We have no choice, so keep your eyes glued to your screens."

"I might have a better idea," Willy rumbled. The engineer had appeared in the doorway to the cockpit, still clad in his spacesuit minus the helmet.

"Go ahead," Dev urged him impatiently.

"The ring around Lagunia," the Dunkelheimer explained, "is also made of ship debris."

Aura waved dismissively. "Yeah, Lagunian and Click ships."

"True, but they're relatively well recorded. Despite the limited capabilities of this crappy system, publicly available data should be in the onboard computer, so at least we'd know where to expect what. As far as I know, there was a moratorium on the export of artifacts from the debris ring under Bradley's aegis. So, whatever was identified should still be there." Willy shrugged. "As far as I can see, there's no Fleet left to enforce the moratorium."

Dev scratched his chin. "Heck, that's not a bad idea at all."

"Exactly. We don't have time to conduct a search here. It'll take at least six to eight hours for us to limp to Lagunia which would give us time to run more scans in the unlikely event that there were battles in orbit."

"And," Aura added, "we can look for the invaders' ships before we set about launching a repair operation, so they don't blow us to hell while we're busy."

"That's what we'll do," Dev ordered. "Good idea."

Instead of the usual bad joke, Willy wordlessly left the bridge.

It took them six hours to escape the battlefield unharmed due to the barely plottable flight vectors of the myriad drifting debris. Dev imagined them passing pieces of hull on which parts of the ships' names could be seen, whole swarms of dead crewmen drifting through the suffocating silence with voiceless screams on their bloodless lips, and here and there the sliced open and cratered hulls of the enemy's huge battleships. Too few of them had been destroyed.

During those hours, though he barely took his eyes off the radar screen to adjust their course, Dev still wondered what might have happened to the *Oberon*. That the Titan had once again abandoned its home world was, in his view as an independent ship captain, the only correct choice. After all, it served no one to get slaughtered for what, in his opinion, would have been vain pathos. In his eyes, that kind of "heroism" was just the stupidity of men who were ruled more by testosterone than by reason.

After they finally cleared the debris field, he cut the engines, which had been under full power, and allowed the ship to drift. If *Quantum Bitch* gave off no exhaust flares, she would be more difficult to detect. Another ten hours later, they were halfway to Lagunia, and for the first time the radar showed a relatively clear picture of what was going on around the water world: virtually nothing.

Twenty invader ships appeared on his screen, at least that's what he thought they were. Their radar signatures were unknown, but the size and shape were about right.

The ships showed no movement, they merely orbited silently around the planet, far below the debris ring.

"We need the damned optical sensors," he cursed, not for the first time.

"We also need oxygen, nanites, neural gel, protein slurry, superconductor cables, copper, helium-3, medibots..."

"Shut up," he interrupted Jezzy gruffly. "Your constant pessimism isn't getting us anywhere now." He paused and thought, then radioed his engineer. "Willy?"

"Yo!" the response came immediately in his ear.

"We now have a radar image that you can check against the debris ring records. If there are any discrepancies, I want to know."

"Will do. Make sure we get there fast. The air in my regulator already tastes like painkillers."

"Wasn't planning on a nap."

Dev adjusted their course with short bursts from the maneuvering thrusters and approached the larger known shipwrecks orbiting Lagunia. For decades, those ships had attracted adventurous researchers from the Federation who cared little for academic recognition and were more interested in genuine, new fields of exploration. It amazed him how small their numbers had been, if the feeds were to be believed. Apparently, most academics were more interested in a cushy professorship at one of the universities on the core worlds or a well-paid job in industry than in searching for truly new knowledge under, admittedly, miserable conditions. Lagunia had never promised more than adventure and relatively loosely regulated projects for artifact hunters. That was the only explanation why the final battle between the extinct Lagunians and the Clicks had not been investigated as closely as it should have been. After all, the Fleet had collected enough data from actual confrontations with the enemy over seventy years of war.

When the early prospectors could not find any active systems aboard the wrecks, the initial enthusiasm had faded. The main prize had always been functioning Click data loggers so they could learn more about the codes they used and their encryption systems—besides an actual Click corpse, of course. It was considered a miracle that neither goal had ever been met. The aliens were very conscientious about never letting anything fall into the hands of the Federation. For this reason, all Fleet and media analysts agreed that a major research investment in the debris ring of Lagunia would be a waste of money and time since, if there had been anything of value, the aliens would have sent a fleet long ago to destroy it instead of allowing mankind to take possession.

It wasn't until hours later, hours of watching the radar screen for any surprises like alien ships accelerating toward them, that Willy woke him from his musings.

"Boss?" the Dunkelheimer radioed from the mess hall.

"Uh, yeah?" Dev blinked and rubbed his burning eyes.

"I found a deviation here. We should check it out."

"Come on over."

"Nah, better come to the mess hall. Bring Aura now but leave the crybaby there."

"We're coming." Dev peeled himself out of his straps and looked at Aura. "Willy's spotted something." Addressing Jezzy, he said, "Keep an eye on the screens. I

77

don't want any of those barges coming after us. All they have to do is blow on us, and we're dead."

He pushed off from his chair, floated out the cockpit door, and into the central corridor. When he reached the mess hall he activated his magnetic boots, which pulled him to the floor with a loud *clonk!*

Willy was already waiting for them at the holotank, which was displaying a large ship with a green cast. The image flickered erratically due to the unreliable power supply or a short somewhere in the relays, but Dev was quite sure it was the silhouette of a Fleet destroyer.

"I hope you didn't spend your time going through the catalog of ships we've had to dodge and whose captains we had to lie to over the years," Aura said with a furrowed brow as they gathered around the image. Her hair formed a halo of greasy strands around her face, which was a picture of loveliness even half-covered. Dev again wished fervently for a functioning wet cell. One got used to one's own stench quite quickly, to other people's less so, but that too came with time. What remained disgusting, however, was the dull feeling on the skin when it was so covered in sebum that it felt like wax when you ran your fingers over it.

"That's the *Danube*," Willy said, not responding to her teasing. Dev thought the engineer looked unusually tired.

"Isn't that the destroyer that sent a detachment of Marines to evacuate the Bellingers after they sent a distress signal?"

"Right." The Dunkelheimer pointed to the sleek space-craft with the massive guns in the graceful design typical of the Harbinger ships. "She was one of the ships that wasn't ordered to the gate and later oversaw the evacuation of the civilians."

"And what does that tell us?" Dev asked.

"I was able to detect her signature in the radar images. Wasn't easy because she's surrounded by rather large chunks of debris."

"Sounds like it's not a coincidence," Aura said thoughtfully.

"My thought exactly. If I wanted to hide, I probably would have chosen that exact position."

"What do you think?" Dev asked his engineer. "Might the crew still be alive?"

"Hmm, doubtful. Our infrared barely works, but I've been on it for several hours now and only have two crude images. No heat radiation at all. As I said—and you should take this with a grain of salt—but if that's right, everything on board would be frozen."

"So, a functioning ship without a crew."

"At best, yes."

"Fuck me raw!" Aura ran a hand through her hair and then unconsciously knotted it into a braid to tame it. "That means we could, with luck—not that we ever have any— take over a fully functional destroyer?"

"Cannibalize it to get the *Bitch* back up to speed," Dev corrected her with a disapproving look.

"That's right. This is the jackpot we've been looking for."

"Damn fine work, Willy," he complimented the Dunkelheimer, unable to keep from smiling. It had been so long since the last time that it made his cheeks feel strangely stiff.

"Shit, yeah!" Aura agreed, grinning.

"But," Dev said, raising both hands placatingly, "I don't think we should rush anything. An abandoned destroyer that's completely operational and undamaged? That should at least set all the alarm bells ringing in our heads. Nobody leaves a weapon like that behind, especially since I see no reason why the crew should abandon their only means of getting away from Lagunia."

"There's only one way to find out. We'll have to get closer and then board the ship," Willy said seriously.

"A ghost ship in the middle of a ring of debris left by two alien races and in the shadow of an invasion fleet? I can't imagine anything better than going on board." Dev sighed as he stared at the green image in front of him, as if he could uncover the secrets that lay dormant inside its hull. "I'll go in with you and Dozer. Get the equipment together, everything we have and can use. Aura, you've got the *Bitch*."

"That's been pretty normal lately." She nodded. "You got it."

"For now, we'll limit ourselves to finding material we need to get the *Bitch* back to a state where we can get out of here as quickly as possible. But we have to be careful. If someone is alive on the *Danube* after all, I don't want to mess with them. I just hope that we realize that we're all human at such times. Still, we're not going in unarmed." He stared at the virtual *Danube* again, wishing he could see what might be waiting for them inside its lifeless shell.

Judging by his feelings, at least, nothing good.

6

"Captain, Commander," Rosenberg greeted them as they entered. The admiral was tall and beefy without appearing fat. His green eyes were alert and wise above the dark bags under his eyes. The space fortress *Carcassonne*'s control center was even larger than *Oberon*'s, but it was not built like an old amphitheater, rather like a doughnut. In the center was the command platform with a holotable and eight seats. The technology and the style of furnishing seemed even older than on the *Oberon* and were testament to the first two decades of the war, when the Federation still had maximum resources and funds at its disposal.

The ring surrounding the pedestal contained workstations for a hundred or more specialists. In addition to organizing the sensor and weapons systems in normal wartime, they were busy monitoring the Tauon transits at the jump point located in the center of the horseshoe-shaped space station. Even now they were working quietly and precisely, despite the loss of Terra and most of Sol. The silence, however, might have been due to the acoustic shielding that enveloped the command area housed within the control center.

"Thank you for inviting me, Admiral," Nicholas replied quickly when Silly did not respond and gazed blankly into nothingness. He nudged her lightly from the side and she blinked a few times.

"Thank you for seeing us, sir," she said finally, shaking Rosenberg's proffered hand after they saluted.

"I must say that I was wondering why it took you a week to accept my invitation."

"The *Oberon* is not in good shape, sir. Not only did we suffer fatalities and injuries, but we also evacuated two platoons of Marines and some recruits who were not doing very well. We felt it necessary to personally supervise and support the rescue and repair efforts," Nicholas said apologetically. It was not a lie, even if it wasn't exactly the truth.

"I had a breakdown, Admiral," Silly said. Nicholas blinked in surprise. Rosenberg raised his eyebrows and his eyes widened.

"Captain?"

"Hostile elements within the Federation... our commander, Konrad Bradley..." she interrupted herself, swallowing audibly. "Saphel Pyrgorates, commander of the Fleet and aide to Vice Admiral Augustus Bretoni, murdered him. Our Marines have provided us with records of the event."

"Captain Bradley is dead?" Rosenberg was startled, though it was not apparent why. Whatever the reason, he quickly regained control of his facial expression.

"That's... yes." Silly nodded with a stony expression and Nicholas understood all too well how much effort it cost her to maintain control at that moment. He only had to listen inside himself. Her every word was like a slap that resonated through his entire body.

"I had a very close relationship with my commander. He was more than my superior, he was my mentor and my friend."

"I'm very sorry to hear that," Rosenberg replied, then pointed to three of the empty seats. He had wisely sent his staff away for this conversation. Nicholas doubted Silly would have been so honest about her feelings otherwise, though he had never expected her to be completely honest with the admiral, either.

After they were seated, Rosenberg spread his hands. "If you provide me with your Marines' helmet camera data, I will issue an appropriate notice to apprehend Commander Pyrgorates."

"It would be better—" Silly began, but Nicholas beat her to it.

"That would be very kind, Admiral." He glanced at her, and her eyes narrowed.

"It is important to me that your allegations are taken seriously, and evidence is secured, Captain," the *Carcassonne*'s commander continued. "And I thank you for your honesty. I want to be just as honest with you. I don't really know what to do with you. According to the latest data available in the Fleet Reconnaissance Network, Federation-wide orders are in effect to detain and decommission the *Oberon* pending Fleet court proceedings. You, Captain Thurnau, have been stripped of your rank and are considered the primary defendant."

Nicholas expected an indignant outburst from Silly, but

she remained silent and merely withstood the admiral's gaze as he examined her closely.

"At the same time, I am faced with the fact that Earth Defense has been obliterated or is offline. Neither the sky fortress nor any of the remaining defense platforms are responding. Even Luna is silent, although according to our sensors it has not been bombed. There are no ships left in orbit that we know of, and there are only a few scattered units in the outer system that have somehow managed to get to safety. The Clicks have imposed a blockade but have done nothing since conducting a few targeted orbital strikes. All the ships that were docked with us were withdrawn before the battle against the alien invaders."

"We are your only ship," Silly concluded.

"Yes. I am therefore inclined to suspend the fleet admiral's orders for the time being. It may cost me my head when this is all over, however, I don't currently see a scenario in which this will be over. I have to use the resources I have, and you have a battle-ready Titan at your disposal."

"More or less battle-ready," Nicholas objected.

"Well, it's certainly in better shape than anything else I see out here, because there's simply nothing left."

"What about the *Caesar*?" Silly asked.

"She's still in orbit around Terra. However, she seems to be inactive. At least we haven't detected an energy signature."

"That's a ruse. Pyrgorates and his minions were prepared. Some shuttles escaped before we sent them to hell just like the others." Her voice was dangerously close to a growl now, and Nicholas worried that her apparently restored ability to maintain her composure was beginning to unravel again.

"Unfortunately, we haven't been able to observe any sign of that," Rosenberg said. "We're not in a good place out here at S2 to have any sort of overview of what's going on in orbit around Terra. But there is one thing we know very well." He gestured to the holotable and quickly tapped on his forearm display. An image of a fleet with several dozen ships of varying sizes trailing long exhaust flares appeared. "This is the last refugee movement from Earth, everything that could be evacuated at the last minute. After the first wave of evacuations, there were barely enough helium-3 pellets left. That's why they're sort of flying on low flame, but they should arrive here in ten hours. We'll make sure they can safely jump out of the system."

"Don't let them fly to a core world," Nicholas said. "Species X is coming out of the hyperspace gates. First Lagunia, then Terra. None of the transit systems we flew through showed any trace of the aliens. Not even Epsilon Eridani."

Rosenberg mused. "We can send them to Dunkelheim. Those people scare me, but they're more capable of resistance than most fringe worlds, and they're armed to the teeth. If anyone is still able to keep some order, it's them. Besides, they've fully industrialized several agricultural moons."

"Good idea."

"He could also be hiding among them," Silly thought aloud, frowning.

"Excuse me?"

"Pyrgorates." She stood and stepped to the holotable.

Then, with rapid gestures, she zoomed in on two of the large cigar-shaped shuttles. "That one. They're identical in design to the ones that escaped into orbit from the valley north of Shanghai. He could be aboard one of them."

"Those are last-generation DeVries line shuttles. Several hundred of them were built," Rosenberg objected, striving for a calm, understanding voice, Nicholas admired his effort. The admiral stood and zoomed out again. "How many left from that valley you were talking about?"

"Three. We were able to destroy seven while still on the ground or during their launch."

"I see." Rosenberg used his finger to mark a total of fifteen ships in the scattered evacuation fleet, which then flashed red. "These are all identical DeVries ships. Any one of them could be the ones you're looking for."

"We could search each ship before they are allowed to jump," she suggested.

"Then we'd have to have the Marines turn each one upside down. You know better than I do that would take days—for each ship."

"Yes." She looked the admiral in the eye and showed no sign of saying more.

He shook his head. "Out of the question. Our most urgent objective is to get these people to safety. On board, in addition to key Fleet officials, are high-ranking politicians and other important figures critical to the maintenance of the Federation and its governing body."

"I'd be willing to bet that the first thing they did was bail out when the enemy came out of the gate."

Rosenberg hesitated.

"Thought so."

"Listen," Rosenberg said in a conciliatory tone, "these people are important to the survival of the Federation, no matter what you or I may think of bureaucrats. I'm going to issue orders to the first transit ship's systems directing the Dunkelheim authorities to take custody of Commander Pyrgorates upon disembarkation, should he be aboard."

"That's kind," Nicholas replied before Silly could say anything rash. To his relief, she took a deep breath and, after a long look in his direction, nodded.

"Good, then that's settled. I will return you to duty for the time being and suspend the fleet admiral's current orders on my authority in lieu of the changed strategic situation. If von Solheim is still alive, he will understand that we need every ship we have left."

"No one has been harmed."

"Excuse me?"

"No one was harmed," Silly repeated, "in our atmospheric jump. *Novigrad* was evacuated enough to drop the last of the capsules before the ring broke up, and ground defenses destroyed the government hub. The wreckage was small enough that when they hit it posed no threat to Shanghai."

"I don't know, I couldn't track it, but your actions were reckless at the very least. Not to mention the property damage, even if by some miracle no one was killed. Your dedication to your Marines and your XO, on the other hand, is something I cannot condemn. That's Fleet spirit." The admiral nodded appreciatively. "I don't even want to know how long you'll be remembered for that in the history books and in academy hallway gossip."

"The Clicks showed that conjunction zones could be

created when they destroyed our homeworld that way," Silly replied calmly. "I just copied their procedure and made calculations according to the mass ratios of the hub to Earth and then got a conjunction phase lasting two seconds in free fall. Actually, it's not as difficult as it sounds."

"It's never been done before, anyway." Rosenberg screwed up his face. "That's because spaceships don't normally crash through an atmosphere."

Silly turned away from the holotable and toward her superior. "Admiral, since we're putting ourselves at your service, could you provide us with your maintenance drones and materials to get the *Oberon* ready for combat again?"

Nicholas hoped the admiral would not take offense at the fact that she did not actually have to cooperate and that, on the contrary, he should be grateful. But Rosenberg seemed to take it with the equanimity of an experienced officer.

"That won't be a problem. It's not like they're needed anywhere else." He waved carelessly. "Stand by on your ship. If an opportunity arises to contact the scattered units in the outer system, I may send you toward Saturn to assemble them into a flotilla. We must do what we can to draw as many enemies away from Terra as possible. If we're lucky and the Clicks remain reasonably inactive for a while longer, we may be able to assemble a fleet from the fringe worlds and liberate Earth."

To Nicholas, that plan sounded like unrealistic wishful thinking. Especially when he thought of the 1,000 enemy ships that had their hands firmly wrapped around humanity's throat and the fact that just about everything operational in the Fleet had been pulled together for Operation

Iron Hammer. But he couldn't blame Rosenberg. At times like this, the only thing a good officer could do was whatever was possible and work toward the impossible, so as not to abandon himself and his subordinates to hopelessness.

Silly seemed to realize this as well because she nodded gravely and saluted.

"We'll do our best, Admiral."

The conversation was followed by a meeting between their respective staffs, discussing the intricacies of system integration, the various exchange channels, and repair procedures.

As they walked through the long corridors of the space fortress back to their shuttle, Silly stopped at one of the large picture windows that pointed inward from the horseshoe-shaped station to the jump point. The *Oberon* was directly in front of them, outside the conjunction zone.

Their Titan was illuminated by spotlights like a prehistoric museum creature. The hull was riddled with impact craters and deep scars that ran along the starboard side, which faced them. Here and there, welders flashed like tiny fireflies and maintenance bots crawled across the hull, identifiable by their red position lights. The Oberon lettering on the bow, as large as a row house, was covered in soot in several places and had peeled off in large sections, probably from her fiery fall through Terra's atmosphere. Some of the anti-aircraft guns along the dorsal main fuselage flashed unsteadily under persistent short circuits, and many were still burning.

"The old lady doesn't look good." Silly voiced what he was thinking.

"She looks like a Titan that did what she was supposed to do."

"She stood up. Did we?"

"There was nothing you could have done. The battle was lost."

"I know it was the right decision. After all, you're standing next to me now." She continued looking straight ahead as he gave her a sidelong glance. "That's what's important."

"Thank you," he said seriously, but she shook her head.

"You would have done the same for me and the crew. Without us, we're nothing but fallen fruit left here to rot— by the Fleet, the Clicks, or that damned Species X. People think *juratis unitatis* is a sign of our stubbornness. But it isn't. *Committed to unity means everything because without our unity we are nothing but dust swept before the wind.* We have no home port, so we must be the home we all long for. That's why there was nothing unusual about my maneuver."

"Silly," Nicholas said, and waited until she turned away from her ship outside the window to look at him. "I know you want to kill Pyrgorates. I feel the same way, I'm sure you can imagine, but Jason is still out there. We had to leave him on Earth."

"I read Ludwig's report. He wrote that Jason voluntarily stayed behind with those *mutants*."

"He gave them his word."

"His."

"We can't leave him behind. I know you don't like each other, but he's my brother and he's a good man."

"He hated your father," she countered with a bitter twist of her mouth.

"The loss of our mother hit him hard, and he blamed Dad for it instead of working through his pain." Nicholas shook his head. "He's all that's left of my family."

Silly didn't answer, instead turning back to *Oberon*. "We should go back."

Later, they stood on the bridge watching the arrival of the refugee fleet on the holoscreen; they were still alone on the command deck. Daussel was part of the detachment overseeing systems and protocol integration on the *Carcassonne*.

The civilian ships had fanned out into a semicircle in front of the open part of the horseshoe-shaped space fortress. Nicholas had never seen so many ships queued to jump through a conjunction point. In Lagunia, there had barely been enough incoming transits per week to count on two hands.

Everything proceeded under great pressure, yet frustratingly slowly. This was due to safety distances and the constant recalculations of onboard computers that jump control had to reconcile. It was an impressive demonstration as to why the Federation had worked so hard on the hyperspace gate technology. Sending an entire fleet into transit simultaneously was a time and tactical advantage that could not be exaggerated. Except that this technology probably destroyed the Federation.

"Jung, tell the colonel he has clearance," Silly said, and Nicholas looked at her in surprise.

"Ludwig? What clearance?" he asked, irritated.

"I had him prepare all the shuttles. Fifteen detachments of Marines that will go aboard the Devries's to track down Pyrgorates and all the conspirators."

"You *what*?"

"I knew you'd try to talk me out of it." She shrugged. "Ludwig wasn't hard to convince because he saw the sense in it."

"But we have orders to the contrary!" he protested.

"Maybe, but Rosenberg has made it clear that he needs us. I don't think he's going to fire on us, and those ships have been stuck in queue so long that we'll have everything done long before it's their turn to transit. Some of those things are so old that just getting their power pattern cells up and calibrated takes an hour."

"He may not shoot at us, but he will..." Nicholas faltered, his features slipping. "*That's* your plan. You want him to relieve you of your command!"

Silly didn't answer, but her expression hardened.

"I won't let you do that! I don't want this post, and I could never do it as well..."

"No!" she snapped at him. "I was never meant for command. Look where it's gotten us!"

"Pyrgorates may not even be on board," he said, trying another angle of attack. He knew full well when he wouldn't get anywhere with Silly. "He saw us jumping. He's not stupid, so he'll know there's not enough for a system jump, but there is enough for one to S1 or S2. Since S2 is out of the question, he'll have reckoned that we could be waiting for him here. I'd like to bet that he's still on *Caesar*."

"In the middle of the Click blockade?" she asked incredulously, shaking her head.

"Maybe he knows more than we do. It wouldn't surprise me, after all. You want to get him too, but he's just a stooge for the exiles who are up to something big. We have to stop that."

"*You* have to stop it."

"No, *we* do. If Pyrgorates isn't aboard one of the shuttles, you'll never get your revenge if you're in the *Carcassonne*'s brig."

Silly grimly pursed his mouth. Distaste was reflected in her eyes, but her lips remained closed.

"Lieutenant," he called without releasing her gaze, "countermand that order. Colonel Meyer is not to launch. I repeat, *do not* launch."

"Understood," came the reply with audible confusion.

"Listen," he said to Silly. "We have an alternative: send the Barracudas out on a test flight and have them attach sentinel mines to the DeVries shuttles. They won't detect them nor will Rosenberg if our guys fly past close enough while they drop them. From then on, we'll be able to track all their movements through the barque network. If any of them separate and arrive at an identical point, we'll know where to strike and where the exiles are hiding. That would be an advantage all the way around, and we'll still be here to destroy the *Caesar*." He added grimly, "Whether Pyrgorates is on board or not."

7

The vector thruster pilot turned out to be even more fanatical than Sirion had expected. It was obvious the Harbingers were not typical followers of Pyrgorates, assuming he was the leader of the local conspirators. Yet the man's stubborn strength, considering the pain he was in, surprised him.

In the end, he had had to use his sequester software. Like any self-respecting pilot, his victim had a data jack so he could interface with the vessel via neural cable and exert direct control over each system. This was a great advantage in operating a ship, but a disadvantage if someone managed to upload sequester software into their augmented brain.

Even though Sirion's body consisted more of implants than flesh and blood, he could definitely see the disadvantages in that. Not only would he not grow old, which he had never wanted anyway, but being half-computer offered a set of attack paths such as those now afflicting the pilot. He was now just a bleeding doll slumped on the front seat behind the windshield. A thread of saliva ran from his open mouth down his chest. Although his brain now had as much personality as a slice of toast, he still deftly and routinely steered the plane just above the swells of the churning Pacific. As soon as Sirion's memory clusters ceased transmitting commands, the man would be brain dead.

The flight took them across the ocean past the gigantic carpet of garbage that spread halfway between North America and Asia, toward the coast of the Terran state of China. For Sirion, it was just another sight of the human condition that so disgusted him.

After several hours, they reached the mainland and flew over the deserted coastal strip below the speed of sound so as not to cause too much noise. The engines could barely be heard over the constant offshore wind, which cost them some speed. Nevertheless, five hours later, he saw the Himalayas looming in the window. The towering snow-capped peaks against the navy blue sky of dawn appeared almost peaceful despite their imposing size. His "work" had led him twice to Fleet Headquarters, where he dispatched a high-ranking officer on each occasion. One had officially died from an exovirus that had turned his gastrointestinal tract into a sieve. The other had unfortunately hanged himself after he was to be tried for profiting from piracy in the Harbingen system. Sirion was not amenable to irony, but that the same conspirators who paid him to kill a captain were the same ones who had paid that officer to allow their ships through made him all the more cautious.

Bradley, he thought, and that grim feeling was as new as it was unpleasant. With his dying breath, the Harbinger captain he had hated so much had done something much worse to him than the indirect murder of his mother.

Sirion had spent his life repressing his pain over her loss to the point that he had eventually been cut off from his own feelings. Not having to deal with remorse or other emotional uncertainties, however, was what had made him the best at what he did. He knew he was a sociopath and had simply accepted being unreceptive to empathy. Bradley had changed that by turning his world upside down. For years, a scene had played in his mind, like a movie, of what the moment would look like when he finished off the captain and watched his life drain from his eyes. Instead, he had found himself wanting to save that very man as he died. He didn't even know why, exactly. Did he want Bradley to tell him more about what happened the day his mother died? Did he want to make sure he was not simply lying to save his skin, even though he now had the opposite impression?

He would never know, at least not from the dead man's own lips. But Konrad Bradley had whispered something to him that could only mean that he had *not* lied. A proof of trust in the very last person he should have trusted, the one who had revealed all his hatred to him.

The codes to Omega's central data storage, he thought, repeating them in his mind. They were long, complicated codes. The captain must have either had a memory cluster built into his brain or a remarkable talent for memorization.

Sirion felt the burden the codes imposed. They weighed so heavily on his shoulders because they indicated two things no one in the Federation was aware of. First, Omega apparently still existed, or at least its central data storage did. That was probably the most valuable warehouse of data potentially available to mankind. Second, there had been exactly one man who had known about it and would have been able to gain access. The question was why he had never done it, even though it could have cleared his name by proving that Omega's order had been to abandon Harbingen and flee with the colony ships.

An incoming communication link sounded, bringing him out of his thoughts. The signal was a barely audible beep coming from the console. That setting had apparently been retrofitted by the pilot since direct neural control normally did not emit any sound at all.

Sirion tried to get the message on one of the screens without plugging in. If the exiles were as good as they thought they were, they would have installed code traps to ward off unauthorized access. Conspirators did not typically like strangers roaming around their networks, and Sirion had taken orders from them long enough to know how paranoid they really were. Even he had not managed to learn much about them. He only knew they had cast a net throughout the core worlds, and even some of the fringe worlds, and that they had invested primarily in the deep space industry, away from the main trade routes. They could have been mistaken for pirates because they did their dirty work so far from the core, but that was exactly what had played into their favor for two decades and cast a shadow in which they had thrived like fungus.

It took him several precious minutes before he managed to find the right controls and pull up a short voice-to-text message which the onboard computer read out in an androgynous voice.

"Unregistered flying object, you are about to enter a Terran Fleet restricted zone. Immediately turn on your transponder and transmit your clearance codes or we will open fire. You have sixty seconds. This is your first and final warning."

Sirion looked at his chronometer and then at the radar screen. Two objects were already approaching at hypersonic speed while his pilot continued stoically on-course to the programmed destination just as the sequester software had commanded his fried brain to do.

He used the few seconds remaining to tear one of the evac-chutes from the cabin wall, strap it on, and pressed the red button to activate the emergency exit. Behind him, the sloping tail ramp was jettisoned as he pulled the rescue pack onto his back. The roar of turbines mixed with the howl of the wind to create an aural assault which his ears immediately dialed down. The automatic ejection system launched the rescue parachute backward through the opening and opened in the wake of the turbines. As if struck head-on by the hand of God, Sirion was thrown back, and within two breaths had put a kilometer between himself and the vector thruster.

The deafening supersonic noise of the interceptor missiles thundered through the freezing air and sped upward, trailing bright trails of smoke. He watched as they impacted with the aircraft a short distance away. Short-lived explosions shredded first the left wing then the entire tail. What was left of the cockpit crashed into the snow and wedged itself inside the end of a long fissure in the towering Himalayan mountainside.

Before Sirion fell backward into the snow, he extended his monofilament blades from his forearms, severed the straps of the evac chute, and fell the last five meters to the snow. His momentum cut a swath of its own. Once he came to a stop he had to lie still for a few seconds. The impact had punched the air out of his lungs and been quite painful despite the soft deep snow. He doubted he would have escaped without injury if not for his titanium-coated skeleton.

After recovering, he looked for the remnants of the chute, which were easy to locate by their orange-red signal colors and residual light enhancement. He sliced them into strips and wrapped them around his boots to form a tread surface wide enough to help him walk in the snow.

Then he set off in the direction of the wreck, which was stuck in one of the mountain slopes about three kilometers away and was emitting black smoke. The dawn was still faint, showing tentatively as a navy glow that faded into deep darkness two fingers' breadth above the horizon.

Every step was exhausting, as if someone had tied weights to his legs. He repeatedly sank up to his knees despite his improvised snowshoes. There was no vegetation out here, so no chance he could find sticks or other material to build better ones. About halfway to the wreck he spotted the light from a vehicle in the valley between two mountains heading directly to the crash site. Despite his two previous missions to the Terran Fleet Headquarters, Sirion only knew that was likely in the northeast area of the mountain range, close to the so-called Quadrant 2, which mainly contained storage facilities and reactors that provided energy to the huge military complex. This fact was responsible for the rather late reaction of the security forces. They were now fighting their way through the wind and snowdrifts to investigate who or what had just entered the restricted security area. Such airspace violations should be virtually impossible. The Fleet took the security of its left ventricle—the sky fortress was the right—very seriously and did not issue second warnings, as he had just experienced.

With half a kilometer to go, he burrowed deep into the snow as a hovercraft flew in an arc around the burning wreckage to scan it. The vehicle looked like a curved caterpillar with a smooth underside and barely kicked up white flakes. Searchlights mounted above the cockpit swept across the crash path and along the immediate vicinity of the vector thruster's destroyed remains, looking for anyone who might have escaped or was hiding.

Sirion used the time to cover the distance, working his way from one piece of wreckage to the next. The burning remains of engines, wings, and cabin elements had formed a cone that terminated in the crushed cockpit. He sought cover behind two seats, that, together with their steel suspension, must have been torn out after one of the missile impacts. The hovercraft soon completed its search pattern and stopped, stern first, ten meters from the cockpit. The hatch turned into a ramp as it folded back, and four soldiers in full armor and bearing assault rifles came running out. They moved quickly and professionally, secured the perimeter, and then marched to the front of the vector thruster, which was less than four meters long and now resembled a cut-open soda can. One of them put out the fire with nanofoam and two of them went inside. The other two stayed outside and scanned the surrounding area.

Sirion crawled to his left, under cover of the deep snow, and advanced in an arc that led him to the hovercraft. The stern ramp had closed again. He was not dealing with beginners. The only question was how valuable his Blacklinks, retrofitted only three months ago, would now prove to be. They had made short work of the air traffic control firewalls on Lagunia, but this challenge was a significantly different order of magnitude.

Since hovercraft distance sensors were built into their air cushions, he crawled underneath them, lying on his back so his body was no higher than the surface of the snow. He found what he was looking for on the vehicle's front: an access panel for maintenance electronics that accessed the peripheral systems. For security reasons, these did not directly interface with the cockpit.

He opened the panel with his right monofilament blade, which cut through the armored steel like butter, then proceeded carefully and slowly so as not to cut any cables behind it. He retracted the blade and pulled out the cable with the round connector head and plugged it into its designated port. His Blacklink routine loaded itself into the vehicle's system and began battling the firewalls as it flooded the log files with cryptic error messages and tried to keep the defense routines busy with deleting tasks intended to avoid memory conflicts. Sirion chose a simple command, pulled out the cable when the upload was complete, and slipped around the hovercraft. The two guards on the wreckage had abandoned their positions and were scanning the area with the lights mounted on their assault rifles.

His cerebral booster was still busy decoding their radio signals, so he could only guess that they had been warned by the pilot that something was wrong and that the wreckage or part of it was transmitting malware. That must have been why they were searching the crash site.

He paused until they were looking away from the ramp and patiently waited until his Blacklink scored a victory and lowered it. He slipped inside the small cabin, past the four soldiers' bucket seats to the narrow cockpit door. He silently turned the latch and slipped through. The pilot was slumped in the straps of his seat. A cable connected his data jack at his left temple to the instruments in front of him. His hands flew over control pads at the end of his armrests, presumably in a desperate attempt to fend off the Blacklink's attack.

Sirion had deliberately given the aggressive subroutines a malfunction in the ramp hydraulics as a lure to lead the soldiers onto a false trail. They would remain calm thinking that the assault on their systems could be suppressed and not a deliberate attack aimed at damaging or sabotaging the craft. The pilot could boast of having averted worse, and the log would record that the defense had been successful.

With his index finger, he injected the prepared killer toxin into the pilot's carotid artery. He placed the smooth ReFace mesh on the victim's face after the brief seizure subsided and he had gone limp. The tiny sensor follicles penetrated the skin and fed data about his molecular composition and micro-metabolic processes to the adaptive neural tissue based on Sirion's DNA. He kept an eye on the ramp for twenty seconds, until the mask lit briefly, and he placed it on his face, taking care to attach the edges to the offset points on his cheeks and chin. He waited for the sharp pain to subside, and the job was done. When he unplugged and unbuckled the dead pilot and pulled him from the seat, he saw a red light come on. He plugged into the control system.

"Topper? Topper!"

Sirion loaded all the pilot's previous radio transmissions into his memory clusters and evaluated the voice. It took a long time. A glance aft showed cones of light in front of the ramp, lighting up the snow like white marble. Using the onboard system, he closed the cockpit door and locked it electronically. A minute later, someone knocked. First twice in quick succession, then more forcefully.

"TOPPER!"

When the evaluation was complete and his transducer had been supplied with the appropriate file, he finally answered, "Yes?"

"What the hell is going on! We radioed you!"

"I just fought off the cyberattack." He struggled to maintain a breathless tone. To get around the subject, he asked, "Did you guys find anything? The signal is gone."

"No, nothing. Absolutely nothing. Why is the door locked? Everything okay in there?" the muffled voice wanted to know.

"Yes. There are still remnants of the attack routines in the system that are causing some malfunctions, but I can't see any problems with the critical components after initial analysis. I'll have that fixed by the time we get back."

A pause.

Sirion looked at the body beside him. Awkward. He

would have preferred to dispose of it here. Now it would be more difficult.

"All right, then, get us out of here."

"You got it."

He ordered the autopilot to fly back on the exact route they had come. If there were no surprises, which he did not expect, he would need no flying skills. The computer gave the flight time as fourteen minutes. He used the time to think of what to do about the body. The front windshield could not be opened, so he couldn't eject the pilot, which probably would have been noticed by an area surveillance sensor anyway. There were no cavities behind the panels in the tiny cockpit except for an indentation that had apparently been retrofitted. It contained two cans of some Terran energy drink.

Improvisation.

Sirion undressed his victim and pulled the military one-piece over his form-fitting body armor. Its three-millimeter thickness tightly hugged his contours. Then he went through sensor recordings from the last few weeks, filtering them for the face of his new identity. From several recordings that displayed "Topper Wilkinson," he memorized the man's gait and how he talked with some maintenance mechanics. Body language was important, the slightest deviation could make another person feel uncomfortable or subconsciously realize that something was not as it should be.

Two minutes before the end of the flight, he exited the augmented reality recordings and watched their final approach. Their destination was a hangar opening in one of the five thousand-meter peaks that surrounded Mount

Everest like watchful guardians, a wide slice of angular darkness amid the rugged white desert. The slope below was just steep enough that the hovercraft could ascend it under full power, its whirring turbines dragging a small storm of snowflakes behind it. The first real light of the day was already illuminating the area with a grayish dawn before the hangar swallowed them up like the mouth of a great whale.

As soon as the automatic hangar control took over, he entered a final command to the door control and pilot software, and then unplugged himself. Next, he packed up his backpack and observed the various parked vehicles and fighter jets secured to parking positions and suspensions on the ground and along the wall. Maintenance drones flew past, their rotors vibrating, joining in the coordinated bustle of the hangar. A narrowing sliver of pale light on the opposite wall told him that the doors were already closing again. He waited a few seconds in front of the cockpit door until it unlocked, then quickly slipped through. It locked again directly behind him. The door would remain locked until the technicians realized something was wrong and began to undo his hack. All he needed was time.

"Any idea what that was out there?" a female soldier asked. She had not yet walked onto the ramp, which was closing again. She had short brown hair and eyes as green as emerald. Her face was sweaty and the visor of her helmet, which she had tucked under her armored arm, was slightly fogged.

"Some automated sabotage software." He shrugged, as many people did all the time, wondering once again why the ramp was closed. As he turned to leave, he noticed her frowning out of the corner of his eye. Something was missing.

"What is it with you guys? Spot anything in the cockpit?" he asked with some inner reluctance.

She shook her head. "No. Just the pilot's body. Barely recognizable as human. We recovered the black box. Rahul already took it to data forensics."

"I wonder who would be stupid enough to race toward Fleet Headquarters?" Sirion shook his head and turned again to leave.

"Hey," the female soldier said, eyeing him in confusion.

"Yeah?"

She glanced at the cockpit door, then gave him a look that seemed to ask if there was something wrong with him.

Sirion's thoughts sped up. He followed the path of her eyes and tried on a disappointed expression. "It's stuck."

"It's stuck? We only have ten minutes before the technicians get here."

"I know." She began to scrutinize him more closely and he decided to take the initiative—and the risk—took a step forward and kissed her. It was a fleeting moment that disgusted him and sent a shiver of discomfort through his body as if he'd been electrocuted.

His instincts hadn't failed him, and he could literally feel her melt into his gesture of affection, which told him even more about their apparent secret relationship.

"Then here, I don't care," she breathed as he pulled away.

"Can't," he countered in a firm voice. "I've already been instructed by the control room to report immediately on the electronic attack."

"But—"

"No," he repeated firmly and walked to the ramp control. He lowered it with a swipe of his fist on the red button. The hydraulics blew air out with a hiss.

Disappointed, she pursed her mouth and nodded reluctantly. Before the edge of the ramp had even touched the ground, he walked quickly down it and immersed himself in the bustle of the ground teams. He had to change disguises before the body was found.

His destination was on the top floor, very close to the orbital elevator. It was a long way there and took him past numerous security gates that required rank insignia.

8

When Jason reluctantly jumped into the water, he was initially surprised that no liquid penetrated his helmet and that the rest of his body did not feel cold or damp.

At least not right away.

The carpet of garbage, which rose and fell with the waves like a viscous liquid of faded colors, felt somewhat like sliding through jelly, except that this jelly stuck to his suit. As he sank, he frantically tried to free himself from it; it felt as if ants were crawling on his skin. The weight of his suit made him sink like a stone.

Unlike on Lagunia, where he had dived often in his youth, the sea here was black and pale at the same time, filled with suspended particles yet without the slightest sign of life. The helmets and flashlights of the mutants around him, falling into the darkness like landing spaceships, made the particles look like the dust one might raise walking through an old book shop.

Two meters below the surface, the layer of garbage was different from what he had expected. It was less dense and interspersed with individual bags and indefinable scraps that became ever-smaller pieces as he descended. As the mutant had said, the Clicks' shuttle was directly below them, a huge shadow that made the hairs on the back of his neck stand on end. His cerebellum seemed unable to rid itself of some prehistoric instinct to flee, one that screamed he was headed for a deadly and ravenous monster in the darkness.

Well, it was monstrous in any case. Their plan once again seemed extremely insane given the size of the eerie spacecraft. For days, Baker had watched the approaches and the subsequent impacts of the Click ships from the beach before coming to Jason with his idea. This one shuttle, which had been larger than the others, convinced the mutant that his insane plan was entirely justified. Jason had had his doubts, but also no better alternative, and now here he was, unsure whether to regret it or not.

The first cones of lamp lights brushed across the surprisingly smooth surface of the extraterrestrial vessel. Jason could barely identify visible joints or welds. It was too dark to make out the flattened teardrop shape he had seen through the binoculars, but he thought they must be somewhere over the bow. One by one, the first mutants landed as if in slow motion. Those who had magnetic boots activated them.

Jason had to stretch out wide to avoid slipping off the hull as he touched it first with his feet, then his stomach and hands. As soon as he straightened, he looked for Baker's silhouette in the jumble of the many lights, slightly taller and broader than the rest and shoulders hunched forward.

When he found him, he walked over to him like an

extremely clumsy astronaut. It was an embarrassingly pitiful act caught in slow motion, and all the while he couldn't stop himself from glancing repeatedly into the darkness surrounding him, looking for some primeval shark to snap at him from the darkness.

"Baker," he said, "the airlock must be somewhere on the highest point of the topside. Click shuttles dock from the bottom up, remember."

The massive figure in front of him tilted his head.

"Can you hear me?" asked Jason.

Baker tapped an index finger against his helmet, about where his ear should be. Then he shook his head.

No radio communication. Great. The silence suddenly grew more oppressive. He glanced to his left and saw flickering plasma flares. The first mutants were already in the process of cutting open the hull. Judging by the bulge, they seemed to be working on the airlock. At least he hoped so because a vibration began to spread through his boots. At first, he thought it was his imagination, maybe he was shivering from the ice-cold water seeping in somewhere around his leg, but then he felt his bones shake from the vibration.

"Shit, they've detected us," he cursed, unheard. He shouldn't have been surprised. Indeed, it was more surprising the Clicks had taken so long to notice them. "They're going to take off!"

A bright blue glow spread beneath the black shadow of the shuttle, revealing, at a stroke, the vessel's dimensions. In space, shuttles like this might look small in the middle of nowhere and compared to much larger warships, but down here with their feet on the hull, their true size was frightening.

The mutants tore away a round piece of the black metal and jumped into the airlock along with the inrushing water. The others converged from various parts of the hull as if someone had set the playback speed of a movie to super slow motion.

The shaking grew worse, and a deafening roar filled the darkness. Jason hurried along with the others to get to the airlock when a heavy blanket seemed to settle on him from above, pressing down on his arms and shoulders. At first, he thought someone had grabbed him, but then a veil settled in front of his visor, behind which the light grew brighter. The weight eased and he tore the plastic mass from his head. They broke through the surface of the water, surrounded by torrents of plastic-infested spray that slid off the black hull.

Jason tottered as his boots threatened to lose their grip. He fell to his hands and knees to avoid slipping off the shuttle, a sure death sentence. Baker, who had caught the edge of the hole with one of his pawlike hands and was lying on his stomach, reached out with his other hand and barely managed to grab Jason as he began to slide off the curved hull under the increasing acceleration pressure of the spacecraft as it took off.

Groaning at the force pulling on his arm and trying to drag him down into the sea—hundreds of miles from any rescue—he gradually allowed himself to be pulled up, finally falling into the airlock that had been cut open. The shuttle must have already gained several hundred meters in altitude based on the approaching clouds. Glancing over the edge, he saw two mutants fall away and disappear.

Those who possessed magnetic boots were now running faster toward them.

"Come on, we've got to make room!" Baker boomed through his helmet, pulling Jason with him away from the ledge where he stood. They landed in a dark passageway where cones of lamp lights were retreating. The massive mutant figures were moving away from them, and the first bursts of weapons fire echoed off the walls. Jason pressed his back against the composite and waited as more and more of Baker's men landed in front of him like meteors of muscle. When no more appeared, Baker tried to pass, but Jason held him back with a hand on his arm.

"Wait!" he yelled, his voice echoing against the din of roaring and rattling assault cannons and machine guns. "I know where the bridge is. We inspected a wreck of this kind of shuttle. We need to hurry before they use the ship's systems against us. If the security bulkheads close, we're stuck!"

"Run ahead!" Baker urged. Jason nodded and made his way to the left, toward the stern.

When he had said "they" had already inspected a similar wreck, he actually meant the pioneers of the Fleet who had searched a half-intact shuttle after the Battle of Geminus and recorded everything. Scientists then analyzed the records and eventually came up with several theories about the purposes of various components and chambers. How valid they were nobody knew because they hardly had any frame of reference, but it was better than nothing.

He recognized corridors like the one they were running in from the pictures, and yet it was something completely different to see them in person. Unlike a Terran ship, there were hardly any corners. The walls converged in arcs and were pleasing to the eye, but that impression was marred by the ugly cables and conduits made of a morphing muscular tissue that constantly pulsed like living worms. If he had ever thought of what an eerie and repulsive spaceship should look like, this one would certainly have come close. There was also a pearlescent sheen that lay on the black walls, as if they were coated with an oily substance. The light was also strange, extremely dim with an unmistakable green tint that reminded him of the algae-rich waters of Lagunia. After a few seconds, they encountered the first two Click corpses, black-armored suits with slats where the face should be, slightly smaller than Jason but noticeably bulkier. Their heads were narrower at the bottom than at the top and extremely large. Both had holes in what passed for a chest, and each was missing one of its four legs. They lay in puddles of water and red liquid.

"Don't look like robots," Baker commented, whirling around as the sound of wind suddenly ceased.

"What was that?" Jason asked in alarm, tearing his gaze away from the Click corpses.

"Guess an emergency bulkhead sealed off the destroyed airlock."

"Go on, keep going," he urged the mutant, stopping in front of what looked like a circular mark in the wall. "Here. Behind this. Can you cut that open?"

"We can cut *anything* open."

Jason sensed that, despite the artificial gravity, acceleration had increased. They were certainly about to go into orbit, so their time was limited. A sideways glance at the bodies was enough to tell him they were about to explode.

Either by self-destruction or from their wounds.

As Baker and one of his men worked on the wall with their powerful fission cutters, he wondered how many soldiers before him had seen alien corpses during previous boarding attempts. They had known that they were not machines despite their robotic appearance, and yet the Federation had remained in the dark because no one had ever survived to pass on the knowledge.

I wonder if the same will happen here.

"Are you all right?" Baker asked. He had removed his helmet and lit a cigar.

"Are you crazy? We can't breathe the air in here!"

"Got an internal air tank," the mutant replied as he continued cutting. Mumbling, he added, "Should be enough for fifteen minutes."

Jason looked at his forearm display and considered the ambient air data. The oxygen content was minimal, but there was a worrying amount of carbon dioxide and nitrogen.

"So, are you all right? You look like you've seen a ghost."

"We're still alive," Jason replied. "Actually, they should have self-destructed by now. Something's different."

"Good for us, I'd say."

"Deviations from the expected are never good. First rule of soldiering."

"If the deviation means I'm still breathing, I don't care," Baker boomed over the hiss of plasma flame between his hands. The glowing circle he and his comrade had drawn in the door was nearly complete. Before that, however, the giant retreated and removed his assault cannon from his shoulder. He addressed his neighbor, "Get out of the way."

Jason already knew the expression on Baker's face and backed away as well. Baker lashed out and kicked what he thought was a door with his oversized boot. The material, an alien composite, Jason knew, immediately gave way and flew into a room that looked like a sphere split down the middle. A lone, pearly figure was holding a gun in its hand and fired past Baker's head.

The laser beam narrowly missed Jason and left an ugly glow in the wall behind him.

"DON'T SHOOT!" he yelled as loud as he could. At first, he didn't think the mutants had heard him or wanted to hear him, but then he saw them rush in, suffused by another beam that was apparently too short-lived to fully penetrate their body armor. Baker slammed his fist into the alien's head. It was thrown back, collided with an armature, and sagged against it like a puppet with its strings cut.

Jason fought his way past the two giants while others rushed in looking for more Clicks. There were four aliens on the bridge hiding behind four tanks of green liquid. They looked smaller than the large one in the pearl-colored armored suit Baker had taken down. Realizing what had happened and that the mutants were targeting them, the four left their cover, lurched toward the dead or unconscious alien figure, and crouched protectively in front of it, their long arms outstretched.

"What's that?" Baker asked, scratching his bald head.

"I've never heard of them having suits other than black," Jason said. One of the giants roughly patted the aliens down for weapons, though they didn't look like they had any pockets on them. The armor, which consisted of innumerable interlocking slats that flipped open and closed like mechanical gills, left no room for them. "Not even on the few helmet camera images Fleet reconnaissance has thanks to the first boarding attempts early in the war."

"Is that maybe why we haven't been blown up yet?" asked one of the mutants, a bull-like specimen with a mighty beard and Neanderthal forehead.

"Quite possibly. These little ones here..."

"Are they children?"

"I don't know. Maybe they're females and the one in the pearly suit is a male?"

"Different question," Baker interjected, "how do you fly one of these things?"

All eyes in the room turned to Jason and he raised his hands defensively.

"I don't know, I'm a logistics officer. I never was a bridge officer, let alone a pilot!"

"But you're a Fleet boy, kid," Baker boomed.

"And you're craftsmen. Still, you can't build a mahogany chaise lounge, can you?"

"A *what*?"

"That's what I mean."

Jason thought feverishly, trying to ignore the unpleasant pulsing sound humming in the background. It reminded him of the bursting methane bubbles on Lagunia that could be heard on every dive. It was an eerie sound, deep and piercing, an audible reminder that they were on their archenemy's ship. These aliens had not only destroyed his home but hadn't even bothered to communicate with humans or returned Terran attempts, except for their devastating response to first contact.

"Should we shoot the critters, boss?" one of the mutants asked. He was holding his vehicle-mounted MG with one hand pointed at the cowering aliens as he scratched his chin indecisively.

"Yeah, best—"

"No!" Jason yelled, stepping forward to push down the machine gun barrel. He might as well have been trying to bend an iron bar with his bare hands. The mutant chortled gleefully.

"Let him," Baker mumbled past his cigar. "These things are unarmed, an' we can rip 'em a second asshole later. Better make sure you keep an eye on your blood oxygen."

Jason knelt in front of the aliens, careful to maintain a healthy distance, worried they might jump on him even though they seemed rather frightened. Their body language was hard to read, probably because of the anthropomorphic prejudice he automatically assigned to them. Their long arms, which ended in three equally long fingers, were spread out so that they formed a kind of cocoon around the pearly Click. Their four legs, each with two knee joints, were bent as if they were crouching. The slatted louvers of their helmets attentively followed his every move.

If they didn't constantly adjust to his movements, he would have mistaken them for statues. Their black silhouettes betrayed no expression. Their suits could be concealing anything. Since there was no sign of a mouth or a respirator, let alone eyes or any optical device for vision, he was not surprised that the Federation had assigned—

though not officially—a high probability of their enemy being a machine civilization.

Jason began to have his doubts as he carefully eyed one of the four. Their helmets had a definitive V-shape and were as large as the mutants' headgear, despite their much smaller bodies. The louvers on the front followed the V-shape, opening and closing at regular intervals, and at their tops were two holes. No, not holes, lenses. Camera lenses? Sensors? When the one he was watching turned its head, he saw a funnellike depression on each side.

The aliens continued watching him, and he wondered what might be behind those featureless slats. Faces? Or were the suits part of their bodies, like the chitinous exoskeletons common to insects throughout the Federation? Such an exoskeleton could mean that they were soft or even gelatinous on the inside. But why were there no eyes or antennae? He figured it had to be metal body armor, though some doubt remained. He would have liked to take off a glove and touch them, but he didn't know how they would react.

That he and the mutants were alive at all bordered on miraculous. He did not understand it, and he didn't want to risk jeopardizing this strange yet gracious circumstance. However, he did want to find out why they were still breathing. Their plan had been crazy and had largely relied on the assumption that the shuttles were unmanned flying objects, because the Clicks had made no effort to drop any ground troops. It had seemed more logical that the vessels had come to gather supplies, even though water could be extracted more easily and cheaply from icy moons, asteroids, or even the moon. Perhaps they ate poisonous algae, of which the oceans had in plenty? After all, their homeworld was just as flooded as Earth, if not more. Jason had only agreed to the plan because he would rather try to sabotage the bridge systems of an alien craft before it self-destructed than perish uselessly in the toxic atmosphere of an alien beach. He had never expected to find Clicks, let alone Clicks that made no effort to press the red button.

He wanted to know why.

9

"Shit, I've been spending way too much time stuck in a crappy spacesuit lately," Dev grumbled as he floated toward the darkened *Danube* with short bursts of cold gas from the mobile jet pack strapped to his back. His only source of illumination was the reflection from Lagunia's blue-green surface—the system's star had disappeared behind one of the moons. It was just enough for him to make out the shimmer of the debris ring outlining the *Danube*'s regular cone shape.

"Now you know how we feel constantly crawling over the hull doing welding work," Willy grumbled over the radio. The engineer was not five meters behind him. Dozer followed with their equipment stowed in a belly pack.

"I belong in a cockpit."

"Could have stayed home."

"With Aura and Jezzy?" Dev asked, snorting. "They're in an even worse mood than I am."

"We can hear you, boss," Aura said, reminding him that

she was in temporary command of the *Bitch* and with it all the radio frequency command codes.

"Good, so we're done with the com check, too," he replied curtly and screwed up his face.

They moved through the vacuum in absolute silence, just a few meters above the edge of the debris. In the distance, the ring seemed to form a uniform surface, resembling ancient music records. But up close, he saw that the larger pieces of wreckage—remnants of engines, reactor block halves that made his radiation readouts spike momentarily when he flew over them, collapsed hull segments—were really widely spaced. The illusion of density stemmed more from the smaller debris of the massive battle that had ended with the destruction of the Lagoon. They were so numerous that they formed a carpet of dust that glittered in the reflected light, except that these "dust grains" were at least the size of a man's head.

The *Danube* was a ninety-meter cigar with a flattened snout and an elongated drive nacelle at the stern. Its main guns splayed out along the top like outstretched fingers. Dev saw no lights from portholes or position lamps. It looked like another cold, silent tomb in the vast cosmic graveyard. Nevertheless, he altered his course toward the last fifty meters and headed for a piece of wreckage directly below him. His HUD calculated its size as fifteen meters across at its widest point. Judging from its irregular shape, it was a hull segment that had taken heavy fire before the ship had exploded. It was colorless, like everything else out here, faded by time and radiation or perhaps just pale in the absence of direct sunlight.

"Where are we headed, boss?" Willy wanted to know.

"I need to get an overview first. That fragment there doesn't rotate, it hardly moves at all. We'll use the cover and check the sensors to see if we missed anything."

"That's a good idea," Dozer said in a monotone.

"Thanks, your encouragement makes me feel a lot better," Dev grumbled. "After all, with the *Bitch*'s sensors, or what's left of them, we wouldn't be able to tell if we've flown into a cornfield or a damned rock garden."

"The girls will figure it out," Willy said optimistically, though it was probably irony knowing the Dunkelheimer.

As they approached the hull fragment from behind, dipping into the cover of the ring instead of flying over its edge, he dared to turn on his helmet lights to avoid colliding with the object in the perfect blackness and smashing against it like an insect against a windshield.

When the two interlocking disks of white light met at the hull fragment's outward-curving surface, he was only a few meters away and his mobility unit automatically slowed him to minimum velocity. The first thing he noticed was that the metal wasn't colorless at all but had a greenish glow that he first thought was reflected light from Lagunia. Then he remembered that hardly any of its light was coming through the ring below him. The second thing he saw—and here he flinched so violently that his suit automatically hardened in anticipation of attack—was an eerie silhouette, like a living shadow.

"SHIT!" he blurted.

"What the hell is that?" Willy asked, tense.

Dev blinked away his fear and looked again. What he had thought was a shadow turned out to be a black image on the inside of the hull section in the form of a creature with four outstretched arms and a large head with something that looked like curved ram's horns.

"A monster," Dozer replied curtly.

"It looks like a nuclear shadow. You know, when vaporized bodies leave shadowy imprints on walls," Willy suggested.

Reluctantly, Dev continued to steer himself toward the remains of the hull until he reached the top edge and held on with outstretched hands, like someone peering over a wall. The *Danube* suddenly didn't seem as scary as it had when he compared it to this thing here. When he tilted his head and looked down, he saw the front end, swollen and irregular like the thick, scarred skin of a deep-sea monster.

"That just can't be," he breathed.

The engineer surfaced beside him, then caught and followed his head movement. "What is it?"

"Look at that. This isn't Click wreckage. It comes from the Lagoon!"

Willy said nothing for a few seconds. "The aliens," he finally muttered. "The invaders from hyperspace. This piece of wreckage belongs to one of their ships."

"Yes. I'll never forget the records of the battle. This belonged to one of them, but there couldn't have been any significant fighting here," Dev thought aloud, licking his suddenly dry lips. Using his helmet sensors, he looked around and let the AI do some quick analysis. "Thirty percent of the debris in the immediate area matches the composition of this one."

"So, no Lagoon fought here." Willy voiced what he was thinking as Dozer arrived and silently drifted beside him.

"No. Back then the Clicks were fighting the same

unknowns that we are. I don't need to do any radiation analysis to know that this debris is not new. Not to mention, there were no ships here that could have done this kind of damage."

"That doesn't make any sense."

"Think about what the Bellingers found in the ocean."

"A hyperspace gate? That's not even confirmed."

"What if," Dev continued undistracted, "the locals back then experienced the same thing we did two weeks ago? This wreckage belongs to one of the alien invader ships and it's over a hundred years old. And there's a destroyed hyperspace gate down on Lagunia."

"That would mean..." Willy fell silent beside him, and only the faint background murmur of radio communication remained. "Shit, man, I have no idea what that means."

"What's that shadow?" Dozer asked.

"I don't even want to know." Dev shuddered, glad they couldn't see the outline of the demon—he couldn't think of a better word—from his position. "I have no idea what any of this means, but we need to get to that ship."

He reached a hand toward the *Danube* and stroked the smooth hull with his helmet lights. It looked almost freshly polished, as if the ship had just flown out of the shipyard, which made it look out of place.

"Without spare parts, fuel, and oxygen we're screwed no matter what happened here," he said.

"Let's hope there aren't any more surprises, then," Willy grumbled.

One by one, they released the edge of the wreckage and floated through the vacuum with short bursts of cold gas. The destroyer grew larger as they approached. Dev remembered too well how he had had to fly a daring maneuver into a tropical storm on Lagunia to shake off the pursuing Marines that had been chasing Sirion. What might have become of them now that the *Danube* was a ghost ship?

We'll probably find out very soon.

"Everything still quiet on your end, Aura?" he asked over the radio as they approached the port airlock. It was located along the destroyer's dorsal seam near the stern, a small hexagon with the white lettering LS-1-BB and a dot code for automatic spacecraft proximity sensors.

"No movement at all," the power node specialist replied. "At least nothing our completely fucked up sensors can pick up. But the radar thinks nothing's changed."

"Good, we're reaching the airlock now." Dev gave Willy a wave as he grabbed one of the edges of the short, connecting nozzle and touched the warship for the first time. He imagined it felt particularly cold.

The engineer came next, attaching a magnetic code funnel to the spot where he thought the internal control automatics were located. He connected the palm-sized device to his forearm display via a short cable and tapped away on it.

"A pirate's life," Willy muttered. "Might take a little longer than usual, military tech and all."

"Just hurry up," Dev said, turning his head. He had turned off his helmet lights so as not to blind his comrades. All he saw now was darkness and the occasional short-lived glint of debris. They had captured, or at least plundered, alien ships dozens of times in situations not much different from this one. Hidden and parked spacecraft with cargo they wanted or needed at a location where they would have been killed outright if discovered. He had always loved the adrenaline rush, the prospect of a snatch-and-grab job that could keep him and his crew afloat for another few months and let them upgrade the *Bitch*. He still felt the adrenaline as a roar in his ears and a tingle in his fingers, but it felt more desperate now, as if his body sensed their very survival was at stake.

The image of the demonic shadow imprint on the wrecked hull flashed through his mind and he swallowed hard. He turned away from the darkness to watch Willy, who was still busy with his forearm display.

"Do it!" he said impatiently.

"This is Fleet code, man!" the Dunkelheimer grumbled indignantly. "We've never broken into a warship before, and there's a damned good reason for it. I can't—"

"All right, all right! Just do your job."

"That's what I'm trying to do!"

Dev wondered for the umpteenth time how he and Dozer could voluntarily spend so much time in vacuum while longing desperately for his cockpit, surrounded by steel, armor, and computers. Out here he felt naked, defenseless, and under constant observation. The tingle on the back of his neck just wouldn't go away, and the longer he spent near the silent *Danube* the worse it got.

After what felt like an eternity, Willy pulled off the code funnel and the outer airlock door slowly slid to the side without any sound. Behind it, they saw a short hexagonal corridor and two meters further in, another door. They floated inside and Dev pressed the red button for the emergency lock, which caused the outer bulkhead to snap shut again. Steam billowed from hidden nozzles in the ceiling. A glance at his forearm display showed him that not only was pressure building, but also a thin but increasing atmosphere.

"Not dead," he said.

"Not yet," Dozer said, hovering in front of him like a giant crab as he opened the bulky pack he was carrying on his stomach. One by one, he pulled out lightly armored suits and helmets that floated around them.

"Nitrogen-oxygen atmosphere. A little more ozone than I'd need to feel comfortable, but we should survive," Willy said, and for the first time Dev heard his voice both on the radio and as a distant echo through his helmet. Carefully, he undid the ring clasp on his neck. There was a brief hiss, and then he pulled off his helmet.

"Ah," he said, taking a deep breath of air. It smelled a little tart, probably due to the ozone content, but not as stale as inside his suit. "That's progress."

"Artificial gravity seems to be out, but there's still power in the control systems and, obviously, in life support," Willy said, as he replaced his spacesuit with the armor.

"Fleet ships are well shielded, so if they don't have any offensive systems activated their power signature might actually be close to zero."

"Or we just didn't see it because the *Bitch* is blind and our helmet sensors are comparatively weak."

Dev pondered the implications. A functioning destroyer along with its crew? If so, they would have long since been blasted away or greeted with drawn weapons.

Right?

The inner door flew aside and startled Dev. At first, he feared someone had detected them, but the short section of hallway beyond was empty and he saw Dozer's hand on a knob.

"Shit, you scared me!"

"Unlocked."

"You don't say." Dev donned his own armored suit and took a short-barreled submachine gun from the mechanic. After loading and disengaging the safety of it, he peered into the hallway. The red emergency lighting created a ghostly twilight that gave him a disturbing impression of a cramped kind of hell, even making him forget the shadowy imprint outside.

"Clear," he said.

"Clear," Willy replied from the other side. "Where should we go first?"

"Reactor," Dev said. "Then we'll know more about the ship's condition, and maybe we can get a log file out of the maintenance computer."

"Mm-hm," the Dunkelheimer agreed.

They carefully worked their way down the corridor toward the stern. The reactor room was, as was usual for a warship, in the aft quarter, closed off by a heavily armored security wall that ran through all decks. Yet, to their surprise, it opened in response to a comparatively simple override code that was over a year old.

"It's a good thing these hillbillies were mostly cut off from twenty years of progress," Willy said after the solid bulkhead had retracted upward into its recess.

The reactor room spanned four decks. The circular reactor was at its center, surrounded by metal walkways from which dozens of cables, instruments, and worksta-tions branched off. All this was directed at the sphere which housed a small star that fused helium-3 atoms together and generated ultra-hot plasma. A continuous whir attested to the fact that it had not shut down. Again, there was no sign of the crew.

The *Danube* was as deserted as it had looked from the outside.

"According to the computer, there are enough pellets on board for ten years of continuous operation," Willy said. He had pulled one of the maintenance displays from its recess and was running his fingers over ancient touch buttons. "Output is at five percent—no wonder there's hardly any radiation. Weapon systems offline, hull electrification offline, sensors offline. Life support looks good. Running on low but running."

"All right. What about stockpiles?"

"This is the reactor room," the engineer reminded him, and Dev screwed up his face.

"According to the log, thirteen days ago the power was greatly reduced, and an evacuation order was issued for the technicians."

"Does it say why?"

"No, just that it came from the bridge."

"Then we should check there."

"Why?" Willy asked, giving him a questioning look as he eased away from the console . "We can go to the storerooms and get what we need."

"I want to know what happened here," Dev insisted. "You and Dozer get to the storerooms and see what we can use and salvage. I'll find the bridge and take your code funnel with me." He held out his hand and waited for Willy to give him the small device. "You can cut into the store-rooms, too."

"That's dangerous."

"Everything we do here is dangerous. I can't shake the feeling that we're missing something, and that wreckage out there... It's been a hundred years and we still don't understand what really happened here."

Willy gave him a long look. "I've never seen you like this, boss. Interested in things other than the *Bitch*."

"We all saw what was going on in Harbingen. Something's not right, and I think there's something here that might explain it all, somehow." Dev pursed his lips and looked at the whirring reactor. "What if this is where the key is? The thing about the claim we found, about the Bellingers and Sirion killing them, and this ship sending down a whole platoon of Marines to stop Sirion..." He shook his head. "I must take a look."

"Take care of yourself."

"I will." He left the reactor room and made his way forward through the deserted technicians' antechambers to where the two main corridors running lengthwise through the ship met and which curved again toward the other end. The silence was now even more haunting without the comfort of his two substantial crew members behind him. The tingle on his neck gradually increased to an unpleasant prickle, almost painful, that spread down his back.

If he had thought the silence in space might defeat him, it was now the sonorous hum of the electronics hidden behind the wall panels that brought sweat to his brow. Everything about this ship seemed dead and abandoned and yet it was still breathing.

Like a dying animal, he thought, repeatedly looking over his shoulder. Sometimes he thought he saw a shadow, sometimes a vague movement, but when he really looked, there were only the same contours of walls and doors, distinctive lettering and complex strings of characters along the maintenance hatches above head height. The red lighting easily played tricks on the eyes.

As in any warship, the bridge was located at its heart, in the most heavily armored spot where no vulnerable points could pose a danger to the commanding brain.

He had followed the signs along the walls and just come upon the corridor that led from the center deck to the right, directly toward the bridge, when a hollow cry made him cringe.

Dev raised his submachine gun and aimed its barrel-mounted searchlight along the corridor, panning the contours and the corridor behind him, first to the right and then—there! A figure! A shadow recoiled from the light and sank back against the wall.

"Shit!" he cursed breathlessly and swallowed. "What the fuck was that? Willy, Dozer?"

"Yeah, boss?" came the reply over the radio. Static hisses and ugly crackles accompanied the unstable connection.

"We're not alone."

"Oh. We're still in the reactor room, but we're just leaving. Do you need backup?"

"No, not yet." He swallowed to relieve his dry throat. *What if I'm getting paranoid?*

Slowly, he retreated from the corridor and walked backward, into the passageway that led to the bridge.

"Where are you?"

He heard a low whisper that drifted behind him and seemed to seep right into his guts. He continued retreating, twitching the muzzle of his weapon, sweeping the searchlight back and forth to spot whatever was approaching. His hands didn't tremble, but his skin felt electrified under the fresh rush of adrenaline pumping through him, urging him to flee.

Dev imagined himself trapped in a nightmare as he nervously blinked drops of sweat from his eyelids. Behind him, he heard a hiss, and before he could turn around something grabbed him and yanked him off his feet. He fell backward onto the floor with a strangled cry. The gun fell from his hands and slid away. A door shut in front of him, blocking the red light. The illumination was glaring and as he struggled to suck air back into his lungs a shadow descended over his face.

"Who are you?" the figure asked. "You're not one of them."

10

Nicholas held his breath as he watched the holoscreen and saw the last Barracuda complete its flyby dangerously close to the rearmost DeVries shuttle. It took a moment before he finally exhaled in relief. The fighter designated "Hellcat," flew a long arc and returned on an approach vector to the *Oberon*.

"That was the last one," he announced, calling up the signal data. "We are now receiving clear position signals from fourteen shuttles."

"Good," Silly said neutrally, but her jaw muscles were visibly clenched. "Any reaction from the *Carcassonne*?"

"Negative," Daussel replied. "We've received some follow-up from space control regarding more specific maneuvering plans for the exercise, but no one transmitted after that."

"A fleet of shuttles is the perfect training scenario for close passes and convoy simulations." Nicholas looked at the chronometer behind Silly, which clearly displayed

Terran standard time for the entire bridge crew to see. "I would like to sign off now, my shift's ended."

She nodded. "Of course. Get some sleep."

He returned the nod and left the bridge. As he passed the security door the two Marines there came to attention, and he heard footsteps behind him. It was Lieutenant Alkad.

"Commander."

"Lieutenant."

"End of shift, huh?" she asked, stifling a yawn. "To think I'd experience something like that again."

"It has indeed been quite a long time." Nicholas's eyelids felt as if they were made of poured lead, heavy and raw. But it wasn't fatigue that pressed down on his lids.

As they reached the elevators, he noticed Alkad's sidelong glance. There was that uncomfortable feeling again that he knew all too well when someone wanted to establish some form of closeness or begin small talk. He never knew how to respond. It unsettled him that he didn't know how to respond to certain emotionally charged situations. He had never been good at expressing emotions, certainly not to people he didn't know well, and he usually ended up saying something awkward.

Still, he turned his head and looked at her, surprising himself with his initiative.

"I was thinking of making a detour to the observation deck," she said, "Would you care to accompany me?"

"I..." he hesitated, and she raised her hands in obvious discomfort. It had happened again.

"I'm sorry, sir, I didn't mean... I mean, I didn't mean...

I'm sorry." The elevator doors opened, and she quickly slipped inside with her head bowed.

Nicholas wanted to stop and wait for the next cabin, as he always did. But again, without any conscious decision, he found himself stepping into elevator as the doors closed.

"It's all right," he said. "Let's go to the observation deck."

Alkad blinked uncertainly, and he briefly wished he hadn't joined her after all. Alkad's second blink and accompanying smile relaxed him somewhat.

They made their way to the bow in silence, immersed in their own somber thoughts. Nicholas wondered if Jason had ever experienced the splendor of the observation deck before his departure for the Fleet Academy on Eden. Jason had been too young. It had always annoyed him that their father had so stubbornly adhered to the ship's rules, even though he had been something of a monarch. Today, he understood it better, not that it made any difference.

When they reached their destination, it was still surprisingly empty, despite the shift change. Perhaps one or two hundred comrades sat on the curved tiers that resembled an ancient amphitheater, some alone, more often in pairs, and sometimes in small groups. Hushed whispers filled the dim deck.

Illumination came through a great window of bullet-proof glass that spanned ten decks and extended sideways to the recessed Carbin gates, which were closed during battle. The sun shone a resplendent orange in the darkness while below, a section of the space fortress was visible. Its numerous windows glittered with interior lighting and would have been a thing of beauty in itself if Sol's central star didn't outshine it with its mystical size and intense color. Nevertheless, the automatic darkening of the armored glass let through a dim twilight that the ship's crew very much appreciated.

In keeping with tradition, one of the reasons he never came here, he removed his rank insignia, the three crossed yellow swords, from his shoulders and stowed them in his pants pocket. Alkad did the same and then pointed to the top row of seats directly to their left where no one was sitting.

"I know most people prefer to sit farther forward because the view is better," she said in a hushed voice, "but I don't like having someone behind me."

"Me either," he replied and followed her. The rows of seats were padded yet simple, configured as a continuous bench and backrest that came to knee-level of the row behind. The plastic was scuffed in places and not as clean as usual, another sign of the unusual situation the *Oberon* had been in for weeks.

They sat near the edge, a spot he would have chosen, away from eyes that might watch him. The observation deck was the only place where crew members could relax —*really* relax. Rank didn't matter here. Only off-duty personnel were allowed and what was said or happened here stayed here. It was perhaps the most necessary space on the Titan, a buzzing hive where everyone had more work than they could handle and where privacy was a foreign concept. Only the senior officers had separate quarters, while the vast majority, even junior officers, had to sleep in multi-bed cabins and the crew ranks in bunk beds.

"My name is Kiya, by the way."

"Nicholas," he said swallowing his discomfort at the prospect of a personal conversation. Tradition or not, it was an unfamiliar situation for him to address his subordinates informally after their daily interactions on the bridge. He never had a direct view of her because she sat in the rows along the back of the bridge while he stood on the command deck. The distance and lighting conditions made her barely visible. Yet the strangeness remained. To overcome this feeling, he decided to do something about it, "Kiya, that's not a German or Anglo-Saxon name, is it?"

"Ethiopian," she responded, without taking her eyes off the panorama before them. "My great-great-great grandparents on my mother's side were Ethiopian immigrants in Germany. On my father's side, Ethiopian immigrants in the U.S., but my great-great-great-grandfather was stationed as a soldier in southern Germany."

"What does it mean?"

"My great-great-"

"Your name."

"Oh." He could practically hear her blush. "Consolation, comfort."

Nicholas's eyes were suddenly wet.

"Mine is from the Greek," he replied, clearing his throat to control the impending onslaught of suppressed emotions. "*Nike* means victory and *laos* is the people: Victory of the people. I used to feel that meaning was apt for an officer, now I don't know if I wouldn't have preferred a more personal meaning."

"That sounds like a burden," she said, voicing exactly what he had wanted to say.

"Yes."

"So is mine."

"Yours? Comfort? Consolation?"

"I don't believe in *nomen est omen* and such, but I used to be the one in the family who tried to provide balance and peace. That just led to me being used like an agony column at school, and no one at home took me seriously because I wouldn't engage in any conflict. It turns out that people like someone to understand their points of view, but not when that understanding extends to someone they have problems with."

"I understand," he said truthfully. "What we think we are and what we are good at we quickly turn into a role that we play over and over again without thinking about whether it's good for us." Nicholas didn't know if it was the quiet atmosphere or the comfortable warmth and closeness of someone who didn't seem to want anything from him except his company, but the words flowed out of him as if a dam inside him had broken open. "I was considered inferior in school because I hardly talked and took a long time to formulate answers to my teachers' questions. The school administration even wanted to have me tested for learning disabilities, but my parents refused. When I was nine, I witnessed an argument between my mother and father in which they yelled at each other so loudly the walls shook. I cried for the whole two hours; I listened until it was over. Since I was sitting with my ears to the door, I quickly ran away when they made up, but not before I realized how they made up. They basically repeated their arguments, only more calmly and more level-headed. I wondered at the time how that could be. The best argument didn't win—the argument was probably trivial anyway, as it so often is in relationships. Every conflagration begins with a little spark."

"Calmness won."

"Yes. Calmness and letting go of emotion. I didn't take it that way, of course, but I internalized something; it pays to think about your reactions and distance yourself from your feelings before you say something."

"I know what you mean."

They were silent for a while, letting the beauty of the view carry them away, punctuated with the subtle nature sounds of chirping birds and a babbling brook.

"My cousin was down there," Alkad said after a while.

"Down there?"

"On Terra, with Colonel Meyer and your brother. To free the Admiral."

"Oh." He swallowed hard. For a moment he had been able to push away his dark thoughts and lose himself in the view—almost, anyway. "Has he..."

"He hasn't returned," she said, answering his question and started to cry softly.

"I'm sorry," he said a little more stiffly than he would have liked.

"I dream about him every night. He was the last of my family to not go to Lagunia and remain on Fleet duty. My comrades look forward to the end of their shifts. For over two weeks I have longed for nothing more than a real end of shift, the prospect of eight hours of undisturbed sleep. Now that that day has come, I dread closing my eyes because I'll see his face."

"I know what you mean," Nicholas replied hoarsely, feeling the corners of his mouth begin to twitch. The dam was crumbling and before he knew it, he was sobbing as well. He tried to keep it quiet so as not to attract attention, but his body took control and tears welled up in his eyes. Alkad did not cause further discomfort by touching him. Instead, she remained seated next to him and said nothing. She simply let what was happening happen. She did not interfere and did not take away any of the necessary force of his pain by playing it down or trying to minimize it.

After several minutes, he wiped his eyes. "I adored my father." He sniffled. "Sometimes I didn't know if it was because everyone did, but in the end, I realized how great he really was, how powerful the shadow he cast was."

"No one is loved so much by a crew of over eight thousand without delivering on what he promises," Alkad said. "Some commanders are respected, some are considered heroes, but hardly any are *loved* down to the lowliest crewman. His shadow may be great and will never be forgotten, but he has left something for all of us: you and Jason."

"We—" Nicholas broke off and shook his head with a sigh. *We can never even emulate him.*

"The crew sees you, Nicholas."

"They want to see my father in me."

"Yes, and no one can blame them for that. You're his son. I don't know you, but I think that's how everyone on board feels. But the way you handle Captain Thurnau... Let's put it this way: the bridge crew sees and hears everything and understands far more than you senior officers think. And word gets around."

"I—" His forearm display lit up and flashed a message. A second later, Alkad's did the same.

"We're to report to the bridge immediately." She gave him a puzzled look.

"This can't be good."

"Not in this war."

Hastily, they left the observation deck and pinned their rank insignia back on. Nicholas's face felt swollen, and his eyes seemed as if they must be bulging. He just hoped they wouldn't be red once they reached the bridge. A complicated knot in his chest that had been causing him near physical pain for the past few days had come undone.

Outside the bridge, they encountered more bridge officers. Their hair and faces showed they had been roused from sleep. On the command deck, he found Silly and Daussel as if he had never been away.

"What's happened?" he asked, examining the holoimage above the table. "There was no alarm."

"No." Silly zoomed out the Sol system and called up a flight vector leading from their position at *Carcassonne* to Saturn. "We've been ordered to leave today."

"Today? But we're in the process of ramping up repairs right now."

"Rosenberg is giving us all the materials we need and even the bots."

"I don't understand. What's at Saturn?"

"Hold on." Silly typed something on her control panel. "The fleet admiral has transmitted a coded message. It was a very, very long Morse message there and back again via the quantum barque. Our computer converted it into a conversation, hence the strange voices."

There was a brief murmur, then the slightly distorted

voices of Admiral Rosenberg and Fleet Admiral von Solheim rang out.

"Genady," Solheim said.

"Admiral, I hadn't expected this."

"The enemy punishes any attempt at communications with immediate fire. They don't seem to recognize Morse code."

"What's the situation on Terra? We're awaiting orders."

"They've slung a close-fitting noose around our necks but haven't tightened it yet. Five of our ships are still operational but shut down to avoid being targeted. The defensive platforms are either destroyed or out of ammunition."

"The *Oberon* has joined us and is cooperating," Rosenberg replied.

"Good."

Nicholas looked up at Silly when he heard the fleet admiral's unexpected reaction but said nothing. "We can use them. There's a plan. I want you to send the *Oberon* to Saturn as soon as Terra is in orbital east around the Sun. We've been informed by directional beam from there that a fleet of fifty free traders has picked up survivors of the Jupiter battle and there are many Fleet members aboard. There are also some frigates and destroyers left, but they are damaged."

Pirates and smugglers, Nicholas translated the message in his mind. *Barely armored, but armed. The survivors might have been mentioned as possible hostages.*

"They've offered their help," Solheim continued. "I want the *Oberon* to round them up and get them in line, as ironic as that may sound. We need every single ship with what's coming. Instruct Captain Thurnau to assemble the fleet and leave immediately for Terra."

"Sir, what hope do you expect one Titan and fifty civilian ships to have against a thousand Clicks?" Rosenberg's voice said on the recording. That question had also occurred to Nicholas.

"We have a plan, which I will describe below."

The file ended with a brief static hiss. The hum and chirp of the bridge returned.

Nicholas looked up and frowned.

"I'd like to know what this plan is supposed to be," he said.

"I guess the fleet admiral's newfound sympathy didn't go that far," Silly said sarcastically.

"He needs us, so he accepts the limited tools he still has at his disposal."

Daussel wiped the flight vector from the holoimage and replaced it with a close-up view of Saturn and its industrial habitats, which were primarily responsible for supplying water and oxygen to the system. The cylindrical ice refineries, hundreds of which protruded from the rings of the gas giant, looked like pins poking through sand.

"Saturn was barely hit, but also has no significant Fleet facilities or munitions depots," Daussel explained. "Our reconnaissance so far has revealed that about twenty Fleet ships, some badly damaged, have been able to retreat to the miners' few populated habitats. The pirates have either placed themselves in service to the Fleet in the face of the alien threat or they're swiping everything they can find."

"I tend to assume the latter," Silly noted.

"Why?" Nicholas wanted to know.

"Because they're pirates. They're all the same."

"They're people trying to make ends meet, and they may have gone down the wrong paths, but they're people," he countered. "These ship owners know they'll have no place to sell their contraband if the Federation is in ruins. I would guess they want to protect the hand that feeds them. Were we able to find out anything about this alleged plan the fleet admiral was talking about?"

"No. Rosenberg wasn't kind enough to send that along." Silly shook her head. "But I'd love to know why it wouldn't be a suicide mission to come to the rescue of a few criminals and risk being intercepted by a thousand Clicks. Not to mention only a few days to repair our ship until then."

"At least rearmament is almost complete," Daussel said, trying for a bit of optimism.

"Von Solheim is not an idiot." Nicholas regarded Saturn thoughtfully. "Someone who has managed to order all defenders to stand down and take the tiny chance that the Clicks won't immediately wipe them out isn't going to set everything on fire just to go down with flags flying."

"That's what I thought, but I can't think of a solution to the Terra problem. They don't have any forces there anymore and the enemy has the power of two strike groups."

"He must have information we don't have," he said, stating the obvious. "I guess we'll have to trust him. And as long as Jason is still on Terra and the *Caesar* is in orbit, that's where we want to be anyway, isn't it?"

"This could be a trap."

"A trap?" asked Daussel. "By Solheim?"

"Or by the Clicks," Silly explained. "Who knows who they might have gotten to sell us out."

"Even if it is a trap," Nicholas said, "we'd still spring it, wouldn't we?"

"You can bet on that."

11

The face was a face, thus, human. Dev breathed a sigh of relief. The look the face gave him was disparaging at best and suspicious at worst, yet not even the sight of a blue Fleet uniform decked with colorful officer's insignia made him think of fleeing.

"Shit!" he cursed, startled, looking toward the bulkhead. Its cold steel armor separated him from the corridor where he had just seen... *what, actually*? "What the fuck was that?"

The Fleet officer crossed himself absently and took a step back, but without lowering his pulse rifle. Its finger-thick muzzle was still pointed at Dev.

"Who are you? And what are you doing here?" The suspicious eyes narrowed. "Is this another one of your tricks?"

"Tricks? What? Whose?"

"Don't play games with me!" the soldier warned him, fixing him with narrowed eyes. "Otherwise..."

"... you'll pop me. All right," Dev grumbled, raising his

hands placatingly as he struggled to his feet. The good news was that the soldier hadn't immediately pulled the trigger. The not-so-good news was that his finger was curled around the trigger far too tightly for his comfort. "Hey, take it easy! I'm an independent ship owner and—"

"A pirate!"

"No!" Dev blurted out of sheer habit. "Independent ship owner."

"That's good enough for me!" The officer took aim and...

"Okay! Okay!" he said hurriedly and hunched slightly to look as non-threatening as possible. "I've smuggled some stuff now and then and made a few, uhhh, cargo adjustments not mutually agreed upon. Here and there we've also made some passenger changes that were not authorized by the transport authority, okay. But these are not crimes, per se, and I would like to explicitly point out that my ship is a legally registered Dunkelheim trader. That does not mean—"

"That's enough! A bloody pirate! What do you want here? Speak up!"

"I would, but you said that's enough and—"

"Next time I'll pull the trigger," the short-tempered soldier assured him. "What do you want on the *Danube*?"

"Helium pellets and oxygen, mostly."

"See? That wasn't so hard. You *can* speak without lying or babbling nonsense."

"Listen, we thought this ship was dead and my *Bitch* is in real bad shape. If we don't get her patched up, not only will she die a cold death, but so will my crew. As long as I can see a way to prevent that I have to take it." Dev merely spoke the truth. "That's all."

"Bitch?"

"That's the name of my ship. The *Quantum Bitch*. Surely, you've heard of her?" he asked, not without pride. For a moment he felt like a stylishly dressed admiral, even though he was kneeling on the floor with his arms stretched out in front him like someone waiting for the executioner's axe.

"I don't think I'd have forgotten such an idiotic name."

Dev wanted to vent his sudden anger with a savage curse but snapped his mouth shut and swallowed the insult, even though it felt too big for his throat.

"But anyone idiotic enough to call his ship *Quantum Bitch* could only be either some sex-starved teenager or a loser with an inferiority complex." The officer lowered the pulse rifle and shook his head.

"I guess you don't have a soft spot for trashy 2-D movies," Dev muttered, but his anger quickly subsided as he stretched his legs and his gaze fell on the bulkhead. "What did I see out there?"

"One of *them*," explained the officer. The name tag on his chest identified him as Lieutenant Eversman. Preoccupied with survival and his effort to say nothing that threatened it, Dev hadn't even noticed it before now. "I have no idea what they are, but I know they're not from our world."

"*They?* There's more than one of them on board?"

"It's hard to say. I mean 'they' in general. The demons."

Dev shuddered. "Demons?"

"Some have horns, others disgusting faces with pointed

teeth, serrated tails, forked tongues, plague boils—I've seen plenty," Eversman replied. "Too much to just continue."

"Continue what?"

The lieutenant eyed him with a frown. "Where do you come from?"

"That's not such an easy question to answer," Dev said, trying to get out of answering.

"Hmm."

"I did witness the battle, though. Those *demons*... you mean the aliens from the hyperspace gate?"

"Yes. They're tough and don't seem to follow any rational logic. Anyway, you can't talk to them. The crew of the *Danube* tried, and now there's no one left alive."

"*The crew of the Danube?*" Del echoed. "So, you are not —were not—part of the crew?"

"Yes. But then again, I wasn't." Eversman waved dismissively and turned around, "It's complicated."

Dev only now noticed that they were actually on the bridge, which was considerably smaller than he would have expected on a destroyer. It was laid out in circular form and there was a holotank in the center, with two seats to the right and left facing the glowing field. Around it, in a recess, specialists usually sat in front of displays corresponding to their various disciplines. These displays faced outward, at least Dev thought they probably did under normal circumstances, although there was no crew present to confirm his guess.

He tried a different approach. "Where's the crew?"

"That's complicated, too."

"I have enough things on my to-do list right now, but since I don't think that you'll let me out of here, or that I *want* to go out there, I guess I have plenty of time for you to explain it to me."

Eversman tossed his rifle onto one of the command seats and turned to face him. Now that the aggressive tension had dropped from him, he looked like a man whose entire life force had long ago drained away like water through a coarse-mesh sieve.

"They've disappeared."

"Disappeared?"

Instead of answering, the lieutenant beckoned him over. He then raised the holoscreen, performed a few quick gestures, and called up the ship's logs. The last entry was eight days old and showed the total number of crew members listed by the ship's life support computer: 110.

Eversman kept scrolling and showed him the next entries, which showed that within the eleven hours that followed, the number dropped to one and stayed there.

"Escape pods?"

"No." The officer called up another display that showed all the capsules were still active and ready to launch. "Only the shuttle is gone, but the captain sent that away before the demon attack to get the refugees to safety."

"So, the evacuation worked?" Dev asked.

"Depends on how you define that. About half of Lagunia's inhabitants were able to make orbit and escaped toward S1, where they should still be hanging around until they run out of oxygen and water, which will be soon."

"You were boarded, you said."

"Yes. One of the alien starships fired projectiles at us. The screens displayed them as much too cold to indicate occupants. But they slowed in front of us, and somehow those demons got on board."

Dev tried not to think about the shadow he had seen in the corridor or the eerie whisper that had followed it.

"Demons," he repeated grimly.

"One of them stayed on board, just like me. That can't be an accident," Eversman concluded with a very grim expression.

"Can they be..."

"Can they be killed?" The lieutenant nodded with no visible optimism. "Yes, they can. But they don't stay that way."

"What does that mean?"

"It's hard to explain."

"Can't you show me?" Dev pointed at the screens.

"No, I can't. Cameras don't seem to like them."

When Dev frowned, Eversman beckoned him closer and swiped across one of the displays and a camera recording showed one of the corridors he had come through. It was impossible to tell if it was the same one since warships had a habit of being featureless—not like his *Bitch*—and, accordingly, looked the same everywhere if you couldn't read the markings on the walls. From one moment to the next, a circular segment of the dark composite dissolved and revealed... nothing. Apart from a flicker of local camera images, which had darkened some, nothing happened. To rule out the possibility that he had just seen an image error, he looked up at Eversman, who seemed to expect his reaction. The lieutenant rewound and set the playback at half speed before pointing an outstretched finger at the spot where the hull dissolved. Dev followed the gesture and squinted. At first, he saw nothing again, then there was an indistinct shadow, frayed and distorted, hardly more than an illusion and yet impossible to miss now that he had noticed something was wrong.

"What am I seeing?"

"I was at the end of that corridor and saw the faces of those demons. But it's like the cameras are lying to us. There's nothing but shadows and image distortions. You can see something isn't normal, but you can't see them. It's almost like the electronics are trying to lie to us."

"Electronic warfare?" speculated Dev.

"No. Or so effective and advanced that our firewalls don't pick up on it. In any case, no intrusion attempt was detected by the *Danube*'s system," Eversman explained as Dev winced. "What is it?"

"My people," he swore and tried to contact Willy and Dozer. He presumed they had switched to passive reception after hearing that they weren't alone. Better safe than sorry, that was their standard operating procedure when plundering a ship. As soon as they suspected one of them was caught, they went to radio silence and tried to get away with what they could take. As smugglers, they were simply too intelligent and opportunistic for heroic rescue operations— i.e., *stupid* ones. For himself, however, the danger of discovery did not apply since he had found refuge on the apparently secure bridge.

"Willy, Dozer, if you can hear me, the *Danube* has been boarded by aliens and must be considered hostile. Withdraw immediately as soon as you have found the most essential things we need. Don't do anything stupid. I am on the bridge and currently safe with a survivor of the

Danube." When he finished, he looked at Eversman, who appeared tired and discouraged. "We can try to get you out of here. At least, if we can find enough of what we need to keep from suffocating. To do that, though, we have to get off the bridge."

The lieutenant shook his head and rubbed his eyes. "I can't go anywhere."

"What do you mean? I don't want to drag you off, I want to take you in exchange for you finding us a way out of here and then drop you off somewhere with the Fleet." Dev pursed his lips. "Then, with any luck, you can put in a good word for us with the Fleet, and they'll believe us when we tell them what we saw."

"What did you see?" Eversman asked without much curiosity.

"You wouldn't believe me if I told you."

"I saw demons."

"True." Dev squinted at the camera's eerie freeze frame and distorted dark image glitches. "We were in Harbingen —why and how is unimportant—anyway, the system was supposed to be empty, right?"

The Fleet officer looked at him more attentively now and eased away from the display but said nothing.

"There were ships everywhere. They didn't ask any questions, they just started trying to shoot our asses off the moment they detected us. That system is crawling with starships and lots of traffic." Dev pointed to Eversman's insignia on his chest, which looked like colorful buttons sewn tightly together. "I don't say this often, but we need to let the Fleet know what's going on. Someone's using the current invasion to get away with some secret shit on one of the darkest spots in the Federation, and I can't shake the feeling that it has something to do with those demons attacking."

"It probably does."

"Excuse me?" Dev asked, irritated by the officer's calm tone.

"What you saw was Harbingen's secret fleet."

"Secret fleet?" He knew it sounded lame, but he couldn't think of anything better to say. "Sure, it was a fleet, or at least a lot of scattered ships, but..."

Eversman snorted and shook his head. "You still don't understand. Harbingen was never dead as long as we exiles still existed. We were in hiding, both in the physical sense— in the darker reaches of the Federation—and behind the cloak of anonymity created by a society spanning two hundred systems."

"*We?*"

"I was born on Harbingen. But my parents didn't want to live under the tyranny of cold algorithm, ruled by data outputs that lacked any trace of God-given empathy. So, they sought refuge along with the exiles even before the official transfer of power to Omega. In my case, to the asteroid habitats of Harbingen's Oort Cloud."

"There are habitats there?"

"None officially. It's a society of exiles united in its beliefs, and it remains united even in the far reaches, scattered over most of the core worlds and even many of the rim worlds." Eversman shrugged. "We learned quickly to accept our situation and build what we lacked. More than two decades is a long time."

"Wait a minute." Dev raised his hands and closed his

eyes briefly. "Are you telling me there was a Harbinger parallel society all these years? I knew about the Omega Exodus, and that those who opposed the AI takeover in the plebiscite were allowed to emigrate if they turned in their IDs. But these were individual families, maybe splinter groups, not a cohesive secret society. Von Borningen and his exile fleet were a unified faction, but they left our spiral arm with their colonist fleet at that time."

"That is true. But you underestimate how strong cohesion is among people who see their homeland burning after a godless AI has taken control. A 'we-told-you-so' is hardly sufficient. Larger clusters had formed before the Clicks attacked, clusters where secret meetings were held. After the attack it took less than three years for the Harbinger network to emerge, united by our chancellor."

"Chancellor?"

"Yes. I don't know his name, but we all know our place in his plan."

"What plan?" Dev wanted to know, still trying to figure out if this man was trying to pull his leg. Yet he neither looked amused nor crazy, and Dev had now seen what he had seen in Harbingen.

"One that will now go into effect without me. There's no way back into the network for me."

"Why not?" He had wanted to ask completely different questions, but he sensed the direct route would lead nowhere with this guy. At worst, he'd shut down. Dev still needed a way off the bridge, even if the thought of facing the demon again made him shudder.

"Because *that* wasn't the plan, the reason I joined Bradley's fleet as a sleeper cell. I sacrificed my life for the goal, and now here we are at the end of a demon invasion." Eversman crossed himself absentmindedly. "This is not salvation, it's madness."

"A sleeper cell. I'm the last person who would scold you for that, but you're still alive and you stayed here. You're telling me all this, so you haven't given up yet. If you think your plan needs to be stopped, then that should be even more reason to get out of here with me and inform the Fleet. I don't know what I saw in Harbingen, but you do."

"The Fleet?"

Dev was amazed that someone could inject more dislike and outright contempt into his voice than he did when the word "Fleet" crossed his lips.

"I think you misunderstood me, pirate. The Terran forces are far worse scum than any demon could be. A creature of the devil is like a wild animal. It must be killed because it is a danger, but one that can be seen acting sincerely within the scope of its wickedness. The Fleet, however, is like a boil that grows uncontrollably, injecting its cancerous cells into every vessel of humanity with its deceitful politics and pseudo-freedoms. A scheming lie, a system that sustains itself by not finishing this war and instead keeps growing, polluting the air of freedom with its fetid breath."

"That's your plan? To destroy the armed forces?"

"You can try to escape. I won't stop you, but I will stay here."

"But why? You hate the Fleet, I get that. And you don't agree with your chancellor, or whatever. Since when is that a reason to hole up in a shipwreck?" Dev didn't really care what happened to this guy, except he would have liked to keep squeezing him for information, preferably with some intoxicating drug. His priority, nonetheless, was to get his men out of here and revive the *Bitch*. If Eversman didn't go along, he would hardly stand a chance; after all, he hadn't even detected that the *Danube* had been boarded. Yet given the virtually nonexistent senses and the strange technology the aliens employed, he could not fault himself.

They simply dissolved a section of the hull, he reminded himself.

"If my people find me, they will kill me immediately as a traitor," the lieutenant explained, not particularly distressed by the thought. "You don't, over two decades, build a secret network that works like a complex cogwheel system and disguises itself through decentralization without developing an effective method for cutting loose ends."

"And the Fleet shouldn't be able to disrupt what you're doing in Harbingen," Dev speculated.

"It won't be able to; it's far too late for that."

"Too late for what?"

"I'll stay here and document as much as I can about the demons. If I'm lucky, the next order will learn about it and be able to use it to rid itself of them," Eversman explained pensively, as if he were talking to himself.

Maybe he was a little crazy after all. Dev could hardly blame him, locked in a room with no windows and no sound, knowing that demons were roaming the corridors outside.

The next order, Dev thought, wishing he could focus on not panicking at the thought of this damned ship as a chamber of horrors. Instead, he was hearing about a conspiracy, a "new order," Harbingers, and...

Something crashed against the bridge's security bulk-head where Eversman had pulled him onto the bridge. Dev winced and caught himself flinching. Then it sounded again, booming through the small bridge and repeating twice in quick succession.

There was a scratch and rustle in the radio bud in his ear. Distorted voices competed to see which sounded the scariest.

"Willy? Dozer?" he croaked around a dry tongue.

"They're not your friends," Eversman said. "That's one of *them*."

"How do you know? That could have been a knock." The pounding was repeated, stronger this time. He had to admit it sounded like someone was trying to tear down the bulkhead. However, Willy and Dozer were also somewhat monsterlike with their size and upgraded muscle power.

Dev took a step forward but felt a firm grip around his right arm as the lieutenant roughly pulled him back.

"No! We can't let a demon in here or we're dead. Besides, then the only chance to learn anything about them would be lost."

"They're trying to kill us! That's more than I need to know," Dev hissed. "If those are my boys there, then I'll fucking make sure they get in here, just like I got in before!"

He jerked free and sprang away so Eversman couldn't grab him again, then awkwardly launched himself forward. He hated gravity, but his instinct drove him and didn't let him down. A shot whipped past where he had been standing a moment ago, and part of him felt more outrage than fright that the officer would shoot him so casually. He landed, nearly dislocating his shoulder, and rose again, flicking his right hand to the emergency release button. He hoped he could still trust his instincts.

The bulkhead hatch shot upward as if sucked in by the ceiling hydraulics, and two bizarre shadows rushed onto the bridge. Dev had to blink twice before he recognized Dozer and Willy. They wasted no time blocking the passage behind them by punching the button.

Another shot whipped through the room, and judging by Eversman's expression, he had fired more in shock than anything else. Dozer jerked to one side, but the projectile slammed into his shoulder and trailed a fountain of black liquid where it exited.

The augment zombie lunged forward and snatched the weapon from the officer... along with his right hand. Without thinking, Dozer drew his fist back and would have caved in Eversman's skull if Dev hadn't stopped him with a loud, "Don't!"

"Behind us..." Willy began breathlessly.

"I know." Dev nodded somberly and looked with some relief at the resealed bulkhead where an eerie scratching could be heard. Looking at Eversman, who was screaming in pain, he added, "Patch him up quickly. I think he's our only way out of here."

12

"How's the integration going?" Nicholas asked the gray-haired recruiting officer. The man was visibly uncomfortable having such a high-ranking visitor. His slightly pained expression, which he labored to suppress, might have also been caused by his uncertainty as to how he should deal with Nicholas's loss. In the last few days, he had encountered expressions of condolence and brief, embarrassed glances. Everyone on board processed the death of, arguably, the post-Harbingen era's most iconic figure differently. This was just as true of his youngest son, the one Konrad Bradley had left behind. That was fine for Nicholas. In fact, he preferred that people he encountered pretended nothing was wrong. That, at least, spared him some awkward emotional moments. These days, he never knew what word, look, or triggered memory would set off something in him that he didn't want to feel.

Major Pankratz, who officially reported to Colonel Meyer, nodded at the change of subject, away from the numbers, dates, and facts about the wounded and disabled incurred in the most recent battles.

"The civilians," he said, nodding again as if trying to get his thoughts straight. "Not as well as hoped and yet better than most expected, I'd say."

"Can you be more specific, Major?"

"Sir, it's like this: the people who stayed when we offered them the choice are largely Harbingers and extremely motivated. They learn quickly because they want to learn, and they don't care that they had to serve in the lowest enlisted ranks. I think they're happy to have a bunk and food and the opportunity to do meaningful work." Pankratz scratched his fastidiously trimmed chin beard. "But we still have nearly a thousand of them who were supposed to disembark as refugees when we arrived over Terra. Nothing came of that, and I think they resent us for it."

"Can't blame them," Nicholas said. "What exactly does that mean for their integration into the ship's ongoing operations?"

"We've assigned them to clean."

"Excuse me?"

"Well, they're not Harbingers, and they complain all the time. It didn't seem wise to me to let them at anything more critical than a broomstick and mop," the major replied evasively.

"We have bots for that."

"We do, but Chief Engie has started converting them to indoor maintenance bots."

"Before or after you put the civilians to work cleaning?"

"After," Pankratz reluctantly admitted.

"I see. Belay that," Nicholas ordered sternly.

"What? But sir, that—"

"—should be your priority. We are members of the Harbinger Fleet, not slave drivers. Create personnel files and find out what training and talents the refugees have, then assign them to appropriate jobs that have no direct bearing on *Oberon*'s combat readiness or security. Understood?"

"Of course, Commander." The major looked extremely unhappy but kept his objection to himself. Nicholas didn't care if he expressed his frustration to his comrades after hours, the main thing was to correct his mistake. The refugees had been through enough.

He left the office and the personnel department, which spanned twenty rooms on Deck 3, to continue his rounds. His father had done this every morning, taking an hour before his shift to tour the ship. Nicholas did well to copy some of his father's routine. By doing so, he hoped he could bring back some of Konrad Bradley's spirit and restore it to this ship that missed his presence so much.

There were pictures hanging on the walls everywhere in violation of regulations that no one reported. Some were hand-drawn in the impressionistic style of Harbingers' recruiting posters. Others were created in woodcut-style lines and crisp colors that suited his father's image. They managed to reflect the mix of sternness and warm-heartedness that had made his countenance so iconic. Banners had been pinned to many corridor intersections, hanging from the walls like monastic vows, waving in the light draft of the air conditioning. They were adorned with important quotes from Konrad that obviously had a special meaning for the people who had recorded them. Crewmen passing by the many pictures seem to have made it a ritual to touch them briefly with their fingers or to indicate a salute by touching their berets.

Nicholas wondered if they could ever revere another commander as they had his father, a man who had suffered the wrath of so many and the love of so few since the destruction of Harbingen that he had survived without breaking. The hatred had come primarily from the Federation, even if the media had possibly exaggerated it. But even the messianic—and sometimes excessive—love shown by his crew and the remaining fighting troops had always had an oppressive feel about it to Nicholas. He felt it evoked expectations that no mortal could ever fulfill. His father, however, had not seemed disturbed by it, at least he had never spoken about it. He had simply done his duty and acted to the best of his knowledge and never hesitated. Nicholas had great respect for that since he felt like every officer in history probably had when faced with a decision: was it the right one or would it lead to disaster? Maybe in the future he would be as independent of his feelings and fears as Konrad Bradley, his dad. Or at least be able to keep it to himself just as well whenever he had doubts, so that his crew would not notice it.

He heard Silly's voice in his ear. "Nicholas?"

"Yes?" he replied as he walked past a group of technicians wearing orange coveralls. They were busy replacing damaged wiring running above their heads, lending the *Oberon* the industrial look of an archaic factory facility.

"You should come to the bridge, there are some... *developments*."

"On my way. What kind of developments?" In less than an hour, they would pass Earth, albeit at a distance of more than two million kilometers. Admiral Rosenberg had set the course because he wanted to know how the Click blockade would react.

"A message from the sky fortress. We now know what the fleet admiral is up to."

"I'll be right there."

On the bridge, Murphy and Meyer, whom he did not expect, were waiting for him, along with Silly and Daussel, whom he had expected. They were standing around the command deck like campers around a fire, looking at a representation of Terra accompanied by its two remaining halos, Luna, and the ring of countless dots formed by the Click ships around the human homeworld. From what he could see it was a still image.

"Ah, XO," the commander greeted him with a formal nod, and the others also murmured a respectful "XO" in his direction.

"You have something important, I assume," Nicholas remarked with a meaningful look at the assembled senior officers.

"Indeed," Daussel nodded briefly.

"New orders from Fleet Admiral von Solheim." The name sounded like a swear word in Silly's mouth. "We are to adjust our course to pass a little closer to Terra."

Nicholas frowned as she waved the holoimage to rotate. Terra itself was hidden under a microcellulose shimmer, but some of the planet's characteristic blue shone through the haze, preserving some of the fragile beauty of the human homeworld. Luna, gray and pale, was just above the sky fortress. It was so small at the current scale that the computer had to enlarge it and outline it in green in the real-time simulation. The Fleet Headquarters in orbit was so far out that the sphere of blockading Click ships, represented as 1,000 tiny points of light, drifted below it, relatively speaking.

"How did we get the message?"

"Morse code with light signals again," Daussel replied.

"Is reconnaissance sure the Clicks can't read this?"

"We haven't exchanged a word in over seventy years. I don't suppose they suddenly speak our language, can understand Morse code based on our comprehension system, and crack our decryption at the same time," Silly commented, shaking her head. "If they did, we'd have a problem."

"Why?" Nicholas asked, looking around at the unusually large crowd. His next question was more rhetorical. "Have we been sent anything else besides these rather unremarkable orders?"

Silly's mouth parted in a hint of a smile, something he hadn't seen her do in days, not that she had ever betrayed signs of cheer very often. Sometimes Nicholas wasn't even sure she was capable of it. However, many of his comrades on this ship were likely to think the same about him, and he didn't know if he could, in good conscience, disagree with them.

"It sounds crazy, but Fleet Command has come up with

a plan to break the blockade and destroy the Clicks," she explained.

"*Destroy* the Clicks?" he repeated, amazed. Judging by the looks on the other officers' faces, they were also hearing this for the first time. Apparently Silly had waited until he was present to give her briefing.

"Somebody pull a secret fleet out of their ass?" Karl Murphy said in his typical rumble. The chief engineer scratched his head, looking for once more like a laborer in uniform.

"No, nuclear weapons."

Now the looks grew even more perplexed.

Silly zoomed in on Terra and wiped away the shimmer of microcellulose to reveal the familiar continents, oceans, and characteristic bands of clouds. Then she brusquely eliminated them as well, and rotated the planet between her hands until she was satisfied. Earth became transparent as Silly marked the orbital elevator that connected the Himalayas to the sky fortress, a 35,000-kilometer-long stump attached to several cables and a counterweight many thousands of kilometers farther out, away from the massive space station. A tiny red dot was moving up from Mount Everest toward the space station.

"A test pilot by the name of Fidel Soares has made his way up from Earth to the fleet admiral in a spacesuit and prototype electric sled to deliver a message," she explained, shaking her head. "No, this is not a joke. Since the Clicks either jam or respond with direct fire to any attempts at communication, I guess they chose a somewhat unconventional way to deliver a message that had to be pretty damned important."

"Now I'm curious," Meyer grumbled. The crusty colonel jammed his thumbs into the belt of his camouflage jumpsuit and narrowed his eyes. "If they're sending some lunatic on a multi-day trip—which would be completely insane even in peacetime—there's probably more to it than some completely stupid idea hatched by those airheads on Terra."

Murphy nodded in agreement and seemed about to respond with some profane remark, but Silly beat him to it.

"There are still nine thousand tactical hypersonic missiles on Earth from the century before last, mothballed in their former silos. *Mothballed*, but not scrapped. Presumably it was more expensive to scrap them than simply secure them. Anyway, they're extremely fast and can reach orbit or even Luna with ease."

"Or enemy ships in mid-orbit," Daussel interjected meaningfully, and Nicholas could practically hear ears pricking up around him.

"That can't be the plan, can it?" he asked. "Hypersonic missiles are all well and good, but even at Mach 30 or 40, the aliens' close-in defense cannons would have more than enough time to blast each missile out of the sky with ease. A missile cannot fly in a direct line into orbit and is highly predictable in its ascent to escape velocity. Our comrades on Terra should really know that."

"They do," Silly assured him. "But that's not all, in any case."

With rapid inputs on her forearm display, she marked the missile silos on Terra, several hundred green dots spread over all the continents, and then the *Artemis* Halo.

"Artemis is heavily armed. Well, *was* heavily armed

before the decisive battle against Species X. They used up almost all their ammunition stores, but only *almost*."

"I thought they were completely empty." Murphy scratched his head. "Surely, they would never have stopped firing otherwise. When the order came from Solheim, it was obvious to everyone that he only gave it because it was all over, and no one had anything left."

"That's correct, and yet they still have missiles on the Halo. At least explosives." Silly waited a moment. Finally, she said, "Supplies. They have plenty of supplies stored for Fleet ships, including state-of-the-art Pagan IV planetary bombs."

"Thermonuclear?" Meyer guessed what they were probably thinking, and with the same sense of confusion. "How are mass destruction weapons designed to fire on a planet going to help against a fleet in orbit?"

"EMP," Nicholas answered in Silly's place. The more he thought about it, the more it made sense. "You throw them out the airlocks and detonate them all at once. The corresponding EMP will be much more powerful than the small warheads in the ship-to-ship missiles could produce."

"Right," the commander confirmed, looking proudly at him. "The electromagnetic pulse won't permanently burn out the Clicks' military sensors, but according to calculations by the eggheads on Terra, it will do the job for at least a few minutes, enough time for ground-launched nuclear missiles to reach orbit. Just two or three per ship would be enough to wipe them all out. Simultaneously."

"What if they've miscalculated?" Murphy asked glumly.

"Or if the bombs are intercepted before they detonate?" the colonel added. "It's hardly going to be like the Clicks to just watch as gigaton explosive devices detach from one of the halos and scoot away."

The chief engineer nodded. "Good point."

"A lot of question marks," Nicholas agreed, then raised a hand admonishingly. "However, it's an opportunity we haven't had until now. Let's not kid ourselves, if the blockade lasts long enough, we'll eventually understand what their mysterious strategy is."

"And that is?" Daussel asked curiously.

"To conserve resources. We expected them to take out all our defenses and then drop nukes on Terra to sterilize the biosphere. But why? The path of least resistance is always the most efficient, as long as there is no time pressure." He was reminding his fellow officers of a basic rule taught at strategy school. "This includes husbanding one's resources. Seventy years of war have dragged us into a permanent recession, and we can barely maintain our existing fleet. New ships are only available for political officers with connections, and research and development have been chronically underfunded for decades, at least since the collapse of our homeworld as the Federation's second economic center.

"The Clicks won't have fared any differently or they would have decided the war a long time ago. Instead, they have been on the defensive for some time. We even had them to the point where we could put most of our resources into hyperspace gate production and still allow us to maintain and replenish our fleet. As long as they can effectively cut off our homeworld, not letting anyone in or out, no aid can flow in either direction. Humanity will slowly suffocate without the Clicks having to waste their expensive munitions. If you've been fighting for seventy years, you can easily wait a few months for anarchy to break out on the surface or for the microcellulose to turn Earth into a global freezer. The decline will only accelerate from there."

"You have no way of knowing if the other worlds were also attacked," Daussel objected.

"Yes, they were, or help would have arrived long ago. New California, Hokkaido, and Hazhuan alone are three core worlds less than 48 hours away."

Silly took up the discussion. "I admit there are a lot of uncertainties. It's not going to be easy and we're going to need a fair bit of luck. But it's a plan, and that's more than we had a few hours ago."

"If I may, CO?" Meyer asked, and Silly nodded graciously. "As I see it, the biggest problem is not that we need some luck. We already got some of that when you bailed us out down there. I'm the last person who's going to question your daring and decision-making skills."

"Why do I suspect a *but* is coming?"

"Communications. We're all experienced enough to know that the talk at the academies about communications and logistics is not just bureaucratic claptrap. Communications and logistics win wars, long before soldiers and weapons come into play. We have two hands: the sky fortress and planetary defenses. Even under ideal circumstances, it would be a gamble to pull off such a stunt with two hundred-year-old, mothballed, hypersonic missiles. But without being able to coordinate the right and left hands of this suicide mission, it could become the shortest military action in history."

"There is no alternative," Silly replied tersely. The colonel opened his mouth then closed it again. His jaw muscles bulged as he did so. "The fact is, we either try to take the initiative or let the Clicks wait until the Federation's heart stops beating."

"In short, we have no choice," Murphy grumbled, translating what he was hearing, and Colonel Meyer nodded slowly.

"I don't think the fleet admiral informed us out of sympathy."

"No," Silly admitted, "he wants us to stand by to clean up."

"So at least von Solheim has enough sense to know that no plan works one hundred percent of the time, and with this one we'll be lucky if it's eighty percent successful." Murphy seemed relieved, though he sounded cynical.

"He's a good commander," Nicholas said. "The battle plan for defending Terra was excellent, and the enemy was destroyed despite the many negative simulations. If the Clicks hadn't shown up..."

"We've been ordered to close in when signaled by the sky fortress and head toward Terra at full thrust. We should be as close as possible when the bombs stored on the *Artemis* Halo are released. The fleet admiral's analysts assume the enemy will maintain its defensive positions and not move to intercept us unless we approach a strategic target. From his point of view, it makes sense since they are already well positioned and should judge our approach as a kamikaze attack. Once the bombs are released and the EMPs from the detonations kick in, we'll take care of those ships that, for whatever reason, were not disabled and could launch counterattacks on Terra. All Barracuda squadrons will be on alert. I want the pilots to stay in their ready rooms and be ready to launch within fifteen minutes. *Hellcat* will become Commander Air Group and is to devise a battle plan that ensures the widest possible coverage north and south of the equator, focusing on the regions above the largest arcologies. He'll have to prioritize and has only two hours to do it," Silly explained, looking to Nicholas.

"I'll take care of it. *Hellcat* is a good choice to succeed *Panther* as CAG," he said, nodding.

"If ever we needed a real go-getter who's done a combat landing inside atmosphere just before a jump, it's now."

13

Sirion straightened the uniform and examined himself in the mirror. His new face was slightly wider with a three-day beard. It was a sign of poor hygiene that he detested. The skin under his eyes was slightly swollen. The veins of his nose were reddened like a drunkard's. The commander whose face it belonged to hung diagonally behind him on a long radiator. He had infected the officer with NeuroStun, then hung him from two towels slung under his arms so he could compare hairstyles in the mirror. Suspending him also tricked the pressure sensors in the floor in the unlikely event that anyone should discover Sirion walking around outside while someone was detected in the commander's quarters.

Unfortunately, the length of their hair was too different. The man apparently hadn't bothered to comply with Fleet regulations, but he could deal with that.

Contrary to his expectations, the NeuroStun had not just sedated his victim, it had placed him into a coma. His first reflex had been to kill him with a neural incision between C1 and C2, but something had stopped him as he thought back to his conversation with Konrad Bradley.

He cursed the late captain once more and looked at his grimly pursed mouth before he neutralized his expression again. Then he went back to the living area and unlocked the terminal by holding the DNA sniffer in front of his comatose victim's mouth.

It took him several hours to figure out that something was up. The Headquarters admiralty had sequestered themselves on the upper floors for days, cut off from the crew. His access to classified information as Admiral Warfield's aide allowed him to discover what was going on, but it didn't make sense. They were in constant contact with Terra's continental defenses, hundreds of missile silos in North and South America, Asia, Europe, and Africa. Sirion knew nothing about the armament of these facilities, but he had learned that the Clicks had disabled the planetary defense centers capable of directly targeting orbiting targets after the PDCs had destroyed twenty alien ships.

"Heroic" was what most of the soldiers stationed here thought. "Stupid" was what Sirion thought.

Despite his highest security privileges—he had identified the right victim—it was impossible to find out what the Admiralty had done. So, he altered his search parameters and tapped into the time stamps of internal communications links. Again, since everything was wired in the age of high-potency jammers, there was a notation in the IT system background logs for each link. The content was not recorded. at least not for the links designated top secret, but the points of contact and the duration of contact were.

A few hours later—he was getting closer to

Commander Erbil's shift start than he would have liked—he was able to put together a picture. The effort had required much of his upgraded cerebral faculties. The Admiralty had been in constant close communication with each other for days. That was to be expected, but there was a discrepancy. In the past six days, the office of Admiral Makoufeh, commander of Headquarters on Terra, had conducted over twenty hours of communication with the planning office of the development department's chief engineer, Commander Mila Shaparova.

Why?

Sirion decided to find out and left the quarters half an hour later. The commander's shift started in eighty minutes, so he still had some time. On his way to the lower floors, he took advantage of the privileges of his rank and authorized the elevator to travel the 800 floors to the research and development workshops without stopping for anyone to board, so the trip only took eleven minutes.

He walked briskly toward the director's office through vast halls filled with people laboring at workbenches. With the help of robotic arms and automated manufacturing bots, they were developing new weapons systems, armor, and other things he had never seen and could not guess what they would one day become. The floor was littered with metal shavings, cables, mobile spectrographs, and lots of open boxes. It was the kind of mess that made him want to clean it up with a flamethrower and start from scratch.

He found Shaparova in her office, a boxy room that looked like an old shipping container. She was on the phone berating someone.

"... of course not, you dumb ox! You should take the

thirteen and shove it so far up your stiffened ass that you can scratch the roof of your mouth with it. *That's* my professional advice!"

Shaparova still looked quite young in her mid-fifties and apparently didn't give a damn about Fleet standards. Her blonde hair hung in lustrous strands over her ears. When she noticed him, she blinked briefly in surprise and took her feet off the table before beckoning him closer.

"No," she said in response to something, and her eyebrows drew menacingly low. "I can have a fifteen brought over, too, and you can choke on it, you fucking asshole!"

Another pause.

"Oh, is that how you're going to come at me? Fine, go ahead and try. Do you know who just walked into my office? No? Well, that's because you're out of the loop. And why is that? Because you're a complete idiot. Don't bother me with this shit anymore!" Shaparova slammed the phone back into its socket and folded her arms in front of her on the table. "Commander Erbil, I would rather be impregnated by a goat than have to bet on ever seeing you down here."

Sirion knew he was operating on very thin ice since he had been able to gather very little data on his victim before he had put him out. Time was pressing, and that could seduce him to haste. Haste meant mistakes. But he had no other choice. He was expected somewhere at the beginning of his shift, and if there was one thing he did know, it was the life of a Fleet officer, including the many small details contained within regulations and expected personal conduct.

Slightly arrogant, but someone who can relate to others. An opportunist who used diplomacy to work his way up, he summed up for himself, imitating the commander's somewhat arrogant expression.

"I can't say I like it any more than you do," he responded.

"Shit, Erbil, you're actually being frank for once! What can I do for you since you've bothered to get the soles of your feet dirty by visiting me here in my little kingdom?"

"I'm sure you can guess why I'm here."

Shaparova eyed him. "I assumed the project was finished."

"It is." Sirion had to proceed cautiously now. He felt like someone feeling his way through a dark cave, able to orient himself only by brief flashes of light. "But we're looking into the prospects of continuation right now."

"Continuation?"

"Yes."

"And how is that going to work? It's been put to bed, hasn't it?"

A completed project. His mind raced, trying to compare and rearrange puzzle pieces. *But communication traffic still spiked. What is it? What? It must have to do with something tangible or they wouldn't have needed this cleaning lady in an officer's uniform. I'm sure no one would work with her if they could help it.*

"I want to see it."

"See what?" she wanted to know.

"The prototype." *There has to be a prototype. A workaround for the jammed communications between Earth and orbit. To the sky fortress or the satellites and Halos. The entire*

Headquarters staff could have no other goal in mind than that. Shaparova chewed thoughtfully on her lower lip as she looked at him through narrowed eyelids, so he added, "We'd rather play it safe."

"Better safe than sorry, huh?" She laughed and stood. "Told you so. You armchair farts better get it right and not put all your eggs in one basket. Especially now that we know the damned rascal didn't get sizzled by any cable."

Sirion tried to fit the new puzzle pieces she mentioned into the big picture, but they still wouldn't fall into place.

"Come with me." She waved at him to follow, and they left the office. Passing work areas populated with engineers and technicians who barely noticed them, they reached the storage rooms. The workshop noise was somewhat less intrusive here. Heavy-duty shelves that served as anchor points for robots that broke down objects at the push of a button were lined up close together over several shelves. It smelled of dust and metal.

"It's in the back." Shaparova led him to a secured area, which she unlocked with DNA access. The small room contained mostly odd-looking weapons, empty warheads, and dozens of other things he couldn't identify. Everything looked improvised and temporary. But she did not conduct him to a weapon he could recognize. Instead, she halted by a gray cylinder with two handle recesses. "There it is."

"That's it?"

"Told you. Surprised Warfield didn't show it to you and sent you here, of all people. What did you do wrong, huh?"

"I had to walk his dog and he peed on Admiral Makoufeh's door," Sirion said. Erbil's records included these regular, and unpopular, favors.

"Ha!" Shaparova laughed. "That little filthy animal. Well, there it is, anyway. What do you want with it?"

"Redundancy," he said.

"So, you finally agree with me!" She was delighted. "Congratulations, you've got it into your head after all. Give me two days and I'll have a new one ready."

Sirion considered.

"We can take the prototype. Time is of the essence."

"Ha! Up your ass!"

"Excuse me?"

"I'm not giving you my damned prototype, am I? If I do that and the part breaks, we won't have a replacement. Then it'll take at least twice as long. As I said, this is the first, fast prototype, clearly more error-prone than the second version that nut Soares used."

"You're right, of course," he quickly relented, nodding. "Then just be as fast as you can."

"Sure. Just have Warfield release the appropriate order in the system for me, I don't want any trouble with procurement, got it?"

"Of course. We can take care of it right in your office."

"Wonderful."

"One more thing, out of interest," he noted, just as she turned to leave.

"Huh?"

"Can you show it to me? How Soares used it, I mean?" He pretended to be a little uncomfortable with the question. "I'm sure you can imagine that I would have liked to see it happen."

Shaparova chuckled. "I guess that's the problem with just being a message boy, huh?"

Sirion shrugged and she sighed.

"Nothing fancy. It opens by applying pressure to the handles." She took the cylinder, grabbed its two handles, and the device opened. A long socket appeared in the center. "That's where the cable goes in. The magnets provide the pressure, and the cylinder closes again. The batteries sit in the rounded parts on the right and left and give off minimal heat. With this one, it starts off as soon as it's closed. For Soares, of course, I built in a little button. Test pilots like him love those. Even made it red."

After Shaparova put the cylinder away again, they left the warehouse secured area and returned to her office. Sirion darkened the window next to the desk with the push of a button before incapacitating the engineer with Neuro-Stun and catching her breath in a thermo mug that smelled of leftover coffee. He had adjusted the dose so that she would be comatose for a few days but not die. Perhaps Pyrgorates had been right, maybe he had gone soft...

Next, he searched her database with the keywords "Soares" and "test pilot" for the person she had mentioned and found the personnel file for an atmospheric jet pilot. A young daredevil with Portuguese roots who, according to the psychological evaluation, had nerves of steel.

Now Sirion only had to put one and one together. He left the office and headed to the warehouse. Using the thermo mug, he satisfied the DNA sniffer and obtained the nondescript cylinder, which he tucked under his arm as if it were nothing special. Since this was apparently Shaparova's project, one she had made her own "baby" due to its secrecy and importance, he didn't think many soldiers working here had been involved or would know what he was carrying, even if they were bothered by seeing someone like him carrying it around.

In any case, no one stopped him before he reached the elevators. He turned aside to take one of the freight lifts. Using his priority code to block access on the way there would have attracted someone's attention since that certainly didn't happen often, and he didn't want to take any chances. He now understood what the Admiralty had done. Since there was no communications link to orbit, they had improvised and sent an astronaut to personally cover the 35,000 kilometers. Sirion would have never thought of that. After all, it had nothing to do with communication and merely involved the delivery of a single message that spent several days in transit at considerable risk.

He meant to keep a low profile, maybe change his appearance once more and then equip himself, because he had a long way to go.

A few hours and one alarm later, he found himself at one of the exit points to the supply hangars on Level 14. This was located several hundred meters below the summit of Mount Everest, where the stalk of the orbital elevator protruded from the artificial cone that looked like a volcano. In an anthill like Fleet Headquarters, with its tens of thousands of soldiers, it was almost too easy for Sirion to duck under cover at the right time, find a restroom, or join a throng of moving comrades to avoid attracting attention. Organizing a spacesuit with an adequate oxygen supply had been the hardest part. It had cost two CPOs their lives, but he had managed that, too.

As soon as he stepped into the snowdrifts, his professional tension fell away, leaving him focused and purposeful. He finally realized what he was about to do. Risking his life in this way was not typical of him, but that was also true of the knowledge he possessed. He should never have been given the codes Konrad Bradley had entrusted to him—or rather *imposed* on him. Now he had to do something with it to free himself from the burden that came with absolute trust. It shook him from head to toe.

It was an unpleasant condition. It deprived him of the clarity of his previous self, a clarity that had always told him what he was doing and why he was doing it.

Quickly, but without undue haste, he worked his way further up the narrow path until he had to start climbing. That turned out to be easier than expected since the wind was not too strong and the snow not too deep. The orbital elevator, or what was left of it, looked like a black band dividing the sky in half, all the way up into the hazy glow that blocked out sun and stars alike.

Sirion made it to the edge of the artificial volcano cone within half an hour. Only his optical enhancements enabled him to see where the main cable disappeared into the station below. There were soldiers there, already waiting for him. They were armed and had trained their weapons on him, but no one opened fire.

So, I'll be expected on the other side, he thought. *And they don't want to risk me blowing up the entire construct.*

The warning he had fed into the system had not failed in its intended effect. Good.

He began his ascent without killing the soldiers below him by leaping onto a cable he chose at random. It wasn't easy to land correctly, because although massive elevators traveled up and down the carbon nanotubes, they were hardly thicker than a finger. Still, it wasn't a problem, and a short time later he was able to open his electric sled, assemble it on his legs crossed beneath him, and settle into position like a monkey on its mother's shoulder.

With the push of a button, the ride began as if slung from a catapult, but his velocity soon leveled off at one hundred kilometers an hour. Nothing happened for the first hour, not even the normally expected radio messages trying to persuade him to return, threatening all sorts of sanctions up to and including being shot down. The Admiralty had to be very afraid of being discovered and bombed by the Clicks. That was warning enough for him to deactivate all his augments' active systems and switch off the automatics on his spacesuit as well.

Once he reached the stratosphere it got very dark, yet he felt an odd relief to see the normal firmament again with its twinkling stars, and he could see the two remaining halos that were not glowing pieces of debris, and Luna. He wondered how many of the "stars" were in fact ships in the Click blockade.

His implanted chronometer displayed a travel time of 87 minutes when he noticed movement out of the corner of his right eye. He had his eye augments to zoom to quadruple magnification. It was enough to show him an alien shuttle lifting out of the atmosphere parallel to the ground, drops of water beading off its smooth black surface.

But there was more. At first, he thought it was an optical illusion. The craft was barely eighteen kilometers below him and still flying below the sound barrier according to his laser tachometer. On its hull, he saw the outlines of humanoid figures moving back and forth.

Sirion looked at his own speed indicator: 1,001 kilometers an hour. With a closer zoom, he identified the figures as Omega mutants carrying large weapons. They appeared to be in an uncharacteristic frenzy. It wasn't hard to guess why, either. Some of them were apparently busy cutting a hole in the hull while others were trying to penetrate it with their handguns. Although parts of the hull flew past them and there were flashes and sparkles, they obviously were not making progress as fast as they had hoped. At their altitude, breathable air had long since disappeared. One of them had already slipped off and plummeted to the ocean below.

The next problem was the lights descending toward them from the darkness above. Sirion didn't need magnification to know they were a Clicks task force.

Strange, he thought. *Interesting.*

A brief analysis revealed six kilometers of transverse distance and nineteen kilometers of longitudinal distance, slowly increasing.

Doable.

14

"You'll survive," Dozer said as he regarded the stump of Eversman's arm, which he had sealed with safety foam. The officer was pale, but the initial shock caused by the amputation had given way to a stoic, somber mood.

"Fine, we'll get him out of here."

"I'm staying here," the lieutenant growled.

"No, you aren't," Dev countered. "I don't like the Federation any more than you do, but they need to know about that thing out there. This isn't just about us or the Fleet, it's about billions of ordinary people who can't do anything about demons falling from the sky."

"Speaking of which," Willy said pointing to the command post displays. "We should go over the sensor data."

"Download what you can," Dev told him. "But make it fast, we've got to leave. Who knows how long it'll take us and what we'll face once we get out of here."

"A demon," Dozer said with a blank expression.

"Yeah, right. Eversman, is there a spacesuit here?"

"No."

Dev wondered if the Harbinger agent was lying but he didn't care. He didn't have time to argue.

"Dozer, give him an evac bladder when the time comes."

The augmented man nodded and extended his weapon implants, a shotgun and a dart launcher with tasers. His gray synthetic skin was studded with obvious cyber prosthetics, the chrome eyes, the ports that stretched like a row of small metal craters from the back of his head all the way down his back and made him look at least as scary as the horned shadow Dev had seen. Added to this was the absence of any body hair or genitals. It all made Dozer look so inhuman that it made him shudder from a subliminal fear of something so unknown that shouldn't even exist.

"Listen," he said turning to Eversman. The lieutenant was trying hard not to look at the hulking augment zombie and didn't look very friendly. "When we get out of here, I'll get you a new hand, if I have a say. But that's only on the table if you help us get out of here. If—"

"Uh, boss?" Willy interrupted, and Dev looked at the engineer in the captain's seat as he rapidly gestured over the holodisplay.

"What?"

"You should see this."

"What should I see?" he asked impatiently.

"The guy didn't block access, so I looked around a bit."

"Looked around for what? We need to get here as soon as possible..."

"For the Bellingers."

"What?"

"The Bellingers! They sent out a distress signal, didn't they? Then the *Danube* wanted to send its Marines after us, right?"

"They didn't just want to, they did," Dev reminded the flight engineer.

"Part of the message is unencrypted, the distress signal. But it had an encrypted attachment," Willy explained. His face was illuminated by the hologram's blue glow.

Dev appeared at his side so quickly that it surprised even him. "So?"

"I don't know, but it's huge. I don't know what those two explorers were up to on Lagunia, but it seems they had a lot to share."

"That can't be right. They hardly had time to spend hours recording a distress signal."

"An attachment, maybe?"

"Can you decode it?"

Willy shook his huge head. "Not here, no. I need the *Bitch*'s software library, and even then, it'll take time."

"Download it," Dev ordered.

"What if it's some sort of malware? I have no clue what kind of shit went on down here, but all that Lagunia crap made me uncomfortable from the beginning. We made a find far too easily, and then we had a fucking assassin breathing down our necks that might have had something to do with shadow wings. Then, not long after, those sick demon aliens came out of hyperspace and fell upon the Federation while a secret fleet was operating in Harbingen. Considering all that, I'd say we can't be too careful."

"Just do it. And download all the sensor images of the *Danube* that you can fit into your memory." As he gave the order, Dev noticed Eversman's eyes narrow to slits. *Yes, we should certainly look at that data.*

The scratching at the door had disappeared by now, leaving a stillness made oppressive by unspoken fears. Dev didn't know if he found the absence of the sound preferable, after all, at least the sound had told him where the terror was lurking. Now it could be anywhere.

"What about the stuff? Did you find enough?"

"Yeah, but we had to leave it all near the airlock," Willy said, peeling himself out of his seat. "That *thing* was rushing toward us, and we didn't want to be stuck in the airlock when it got to us. We got here via the dorsal corridor, and we were faster, apparently."

"Eversman, are there any ventilation shafts or anything?" Dev asked the lieutenant.

"None that these two freaks could fit through," he grumbled. "Not even us."

"Then we'll take the opposite door," he decided, pointing to the bulkhead on the other side of the command post in the center of the bridge.

"Leave me here," Eversman pleaded. "I need to know more about—"

"No," Dev interrupted him. "Even if you could study the thing, which I don't think is logical, you'd be trapped in here with no food. No one would know what you learn. What good would that do? I guess an unseen martyr isn't a real martyr, huh? You're coming along. If you refuse, I'll have Dozer wrap you up like a fucking Star Logistics package. Now open the fucking bulkhead."

Willy and Dozer split left and right and leveled their weapons at the locked passageway while Dev kept an eye on their unwilling companion to make sure he didn't do anything stupid. Reluctantly, Eversman tapped a few short inputs on his forearm display and the bulkhead hatch rose. The corridor beyond appeared safe, to their relief. Dark, but there was no sign of anything with horns. Willy and Dozer switched on their lamps and dispelled the gloom with cold white light that spread in elongated cones across the rough wall panels.

"Let's go," Dev urged and followed with quiet steps. They tiptoed through the silence as if to not disturb the sleeping spirits of the abandoned ship. The primary systems were no longer online, so there was no soothing hum and whine of engines and computers. Again, he felt as if he were walking through a claustrophobic graveyard, and for the first time he longed to be out in the vacuum of space instead of aboard a starship.

They proceeded, step by step, through the ghostly silence, illuminating every shadow, no matter how small, lest something suddenly jump out at them. The numerous wires and cable strands running along the ceiling stretched away from them like tentacles into the darkness, occasionally interrupted by tiny, light-emitting diodes that drew their power from the minimal supply provided by current transformers.

Since Dev could hardly see anything behind the powerful backs of his two heavily augmented crew members, he confined himself to pricking up his ears and listening for even the smallest noise. That's why he almost jumped when Eversman whispered: "Stay in the light and look behind you regularly. They can only exist in the dark."

"Like vampires, or something?" Willy said in a low growl.

"Something like that."

"Shit, this just keeps getting better."

"Easy now," Dev said to calm them.

As soon as they reached the starboard corridor, they turned left after shining their lights in both directions and making sure they didn't detect any movement. The *Danube* was long and curved, so the corridor curved as well, as if trying to conceal its secrets just beyond the bend.

Dev looked up whenever he spied a ring on the wall, which appeared every ten meters. It looked like the various modules of the corridor had been assembled there. In front of one of them, he suddenly noticed that something was different and turned around. Eversman was bent over and holding the stump of his arm. His shoulder was leaning against one of the wall panels, as if he were exhausted.

"What is it?" Dev hissed impatiently, looking at Willy and Dozer. Their backs had already moved a few steps further along the corridor. In that instant, something in the wall whistled like a long, drawn-out sigh, and the ring in front of him suddenly expanded into a massive barrier. "Shit!"

He jerked his head back to Eversman, who had flipped open the wall panel and was thumbing around on a display behind it.

"Bastard!" Dev cursed and dashed toward the lieutenant, but Eversman saw him coming, rolled backward, and started running.

What a fucking piece of shit!

Dev looked at the security bulkhead, heard the muffled

thuds, presumably from the butt of Willy's submachine gun, and then to the fleeing officer. He decided to chase him.

"Stop right there, you son of a bitch!" he shouted, running into the darkness. Eversman looked like a silhouette from an oil painting come to life, with distorted arms and legs barely recognizable as Dev's eyes only slowly adjusted to the minimal light. At the first turn to the right, he thought the lieutenant would disappear and barricade himself on the bridge again. When an infernal screech sounded from that direction, he was not surprised to see Eversman running ahead of him.

Several times Dev almost caught him, but the bastard was nimbler than he expected and able to keep his distance, even as he ran through the shadows, right past the yellow-marked reactor area Dev had seen before. He wanted to call out after Eversman but feared the noise might arouse something he preferred not to awaken.

He was panting by now, unaccustomed to the physical exertion. Then he saw a light in the darkness, far ahead of Eversman. It was a cold, unsteady glow that seemed to have no source. He thought he saw two glowing eyes and shuddered. The officer was startled for a heartbeat and stumbled. That was all the opportunity Dev needed. He leaped forward and threw himself at the exiled Harbinger. In a tangle of arms and legs, they tumbled over each other, grunting as they rolled along the cold composite of the corridor and landed side by side in the darkness.

"Son of a bitch," Dev croaked. He quickly scrambled to his feet and rammed his elbow into the lieutenant's head as he started to stand. The officer staggered, dazed, to the side... and straight into the outstretched arms of a demon that silently peeled itself from shadows at the edge of the corridor that were deeper, untouched by the diffused emergency lighting.

What he saw were pitch-black veins under red skin stretched over knotted muscles. Instead of fingers, the creature possessed flashing blades as long as his forearms. It was huge, towering over Eversman by at least two heads. Its face was crowned with bizarre ramlike horns. It had a lipless mouth with sharpened teeth and glittering, slanted eyes that glared pure murderous lust at him. Dev found himself facing a terrible apparition that could have come straight out of the hell of his darkest nightmares.

It reached for Eversman, who cried out in horror as the demon's fingers snatched him and sliced into his arms as their eyes met. The lieutenant's screams became more bloodcurdling and penetrated Dev's bones.

Then something happened that Dev didn't understand. The struggling lieutenant was suffused by an ethereal glow that *flowed* into the red demon, who greedily opened his mouth as if delighting in the carnage. In the next moment, Eversman's body went limp and slipped through the creature's blades. Before the corpse hit the ground, it turned pitch black, then translucent before vanishing entirely accompanied by a chorus of voices that slobbered and shrieked out of nowhere, as incorporeal as a fleeting thought.

Then Dev, who had unconsciously retreated to the opposite wall, was alone with the demon. Saliva dripped from its sharpened yellow teeth.

"Now, for you," the hellish being said in a distorted hiss that was barely understandable.

Naked fear spread through Dev's limbs and froze him in place. Unable to move, he stared at the shining eyes as they drew ever closer, thirsting for his death. One look into the yellow flames within led him directly into the sixth circle of hell, searing, excruciating, like a maelstrom that sucked every bit of warmth and life out of him and swept him away. Part of him groaned in frustration at his paralysis, cried out to fight back, futile though it might be. He didn't want to die without a fight and vanish into nothingness like Eversman, yet his body refused to obey him, and he sank to the floor.

Suddenly, a flash of light struck the demon and it lurched to one side. Another bolt of lightning, preceded by a clap of thunder, sprang from the creature's chest and tore a fist-sized chunk of flesh from it, turning it into a pool of black ooze that splashed at Dev. He raised his hand to ward himself, but the thick drops turned dark as oil and disappeared just before they hit him.

Through fingers held before his eyes, he watched as the demon hissed and sizzled furiously like a steam engine. Then, suddenly, Dozer was there, charging from the left and hammering the alien with his weapon attachments. The creature defended itself with clicking finger blades. The augment zombie, whose chrome-cold eyes seemed the exact opposite of his adversary's, laboriously fended them off with his shotgun. He was fast, but not fast enough, and several of the razor-sharp blades dug into his forearm and flank. Since he was able to deactivate the stimuli in his synthetic skin and the equally artificial muscles beneath, Dozer seemed unaffected. The only effect of the assault was the white nutrient fluid that spurted like liquid snow from his wounds.

Dev shook off his paralysis and did what any good pirate would do. He kicked at the demon's bent back lower leg with all the force he could muster from his slumped, sitting position. The fiend stumbled. At the same moment, Willy appeared next to Dozer, his rifle trained directly at the red face. He pulled the trigger and the horned head dissolved in a cloud of blood that reverted to black ink. Before the liquid hit the walls, the demon underwent a metamorphosis, becoming transparent and dark, an ethereal shadow. Again, the chorus of eerie voices arose, then the alien's dark, distorted form was pulled back by an invisible force and collapsed into a tiny dot that seemed to recede infinitely far away.

Silence ensued. There was no sign of the demon or Lieutenant Eversman. It was as if they had never existed. Were it not for the fact that Dozer was bleeding white fluid from several deep lacerations, Dev would have believed he had succumbed to a nightmare, entirely imaginary except for his naked fear and panic.

"Shit!" was the first word that came to mind as he struggled for breath and took Willy's hand, who pulled him to his feet.

"Everything all right, boss?" the Dunkelheimer asked as he looked around the corridor with an unusually pale face.

"Nothing's all right. I almost got made into sushi by a goddamned demon with scissor hands!"

In the background, Dozer sprayed a transparent liquid on the wounds on his augment body. The hiss of the pressurized container shook him as if heralding the return of the demon.

"I don't know what that was, but if it was an alien, I don't ever want to see its homeworld," Willy said somberly as he checked Dev for injuries like a mother would a child. Dev remained impassive, not even responding, and looked at Dozer.

"All right?"

"Acceptable," the mechanic replied, checking the seal on his skin for damage, then tossing the can carelessly aside. "Let's go."

"Good idea," Dev agreed, looked to his right and left, and gulped. "Eversman believed there was only one of them trying to kill him, but I don't feel like sticking around long enough to find out if he was wrong."

"No objections," Willy rumbled, waving to Dozer to go ahead.

Directly in front of the airlock, fortunately only a dozen or so yards away, were several military crates and zero-G nets holding gray steel containers. The pile looked like a hastily packed campsite. In the lamplight, it cast long, uneasy shadows on the walls that made Dev's blood rush to his ears.

"I hope you recorded that shit with one of those expensive eye implants you had screwed in with your prize money," he said. The taste of curses on his tongue eased him back a little from the fear that had paralyzed him. Something of his old self returned with them. It was like being reborn after a difficult pregnancy.

"I have a buffer that automatically records everything I see and erases it after five minutes if the memory gets too full," Willy said tersely as he helped Dozer heave their bulky luggage into the airlock, which took longer than Dev would have liked. In the meantime, he had taken the engineer's gun and was trying to keep an eye on the right and left sides of the corridor at the same time, ready to shoot at anything that even looked like it was moving.

Ten minutes later, with silent blasts of cold gas from their mobility units, they slid away from the *Danube*'s cold corpse through the ring of debris and past the hull section where distorted shadows appeared as sooty figures.

Figures that make an awful lot of sense now, he thought to himself.

"Son of a bitch! There you are. Finally!" Aura shouted over the radio with some distress. "We thought we were about to suffocate!"

"We had some... *problems*," Dev said, tight-lipped, not giving in to the itch on the back of his neck that urged him to look over his shoulder. "But we're coming back now, and we've got everything we need."

"Plus, a shitload of new problems," Willy added. He seemed to have recovered his typical pessimism.

"If you have oxygen with you, we can talk about everything else afterward," Aura responded. "It can't be worse than being stuck in a half-shredded tin can and not knowing whether you'll freeze to death or suffocate first in the next thirty minutes."

"I wouldn't be so sure about that," Dev said and exhaled loudly.

15

"Baker?" One of the mutants called to them from the door they had cut open.

"Mmm?" Baker rumbled around the cigar in his mouth.

"We're missing eight guys."

Baker took the cigar out of his mouth. "Missing?"

"Took a head count." The mutant rubbed his beard with the barrel of his assault cannon, then nodded. "Yeah. Eight missing. Grisha was cutting up front. Some aliens were there."

"Did he take them out?" Baker said.

"Blew them away. Looks like somebody blasted them with a goulash cannon."

Jason looked up in disgust as the two mutants chuckled in satisfaction. The sound made him think of someone shaking a bag of rocks.

"Watch the little guys here," Baker ordered. As he turned to leave, he looked at Jason. "I'll go see what's going on. Maybe they didn't make it through the airlock before the emergency seal activated. Watch yourself."

"Likewise. Tell your pal we don't need any goulash here."

Baker rumbled a laugh and left the bridge with his cigar glowing in his mouth again.

Jason tried not to feel irritated by the floor vibrating beneath his feet and continued to look at the four smaller Clicks in black armor. They had formed a protective shield in front of the much larger, pearly specimen. Their four legs were constantly shuffling back and forth in such a bizarre way it made his eyes water. They held their long arms in a pose that reminded him of goalkeepers getting into position to block a shot. There was something menacing in their body language, but he wondered if he was subconsciously attributing human behavior to them.

"I could blow away one of them and see what they do," said the mutant Baker had left to protect him. He was huge, like the others, about seven feet tall. His eyes were chrome-plated and the skull above his eyebrows had been replaced with a scratched and faded steel augment. His grin revealed a row of gleaming, metallic teeth, but the appearance was neither sarcastic nor even sadistic. What alarmed Jason was the casual way he spoke, as if he was suggesting that they might make some coffee. When Jason said nothing, he shrugged his massive shoulders and lowered his man-sized assault cannon. "Just a suggestion, to keep things moving along and all. Heh, heh."

"You people solve every problem with guns, don't you?"

"No, we also have swords, machetes, and, believe it or

not, scalpels. Markhaz can carve a smile on the capillaries in a slice of kidney."

Jason shook his head and turned away. He blinked when he saw the pearly alien move. At first, it just made a slight turn of its head—or helmet—then the three armored fingers of each hand moved as well, and it slowly straightened. The change did not escape the attention of the four smaller Clicks, their excitement was unmistakable. They moved right and left like crabs that couldn't decide where to go. Clicks emanated from them. The sound had been there before, but he thought it came from the computer systems. Every console around him was blinking and flashing in pale pastel colors that his eyes could barely make out. The clicking intensified. It reminded him of the crackling sound he heard when diving on Lagunia, that emanated there from the extensive coral reefs that covered its ocean floor. Or again, of his time as logistics officer on the *Zarathustra* when the crew had spent several months battling recurring short circuits in the magazine's wiring.

"Click, click," the mutant behind him aped the sound.

"What's your name?" Jason said without turning to him.

"Rochshaz," he replied in a deep voice.

"Rochshaz, could you do me a favor and put your gun away?"

"Are you crazy?"

"These five are definitely unarmed, right?"

"Can't speak for their suits, no idea what's in them."

"We can assume they would have shot at us long ago with anything they might have on them. There are only two of us, but they still haven't made a move to attack us up to now—"

"I see where you're going with this, but I'm not putting my gun down."

"How long would it take you to take them down with your bare hands?" Jason asked.

"The four little ones? Two seconds to reach them, a third to send the milk spurting out of them. The big one will probably faint by then. It already looks like it's on its last legs."

"Now let's try to put one and one together. We're on their shuttle and have no idea about their technology. Right now, we're going into orbit where a thousand Click ships have Terra in such a tight stranglehold that we can't even let a fart go without them smelling it. Normally, we should be dead by now. We'd have been shot down by a laser from orbit or the shuttle could have self-destructed, whatever. But we're still alive," Jason said without taking his eyes off the agitatedly chittering aliens. They seemed to be trying to keep an eye on him and their larger comrade at the same time, if the two lenses on the right and left of their V-shaped heads were indeed eyes. "What do you think that's about?"

"We've only heard of black Clicks," Rochshaz said.

"Exactly. That one"—Jason pointed to the shimmering mother-of-pearl armor, its wearer slowly straightening with ponderous movements, as if dazed—"doesn't look black."

"Like it's been doused with oil. Funny shimmer."

"What if he's a VIP or something and that's why they didn't self-destruct."

"Or maybe they just couldn't push the button. Malfunction or alien error," the mutant said.

"But that still doesn't explain why they haven't vaporized us from orbit," Jason insisted.

"Hmm."

He turned his head briefly and saw Rochshaz reluctantly shoulder his assault cannon and lean against the wall, seemingly relaxed. He then put on his helmet and connected it to his oxygen supply.

If Jason expected a change in the aliens' behavior, he was disappointed. They seemed just as agitated as before. He spread his arms in imitation and tried to look as nonthreatening as possible, at least to a human. What if they interpreted his pose as he would someone baring his teeth and snarling?

The surreal nature of the moment hit him like a bolt of lightning. He was perhaps the first person to face—or better, sit across from—a Click for more than a few seconds and attempt de-escalating body language instead of burning holes in their armor with a laser rifle. What could possibly be more ironic?

"Okay, you passed out," he said, looking at the big one with the pearly armor. "And you're clicking around, just like your little friends. Or they're mute and you're clicking? Or vice versa? Where do you start when there's nothing to start with?"

Rochshaz's radio crackled, then beeped.

"Yeah?"

"Baker here, we're under attack. Drop troopers, it looks like."

"Want me to come over and make some flak?"

"No, watch the little guy."

Rochshaz emitted a disgruntled growl but stayed where he was.

"Shimmer's" movements seemed more purposeful and conscious, now. The alien came to its four feet, its lower knees bent as if praying. The four black Clicks wiggled their whirring fingers back and forth like knives and seemed to stare at Jason in a way that made the hair on the back of his neck rise.

"Want to change your mind?" the mutant behind him remarked.

"No. I just don't know where to start," he replied, frustrated. The muffled rumble and clatter of automatic weapons reached them on the bridge. The Clicks simultaneously turned their heads to the cleared passageway but showed no other reaction. "There are experts in this sort of thing. I'm not one of them."

"These *experts* haven't been able to do anything in over seventy years. I can't imagine they'd be any better at it now."

"That's only because they haven't had the chance."

"If you say so." Rochshaz's apparent disinterest in this first contact, even if it wasn't one in purely factual terms, irritated Jason. Could this giant hunk of flesh be so uncaring about the fact that they were actually sitting across from aliens? Beings, though enemies, that had evolved on an alien world and were apparently intelligent? Perhaps he had overestimated the mutants' cerebral capacity. After all, they were criminals whose work consisted of cannibalizing corpses to sell their organs and eyes on the black market.

"There must be areas where we overlap, things we have

in common. They use almost the same technology we do," Jason said more to himself, and eyed Shimmer's every little movement. Its four little helpers had apparently calmed a bit because the clicking noises had noticeably subsided. "Fusion reactors and thrusters, the materials of their hulls are made of composites similar to ours. They also work with Carbotanium and Carbin, albeit in smaller quantities. All this around us here"—he made a sweeping gesture, which the aliens closely followed—"could almost be one of our ships. That can only mean that mathematics is the language of the universe for them, too; we could communicate with them. Not to mention manufacturing processes, an understanding of physics necessary for space travel, and optical stimulus conduction. How else would they develop complex sensor graphics, navigate, and write targeting routines?"

Jason thought for a while. It wasn't that he had never had any of these thoughts before. But now, for the first time, they were relevant because a situation had arisen that he had never thought possible.

"Can you hear me?" he asked in Shimmer's direction and would have liked to slap himself for it. It sounded so stupid coming out of his mouth. The Click continued to glare at him, the slats on the front of its helmet opened and closed in a steady rhythm.

Neither a mouth nor a corresponding opening. These louvers are apparently for breathing. There's little oxygen in the air, but that shouldn't matter to them, they're wearing sealed suits like I am. My helmet also has no obvious facial features.

He tried something else. He tapped his chest with a fist,

and then the bridge's rough floor, the pattern unsteady like a blurred image.

Shimmer tilted its head back a little and the clicking resumed, echoing faintly in Jason's helmet. Then, tentatively, the alien imitated his gesture.

"And what's that supposed to signify?" Rochshaz said.

"That we're reacting to each other," Jason said absently. "It sees me, I see him."

"It's imitating you, an ape can do that. But a parrot is even smarter because it can repeat all your bullshit."

"The fact that it repeats my gestures says a lot," he said, contradicting the mutant. "It has an optical stimulus processing organ, otherwise it wouldn't have seen my movements."

"We already knew that, or they wouldn't have fired at us in the hallway."

"And it shows it's interested in communicating," Jason continued.

"Sure, because it knows its skin is on the line. Baker gave him a big knuckle sandwich."

"Just be quiet, that would be most helpful." He considered his next steps, only to conclude that he hadn't the faintest idea. So, he stood. Shimmer also stood, and the four black Clicks became nervous again, or so it seemed to him.

The bridge was about the size of the living room in Jason's parents' house on Harbingen, not very impressive. Unlike Federation shuttles, which were much smaller than this one. There was no cockpit with a pilot's seat nor windows looking outside, which was odd enough. In addition, there were the four tanks containing green liquid that bubbled sluggishly. They were neatly lined up like slim advertising columns and took up almost a quarter of the space. His first thought was that they were acceleration tanks. A century ago, the Fleet had experimented with solutions using smart nanofluids that thickened with increasing acceleration forces and mitigated the worst effects on the human body. And though somewhat higher final acceleration values had been achieved, their use had been too impractical and, ultimately, too expensive. Space travelers had to be oxygenated, their excretions removed, and their skin protected from softening and rotting. This had all required additional chemicals. Moreover, they could not simply go to their quarters and sleep at the end of their shifts, although the neural interface control had not posed a problem. In the end, the development of inertial dampening had put the final nail in the coffin of the acceleration tank concept.

Jason didn't know if the Clicks had artificial gravity on their ships since they were probably still deep in Terra's gravity well, if they had even left the atmosphere behind. As for fittings, there was an oblong console in front of the tanks in the rear that illuminated the room with a greenish light that reflected unsteadily off the dark walls. As he circled it, the crackling in his helmet grew louder, but the Clicks didn't stir other than intently following his movements.

There were controls—or what he thought were controls —curved levers with flat tops, some cogs, and lots of buttons, like in old Federation ships. They were arranged in a circle that rippled out at the edges, forming a mandala of input points so complicated that it made his head spin.

Each one seemed to radiate its own, albeit very pale, color, as if a hazy glow lay over it.

Everything seemed similar enough to understand what a button, switch, or control stick was, yet at the same time sufficiently alien that he didn't have the vaguest idea what they were for. It occurred to him to wave Shimmer over and get him to operate something. Aside from being an exceedingly stupid idea, however, he didn't think he would comprehend anything, even if he saw it demonstrated with his own eyes. On a Fleet ship, he could have asked an engineer to show him the inner workings of an engine and still not understood a word, even though they spoke the same language.

The two other consoles were farther forward and lower than the one where he was standing. The complex pattern of input options was also much less varied and confusing.

Jason looked at Shimmer, pointed at him, and then at the console in front of him. He circled it, pointed to one of the smaller black Clicks that were still almost as big as he was, and finally to the small console nearest him.

The pearly alien followed his gestures and then lifted the arms hanging down his body a little. Just a little, but the movement was impossible to miss.

An explosion roared along the corridor. He flinched, startled.

"That was close," he said.

Rochshaz nodded, took his assault cannon from his shoulder and peered into the corridor. The Clicks hastily crowded closer to Shimmer as he peered out into the corridor.

"Farther forward," the mutant reported, and reverberating bursts of fire followed his words. "Baker will take care of it."

Rochshaz turned back around and waved his weapon over the aliens as he did so. Jason motioned for him to shoulder the assault cannon and the mutant complied, rolling eyes.

This time the four relaxed more quickly than before. Shimmer slowly rose behind them. Unfolding first its lower knee joints and then its upper ones, he rose to his full height, which was somewhere between Jason's height and the mutant's. Given the mass of its armor, that was quite impressive. Jason had to summon all his willpower to not instinctively recoil or imagine a monster waking from hibernation. The four black Clicks began their crab-like dance again with wiggling fingers until Shimmer clenched a fist and they stopped their movements almost completely.

The alien's backward-curving feet began to tremble, then it pushed two of its kind aside and stepped toward Jason, who put a hand up to prevent Rochshaz from reacting hastily, though he swallowed hard. When he found himself taking a half step back, Shimmer immediately froze.

Did it frighten itself? Or does it understand my impulse for what it was? The thought flashed through Jason's mind. A cascade of clicks echoed through his helmet. They sounded like someone dragging a stick across a washboard, only it sounded much more sinister.

Records of signals emanating from Click ships existed in archives by the hundreds, although most of them were very brief. But decades of decryption and translation efforts had been fruitless. In the early years of the war, the Federation had paid vast sums to linguists and xenologists to decipher the underlying language, without success. The only results were more theories, all of which were so outlandish that Jason had not remembered anything of them except that no recurring pattern had been discovered. None of the clicking sounds were identical to each other. Sometimes there were short sequences that resembled each other, but they never occurred in the same combination twice. This had led Fleet Command to conclude that they were dealing with simple jamming attacks.

Here and now, Jason wasn't convinced that was true because the same sounds were definitely coming from the alien in front of him and not from a jammer. Even as he pondered how to signal that he wasn't afraid—how he could lie—a gunshot sounded nearby and all seven present —human, mutant, and alien—flinched in a universal moment of shock.

The four Clicks gathered around Shimmer faster than Jason could blink. Simultaneously, the doorway opposite Rochshaz opened where only a barely discernible circular gap had been visible a moment before. Two halves of the door, resembling the interlocking tears of yin and yang, jerked apart, and an extremely beefy Click wearing white armor deftly rolled under a blast from Rochshaz's assault cannon. The projectile detonated on the corridor wall and sent out a storm of shrapnel. The alien returned fire and Jason watched, his head tucked, as a hit on Rochshaz's chest plate punched him back.

Horrified, he watched as the thumb-sized muzzle opening swung in his direction.

16

"I don't even know where to begin," Aura said. Her picture album face had developed deep wrinkles around her eyes and corners of her mouth. They didn't detract from her beauty, on the contrary, they enhanced it with an attractive maturity. Dev, however, interpreted them as another unmistakable sign that his crew, including himself, had been through too much.

They were standing around the holoscreen in the mess hall. The repair work had gone on for two days. Willy, Dozer, and Jezzy had foregone sleep as they hurried to install the spare parts, integrate them into the system, and provide life support with what it needed. To do the necessary welding on the hull, Dev had maneuvered the *Bitch* into a shot-up hangar that had once been part of a warship. The shielding the wrecked bay provided, though full of holes, meant they could work undetected despite the plasma flames, and thus bought them some time.

While they labored sleeplessly, their onboard software deciphered the Bellingers' encrypted message and the

Danube's sensor data. Aura had compiled and processed it and was now able to share it with him. Dev decided not to include the other three, so they wouldn't be distracted from their work. After all, despite their best efforts, lack of sleep, and excessive use of stim tablets, it would still take some time for the *Quantum Bitch* to function anywhere near the way it had before half the Milky Way had decided to bombard it with everything it had.

"Start with the debris ring," Dev suggested and crossed his arms over his chest. The whir of not-quite-tightened screws in the ventilation circuit comforted him like a reassuring embrace. That familiar kind of imperfection provided satisfying evidence that everything was as it should be, because that's how it always had been.

"The sensor images from the *Danube* are numerous and detailed. You can tell that the barge has been patrolling over the ring far too long," Aura explained without betraying any fatigue. "More than four hundred overflights are sufficient for piecing together a complex picture with hardly any gaps."

To punctuate her statement, she called up a high-resolution holo-image in the tank that showed Lagunia and the ring around its equator that resembled a band of shimmering diamonds in the reddish light cast by the central star. When she tapped various pieces of debris with her index finger, they detached themselves from the shimmering image and hovered above the ring. After she repeated the process twenty times with marked objects, they assembled themselves into a ship he had seen before. To make sure he hadn't just imagined it, he tapped his forearm display and called up the representation of the alien ship they had the onboard computer construct after the Battle of Lagunia. As soon as both images hovered side by side before him, he took a deep breath.

"They're identical."

"*Almost* identical," Aura corrected him, pointing to a few areas the holotank highlighted to make them stand out. Dev had to blink a few times before he understood what she was getting at. Their size was the same, as was their basic shape. Bulgelike irregularities on the hull created an impression of a sperm whale. He spotted small openings from which plasma launchers had shot at the *Bitch*, as well as the strange propulsion section with its dark holes. Aura's indicated differences were small at first glance. Scars that had been black in the previous likeness seemed reversed with glaring white in the other. Instead of black stains on the craters, there were greenish growths, as if the hull was covered with algae. Several areas revealed holes and gashes reminiscent of bite marks.

"Definitely the same kind of ship," he finally concluded, stifling a yawn. "Just beat up differently, maybe."

"Maybe," she conceded but sounded unconvinced. "In any case, the wreckage that the Federation couldn't attribute to the Clicks actually belongs to the Demons, not the Lagoon."

Dev gulped at the mention of the name they had given the aliens after they returned from the *Danube*. Auras said it easily, almost casually, but she hadn't been there either, hadn't seen what he'd seen.

"So, a battle between... *them* and the Clicks."

"Yes. About a hundred years ago. I guess the dating

parameters don't change. The Federation researchers have done a good job determining the age of the various materials. And incidentally, we've just solved one of the biggest mysteries in Lagunia research."

He gave her a questioning look through the holotank. "How so?"

"I did a little research." Aura marked all the debris that had so far been attributed to the extinct Lagoon but were now assigned to the Demons that had raided several Federation worlds. Next in green were those identified as Click. All objects in orbit around Lagunia therefore glowed either green or red. "The Click fleet's debris are different ages, which is expected. You rarely build a fleet in a day. The oldest wreckage has been dated to about one hundred forty years old, others to only one hundred ten or one hundred years. Those believed to be Lagoon ships have been dated to be exactly one hundred years old, give or take a few months. Two different dating methods were used, but both were based on isotopic decay. Once rubidium-strontium for the Click ships and then potassium-argon. Basically, just because they didn't know why the results were so different."

"They thought they were doing something wrong because no fleet can entirely be made up of ships exactly the same age," Dev speculated.

"Yes. At least, I guess so. But no matter what decay dating method was used, you always got the same result. That's why they started looking for hidden superyards in the system." The rings under Aura's eyes, enhanced by the tilt of her head in the reflected light of the holotank, looked like the fur coloration around a panda bear's eyes. "I guess they could have saved themselves the search."

"They were invaded out of hyperspace, just like we were. But even then it doesn't make sense that all these alien ships were the same age. Could it be that the transiting effect somehow alters the materials and only the date of entry into the system applies? That might distort the age of the hull materials." He knew full well his question was pretty silly.

She confirmed his suspicions. "No. Not only is that physically illogical, but after centuries of jump technology, we have never noticed such an effect in our own ships."

"So, the Demons have a super shipyard on the other side, wherever that is."

"Or they build their ships using a different principle. After all, both their armor and weapons work differently than ours and the Clicks'. In any case"—she made a gruff gesture with her right hand—"a strangely huge battle took place here between the Clicks and the unknown aliens, and not, as once assumed, between the Lagoon and the Clicks."

Dev thought about what she had said and began chewing on his lower lip. "Then maybe they were a force protecting the Lagoon? Or the natives were their vassals?"

"I don't know." Aura shrugged. Next, she called up the image of what the Bellingers had found deep in the ocean: a ruined horseshoe two kilometers across covered in shells and seaweed. "But this is most definitely a hyperspace gate. Now that we know the Demons struck here, too, I have even less doubt that it can't be anything else. We sold the Bellingers the best claim because it was once a hyperspace gate."

"A hyperspace gate that existed a hundred years before ours."

"Yes. So much for our technological superiority."

"If the Fleet had had this information—"

"—it might have waited to activate the gates and Iron Hammer to find out why the Clicks knew of the existence of this technology but never used it themselves."

"Provided that someone with a lot of tinsel on their chest made a wise decision."

"So unlikely," she concluded, and he nodded in agreement.

"All right. Let's assume that there are the remains of a hyperspace gate down there. This only raises further questions. How can such a large cave form beneath coral reefs on the ocean floor within just a hundred years? That seems like a very short period of time to me. It must have been at one of the jump points. So, how did it get here? I don't understand."

"There are many more questions. Why install a jump gate near a world inhabited by an aquatic species that, one would think, doesn't build spaceships itself."

"At least now we can establish once and for all that aquatic species *are* capable of space travel," Dev said. "I've always wondered how such a species would conduct its first high-voltage experiment without frying its entire population."

"Until there's a better explanation, the eggheads just assume there's some factor they haven't discovered yet." Aura shrugged. "Of course, there's another possibility."

"Yes?"

"There was and is no Lagoon."

Dev raised his brows and frowned. "Remains of them

were found. Even several well-preserved body parts. There were also aquatic cities on the ocean floor."

"I know that. But what if they didn't belong to the Lagoon? What if they're Click?"

"You're saying that Lagunia is actually Clicktown?"

"Sounds ridiculous," she admitted, "but think about it. If you develop a hyperspace gate and build a prototype, where do you put it? Certainly not near a planet inhabited by another sentient species, especially given that the scale of resources and labor required to build such a monster machine would be enormous. The hypothetical Lagoon certainly weren't capable of it, and the number of resources and facilities that must have been brought here is gigantic."

"If it were true, where are they now?"

"Who?"

"Not who, what. The industrial facilities. Lagunia was largely empty when the first prospectors arrived."

"Gone," she said as if it were obvious. "After the battle, they packed up and left the system."

"Why would they have done that if they were able to win the battle here?"

"Maybe they didn't."

"They're still around," he pointed out. "The Clicks, I mean."

"The Demons, too, apparently. Though perhaps not here. We just don't know enough. But either the Clicks got rid of their industry after experiencing the same debacle with hyperspace gate technology that we did, or the other aliens shot everything here to smithereens once before and have now returned after we practically *invited* them back with a gate. Either would be reason enough for the Clicks to never return. I submit that their homeworld, or what we've thought is their homeworld until now, is also mostly covered by oceans. What if what we've assumed is wrong? Maybe their watery world was not a result of industrial climate change melting their polar ice caps as it did on Earth."

"You mean they feel comfortable there?" Dev wasn't convinced.

"Yes, it's possible. I agree with the logical idea that aquatic species cannot develop electricity. It's hard to do underwater. But it could be bioelectricity or something like that."

"Living things that rely purely on biological mechanisms don't have a habit of inventing things that operate outside their bodies," he objected, shaking his head. "Besides, we see the Clicks flying around in spaceships, and they either wear powered mechanical armor or they're robots, which I still think is more likely."

"They could have evolved. Or they had outside help. Until the AI revolution, we built humanoid robots that were so complex that we could hardly distinguish their behavior from human, even if it was merely the product of complex algorithms. Someone might have done something similar with the Clicks. Imagine if we augmented primates and made them only twenty percent smarter. Who knows how they would turn out."

"That seems like a stretch," Dev said. Yet his protest lacked the conviction it would have had a day ago, or even a month ago.

"A greater stretch than a supposed robotic species flying all the way to the home planet of a pre-industrial aquatic civilization to build a hyperspace gate? A location that requires them to fly an entire fleet far from their home just to make use of it? The cost in resources, money, and time alone would be exorbitant and anything but logical or efficient—two characteristics usually attributed to robots," Aura countered.

"You know more, don't you?" Dev said suspiciously. "What about the Bellingers' distress signal?"

Aura sighed and tapped her forearm display.

"Standard distress message to a satellite in orbit," she explained, and the image of a small satellite with a large receiving dish zoomed in. It was a tiny satellite circling alone in high orbit. "As you mentioned, however, the data packet was much larger. Although Valeska Bellinger apparently hadn't had time to send a voice message, she sent along an attachment. Well, at least something like that."

"Something *like that*?" he asked.

"It's an automatic security release for her implanted data storage. The officer in charge on the bridge of the *Danube* didn't know what to do with it, but he was smart enough to realize it was unusual and downloaded everything he could extract from the implant. A whole lot of data, although it was all encrypted. The *Danube* crew didn't bother with it any further. Presumably, the captain postponed anything related to it until after Iron Hammer, which would be understandable. The Bellingers were respected explorers, but were small fry compared to the Fleet's final, war-ending offensive."

"And? What did you find out?" Dev asked with undisguised impatience. Aura was rarely chatty, and her speech was all the more remarkable for the lack of colorful cursing, which was something of a standard practice on the *Quantum Bitch*. If the alternative was beating around the bush, he'd rather have the old, bad-tempered Aura back.

"Several things. The Bellingers were able to figure out that the damage to the sunken hyperspace gate was inflicted by shipboard weapons of Click origin, just like the hyperspace gate itself is."

"So, you already knew."

"Yeah," she admitted, dismissing his exasperated expression with a curt gesture. "Don't piss yourself, man. I had to at least see how a conversation would go, if we're willing to question everything we know so far. At least that'll help us when we sell this info to the Federation guys at a high price."

"Hmm," he said reluctantly and gestured for her to continue.

"They also learned that the gate had only been active for a few hours before they destroyed it themselves and sank it there. Valeska Bellinger, according to her own logs, felt that once the technology had been activated, the Clicks had deemed the danger too great to maintain it. So, they destroyed it and never pursued research into it again. They abandoned the planet after hiding the remains."

"That would explain why they attacked Harbingen with everything they had." The scales fell from Dev's eyes. "Their attacks on the moon Kor, where Harbingen's main research facilities were located and work on hyperspace technology was conducted... It was the groundwork done there that the Federation eventually owed, unofficially, the breakthrough made twenty years later."

"Yes. That was the Bellingers' theory, too. The Clicks

wanted to prevent what happened at Lagunia from happening again by any means necessary. The only thing they didn't know was why. The researchers had no idea about the Demons and believed it had something to do with hyperspace sleep and that the permanent activation of a hyperspace link could lead to similar effects in the environment. In the last entry of her memory cluster, she is recorded as saying to her husband that she had to warn the authorities immediately, before they opened the gate. That was a few hours before Augustus gave the order for the activation sequence. She never got around to it."

"Sirion," Dev growled. "That son of a bitch has to answer for the whole system. Maybe the entire Federation once the fringe worlds that are cut off from the core starve or drown in chaos."

Aura nodded grimly. "Yes."

"That means that the Clicks' only previous major offensive into human territory was an attempt to protect us from ourselves by destroying our most promising gate research?" Dev summarized, scratching the stubble on the top of his head. "It can't be."

"Did they mean well? That would be a pretty brutal paradox, but I doubt it. We only have to think of First Contact when they destroyed an unarmed research ship without warning."

"Still, this sheds new light on them. After all, they could have just let us die then, just as we are now. When it comes to destroying us, those damned Demons are achieving more now than the Clicks have in almost seventy years."

"Maybe that was never their goal. Maybe they're afraid they'll be next."

"But if the Demons can jump without hyperspace gates, why haven't they shown up in the rim systems we jumped through? If they can use normal jump points, why didn't they start their invasion earlier? Why haven't they ever shown up anywhere?" Dev asked, eyeing her, but Aura just shrugged. "All indications are that they need a stable link into hyperspace to invade our systems."

"I don't know. Seems like it, but so far, we know little about the Clicks, which is still a hell of a lot more than we can say for sure about these *Demons*."

"We're going to Terra," Dev decided. "As soon as the *Bitch* is spaceworthy again, we'll be on our way."

"There's one more thing we should talk about."

"What?"

"The guys brought repair materials, mostly, but also ammunition."

"I know." he said with an impatient wave. "I've already looked at the updated inventory lists."

"There's one sequence number missing from it, though." Aura called up an image of a short, squat warhead. "Willy must have thought it was a fusion torpedo, albeit an oddly thick one, but magnetic spectrography revealed something else."

"What?"

"Antimatter containment chambers."

"An antimatter torpedo?" he blurted, horrified. "Is he crazy? If someone caught us with that—"

"I know, boss. He didn't know what it was. Shall we jettison it?"

"No," he said reluctantly. "If the *Danube* had one loaded, the Fleet might want to find out where *they* got it.

Those weapons have been outlawed for decades and should be traceable, as few as there are of them. But hide that thing well. And tell Willy I want him to be one thousand percent sure the solenoids are working."

"There's more," Aura said, and he didn't know what to be more concerned about, that she sounded embarrassed for the first time, which was unlike her, or that there was more bad news. "*Danube*'s sensor data included telescopic images from the few surviving satellites, plus recordings from surveillance cameras all over Lagunia that captured how the invasion went down."

Dev swallowed.

"I wish I hadn't seen what I saw," she said quietly. "It was a slaughter. But what's worse is that they disappeared."

"*Who* disappeared?"

"All of them, boss. All of them... just disappeared."

17

When Sirion sprang from the electric sled it felt like gravity didn't quite know what to do with him for a few seconds. His 1,000 kilometers per hour of upward acceleration diminished rapidly against Terra's relentless effort to pull him back down. For a moment, he was weightless until the relative wind took hold and pushed him downward. He did not let those precious seconds go to waste. He placed his legs shoulder-width apart, stretched his feet downward to full length, spread his arms out to the sides and pulled his head back onto his neck as he bowed forward slightly to create a small cavity on his belly to capture air resistance.

He had not thought he would have to prove his freefall abilities again in such a short time. It had already been tested when his shuttle fell, or rather was shot down, into the Himalayan mountainside. Although he was about to jump, or rather plunge, from a jury-rigged contraption attached to a 35,000-kilometer-long cable in the direction of an ascending shuttle, this was certainly the simpler challenge.

He was able to estimate the shuttle's rate of ascent, so he could lead his target. This allowed him to achieve a respectable horizontal velocity and descend at an angle.

The alien shuttle was still four kilometers away, climbing in a straight line. Despite the closed spacesuit, Sirion could hear the muffled rush of the relative wind as it streamed around his helmet. He cupped his hands and steered his fall right and left, making small adjustments now and then, and hoping the Clicks didn't alter their course.

Drop troopers were a special breed of Marines trained to infiltrate orbital stations and secret military ground installations that, for some reason, could not or would not be bombarded from space. They had special combat suits and jetpacks that turned them into little meteorites, and which required a rather unique attitude toward life. There weren't many of them, maybe a few hundred in the entire fleet if the more credible rumors were accurate. The survival rate was not particularly high, but missions were few. The fact that the Clicks apparently had such units themselves did not surprise him, since they were technologically at about the same level as the Federation. That phenomenon had long puzzled researchers. How likely was it to encounter another intelligent species that was at the same level of development? The probability must have been about as low as witnessing alien drop troopers in Terra's outer atmosphere targeting mutants trying to cut open the hull of an alien shuttlecraft.

The glowing double flames from the jetpacks the aliens wore had become long fingers of plasma as they descended the last hundred meters, breaking as abruptly as bungee jumpers at the end of their cables. The mutants were preoccupied with their hectic attempts at forcing an entrance entry into the interior of the space shuttle before they succumbed to the airless atmosphere. When they finally noticed the bulky invaders descending on them, they had too little time to react effectively. They hit four alien troopers out of two dozen with machine gun fire and grenades that either shredded them completely or flung them out of their trajectories like stuffed dolls. The rest, however, landed on the shuttle's hull like a hailstorm and engaged the mutants in a brutal battle.

One of the aliens simply crushed a mutant when it landed on him. The mutant briefly disappeared in a red cloud before his remains slid off the shuttle. Another mutant rolled out of the immediate field of fire—too far. He rolled to the very edge of the shuttle, lost his grip, and plummeted toward the earth, his arms flailing.

Three mutants farther forward had thrown away their welding torches and drawn melee weapons, a saber, an axe, and a huge vibroblade, and engaged ten aliens that had landed in a circle around them. The carnage was short and fierce, costing lives on both sides, yet the outnumbered gene-modified humans quickly got the worse of it. One of them managed to cut one of the troopers in half, only to find himself without a head the next moment—it had magically disintegrated. His body tipped forward and slipped off the hull.

Amid this chaos, Sirion flew toward them like a speeding arrow. He braked by bringing his arms forward and increasing the arch of his back. When he saw he was about to overshoot the shuttle, he moved into a sitting position with his arms splayed up out his sides and fired the control jets of his tight-fitting spacesuit. He burned his entire supply of cold gas in five seconds for the braking thrust he needed to avoid ending up as a red blur and to keep the deceleration from tearing him apart. Even with his titanium-coated bones and muscle-enhancing augments, the force acting on him was brutal. He felt like he was being quartered.

But it worked, his timing was perfect. He landed— albeit a little harder than he'd hoped—at about the middle of the shuttle as it raced through the darkness toward the twinkling stars. Around the opposing figures, the shimmer of Earth expanded, enclosed in a hazy fog of modified microcellulose. The two remaining Halos, whose orbits intersected, now seemed very close, like luminous streaks in the firmament rather than the thin, silvery filaments they resembled when farther distant.

Sirion had just enough time to pull the small satchel from his back to shield him from a laser beam that ate through the material in a single breath. He rolled forward and dodged to one side as the shooter, one of the four-legged aliens, made the hull right behind him glow.

He had never fought Clicks before and would have to adjust, but that was also true of his opponent. He kicked the knee joint closest to him and threw his attacker off-balance just long enough for him to deploy the vibrating monofilament blades from his forearm sheaths and relieve the alien of two of its legs. As the armored figure lunged forward, Sirion ducked under it and thrust his bladed arms upward and pierced through the alien's chest armor. With a quick jerk, he yanked it aside and was immediately enveloped in a shower of blood and water that instantly turned to ice crystals and fell away.

The next Click nearly riddled him with rapid fire when he was almost too slow taking cover behind the twitching legs of the alien corpse. Sirion grabbed the dead alien's laser rifle to fire at the shooter, only to find the trigger did not function.

Induction enabled, he thought, waiting for the next volley. As the munition threw sparks from the corpse's armor, he rolled out of his cover and spotted the alien targeting him. It was five meters away. Behind it, he saw another one engaged in brutal hand-to-hand combat with a mutant. Sirion hurled the useless firearm at its V-shaped head and ran toward it. He used the two seconds it took the alien to avoid the improvised projectile and recover its bearings to close the distance. As he moved, he pulled a blade from its thigh sheath and thrust the weapon upward from his right hip toward its neck, but the alien used its long arms and greater reach to parry the blow with its own weapon. The blade must have been coated because his own did not slice through it.

Sirion ducked under a riposte that would have cost him an arm and rammed a free monofilament knife into one of the Click's four thighs. He managed to twist his hand to prevent the wound from closing and was already whirling around the alien's back. It moved more ponderously than he did thanks to his activated reflex booster. It was a formidable opponent, although it appeared non-augmented. It simply could not match Sirion's stimulant-flooded system working at full speed with eightfold stimulus conduction. Before he even completed his turn, he removed the top of the alien's skull from its head with a backhanded swipe of his knife. A fountain of blood and water turned into a geyser of red and white ice crystals as the alien sank backward. The small particles danced across the hull and directly toward a hole where the last trooper was leaping into the shuttle. Several corpses, human and alien alike, slid off the hull, leaving it so deserted that one might think nothing had happened if it weren't for the numerous craters and gouges around him.

He resisted the urge to immediately leap after them, although the twinkling of the stars above him could only mean they were getting closer to the warship net the Clicks had arrayed around Terra. Again, he wondered why they had not opened fire long ago. The possible answer to that question was, after all, the reason why he had changed his *initial* suicide plan to the *current* suicide plan.

He crouched at the edge of what was once an airlock. The outer and inner doors had been crudely cut and destroyed. He peered inside and could clearly see erratic muzzle flashes reflecting off the walls. The shadows of aliens dispersed along the corridor, which he recognized by their human-sized but beefier proportions, flitted right and left. An explosion near the hole sent a short-lived cloud of smoke billowing toward him. He used it as cover to enter the ship.

He hung upside down from the handholds of the inner airlock and hooked his feet into handholds on two walls to keep from falling. Then, very slowly, he lowered himself until his head slid into the passage. There was fighting to his right. Some aliens had taken cover behind extended force field shields and were firing laser beams at targets farther back. Yellow fireballs answered and hammered at their shields. Ricochets whizzed just past him, flaying insulating material from the walls.

Sirion waited until the aliens fired another massive volley, then released his feet from their improvised anchors, lowered himself like a spider, and landed in a crouch. Close to the wall, he ran in the opposite direction, where the bow should be and where no fighting was evident. Less than ten steps later he came to a bend where he encountered two mutants who, apparently at the cost of one of their own, had overpowered three aliens who now lay behind them, their armor smoking.

The two giants seemed as surprised as he was. They froze, halting their slow, silent progress along the passage. Sirion did not hesitate. He raised one of his blades and plunged it through the Adam's apple of the one closest to him, a hulking broad-faced man with two horns implanted on his forehead and a bare, tattooed chest. His skin had the rough matte texture of dermal armor and was now soaked with the blood streaming from his throat.

The second mutant growled in rage and swung a monstrously large axe at him. The blade whistled so close over his head that it lopped the sentient receiver from his helmet. He thought he could feel the passing breath of air, even through his armor. The resulting fight proved his augmented opponent stronger than he was; Sirion had to rely on his speed, his own hardware was certainly better. He didn't think he could meet another human in the Federation who had invested more credits in his systems than he. Still, his opponent clearly had more room for implants. The mountain of muscles handled the axe nimbly, swinging it as if it were a toy, and his body armor boasted ablative elements that warded off several blows from his monofilament blades. Although blood trickled from the wounds beneath, the mutant's furious frenzy only intensified, presumably incited by battle stims. It was only when Sirion feigned a parry, retracted his blade, ducked away, and snatched a pistol from his opponent's thigh holster that his strategy paid off.

The second mutant soon lay with a smoking hole in the back of his head. Sirion wasted no time and took off along the passageway on the other side of the shuttle. The shouts, explosions, and rattling rifle volleys of genetically modified humans and aliens contended for control of the shuttle behind him. Sirion was not interested in them, but in what they were trying to control. And in space, that always meant the bridge.

After only a few steps, close to the dark wall, he saw lights at the other end of the corridor moving with the typically erratic rise and fall of helmet lamps. Instinctively, he pressed himself into a recess at one side. At its base, wisps of steam shot up from a grate, which lent him surprisingly good cover. Since the steam was as hot as it was dense, he could not utilize any of the obstructed vision enhancements in his eyes, so he pushed his face forward just far enough to make out anything.

A lone Click warrior was coming his way, surprisingly fast on its four powerful, double-jointed legs before it abruptly stopped. The alien attached finger-sized objects to several spots on the wall then dashed back from where it had come. Four simultaneous low-pressure explosions thundered through the corridor and briefly drowned out the noise of fighting on the other side of the shuttle. Sirion extended his blades in perfect silence like the fangs of a predator and, with long strides on the balls of his feet, crept up to his prey as it leaped into the cleared passageway and opened fire against its unseen pursuers. It jerked deftly to the side, just enough to dodge a grenade that blew open half the wall behind it, exposing cables and pipes that sprayed water, steaming coolant, and hot gas. Amid the roar, Sirion quickened his final steps, performed a leaping kick against the first hollow of the Click's knee, followed it with a round-house kick against the next higher one on the left, then grabbed the alien's chin from behind and drove his right monofilament blade its full thirty-centimeter length into the alien's neck and cut diagonally through the spine, or at least where the spine would be in a human.

In any case, the effect was virtually identical, the alien immediately collapsed as if the cord holding it upright had been severed. Water and blood ran from the narrow wound as Sirion withdrew the blade and balanced himself to stomp on the corpse's back at the end of its fall. A room opened before him, one he had actually expected to see further ahead: the bridge. Three consoles were arranged in front of a wall that was smoother than the others, a display, perhaps? The illumination was a diffused greenish hue, like on the rest of the shuttle, and made for a blurry image, like someone deprived of a visual aid.

Sirion was not often surprised, but this time was an exception. In addition to four Clicks standing before him like a wall of black chitinous creatures, he spied two other figures in the round chamber. One was a Click that was noticeably larger than the others. It wore pearly armor that shimmered as if it could not decide whether it wanted to be green, blue, or purple and was crouched like a cat about to spring. The other was a normal-looking human. He wore black armor that looked as if it had been soldered together from scrap metal, uneven, dented, and stained. His face was hidden by a visor with a clunky breathing device stuck to it. Through the scratched glass, he made out soft eyes that sharply contrasted sharply with a curved nose that resembled the beak of a bird of prey. Something about the look in those eyes seemed strangely familiar, which was just as true of the nose.

Even stranger than that was the fact that his fellow human was armed but had his rifle shouldered. Instead of looking frightened, he seemed strangely relieved. That quickly changed as Sirion took out the four Clicks standing in his way. Since they were unarmed and acting much more heroically than their unmodified abilities should have allowed, it took him less than two breaths to finish them off.

His blades dripped blood as he stood before both human and alien and lowered his gaze.

"I'll only ask this once," he said. "What is going on here, and which one of you controls this ship?"

His human counterpart tried to yank his weapon forward amid insistent clicking sounds that crackled through the bridge, but his movements were downright sluggish to Sirion. With a swipe of his right blade, he severed the barrel of the rifle while it was still pointing at the floor.

"Bad idea."

"I've got a better one for you, kid," a deep bass voice rumbled.

Sirion extended his left blade in the direction of the two beings before him so they wouldn't get any ideas, then he turned toward the welded passage on the other side of the corridor. The noise of the battle had died down—apparently the mutants had won. One was standing there, just placing an assault cannon on the floor that was so large it was probably normally mounted on vehicles instead of being used as a hand weapon. His skull was shaved, and chrome shone through several places on his body. Chrome also covered eyeballs that stared at him like cold moons. He had bared his platinum-coated teeth in a battle-scarred grin after spitting a glowing cigar stub from the corner of his mouth. Even the massive plates of his armor could not hide the bulging mounds of muscle that stretched beneath and would probably have made anyone other than Sirion instinctively recoil.

"I'd normally say I'll make a man out of you, but you've got a couple of my boys on your conscience, so let's do it another way," the mutant said, curling his fingers into fists the size of dinner plates. As he did so, curved augment spurs slowly extended from his knuckles and Sirion immediately recognized their shimmering sheen as monofilament. They were at least twice as long as his own blades, and the giant's movements were accompanied by a telltale tremor indicative of an implanted reflex booster. "I'm going to shove my spurs so far up your tiny ass that I'll be able to pull out your baby teeth."

18

Dev tried to banish the images from his mind. Visions of crowds running in panic through the damp streets of Atlantis, of mothers holding their infants close to their chests, their eyes filled with sheer terror. He saw the woody seaweed, trimmed in a pitiful attempt at aesthetics, the flog that bore the capital of Lagunia across the endless ocean. The cuttings served as a kind of railing for the few pedestrian walkways to offer protection from the vehicle traffic that had long since degenerated into a chaos of pileups and gridlock. Not that they could have escaped anywhere on an island. There were neither cellars nor bunkers on a flog, but there was plenty of open sky, from which meteorites fell, flaming through the clouds. Wherever they hit, nightmare creatures rose from the black smoke. Sometimes they took the form of horned devils, sometimes hybrid spawn that were half human, half animal. He also saw ghostly apparitions with distorted grimaces, men and women wearing horrible masks and bearing even more horrible weapons.

As different as the aliens were in appearance—if they were alien, Dev, at least, thought they looked far too human, or at least humanoid—they were united in their lust for murder. Wherever they appeared and emerged from the blisters, which dissolved into black nothingness in their craters. They hacked mercilessly at the fleeing humanity and slaughtered their way through men, women, and children alike. It was the purest bloodlust that compelled them and filled the massive gutters with the blood of the civilians of Atlantis who had remained behind. The city, otherwise plagued by heavy monsoon rains, turned red as a meat grinder of sheer hatred processed its inhabitants. It was a hatred that blazed in every invader's eyes, unlike from each other as they were in other aspects.

Dev had seen a lot of violence in his life and had developed a soul more hardened than he sometimes liked, but the scenes Aura had played for him in the mess hall still made him feel sick, though he was fully occupied in the cockpit completing systems integration of the new components. Even worse than the blood and helpless panic of the defenseless Lagunians, those unlucky enough not to get one of the limited seats during the hasty evacuation, was what had happened to them. Like Eversman on the *Danube*, they became translucent shadows shortly after their deaths, distorted ghostly shapes that seemed to be pulled aloft and condensed into an infinitesimally small point before disappearing. With them, any indication that they had ever existed, even the smallest drop of blood, vanished. The last images from the city cameras showed deserted streets. Even the Demons seemed to have hunkered down in the darkness of the ruins and abandoned houses, now that there were no more inhabitants they could unload their frenzy on.

Atlantis had been wiped out entirely within hours. And by wiped out he meant *eradicated* from the history books. There was no trace of the dead, and as frightening as the mere thought of simply disappearing was, the thought of how it was possible for a person's material remains to just vanish into thin air obsessed him. He simply did not know, but who was he? A smuggler allergic to the more accurate word "pirate" was hardly the right person to talk to when it came to exploring the border between physics and metaphysics.

"Boss?" Jezzy's voice snapped him out of his thoughts. Apparently, she had been talking to him for some time.

"What, huh?" he asked and sat up in his seat. His movement was quickly arrested by the three-point harnesses that kept him from floating away at the slightest impulse.

"The power pattern cell relays," she repeated, "is the error message still there?"

Dev shook his head and gestured through the appropriate diagnostic menu.

"No, everything looks fine," he said absently.

"Good, let's move on to the starboard cooling units," she suggested.

He scrolled through the menus almost in a trance, queried each item, and then activated the onboard computer's diagnostic software before skimming the logs his console spat out and convinced himself there were no glitches in the heuristics. While most of the damage to his *Bitch* was purely analog in nature, short circuits and faulty applications of secondary systems could cause discrepancies in the primary software more often than desired, and this time he had to play it safe.

All the while, he answered Jezzy's increasingly frequent queries with "Yes," "All good," or "Green." In fact, he should have been pleased, almost ecstatic, to see so many good messages follow each other on his screens. They told him everything he hoped to hear, but they were still hidden in the debris ring, and that meant in orbit around Lagunia, the one place in the universe he wished to leave as soon as possible.

"Willy? How's it looking out there?" he asked over the radio.

"Welding down the last of the printed Carbotanium plates right now," the engineer reported, his voice reverberating in his space helmet. "Dozer is handling the integration with the molecular bond generators. We should be finished in ten to twelve hours."

"Thank you." Dev switched to Aura. "Reactor status?"

"Not bad for a beaten-up donor heart," the energy node specialist replied. She had recovered her foul mood, which almost made him sigh in relief. "At least the Helium-3 pellets are up to half full, which is good. With the ice we've sucked out of the ring so far, we should have enough propellant, too. The reactor is humming along and displaying only standard error messages, but that's due to incompatible software interfaces, and most of them are the result of missing security certificates rather than real system incompatibility."

"Good, so we're ready to go from your end?"

"Hmm. I want to get out of here as soon as possible,

too, boss, but we should at least conduct a few test runs with the high energy output before we pull our pants down. The energy pattern cells took a good beating, and we should figure out which ones are going to fail when we turn up the juice, so there won't be any undesirable side effects. By that I mean, when so much shit flies into the fan that we dissolve into a giant cloud of manure."

"Noted," he said and focused again on his pilot controls. After making sure the final sensor checks were positive, he raised a fist as they regained control of the two Sentinel ejection bays. Until an hour ago, the control pumps for the doors had stopped working after a high-energy laser from one of the Broadswords made short work of the control relay clusters on the bow.

"You don't want to fool around, do you?" Jezzy asked in alarm. Her voice was so close to his ear that he flinched.

She correctly interpreted his what-are-you-doing look and pushed herself off his backrest to put some distance between them before pointing upward to where the panel to the flux actuators stood open.

"Half of them aren't doing their jobs anymore," she said.

"Never mind, triple redundancy. Which I insisted on, I'd like to point out," he grumbled.

"Now we don't have any at all."

"Hmph. Anyway, we've been sitting here deaf and blind for far too long. We need to know what's going on out there."

"If there's one thing we've learned about the aliens with their strange dark drives, it's that they're pretty stolid. I don't think much has changed since we got here." Jezzy sighed wearily, and with the filigree soldering iron crackling in her hand, began working on the wires. With her knee on her neck to anchor herself in the weightlessness, he cursed the day he had encouraged his crew to have no regard for rank whenever something urgent needed to be done for the *Quantum Bitch*. "The flight here," she continued with a groan, "didn't arouse their attention."

"But maybe the death of one of their own kind did," Dev said. In truth, he agreed with her, but he didn't want to be the only useless one here, just sitting around. So, he waited until Jezzy fell silent and gave herself over completely to her obviously frustrating work, just hissing and humming, then he pressed the eject command for the spy drone, which was about the size of an Edenite pineapple. He felt almost liberated when he saw the tiny green dot across the radar screen. In the ruined hangar behind them, they were practically blind since most radar beams reflected off the cold metal and the holes and cracks didn't provide enough surface area to produce a coherent image. That changed immediately as the Sentinel, which dutifully provided updates of its complex sensor image every two seconds, began transmitting surprisingly large amounts of data considering its small size.

Dev leaned forward as if that would help him see more detail in the image. The ring of ruins lay quiet. The fleet of Demons had mostly gathered at the poles and appeared motionless. He could not see any of the ships that had been heading toward the inner jump point when they jumped— or rather, limped—into the system. That was because the S1 was on the far side of Lagunia. The blue-green ball hovered almost peacefully below them; the cloud bands trotted like a flock of plush sheep over the seemingly endless green mass of water. The sight offered a mirage of harmony and silence that stood in sharp contrast to what he had seen on the camera and satellite images.

That illusion of tranquility provided something soothing for his tortured mind. The simulated image of a computer-generated mock version of the real world around them, created from data offsets, offered an escape from himself. The relief he experienced was quickly shattered when three dots shined red, and the Sentinel's intelligent control software assessed them as potentially hostile.

It was entirely accurate.

"Oh, shit," he cursed.

"What is it, now?" Jezzy asked in her whiny, pessimistic tone.

"Looks like they're looking for us," Dev said and raised a hand to stop any more questions until he could tell what was going on. One of the Demons' massive warships was flying toward the S2 near the gas giant Artros. Another flew very close over the ring of debris, relative west of their current position, and still another was coming from relative east. "It looks like they want to get us in a pincer."

He made a few inputs on his command console and then slid his fingers into the neural cushions at the ends of his armrests to work faster. The western ship would overfly their current position in forty minutes if it did not alter its velocity, and the eastern one would arrive in just over seventy.

"Shit!" he repeated grimly and recalled the Sentinel. While even the Fleet's most advanced frigates had trouble detecting the little buggers, he didn't want to find out how advanced the invaders' sensor technology was, especially since they didn't seem to care much about natural laws. "Jezzy, stop working."

"I already have," she murmured close to his ear.

"In your seat." He opened a radio channel to the rest of the crew. "Everyone to your stations, we're getting out of here."

To his surprise, he heard no objections. Aura appeared in the cockpit five minutes later and took a seat behind him to his right. Willy followed a little later just as the systems checks for flight takeoff were completed, and Dozer reported from the mess hall that he was strapped in.

"How bad is it?" Willy asked.

"I'll be damned if they're not scanning the debris ring," Dev said as he flipped the final toggle switches. Their haptic feedback calmed him a bit. He shared the Sentinel's sensor images with everyone and calculated the flight time of the ship that had set out for S2 near the gas giant, based on its current acceleration. He tried not to gulp at the sight of the darkness the eerie monster's engines were sucking in. The effect made the surrounding void shine bright in contrast.

"Can we make it?" Aura asked.

"It'll be tight," Jezzy objected.

"Everything's always tight for you, princess."

"Somebody's got to be realistic."

"We're still alive, right?" Dev said. "How realistic is that? Aura, I hope the reactor delivers what you promised."

"I didn't promise anything, and that goes especially for the engines. Besides, I said that we—"

"—have to conduct tests. All right," he interrupted,

growling. "Then, for my sake, we'll consider this a dress rehearsal, but we've got to get out of here."

"Our hiding place is pretty good. If we shut everything down at the right moment, I don't think they'll find us. At least not unless they intend to spend days turning over every piece of junk with drones, and I haven't seen any of those yet," Willy said.

"I'm not just talking about saving our sorry asses, but we have a commitment to get the information we've gathered out of the system." Dev took a deep breath. "We know something that humanity needs to know before it's too late."

"If it's not already too late," Jezzy muttered, earning an annoyed sound from Aura.

"Never thought I'd say this, but we really should do the right thing," the flight engineer jumped in. "These... *things*..." He paused. "We can't have a repeat of what happened on Lagunia."

"Or on the core systems we flew through," Aura said darkly. "You all heard the radio transmissions we picked up. What happened here happened there. Everywhere."

"Then what can we even do?" Jezzy demanded. "The gates have been opened and now these invaders are here."

"That's up to the Fleet," Dev said firmly. "We're not the Fleet. We're an independent trader and we do what we can and must, at least this once. If the whole fucking Federation goes to hell, we won't have anything to live on either, if you need a solid reason."

No one replied, and as soon as engine power-up was complete, he maneuvered the *Quantum Bitch* out of the hangar wreckage, sliding her sideways through a large hole.

Its deformed edges suggested that it had been melted by a sustained laser blast. The ring of debris was extremely dense at their current position, and the gaps between the larger objects measured only a few dozen meters. In their brief search for this hiding place, Dev had imagined two mighty ships—a Click cruiser and a sinister Demon ship—firing broadsides that ended in two simultaneous fireballs, only to fall to the endless embrace of the halo of debris, both the remains of a violent inferno, bound forever to each other.

But now he merely imagined how the Clicks had fought for their survival and saved humans from the same fate. Probably more for their own protection than out of any altruism. After all, instead of warning the humans, they had... thoughtlessly?... destroyed Harbingen and its many millions of inhabitants. Nevertheless, he felt like a member of a very stupid species that had schemed itself away from the truth.

A circumstance he intended to correct. But it would be close. Again.

As he lifted the *Bitch* above the ring, the two huge invader ships immediately accelerated toward her. So, their sensors couldn't be as bad as he hoped, but neither was their acceleration as good as he feared. Therefore, he allowed himself the luxury of several minutes to calculate a course, then had the onboard computer check it before he accelerated to full thrust toward Lagunia's outermost jump point. He briefly closed his eyes, fearing the engines might explode. Since he was able to open them again after a few breaths, nothing of the sort seemed to have happened. He suppressed a relieved sigh.

Instead, he told the cockpit, "Good job."

For the first hour of their flight, they were primarily concerned with dodging the green discharges their two pursuers threw at them, which they had already seen during the battle at the hyperspace gate. Fortunately, what they presumed to be plasma launchers turned out to be much more deadly at short range than at the many 100,000 kilometers currently separating them. Occasional course corrections were enough to effortlessly escape the fire.

After the third hour this became more difficult when the ship ahead of them felt it had to join in. Sheer destruction reached for them from three directions and the *Quantum Bitch* could do nothing about it. The situation was made even worse by the fact that the enemy knew exactly where they were headed.

We're not the Oberon, *which could easily take a dozen strikes from that stuff*, he thought tensely as he dodged for the umpteenth time and counted the kilometers remaining to the jump point. Sensors already displayed the first outliers of the vast debris field from the massive battle that had led to the demise of the legendary Strike Group 2, and of all Federation hopes of victory over their longtime enemy, the Clicks.

"This is going to be close." Jezzy was already starting in with her doom-and-gloom when they were still 60,000 clicks from the alien warship they would overtake in the next thirty minutes in the direction of the S2, if the onboard computer was not mistaken.

"It's *always* close," Dev grumbled, turning the energy matrix cells to maximum flow.

"Not a good idea, boss," Aura warned.

"It's *never* a good idea."

"Shit, he's up to something again," Willy said, correctly interpreting Dev's grumbling tone.

"Have you guys reloaded the ammo yet?" Dev asked.

"No. It was at the bottom of the list."

"Good, bundle it all together with armor tape or something and get it to the shuttle."

"To the shuttle?"

"That's what I just said."

Willy growled, sounding like a bull about to charge a torero's red cape, but Dev heard the *click* of seat belts opening not two heartbeats later.

"What are you up to, boss?" Aura asked.

"You'll see in a minute." He waited until the enemy ship fired again, this time from as many as twelve plasma launchers on its port side, and then changed course, jerking the *Bitch* hard to the right and heading for the stern of the alien space whale. His ship looked like a gnat in comparison. "Aura, when I say *now*, you take the controls, all right?"

"Uh..."

"Good. I'll handle the shuttle's remote control. Is it fueled up?"

"Yes, but—"

"Good. When I say *now* a second time, you're going to fly a circle around the drive nacelle of that thing and you're going to do it at a close distance, maximum... let's say ten meters. Do you understand?"

"No, I don't understand anything."

"Understand?" he repeated much more sharply.

"Yes, boss." Now she sounded more tense than a moment before. He guessed she had caught on to what he was up to. But she didn't protest, which was a good sign.

Not that it mattered. Rather, he hoped his captain's instincts hadn't failed him.

One more time, Devlin Myers, just one more time...!

The green plasma blobs the alien ship was throwing at them weren't hurtling toward them as fast as railgun rounds and were much easier for the sensors to detect. Still, their increasing density was a problem as they neared the enemy.

The onboard computer emitted a shrill warning, signaling that none of its preprogrammed evasion patterns offered more than a fifty percent probability of success. He shrugged inwardly, bit his tongue, and steered manually. Some would say that was suicidal, but Dev relied on the element of unpredictability as he initiated a series of wild evasive maneuvers that tossed him right and left in his harness.

The Demon's drive caused the two-kilometer-long vacuum trail behind its oddly arranged drive nacelles at the rear to flicker. It looked like it was sucking up the darkness itself and swallowing any photons that dared come near it. It was a strange sight that looked *wrong* and made Dev want to shoot at it with everything he had on board.

Everything, however, came to practically nothing. The weapons systems had not been powered up again because they had prioritized other systems to get out of Lagunia as quickly as possible. All they had left was the ammunition from the stores and the few warheads from the *Danube*, which Willy and Dozer had hopefully just loaded into their shuttle.

Green flowers of plasma fire, hot as the sun if the screeching sensors were to be believed, narrowly missed them. They passed the cockpit window and grew denser as they neared the stern of the huge warship. Damage reports howled for attention, indicating several spots on the hull that had burned up. A fuel line, a superconductor joint, the landing gear hydraulics, the hatch of the tiny shuttle under the bow, one of the two Sentinel ejection shafts—nothing critical. He dodged two more shots. At these speeds, he avoided them more out of luck or instinct than any conscious decision. Then he noticed one last blast and flew straight toward it, before abruptly swinging the *Quantum Bitch* 180 degrees and switching to full thrust. The plan worked, and the boiling gas of the alien weapon evaporated into a maelstrom of dancing atoms in the even hotter exhaust flare.

"Fuck yeah!" he yowled when he realized they were still alive, and brutally yanked the *Bitch* to one side and into a kamikaze turn upward, just above the edge of the contracting darkness behind the drive nacelles. Over the radio, he called out, "Willy?"

"Closing the hatch now!" came the reply, and Dev deduced from the echo that the Dunkelheimer had wisely put on a helmet. He would have to risk it, or the brief instant in which the next move could succeed would pass.

"Now, Aura!"

Dev switched to shuttle control, ejected the vessel by releasing the clamps, and sent it shooting downward at the maximum thrust its cold gas jets could manage. He lowered the nose of the shuttle just before Aura steered the *Bitch* into a tight circular motion along the edge of the alien ship's stern that flung him sideways into his straps. A blink of an eye later, it would have been vaporized as a plasma lanced past just below his ship, burning half the dorsal sensors to cinders.

"I'm shitting myself!" Aura yelled, holding the ship just a few feet above the alien stern's terminating bulge like a wildly spinning gyroscope. The angle was too small for the enemy's plasma launchers, and they repeatedly missed the *Bitch* by the same few degrees. Relieved, Dev steered the shuttle directly into the main flow of the inexplicable suction effect below them, which they were much closer to than he would have preferred. A few seconds later, he lost control of the small craft and it met the same fate he had seen befall the numerous dead on Atlantis: it turned into a shadow, a tiny dot, and then disappeared toward one of the drive nacelles.

At first, nothing happened and he was about to curse when an explosion flared, and the billowing tail of darkness disappeared. Secondary explosions followed, ripping whole sections of the hull out of the stern. He instinctively picked out the largest of these and took over the controls before bringing the *Bitch* behind the jagged disk of shimmering green armor.

He let the computer take over to match the tumbling motion of the ruined hull section. This moved them at an angle away from the aliens, but they gained both cover from fire and effective stealth. At first, several plasma lances crashed into the alien hull section and caused the *Bitch*'s sensors to protest, but fortunately, nothing melted. Then, after a quarter of an hour of tense silence on board, he dared to break cover and raced toward S2. The Demons were able to follow them yet. Soon the distance was also enough to evade the remaining incoming plasma fire, although it was close several times.

"Now we just have to make it," he sighed in relief.

"Where to, anyway?" Aura asked.

"To Sol. If there's one place that can withstand this invasion, it's Terra."

19

With a mixture of astonishment and surprise, Jason realized that Shimmer and he had, as if by instinct, moved closer together as they retreated from the stranger who had slaughtered the other Clicks like some unstoppable automaton. Although the stranger wore no armor—at least none that was visible—he was clad in an advanced spacesuit made of programmable nanofiber that clung to his body like a second skin. The face behind the narrow helmet was oval, and the eyes were darker than the blackest space and at least as cold. But there was also a spark in them that he almost missed amid the brutality. Within those almond-shaped, obsidian eyes, a light flickered like a candle surrounded by looming shadows. Nevertheless, the mere presence of this man frightened him. His fright stemmed not only from the sight of the dead aliens he had murdered in a flurry of implanted blades, it was also the paralysis Jason felt that was born of helplessness. If Baker hadn't shown up at the right time, both of them would probably be dead by now.

"... shove my spurs so deep up your tiny ass I be able to pull out your baby teeth," Baker rumbled and lowered his head like a bull ready to charge. The stranger calmly watched the mutant, barely shifting his weight. He gave a barely perceptible nod and spread his blades, which hung like gleaming extensions of his arms at his sides. All the while not uttering a sound.

Baker struck like a force of nature. Jason was amazed at how fast a half-ton of muscles, coated bones, and implants could move. It made him gasp. The mutant's spurs sliced through the air like the long claws of a predator. The stranger dodged them by taking short steps and throwing his upper body unnaturally far and fast from side to side. He escaped a blow by rolling forward between the mutant's trunk-like legs and executed an x-shaped upward slash with his monofilament blades. Baker threw himself to one side, avoiding the blow, and rolling on his shoulder.

Both opponents were so fast that Jason got a queasy feeling in his guts, as if he were in a VR environment where the frame rate had been set too high. Their bodies hummed with power as if they were electrified. He thought it entirely possible. He knew about the neural implants his people had developed to upgrade the Black Legion in the last few decades before Harbingen's destruction. Yet he had never seen any in use apart from the brief, distorted impressions he got in Shanghai North through the explosions and dust when Colonel Meyers's Marines were fighting for their lives. These two contenders, at any rate, seemed to be equipped with stimulus conduction accelerators, which had been outlawed in the Federation and traded as "reflex boosters" only by the best-connected black-market cartels. He hadn't known Baker possessed one—the mutant had presumably not turned it on until now. He was not surprised, unlike the stranger, whose mere presence sent a shiver down his spine.

"Fast little sucker," Baker murmured in acknowledgment. "But that will just delay the inevitable."

The brutally intense ballet of death resumed. The stranger slashed one of the front consoles in half, leaving two smoking pieces of junk, and the shorted circuits sprayed violent sparks. Baker tried to feint and smash his opponent's skull, but he ducked away at the last moment, and the blow left an inch-deep dent in the wall next to the door. The mutant launched a kick but struck only air, sending him flying and leaving a gash on his left thigh. The stranger tried to take advantage and drive his right blade into his neck, Baker grabbed his wrist and flung him off with a violent heave. The much smaller killer flew across the bridge. His shoulder slammed through the remains of the console and stopped against the wall. Jason thought it was the end of the fight since the very idea of being on the receiving end of Baker's powerful arms made him think of torn and shredded paper.

The killer landed on his hands, sprang to his feet like a cat, and jerked his head up to pin his opponent, who was already following up and running through the destroyed console as if it were made of foam. Composite parts and cables exploded in a shower of debris. Baker's spurs whipped murderously through the air, but missed again, and, despite the violent impact, his opponent was already back on his feet and dancing effortlessly toward the access door that had been blown open by the Click trooper. He deflected a passing blow from the mutant aimed at his helmet with a parry from one of his own blades.

Jason thought the killer was coming for him and Shimmer as he jumped over the body of an alien he had stabbed earlier. As he advanced, he stepped on the barrel of the gun in the alien's dead three-fingered hands with one foot and lifted the butt, or what Jason thought was the butt, with the heel of the other. The gun flew behind his back, over his shoulder, and he snatched it from the air with both hands. As he turned, however, he did not fire it at Baker, who was close behind him, but hurled it like a club at the giant's face. The giant raised an arm so huge that the rifle looked like a miniature toy. The stranger used the distraction to leap forward, his legs outstretched. He crashed onto the inside of Baker's left knee, and as they fell he drove one of his blades through the mutant's left arm. It exited the other side, bloodied and vibrating.

Baker's reaction surprised Jason. He growled in pain and anger, then, instead of aiming a blow at the killer's head, which he seemed to anticipate and ducked, the mutant stepped on his opponent's foot with one of his huge boots, pinning him to the ground, and then brutally twisted his injured arm backward. There was an ugly sucking sound as the blade cut through more flesh and sinew, but the move created so much tension on the stranger's arm that he was unable to extract his weapon.

"And now," Baker growled, "you can go light a fire in hell and warm up the place."

The mutant slashed, lightning-fast, with his healthy

hand. The long, curved spurs that shot from his knuckles whistled toward the stranger's wrist. They would have instantly cut through any normal human's arm, and most materials found on a ship could not have withstood the hardened blades powered by Baker's strength. The result was almost anticlimactic. The killer's wrist sagged unnaturally, and a gush of blood spurted out. His entire body, stretched as it was between the giant's raised arm and his foot on the ground, sagged a bit. But even as Baker withdrew his spurs and aimed the next blow at his head, the stranger surprised Jason. He didn't respond by striking his opponent with his free blade, instead he brought it down through his half-severed wrist and cut off his hand. Now released from Baker's grasp, he dropped and, with a surprised gasp from Baker, kicked the foot pinning him to the floor. Suddenly free, he rolled backward and landed near the unconscious Rochshaz. With his healthy hand, he grabbed the assault cannon and fired a round at Baker. The weapon, as big as the man, barked out a mighty flash and then he fell to his side. The gun was far too heavy, even for an augmented human like him.

The mutant hoisted two of the Click bodies close to him and used them as improvised shields. The blast tore them into shreds of armor, flesh, and water, turning the bridge into a slaughterhouse. Baker was thrown back by the blast wave and crashed into the wall. His armor smoked and was littered with shrapnel strikes. Jason had instinctively ducked, taking the Shimmer with him. Only now did he realize the alien could have misinterpreted it as an attack, but like him, the Click seemed paralyzed by the violence between the two humans, so it showed no reaction when Jason withdrew his hand as if he had been burned.

The killer remained silent, he didn't even groan as he got to his feet. By some, presumably technical, miracle, his arm stump no longer dripped blood and he calmly moved his right hand with the monofilament blade as if to balance it. Then he walked toward Baker, who was shaking his head like someone who had just woken up. The mutant swung his left arm back and forth, as if in imitation of his opponent. His own right arm was no longer bleeding either, but it hung limp.

"Round two," Baker said with a grin as if he were looking forward to it, which Jason thought was a distinct possibility. "Kid, you'd better get the hell out of here. Now."

The stranger didn't respond and continued walking toward his hulking adversary like a robot.

"Bradley! I mean you!"

Jason blinked in alarm. That meant Baker thought it was possible he might not emerge victorious from this fight. But where could he go?

"I'm not leaving without him," he shouted, pointing at Click. The alien was now emitting a steady, high-pitched crackle, though it didn't move. "He's our only way out of here."

"Bradley?" the killer said. It was the first time he had opened his mouth. He turned his head slightly as if to keep Baker and Jason in view at the same time, while the two adversaries maintained their distance from each other.

Jason didn't know what to say and blinked in surprise

at the sudden silence amid the explosion of violence that still had his head spinning.

"What?"

"Bradley?" the stranger repeated. Baker fixed his opponent with narrowed eyes but appeared flustered by the sudden turn of events.

"Yes. Jason Bradley, Lieutenant Commander."

"Harbinger accent."

Jason looked at the mutant, but Baker paid no attention to him, so he turned back to the alien assassin.

"Yes?"

"That's an amazing coincidence." The killer very slowly lowered the monofilament blade while keeping an eye on Baker. For his part, the mutant was still trying to fathom what was happening.

"I don't understand. Who are you?"

"Sirion. I met your father just before he died."

Jason swallowed and felt a pressure building in his throat that grew so strong that it felt like it would completely block his larynx and suffocate him. "What?"

"Konrad Bradley was my final target, and I failed. He left me with a burden that I must unload," Sirion explained. His voice was as cold as an autumn morning and as somber as the night of a new moon. But there was also an undercurrent that ran counter to this that Jason couldn't quite make out.

"I-I don't know what that means," Jason stammered, bewildered by the sudden absurdity of the situation.

"Your father, I wanted to kill him for what he did to my mother, but I couldn't do it." Sirion's mouth twitched slightly. "In my attempt to get him from a Harbinger conspirator named Pyrgorates, I was—"

"Wait, you ran into Pyrgorates?"

"Yes. He assassinated Admiral Bretoni, took command of the *Caesar*, and—"

"Bretoni is dead?" Jason interrupted the stranger again.

"That's what I just said. I was removed before I could take your father with me, but he put a burden on me that doesn't belong to me, and I want to get rid of it."

"What?"

"The access codes to Omega's memory core," Sirion said.

Jason gasped. "Impossible! He would never give up the codes. He's the last captain with that knowledge and the only one who knows where the memory core is hidden."

"No. He *was* the only one," the killer corrected him, unmoved. "And now I am. Pyrgorates and his conspirators wanted to find out about your father, so they kidnapped him. They betrayed me, and now it is my wish that they fail before I end the commander's life."

"You mean—"

"Pyrgorates." Sirion's gaze grew colder, if that was even possible. "He will die."

"Then we have the same goal," Jason said carefully, slowly raising both hands. "There's no reason for any more bloodshed."

"I could think of a few," Baker said, wiggling his fingers so his nails rang against the spurs.

"Not now, Baker." He turned back to Sirion. "I wasn't my father's biggest fan, but I want to see his killer brought to justice as much as you do, though perhaps for different reasons."

"Both," the killer said, but Jason didn't know what to make of that statement and decided to ignore it for now.

"If you can take out Pyrgorates, it would certainly help the entire Federation. The exiles are up to something, and I can't shake the feeling that they had something to do with this whole invasion. They were prepared—far too well prepared."

"That's correct."

"You know something, don't you?"

"Not directly. I took out targets for them so they didn't have to emerge from the shadows," Sirion replied coolly. "But the nature of my orders has allowed me to draw some conclusions. For example, they knew something about hyperspace gate technology that they tried to hide. I myself made sure that a warning was not delivered just before the invasion of the Lagunia system."

"A warning?"

Sirion nodded but said nothing more about it.

"All the more reason to shorten you by a head," Baker said. The killer returned his gaze without visible emotion. Nevertheless, the barely restrained readiness to use violence between the two, especially on the part of the mutant, was palpable.

"If that is true, then the Fleet must know what you know," Jason said. "And we need to get those codes."

"Or destroy them," Baker added, apparently ready and willing to see to it himself, but Jason held him back.

"No. It's true what I said, my father was the last officer to have those codes. They can't be extracted from his head storage or reconstructed in any other way because he memorized them."

"But they are stored in his."

"Yes," Sirion replied. "But no one will get to them without my permission."

"And how do you know that?"

"I'll see to it."

"Give me the codes," Jason urged him, but the man in the spacesuit shook his head.

"No."

"Why not?"

"Because your father asked me to give them only to *you* and *your brother* together."

"He said that? Nicholas and Jason?" he asked, surprised, and the lump in his throat suddenly grew a little heavier.

"Jason and Nicholas, to be exact," Sirion corrected him.

"Nicholas has left the system, I think. The *Oberon* jumped."

"I heard that. That makes it more complicated."

"We may not have that much time left."

"Do you have control of this shuttle? I propose to fly to the sky fortress to obtain reconnaissance data we can use to track your brother."

"That's your plan?" Baker asked, laughing contemptuously. "Almost as stupid as showing up here and messing with the big boys."

That provocation seemed to roll off Sirion's back, and he didn't even shrug as he replied, "The alternative didn't have much more chance of success, but the possibilities of getting into orbit are currently limited."

"We don't have control," Jason admitted. "Our plan"—he looked meaningfully at Baker—"wasn't much more sophisticated, let alone well thought out."

"What about him?" Sirion nodded at Shimmer. The Click had remained relatively motionless the entire time, except for the constant, minute bobbing of its four legs, which contracted and stretched at the double knee joints as if to a silent melody. Its head barely moved, although Jason could sense that the creature had been watching them intently the entire time. He wondered what it was thinking.

He was probably the last alien on board and had seen his fellow aliens murdered before his eyes. The humans present, one of whom must have looked like a monster, were trying to bash each other's heads in. In any case, if the first contact between the Fleet and the Clicks had been even remotely similar, he wasn't surprised their two species had been in a bitter, merciless war ever since.

"I don't know. We haven't gotten to the point of communicating with each other in any way, if that's even possible." Jason sighed. "I don't know what we were expecting, to put a gun to its head and hope it understood that it should get us out of here?"

"We don't have much time, anyway," Sirion said.

"What do you mean?"

"The Fleet has a plan to end the Click blockade, and I believe that plan will be implemented sooner rather than later."

"What kind of plan?" Baker said suspiciously. He had lit a cigar and stuck the spout of a thick tube into his upper arm wound. "Is that good for us or bad for us?"

"Considering the altitude we're likely at, most likely bad."

"What kind of plan?" Jason repeated Baker's question, and Sirion explained in short sentences exactly what Fleet HQ on Earth had hatched and was about to do, if it wasn't already too late. The more he heard, the colder he felt. Most importantly, he realized they were in completely the wrong place at the wrong time and had to react quickly if they didn't want to end up as a volatile cloud of gas in orbit before they could even begin trying to leave Earth and get to safety.

20

"We'd better get out of here," Baker said curtly, and was about to point at Sirion, but Jason interrupted him before the mutant issued another challenge.

"Right. What about your people?"

"They're up in the bow gathering the wounded and tending to them."

"All right." Jason raised a finger. "We don't know precisely when the Fleet is going to initiate this crazy plan, but we do know where. So, we'll need to figure out what trajectory we're on to know when we're in danger." A second finger went up. "To accomplish that, we need to access the shuttle's systems." A third finger rose. "But we can't do that without this guy." He pointed to the large Click, who was all but motionless, presumably watching them.

"We can't even talk to that thing," Baker said, stating the problem.

"I could..." Sirion started to say, but Jason immediately said "No!".

"Then I could…" the mutant began.

"No! We've tried that for seventy years and it's led us to this slaughter. If the threat of violence and fear would make him talk, he would have done it long ago. But maybe he *can't* talk to us at all, remember? What's the point of trying to force someone to do something he is incapable of?"

"Do you have a better idea?" Baker demanded, and Sirion gave him a questioning look. Something in the killer's eyes troubled Jason. What disturbed him wasn't so much the frightening darkness, unfathomable depths that struck him as two black holes sucking all life out of them. What unsettled him was the spark to which he could not assign a meaning.

Jason sighed. "Yes, leave me alone with him."

"Isn't that just a bit reckless? No offense to your skills, but that creature could tear you apart in no time." Baker eyed him and then looked at Shimmer before nodding as if confirming what he suspected.

"Maybe, but if we all get blasted apart when the fleet mines Earth's orbit, it won't matter anyway."

"We killed its people," Sirion said coolly. If he felt any emotion, he did not show it. "As a rule, that doesn't exactly encourage benign cooperation."

"As a *human* rule," Jason pointed out.

"Just what the situation calls for, naïve optimism," Baker said sarcastically.

"I know, but maybe after seventy years of futility it's time to try something different. Anyone who always does the same thing and expects a different result is much more likely to be the naïve one, isn't he?"

"Sounds like a Chinese fortune cookie."

"Well, it's an old saying, but no less true for that. We need a radio signal to contact the Fleet and we need to pass on Sirion's information in case we're destroyed. We can't let it die with us, not while conspirators are targeting Harbingen, whatever their objective is."

"Maybe we rig something together."

Jason looked to the assassin and swallowed before continuing, "Sirion, someone needs to check to see if anyone, or anything, hostile is still on board."

To Jason's surprise, Sirion looked appraisingly between him and the alien, then seemed to reach a conclusion he hadn't expected because he nodded.

"Please, no more deaths. That won't help us."

Again, a nod that surprised him even more. He didn't doubt that someone like the Shadowwing, someone Fleet members told creepy stories about and widely believed to be a myth, didn't take orders from anyone except his principals. But Jason was not entirely sure of that, since it was more likely that Sirion accepted only those tasks he saw as a challenge or were in line with his own objectives. That he now agreed with Jason probably meant they had the same goal.

But what is it exactly? he asked himself and looked out of the corner of his eye at Shimmer. The pearly alien was standing near one of the tanks with the green liquid and not moving. Although he imagined the helmet was tilted slightly in his direction, it might have been his imagination.

"We don't have much time," Jason said more to himself than the others.

"Do you even know what you're doing, kid?" Baker said intently. The mutant looked grimly after Sirion as he disappeared from the bridge like a fleeting shadow. Fortunately, he didn't seem tempted to chase after him and finish him off.

"No," he admitted bluntly. "But I see no alternative to trying everything possible. This is a historic opportunity. When was the last time a Click and a human were in the same room together? I'll tell you: never. How's your arm?"

Baker shrugged. "I'll live. Tough guy, that son of a bitch, especially for such a skinny guy. Would love to gut him when this is over just to look at his hardware."

"Maybe we could leave that, too."

"For now. He killed my boys." The mutant lit a fresh cigar and sucked on it. "Besides, I want to show him. Never had to break a sweat fighting one of you dwarves before."

"For now, then." Jason sighed and shooed the giant away. "If you get a radio signal out, let me know. Maybe with the right frequency and my priority codes as a Fleet officer, I can get something done."

"Watch your ass, kid," Baker mumbled around his cigar, then shifted it to the right corner of his mouth with his bulging lips. "What you've got in mind isn't worth shit."

"Thanks for the pep talk," Jason grumbled and watched as the battered mutant disappeared through the left-hand passageway and picked up Rochshaz. The dazed mutant had just regained consciousness and was muttering something about being hungry and why hadn't his sister brought any salt to bake bread with. He had obviously suffered more than a mild concussion, but he was still breathing.

"Just the two of us now, then," Jason said once silence fell, and then swallowed as he turned to face the alien. Despite the creature's—or robot's?—crudely familiar appearance, its numerous alien features made him shiver. Its four legs were the most obvious, but more irritating were the two knee joints on each leg. That meant the lower legs bent backward and ended in long, backward-bending toes. They reminded him of ancient prostheses. Its overlong arms with three fingers each also caused stirrings in his brain that presaged a flight or fight reaction and urged him to act.

Jason frantically considered how to begin and waited a few moments for the Click to stir. He hoped the alien would do *something*, even lunge at him. But Shimmer remained immobile, looking at him out of what he guessed were eyes or sensors above the facial slats.

Maybe he's in a stupor? Or has he switched off? he wondered. *Speculating is useless. You have to do something. But what?*

Then an idea came to him. He picked up his gun, which he had placed on the floor, ran to the door, and threw it out. Then he dragged the four corpses of the smaller, black-armored Clicks out of sight. He also removed Rochshaz's assault cannon, which he had left behind, and the laser rifle of the Click drop trooper Sirion had killed. While he did all this, panting and groaning, he watched Shimmer out of the corner of his eye. The alien's helmet swiveled, following his every move closely.

Once all the weapons and bodies were now out of sight only pools of blood remained, but he hoped the message had gotten through. To emphasize it, he raised his arms and held out his hands, or rather his gloves, with the palms facing the Click.

"No danger," he said slowly, but Shimmer didn't

respond, it just continued to look at Jason. He swiftly reviewed the de-escalation gestures he knew from numerous cultures when Terra was home to a variety of peoples with different customs. First, he tried lowering his head and exposing his throat as a sign of submission, a gesture also found in the animal kingdom.

No reaction.

Next, he went on all fours like a dog, feeling somewhat ridiculous. He continued trying more gestures: waving his arms right and left, stretching his legs, lying on his back, constantly under observation by the alien's cold sensor-eyes. Shimmer tilted his head slightly here and there and seemed to follow him, but otherwise showed no reaction to the show.

"Well, we're not getting anywhere with this," Jason said to himself, trying to dispel the strange silence, broken only by the low hum of the engines.

Then another idea occurred to him.

"You didn't try to kill me," he began as if reciting a list. "You didn't try to escape or strike during my strange performance. You would have good reason to do so after the slaughter that happened here. You don't understand my body language, or if you do, you're not telling me. But if you're not a robot we do have one thing in common."

Jason took a deep breath, patted his sealed body armor, then took a step toward Shimmer. The Click backed away until Jason slowly extended his hand and very lightly touched the chest area of the alien armor. It felt cold and damp. A vibration ran through the armor and made him flinch. Again, the clicking sounds he had heard before started, only it was more intense and rapid this time.

"Okay, okay, that was obviously not good," he said placatingly. After Shimmer seemed to calm down and was standing still again, he pointed first at its armor and then at his own. "We're both in a suit."

He took a deep breath and began to undress. He was sure the aliens had autopsied humans before since as a species they didn't seem to be as attached to suicide as Clicks. The aliens seemed to consider capture—dead or alive—by an enemy as an impossibility. Still, the message might get through. He thought he detected at least a basic willingness to communicate. Since they weren't fighting each other, that must be the case.

He released the valves on his suit after checking his forearm display to ensure there was pressure and atmosphere on the shuttle. Next, he removed the lower leg pieces, his boots, the fasteners on his knees, the thigh pieces, and the rather rigid corset around his torso. Last, he freed his arms and slid the forearm display with the smart nanoband back onto his bare skin. He was cold and felt completely defenseless in his purely functional underwear. They had been soaked with sweat for days and had to stink.

But against his instincts, he stuck to his resolve and removed his helmet. He held his breath and finally took off his underwear. Only in this way would the gesture make any sense. And it seemed to work. For the first time, the alien stirred by putting both three-fingered hands on its abdomen and spread its elbows slightly, like a bird.

Okay, at least we're headed in the right direction, he thought. With cold fingers he fumbled as he took the mouthpiece off his helmet so he could at least breathe. Their air filters might allow mutants to tolerate the less-than-ideal atmosphere for several minutes, but he could not. Eventually, when his lungs felt like a crumpled paper bag, he slipped the mouthpiece over his nose and mouth. He inhaled with relief and pulled the oxygen tank, a small box on the back of his suit, out of its holder and held it in his hand. He was already beginning to shiver from the cold.

"Now it's your turn, buddy, or I'll not only look really stupid, like some sort of pervert, but soon I'll be a *frozen* pervert," he said, his voice muffled by the breathing apparatus. *If this goes on much longer, I'll be glad to freeze to death before anyone sees me like this and go down in history for the most ridiculous attempt at communication with an alien.*

Shimmer didn't disappoint him. The alien turned and gracefully extended one of its three fingers. It tapped its tip, which resembled a curved metal claw, against one of the tanks in a complex pattern that sounded like an extremely complicated melody, alien and driving, and frequently, to his sensibilities, out of rhythm, if there was supposed to be a rhythm at all.

Then the Click moved so fast that Jason was startled and stumbled back. His cerebellum, terrified, screamed fight-or-flight. Yet the alien did not erupt into sudden violence. It simply climbed nimbly up the tank like a spider. Its four feet were so deft and purposeful that Jason could only marvel at it. Until now, Shimmer had been so economical in its movements that he had feared it might have suffered severe brain or processor damage from Baker's punch.

Jason recovered and watched as the top cover of the tank detached itself from the armored glass and rose as if on invisible threads. A depression in the ceiling opened that matched the diameter of the "lid." Four robotic arms extended from dark flaps beside it, then slowly but purposefully unraveled until Jason could make out four six-fingered metal hands. The sudden movement on the bridge, the hydraulic hiss, the hum of servo motors behind the covers, and the Click now perched above him on the tank like a monster ready to leap, made him freeze.

Had he made a mistake? Had he placed too much hope in an idiotic idea? Or had the mutant carnage softened his brain into infantile naivete?

"I don't know what you're up to, buddy, but I bet Baker is going to be really pissed at me," he said, looking down at his scattered pieces of armor. He thought he'd better put them back on before anyone else saw him like this, or he'd be completely defenseless if Shimmer decided to maul him after all.

But the Click didn't attack. Instead, it grabbed the edges of the tank with its backward-curved feet that now looked like claws, repositioned itself, and slid into the tank. It was hard to imagine how it could fit in a space so narrow, but in the next instant, the creature was floating in the green liquid. The lens effect of the tank's transparent sides made the alien appear bloated and more colorless than before. The pearlescent glow was now more a turquoise sheen.

"Okay. That's the way to go, I guess. What do you have in mind? Is that an acceleration tank? Are you trying to get out of here?" Jason asked despite knowing the alien would now be able to understand him even less than before. What difference did it make? "Do you know about this insane plan? Because stepping on the gas wouldn't be a bad idea at all, you know."

Jason looked for signs that something was happening to the shuttle. He should get slammed into the wall, or rather *pulled*, when they accelerated. After all, acceleration tanks made no sense on a ship with artificial gravity. But nothing changed until the four robotic arms hanging from the ceiling started to move. They reached into the tank and grabbed the Click by its shoulders, both in front and behind. The alien's armor jerked violently, and bright streaks appeared on its flanks and collar and along its limbs.

The armor! It's coming off, shot through Jason's head. Instead of putting his clothes back on, he stepped toward the tank, transfixed, and watched as the Click's suit peeled away, releasing a gush of bright liquid into the dominant green. Suction hoses around the edges at ankle height pumped it out. It seemed able to separate one liquid from the other because the color returned to the green hue. The grasping arms pulled the carapace upward like an insect exoskeleton, leaving behind a *real* alien. And Jason was now certain, it was *not* a robot.

Its four legs, each in three parts with two knee joints, were slender and chalky white with smooth, shiny skin. In any case, the alien's overall appearance was far slighter than the beefy armor it had worn. Its torso was short and stretched back as if over an inverted hollow back. Striped gills on its sides opened and closed in a fluttering fashion. Its arms hung in the water at its sides, and the three delicate fingers of both hands were raised in Jason's direction. Where the torso should have merged into a neck there was a metallic collar with rubber elements and tiny threads were just retracting into them. Jason guessed they served as some kind of interface between body and suit. The Click's head looked like a bell and was semi-transparent like a jellyfish. Instead of a mouth, it had six more gills, but they were narrower and barely opened. The eyes above were set wide apart and huge compared to the two lenses of the helmet. They glowed aquamarine and were as expressive as anything Jason had ever seen. Entire worlds—entire universes!—seemed to be staring back at him. The raised forehead above was covered with tiny feelers that moved back and forth in the green liquid like seaweed. Even more fascinating than the Click's wholly alien appearance and its fist-sized eyes was the fact that Jason could effortlessly peer through its jelly-like skin and see its brain. Flashes of blue twitched back and forth in the dark mass, interspersed with many other colors that seemed to connect between the various areas and were so ephemeral that they more afterimages on his retina than real, conscious impressions.

"Holy Mary, Mother of God!" Jason gasped. He wanted to close his mouth, but he couldn't bring himself to do anything but stare. All at once he felt crude and downright boring as a human being, like a dull stone compared to a colorful parrot perched upon it. The Click was ugly, the pale skin, the overly long fingers and toes that were strangely bent back, the jellyfishlike head, the bony torso. The sight of its gills, the way they wiggled back and forth in the liquid, almost made him tremble. There were enough things about the alien that his basic human programming found repulsive precisely because it *was* so alien. Nevertheless, his fascination prevailed against the urge to retreat and look for a weapon.

Whether Shimmer understood, he didn't know, but the Click raised a hand to one side and tapped the claw of its longest finger against the left wall of the tank.

Did you just point to the neighboring tank? Jason thought and turned his head. *What harm could one more stupid idea do? Besides, in retrospect, the previous ones weren't so stupid, were they?*

"Time to find out."

21

SKY FORTRESS, SITUATION ROOM

Fleet Admiral Hannibal von Solheim stood at the heart of the Terran Fleet's command structure with his hands clasped behind his back. The Situation Room resembled the bridge of a modern fast cruiser where the seating and consoles for specialists formed a ring with their backs facing the podium in the center. The difference was that the Situation Room was the size of half a soccer field and housed more than 400 officers and NCOs. They were all seated at modern AR holos, busy navigating through their virtual displays using mind and gesture controls. Their seats looked like comfortable armchairs and the tasks they were performing did not appear very demanding. Only the two-dimensional holodisplays in front of them indicated the complexity of their work, and the live visual feeds they provided allowed the command staff to see what they were doing at all times.

The staff sat around the oval table. The eight admirals present looked fatigued and demoralized. Their condition was the result of days spent helplessly watching as their homeworld slowly became deprived of air. In "normal" times of war, they had been accustomed to commanding entire fleets, or skillfully exploiting their connections to pull strings in the Jupiter Parliament of the SCR to secure the necessary funds and grants the military needed to keep humanity alive. Now they were stuck on a space station, a place they usually visited only for meetings and press conferences, while the specialists served as the vessels that transported the blood through the Fleet's complex body. They issued federation-wide orders with the necessary bureaucratic attachments, prepared analyses and strategic overviews, and processed thousands of requests and transit permits per minute. Until yesterday, they had been unable to do any of this because they were cut off from the rest of the Federation and Sol was burned. The sky fortress had become a brain without a body.

Until now.

"The *Oberon*," von Solheim said as he turned to face his admirals. The holotable around which they sat glowed dimly like a small pond of reflecting water. "Is she in position?"

"Yes, Fleet Admiral," Admiral Legutke confirmed. The gaunt man from the core world De Gaulle always reminded von Solheim of a scarecrow. But a very loyal and extremely conscientious one. "They've been flying at eighty percent thrust so far, as we recommended. If they go to full thrust, they'll be well within firing range in fifteen minutes."

"Good. Still no direct response from the Clicks?"

Legutke shook his head. "No. They're maintaining their positions, except for a few minimal adjustments to pull the net tighter in the sector the *Oberon* is approaching."

"Good," he repeated, then turned to Admiral Hachiro. "Shinto? Give the order to *Artemis*. Either Fidel Soares managed to reach them and they're ready or it's too late anyway. Once this boulder starts rolling, it won't roll back."

"*Hai*, Fleet Admiral." Hachiro maintained his stony countenance as he nodded. The only hint of possible tension was in his sudden formality. Perhaps, however, he was just aware of the high stakes they were playing for— Terra. That was true even though he still believed that failure was better than dying of thirst up here while they watched the same thing happen to billions of people on Earth.

Admiral Saunders spoke up and raised a meaty hand. "What about the *Oberon*?"

"What about her?"

"You've collectively served her command with arrest warrants. For treason."

"I'm aware of that. They abandoned their assigned position despite multiple warnings and performed a zero-Tau jump in Terra's atmosphere. That cost us the *Novigrad* Halo, a habitat that was over a hundred years old, and cost more than the gross system product of ten core worlds." He looked into the faces of his highest-ranking admirals and managed not to roll his eyes when he saw their undisguised appreciation and admiration. One way or another, the act committed by Captain Thurnau and her crew would go down in the history books and Fleet folklore, he was sure. "A crime is still a crime. If we close our eyes just because an act of insubordination, the negligent endangerment of an entire planet, and the destruction of a habitat didn't have as big a consequence as expected, the Fleet will have a problem."

There were nods of agreement all around.

"I'd also like to remind you that the planetary defense centers and orbital platforms had to sacrifice a large portion of their ammunition supplies to blast the *Novigrad*'s falling debris before it devastated the surface. Yes, Michael?"

"Rosenberg has put the *Oberon* back into service despite your instructions. We should at least know how to handle her if this plan is going to work. I honestly have a hard time with the thought of bringing her in for this dangerous job and then trying to detain her," Admiral Saunders said.

"Not to mention that we wouldn't even have the military capacity to do that if it weren't for the *Oberon*."

"Both valid points," von Solheim agreed with them, looking at his chronometer. Ten minutes. He was reluctant to discuss the aftermath now, just as a battle plan was just about to be executed. But in this battle, they were doomed to idly stand by. Either it worked or it didn't. "Under my tenure, there will be stabs in the back. If the *Oberon* does their part, I'll provide a way out for both sides. I could see demoting Captain Thurnau and then promoting Bradley's son, Nicholas, to command the Titan. The crew will agree to that, and from what I understand, Thurnau is happier in the XO role anyway. So, we establish consequences for their actions while acknowledging their role in this fight for survival. After all, they managed to evacuate *Novigrad* even though it was considered impossible—however they managed it."

The admirals nodded in agreement.

"All that remains is for us to hope that they follow orders this time and don't do what those stubborn Harbinger bastards think is right, again," von Solheim said. He called up the current location of the Earth orbitals with a wave. "Let the battle begin and may God and Fortuna be on our side."

22

It was harder to get into the tank than Jason imagined. It was only about two and a half meters high, but that was more than he could manage. The lid had already retracted into the ceiling, but when he tried jumping to reach the rim, a sight that must have looked pretty ridiculous to anyone watching, he couldn't get a grip on it. Pulling himself to the top was out of the question. He gestured wildly at Shimmer, trying to signal for the grappling arms that were surely located above this tank as well. But either the Click didn't understand him or the robotic aid had a very limited range intended only to collect armor from Clicks who were already in the tank taking a bath.

"You want me to climb in there, don't you?" he asked aloud, pointing to the empty tank. Shimmer responded to his gesture by tapping his outstretched finger against his armored glass again.

"Looks to me like you're pointing at it," Jason grumbled and looked up. "A little help would be nice."

Shimmer scrutinized him with a thousand facets of

expressions he didn't know how to interpret, and yet they stirred something in him. The feelings they awakened were hard to define and too varied to name or classify appropriately. He had no clue what good a bath in the green tank was supposed to do, but he had to do something, and if there was one thing he understood, it was an outstretched forefinger.

"Fine, no help then." Jason looked around and spotted the console behind him. "A bad idea, a really, really bad idea."

It looked like a table, albeit somewhat curved and covered with odd buttons and switches. After judging the distance to the tank at about a meter and a half, he repeated his estimation. "A *very* bad idea."

Nevertheless, he climbed onto the console, careful not to damage his precious oxygen supply. When he straightened and balanced himself, the edge of the tank seemed much closer, at least with respect to his height. The next problem was the distance.

Doable, but difficult, he said to himself. One problem would be the breathing apparatus, because if, or rather, as soon as, he banged against the tank, it would fall off since he needed both hands to grab the rim. So, he decided on another unavoidable act of stupidity. He held his breath, wrapped the hose around his oxygen tank until the mouth-nose piece rested on top, and then weighed it with his throwing arm.

"If it lands inside and I don't, I'll suffocate," he explained to himself, losing precious breathable air. The silence was worse, though. "If it falls, it might break and I'll suffocate."

When, compelled by the rapidly diminishing time left to him, he finally dared to throw it, his throat tightened. The device soared in a high arc, so far that he thought it would shatter on the floor behind the tank. But it landed in the green liquid and slowly sank.

Any impulse to celebrate his success was quickly swept away by the realization that he had only one chance, two at most, to get into the tank and put his breathing apparatus back on. So, he crouched, gathered his strength and leaped.

When he was a child, he had once dreamed of being a mayfly smacking into the windshield of his father's car. Now he knew what it must feel like. The only difference was that this time he didn't wake up, but found himself groaning on the cold floor, watching huge alien eyes in a green tank filled with some substance he didn't know.

The urgent impulse to breathe was already building up in his throat, slowly hardening into a primal compulsion he wouldn't be able to avoid for much longer. There was only one thing he could do, get up and try again. In any other situation, he would have been on his way to some sickbay. This time he caught the rim and his fingers clenched around the wide bulletproof glass with a strength born of desperation. Naked and freezing, he dangled from the rim. Presenting such a pitiful sight, he briefly wondered what the Click thought of humans now as he gathered his strength to pull himself up. He had always kept fit and spent more time in shipboard gyms than many others of his rank who, after their first officer years, no longer felt compelled to seek every opportunity to gain recognition from their superiors. Still, without the proper augments, pulling his own body weight up with only his fingers was no easy feat.

What mobilized all his reserves didn't matter to him, whether it was despair or a primal impulse to survive that grew stronger along with the feeling of suffocation in his chest. The only thing that mattered was that the next moment found him in the green liquid, which was surprisingly viscous. When he opened his eyes, they burned slightly, as if in salt water. He could barely see, but he was pretty sure he was floating upside down, so he groped downward for the oxygen apparatus. First, he found the bottom, then finally the square metal casing and the tube. Just as the urge to open his mouth and inhale became unbearable, he put the mouthpiece over his head and took a deep breath. Since it sat tightly against his lips and nostrils, very little fluid entered his trachea, and he quickly brought his coughing fit under control. Still driven by residual panic, he tried to sit up and turn around in the claustrophobic tank. Only when he had managed to float upright in the liquid mass, which held him as if weightless and was pleasantly warm, did the feeling of confinement and helplessness subside somewhat.

Only now, as he calmed down, did it occur to him that he was hearing complex melodies distantly reminiscent of the clicks of Morse code, only more drawn-out and varied. Each sound echoed in his ears, resonating longer and longer, blending with the following tones to form a pleasant arrangement of sounds that created a pattern made up of each of them, yet seemed to exist only through their totality. Although the two sounds had little in common, he knew immediately that it was the alien's clicking he was hearing that gave them their human moniker. initially colloquial, now canonical: *Clicks.*

His eyes slowly adjusted to the new visual conditions, blurry with a green cast, but good enough to make out Shimmer in the neighboring tank. He felt an uncomfortable itch all over his skin that he knew would soon become a burning sensation, and a throbbing headache spread behind his forehead and temples.

Okay, what now? he thought, trying to block out the fact that they could be blown up by nukes at any time.

Jason thought back to his dives on Lagunia, the extended reef trips with all the colorful fish and the similar green tint in the sea that had given everything a vivid hue. Except that he didn't recognize the reefs. It was darker and he saw strange formations reminiscent of Sumerian ziggurats. He tried to shake off the mental images but could not. He remembered looking down at his diving suit, but it was no longer a diving suit, instead it was four chalky white legs stretched out behind him as he moved through the water.

Shit! The curse shot through his head. The pain under his temples grew worse. *What is this?*

A new memory—*no, not a memory, not a memory!*—solidified in his mind, revealing a plate, blurry, dull and—*No, not a plate. It's a carpet. No, everything is blurred. A flog! That's a flog from below!*

Jason remembered the sight. He had once paid a lot of money for a two-hour dive under Atlantis. It had been as frightening as it was exciting. But the perspective wasn't right. It hadn't been so dark then. He had to be deeper because he could now see the rim of the algae island. Back then it had been much too big for that.

What is that?

As if on cue, he looked down at himself again, and saw the four alien legs that weren't his.

No, this is wrong! Wrong!

The headache swelled, approaching a point that he could no longer bear.

Stop! What is this? Is there some sort of hallucinogen in the tank? he thought through gritted teeth. He wanted to bite his tongue to distract himself from the pounding pain. In the next moment, the distorted memories disappeared and the headache slowly subsided. Relieved, he breathed in and out.

The clicking melodies were gone. No, they hadn't disappeared, but they had become quieter, like background noise in the far distance.

"Was that you?" he thought but got no answer. Of course not. Jason closed his eyes and tried to envision an image of Shimmer without his armor. He managed it to some extent, even if the alien looked perhaps more grotesque than in reality. The inner image solidified and then disappeared without his effort, only to be replaced by a much more detailed version that he immediately knew was more accurate, as if a puzzle piece had been inserted into the matching shape.

"It was really you! Are you in my head?" The implications of this thought made him breathe excitedly. He was surely consuming too much oxygen, but it did not matter. *Holy shit!*

Jason thought of himself and his appearance and waited for the image to change to a variation of it: blurrier and more translucent, as if a multicolored glow lay over his skin, radiating from within him and lost in the surroundings like a delicate aura. His head seemed too big, his fingers too short, and, well... it wasn't quite accurate, not from his point of view, anyway.

"Is that how you see me? Apparently, you don't find me very handsome, either."

Realizing what had just happened, Jason tore open the eyes he had closed because of the pain and stared through his tank into the alien's eyes, which he made out as blurry aquamarine ovals looking back at him.

"Telepathy! That was telepathy, wasn't it?" Excitement drove away the headache like withered leaves in a hurricane. What remained was a tingling sensation in his fingertips and under his scalp that made him forget even the increasing burning sensation on his skin. *Real telepathy. It was sending me images.*

"You sent me pictures. Memories!"

Again, he remembered—no, he *felt*—something... a sensation of agreement. It wasn't quite what Jason associated with it, at least not one hundred percent, but it came close to what he would identify as "agreement," a vague impression of something falling into place that filled him with calm. Now that he was thinking about what agreement really *felt* like, he was intrigued by the fact that he had never explored the feeling behind the thought until now. When he thought "yes" to something, he didn't question the feelings associated with it. Now that he did, it struck him that through the telepathic transmission from the alien, he precisely understood the feeling behind it.

Yes, he thought. *Telepathy.*

Agreement was how he translated the renewed alien

feeling. It was as if it were rising in him, but with a touch of *falseness*, as in a dream that seemed perfectly real and yet frayed at the edges, making him aware that he was dreaming. This knowledge did not make the dreams less "real" and yet dissociated him from them.

"My name is Jason," he said in his mind, and automatically a whole flood of memories, emotions and feelings of self, flowed in with it.

Optimistic broodmother, egg-laying importance, beautiful brightness ray of warm layers, was the answer he received, and his head felt as if it would explode at any moment, so complex were the emotions and memories that flowed into his head and heart like lava. Of the package of sensory impressions, of squeezing sensations in an abdomen that was not his, he interpreted as thousands of eggs pouring out of him, masses of water through which a ray of light fell on *his* future brood, and equally ugly—which he perceived as normal for that period of time—as numerous Clicks swimming around him in the water, into a unified overall feeling of ego sensations he could name. These interpretations did not do justice to anything. They seemed like a brutal act of reduction, for which he was thoroughly ashamed, although it happened all by itself.

"A female. You are a female!"

Agreement.

"And you are an important person among your people."

Agreement.

"The other four who protected you, they were your bodyguards?"

Jason tried to banish the images of musclemen in suits that were part of his definition of bodyguards and focus on the feeling of protection and security that their fictional presence evoked in him.

Bodyguard feeling. Agreement. Male.

Jason's mind got better at finding corresponding feelings to the transmissions and filling in the gaps. He concentrated on that as much as possible, despite the risk of reduction, which made everything less accurate but made his headache more bearable. He felt like a vessel that had been filled with more content than it was intended to hold and was in danger of bursting. He needed an overflow valve, and his mind seemed to be looking for it right now.

"I am military male."

Warrior. Clicks in the black armor that made them look robotic, carrying heavy weapons, marched through his mind, operating controls on complex bridge systems, and being loaded onto shuttles that landed on artificial islands in a storm.

"Lagunia," Jason thought. *"Your memories. I thought they were mine at first. I was in the water on Lagunia. You were there too?"*

Home, the alien replied, and a surge of comfort and profound peace was followed by turmoil, loss, and pain. The definition of home was virtually simultaneous within him, as he shared the complex feeling the Click associated with it in almost exactly the same way. When he thought of Harbingen, there were the heartwarming early days with his family, the knowledge of belonging and having a place for himself, followed and destroyed by the heavy loss and suffering that came with it, leaving a pain that no scar on the body, no matter how bad, could create.

"Lagunia is your home?" he asked incomprehensively.

Home of my kind.

"Home of the Clicks. That... can't be. It is the home of the Lagoon."

Jason thought of the fossil finds of the aquatic inhabitants on his exile home, finds made every year by disreputable explorers who had strayed to Lagunia to prove something to themselves and to science, or to make a few credits, although most of the research institutes in the Federation had quickly lost interest. In times when the military utility behind each credit was questioned, a majority worked in Fleet research and development or on improving manufacturing techniques and resource recycling.

Home of my kind, repeated *optimistic broodmother, egg-laying importance, beautiful brightness ray of warm layers.* Jason had to come up with something shorter than this torrent of sensations. Each time felt like an exploding singularity, timelessly brief yet so full of time and depth that his brain seemed to spin.

"Mother," he thought.

Mother, she repeated as he reinforced his sensory reaction, compressed by his mind, to her self-image.

"Are you a leader?" he asked, feeling a twinge of sadness as an image of his father rose in him, followed by a hint of anger and frustration because his father was the first person his subconscious seemed to associate with the word "leadership."

No, Mother answered. **Not that.**

"I'm sorry, I think I 'worded' my question incorrectly." Jason tried to recall memories of himself and his feelings when he had given orders, for example, to the recruits on

the hangar, his organization of the refugee crisis on the *Oberon*, and how he was obeyed and shown respect.

That. Agreement. Leader.

"Are there many of you?" When he didn't get an answer, he felt a twinge of shame. Did she feel she was being interrogated like a prisoner of war? He probably would have. So, he tried another approach and let his honest curiosity get in the way of their common bond, whatever it was. The good thing about telepathy was that lying was impossible. At least for him. Did Clicks learn how to shield their thoughts and willfully alter them to what could amount to a lie?

"So much to learn. So much fascination."

Fascination. Agreement.

"I am happy that we are communicating." He broadcast his relief and satisfaction at their exchange. His excitement also flowed into his thoughts, and he couldn't do anything to stop that.

Agreement. Mother is satisfied-relieved-sad-confused about contact with Coldhearts.

The complex concept of what his mind translated into the word coldhearts made him shiver. He was overcome by a heartless, empathy-less fog of emotional coldness, a black hole closing in on him, turning into missiles and flashing flowers of fire.

He found himself on a bridge—thousands of bridges—monitoring ships and their crews. He felt as if they were standing next to him. Their feelings and emotional closeness touched him and hovered around his mind like a comforting embrace that warmed the entire universe. He stretched out his spiritual feelers. They seemed like ethereal umbilical cords that gently stretched and flowed through the nothingness of the vacuum like a superconductor. They reached for the death-bringing black hole. There were many of these holes. His increasingly desperate attempts to get an answer, a confirmation that something there noticed and acknowledged his feelings, his existence, came to nothing. There was nothing, only emotive coldness, lack of feedback, loneliness.

"Coldhearts." He replayed the intricate web of sensations that caused an emptiness to expand within him. The very idea of being attacked by other people and asking them to have compassion on him, and not seeing a reaction from them to his suffering, made him shiver. Facing aliens who, by his standards, didn't even perceive him was even worse. *"We always thought you communicated by clicks. We didn't know what they meant. There is no equivalent among us, except in the animal kingdom underwater, in shellfish, but we never deciphered those either."*

He tried to remember the clicking sounds and recreate his confusion whenever he heard corresponding recordings. Every school child knew the black box data with the reconstructions of the fatal first contact inside and out.

Sounds. Mother repeated his representation with a mixture of confusion and understanding. **Sounds for orientation. Localization in space. Show physical proximity or distance. No concept-reality exchange.**

"No telepathy. You must have thought we were mute."

Mute. Agreement. Coldhearts mute. Violent.

"Clicks destroyed our research ship Vasco da Gama. *This ship was unarmed."*

Not true, came the abrupt answer, and it was so emotionally charged that Jason's headache worsened. **Cold-**

hearts worst weapon brought to breeding place. Great danger.

Jason saw what Mother saw, felt and sensed the *Vasco da Gama*. He recognized the ship by her silhouette, as Mother captured objects as outlines, detailed but devoid of color and aesthetics. If the research vessel were not the most famous ship in the history of the Terran Federation, he would not have been able to recognize it with Mother's senses.

Fear spread through him as he thought of the ring that surrounded the hull as a habitat. When lights on the ring switched on, he perceived them from Mother's view as waves of fast particles on a sensor. When they began to rotate, all alarm bells shrilled in him. He saw floods of monstrous Clicks, males with distorted eyes and opaque heads, and they felt more sinister to him than anything in his experience. The Coldhearts had brought the demons here.

Behind him lay *breeding place*, a world with the purest seas the world-shapers had ever spawned and nurtured, where millions of eggs lay at the bottom of the sea. He had personally laid nearly ten percent of them and supplied them with their genetic code. Generations of Clicks would rise from the protective darkness of the deep, warmed by subterranean geysers, and feast on the sun-drenched shallows, swimming in freedom and sharing ever more complex patterns of sensations and dreams.

But the image burst under an onslaught of grotesque monsters pouring out of the ring, bringing death and destruction, at the end of which *breeding place* lay empty and abandoned. Without life. Without warmth. Without the delight of the complex sensation of a consciousness born of a universe that awakens to itself through them.

"A hyperspace gate. You thought the Vasco da Gama *brought a mobile hyperspace gate,"* Jason thought. *"You were fighting Species X yourselves at Lagunia, and you were afraid of the gate technology."* The tragic irony came down on him like a hammer blow, and he would have liked to scream and cry at the same time. *"A habitat ring. This was a habitat ring in which the researchers lived, worked, and slept."*

Their grief flowed and mingled and became a maelstrom. Yet at its bottom lay a foundation of certainty that there were no boundaries between them. Every single sensation produced a resonance that automatically generated understanding and security because it did not echo in emptiness as he was used to because thoughts were something personal.

Misfortune. Great misfortune, grief, bitterness.

"Yes. A misunderstanding." With millions of deaths. The bitterness of this fact was literally inexpressible in words, but it didn't require them because the kaleidoscope of sensations that flowed through their common bond expressed it all much better and more precisely, and more overwhelmingly. Jason could not understand how a sentient being could constantly endure the sheer volume of sensations. He was on the verge of breaking under it. *"There is a problem, Mother."*

Problem, now?

"Yes, big problem." Jason recalled what Sirion had told him about the Fleet's plan, and the corresponding inner images arose automatically.

Destruction of my warrior males.

"Yes. I must stop them."

Gratitude.

Jason received what he understood as gratitude, but it was much more. There was sadness, and something like frustration about the Clicks who had died on board.

The four on the bridge had apparently hatched from her eggs and thus had been something like her children. But it did not match the abysmal calamity a human mother would have felt over her four slain children. The pain was there, but different, more distant, and at the same time closer, because the telepathic bond between them had created more closeness and identification than humans were ever able to experience. But the view of death was different. It represented an end that was a new beginning and part of a natural cycle whose possible endings also included a violent death. Even that was not perceived as some stroke of fate, but as destiny. Likewise, the resonating empathy about the loss did not come with the sensation that she did not want to feel the pain. Indeed, she seemed to accept it as something normal that did not require vengeance. Jason was fascinated by this and at the same time felt a fierce shame rising within him. After his mother's death, he had felt nothing but hatred, because it had been his strategy for dealing with the unbearable pain and had already cursed everyone and everything for it.

"I must try."

Gratitude. Important transmission: shuttle damage-destruction. Proximity.

"The shuttle is damaged and will explode? Are there any escape pods?"

Agreement. Four-twelve-units.

Jason didn't understand the time expression, which evoked a picture of bubbles arranged in two groups of six, one below the other, but the accompanying feeling was one of haste, and that seemed all too familiar.

He reached up to the edge of the tank. Its lid had apparently opened again at Mother's command, and he climbed out. Immediately he felt cold, as if he were being cast out of his mother's warm womb.

"Well, shit me!" someone shouted. Naked, wet, and shivering, it took Jason a moment to identify Baker's rumbling voice. The mountain of muscle stomped onto the bridge and grabbed him by the arms before he could fall. "What happened here?"

"Mother... she..."

"Mother?" Baker repeated mumbling past his cigar stub and looked at Mother. She was still in her tank yet clad in her massive armor again. "Had to take an alien goo bath first, and now she's your new mom?"

"Radio... did you...?" Jason gasped for breath. His skin was scarlet red and burned like hell. It felt like someone had covered him with stinging jellyfish.

"I did. It's improvised but strong. There's nothing wrong with encryption, but if you've got a frequency and can manage to get through somehow..."

"Take me there." Jason noticed Rochshaz at the door and pointed at the astonished-looking mutant. "The Mother must be protected at all costs."

23

"Battle range achieved," Daussel reported. The bridge was already immersed in the red combat light that once again embraced the crew there in the cloak of danger. In recent weeks, it had become as familiar to them as breathing. Originally intended to stimulate concentration and alertness by association, Nicholas already saw the danger of attrition in the crew. Each of them looked like someone who had drunk too much alcohol to get drunk anymore.

"We wait," Silly ordered from the other side of the command deck, partially hidden by a hologram representation of Terra and the grid of one thousand Click ships that surrounded the planet like a shell. "Let them believe, as long as possible, that we're out of ammunition like everyone else and we're bluffing."

"Bombardment in two minutes."

"XO?"

Nicholas nodded and reached for his handset and pressed 3 to direct dial the CAG. He did not even get a call sign before Lieutenant Commander Richard "Hellcat" Bales answered.

"Sir? Are we a go?"

"Not yet. Two minutes."

"We're ready, sir."

"Good. Remember to focus on bombs. I don't want to see any deviation just because a high-value target presents itself. Your mission is to protect Terra's civilian population. Any bomb that makes it to the surface in response is on us."

"Understood," Bales assured him.

"Good luck, Hellcat. Get home safe." Nicholas hung up and nodded to Silly, "All set."

"Very good."

They spent the remaining ninety seconds in silence except for the hum of the bridge and the muffled voices of the operators in the ranks. A red number in the holotank counted down. As it dropped to zero, thousands of symbols blinked to life. Yellow dashes, each labeled PNW, for Planetary Nuclear Weapon, and an associated number, moved away from the *Artemis* halo like tadpoles.

"Clear for launch!" Silly barked, and the launch catapults in the port and starboard grooves of the *Oberon* ejected eighty of the darting fighters at a time. Geysers of fire and smoke followed but dissipated in the vacuum within seconds.

"Captain!" Lieutenant Jung called. "Incoming communication."

"The fleet admiral?"

"No, ma'am, it's from a Click shuttle transmitting on an old frequency. It's recorded in our system but was updated eleven years ago."

Silly and Nicholas exchanged a puzzled look.

"Why wasn't the signal jammed by electronic defenses?" she asked, sternly.

"Because it has a priority code on it."

"Whose?"

"That's the funny thing, according to the computer it belongs to Lieutenant Commander Jason Bradley, ma'am."

"What?" Nicholas and Silly blurted simultaneously.

"Put him through!" he ordered, ignoring the chain of command. The commander nodded urgently.

A crackle and scrape came from the speakers on the command deck, then Jason's voice rang out, vibrating as if he were freezing to death, yet clearly recognizable, "This is Lieutenant Commander Jason Bradley to anyone who can hear me. Abort the attack! I repeat, abort the attack! I have managed to establish contact with a Click leader. Talks are not possible, but the attack must be called off before it is too late! I—" The transmission ended in static.

"Something's missing!" Silly snapped.

"The signal's being jammed, ma'am," Lieutenant Feugers reported.

"By whom?"

"Impossible to say. Possibly by orbital defense."

"Damn!"

"That was him," Nicholas breathed. "That was Jason."

"Yes," Silly agreed. "And his message..."

"We have to abort!"

"Slow down!" Silly raised a hand. "We don't know if it's a Click ruse."

"Since when do Clicks send fake messages in our language?" Nicholas shook his head.

"Since when did they attack Terra and blockade it?"

"That was Jason," he insisted.

"I heard him, too, but what if he's under enemy influence? We can only try this maneuver once, and if it goes wrong, that's it for good."

"Captain Thurnau is right," Daussel agreed, but Nicholas ignored him and leaned toward Silly.

"I know you guys have your differences, but Jason would never, even under torture, unwillingly record a message like that. I don't know what he's found out or what it means, but I know we only have one chance, and it's dwindling by the second. If he's right, and he wouldn't say it if he didn't believe it, then we cannot proceed."

"Any new orders from the fleet admiral?" she asked.

"Negative," Jung reported, and Silly struggled with herself. Nicholas knew it was not her custom to refrain from attacking as soon as she thought an opportunity presented itself.

"Please, commander," Nicholas said. "At least trust me, if not him."

"Too late," she said, pointing at the holoscreen. One PNW symbol after another disappeared from the display faster than he could follow.

The nuclear bombs, which were actually munitions meant for docked Fleet ships, were purely designed to be dropped. They had no propulsion of their own and only moved at the velocity achieved at ejection from the airlocks and improvised launch bays, which was not very much. They detonated almost simultaneously over an eleven-second period, creating a sphere of flashes in low Earth orbit that first burned large portions of the microcellulose in the higher atmospheric layers, clearing the view to target the ground-based nuclear missiles. If there were no pressure waves in the vacuum, there remained the short-lived fireballs of hard radiation, a diabolical heat that melted many nearby civilian and military satellites to cinders. Collateral damage that under normal circumstances would have been massive, but in humanity's desperate plight was considered marginal. More important were the electromagnetic impulses that emanated from the fission process and interfered with the Click fleet's sensor coverage over a large area.

"I can still redirect the fighter squadrons to the western hemisphere, and we can take care of the eastern," Nicholas suggested. "Please."

"All right," she said, baring her teeth. "Change course, prepare intercept of planet-based missiles, align all port railguns! Prepare flak shield, maximum extension, minimum density!"

"Thank you," Nicholas breathed with relief, literally ripping the receiver from its cradle as he pounded on 3.

"Hellcat here!" came the voice of the Commander, Air Group, backed by the loud hiss and roar of his Barracuda.

"Change of orders!" Nicholas shouted. "Swing to the western hemisphere and intercept all ground-based weapons aimed at the enemy."

"Uh..."

"Do it!"

"Roger that, Commander!" Hellcat confirmed without further question, to Nicholas's relief.

"We'll send you the perimeter of your area of operations any moment now. Don't let any get through, Lieutenant Commander!"

"Juratis Unitatis!"

"Juratis Unitatis." He hung up and nodded to Silly.

Hellcat pushed the nose of his Barracuda down and let out a yowl as the slender hunter leaned toward the planet, which finally glowed blue again. Below him, the silhouette of Europe peeled out of a curving band of clouds, the home of his maternal ancestors who had baked bread in Alsace, as his grandfather had once told him.

"You have the new orders," he said, deliberately bypassing the squadron leaders and radioing directly to his air group consisting of twenty-two squadrons of twenty airmen each. Urgency in combat knew no chain of command in extreme doubt, as every cadet learned at Harbingen.

Well, what every cadet *had* learned at Harbingen.

"We're going to go in and take out anything unmanned trying to get into orbit from Earth. They'll be ancient hypersonic missiles, so don't expect any effective ECM signals. Fire your Fenneks and don't hold any back. Only then go to the Vulcans," he ordered. "Good hunting! Juratis Unitatis!"

Bales readied the eight Fenneks under his hull, tiny shrapnel-headed guided missiles designed to intercept small, lightly armored vehicles like reconnaissance drones. They were equipped with a proximity sensor that triggered the charge a few meters from the target, shattering it with a spreading, funnel-shaped cloud of tiny metal spheres. Perfect against planetary bombs, but, fortunately, just as effective in countering guided weapons like hypersonic missiles. They were significantly lighter than the armor-piercing Tommyknockers they usually used in starship combat, so they could carry many more of them on board.

The interconnected radar system of all his Barracudas formed a perfect coverage from one pole to the other and showed the Clicks' massive warships hovering between two hundred and three hundred kilometers above them and not moving. It was a strange sight. He was used to them hitting him with everything they could muster but the brief sensor overload from the EMPs that had just been triggered was apparently still affecting them.

A glance to the left and right showed him the shadows of his comrades in their own Barracudas. Like a black flock of birds of prey in a perfect jagged formation, they raced along the upper atmospheric layers on afterburners, trailing tiny streaks to get away from the behemoth called *Oberon* as quickly as possible, which happened to be their home.

"Multiple rocket launches!" his wingman, Alphastar, exclaimed excitedly. "Are we really shooting our own toys out of the sky?"

"Looks like it."

"Well, let's do it."

On optical sensors, Bales watched as hundreds of tiny lights flared on the sickly brown carpet that was Europe. That he could see them now with the telescopes meant they had been on the move for some time.

Less than two minutes later, as they sped across the Atlantic at 55,000 kilometers an hour, his targeting system screeched loudly, informing him of friendly transponder codes on approach vectors.

Collision danger. Bales laughed with a snort, switched on eight of his bombs and waited two breaths for his air group's interlocked Warframe battle system to confirm to avoid duplicate targets.

"Bombs away!" he shouted out of habit and pressed the release button on his flight stick. The eight Fenneks, long as a human arm and about as slender, disengaged from their weapons bays, catapulted downward by cold gas jets, then fired their own thrusters, propelling them forward at a peak acceleration of 120 Gs. Like slippery eels, they slid away from the outer atmosphere and altered their trajectories before plummeting to meet their ancient ancestors.

Less than eighty seconds later, the first blooms of fire flared before him, distant yet bright and unusually long-lived to someone who normally fought in space. There were dozens, hundreds, and soon thousands, almost as dense as the lightning storm of their beloved *Oberon*'s anti-aircraft screen.

"Interception rate ninety-seven percent," Alphastar reported with satisfaction.

"I see," he replied absently as an incoming priority message appeared on his primary screen and cut directly into his AR vision. The Fleet Admiral's seal preceded the message.

"Lieutenant Commander," an angry voice called out, "break off the attack! What the hell are you doing?"

"I don't know," he said to himself, cutting the connection before he could make a silly remark. The fact was, he didn't know himself, but orders were orders, and Commander Bradley was known neither as a hotshot nor a fool, so he would have his reasons.

"All Fenneks discharged," Alphastar announced.

"Switch all squadrons to Vulcans, don't enter the atmosphere, we can't save you there. Intercept anything that sticks its head into the vacuum. Group One, keep moving forward. Group Two, break out and turn around. We're not letting a missile through!"

"All launch bays, open fire!" Silly ordered and watched as the hundreds of launch bay hatches on the port and starboard ports opened and spat out guided missiles like darts. It was an excessive amount of firepower to take out single missiles, and ancient ones at that, but whatever the *Oberon* did, it usually did extremely accurately and thoroughly.

The ramps located on the top side also opened and fired eighty missiles per minute into the vacuum at the same time. They banked right and left in curving vectors and then hurtled downward to enter the atmosphere and bring a fiery end to their ancient counterparts. "Fire railguns at your discretion, but only after the targets have emerged from the atmosphere. We don't want collateral damage on the ground."

"Roger that, ma'am," Lieutenant Bauer acknowledged from Fire Control.

"Incoming communication from—" Lieutenant Jung began.

"Ignore it," Silly interrupted him gruffly. At Daussel's look, she added, "I already know what Fleet Command will accuse me of. I've gained enough experience, remember?"

Daussel's face showed a rare grin.

"If this goes wrong—"

"It won't," Nicholas assured her. "I know my brother."

"Your word in Omega's ear."

The *Oberon*'s interception efforts followed a simple pattern. Forced to cover an entire hemisphere, which was a downright impossible task, all the missiles in their arsenal targeted the sector behind them, while the railguns covered the front. At first, it was a strange feeling for Nicholas to watch idly as the railguns were deployed but remained inactive while their arsenal of missiles rapidly emptied, racing away on glowing flares of exhaust. Soon, however, countless explosions in the stratosphere bloomed as the inferno began.

Ahead of them, the first hypersonic missiles emerged from the atmosphere and the *Oberon*'s targeting systems followed their programmed commands once fire control gave the go-ahead. The hundreds of railguns, twelve-meter-long twin sleds on rotary mounts that accelerated their kinetic projectiles to relativistic velocities, began their tungsten assault on the nuclear-tipped guided missiles, shredding them one by one. Hundreds disintegrated in funnel-shaped clouds of debris, and the hurricane of destruction spread like a fan, speeding away from the *Oberon*.

There were no cheers on the bridge. The crew was too focused or confused for that. Nicholas guessed a mixture of both since the same was true for him.

"Ma'am, two Click frigates are veering off their standard course and have us on target."

"So much for EMP," Silly grumbled. "Realign flak screen, seventy-five percent coverage."

"As long as it's only two," Nicholas agreed, studying the holodisplay between them. A thousand or so other red-marked objects stoically held their orbit. He guessed that could only mean that their sensors hadn't yet come back up after what he presumed was an emergency shutdown in response to the electron fireworks that had raged in orbit.

"It won't stay that way," Silly predicted. "But we'll be fine. For now. I don't know what Jason has in mind, but there will be a limit to what we can do here."

He realized quite quickly what she meant by that when the two Click frigates opened fire, sending two dense swarms of kinetic missiles toward them. The anti-aircraft screen enveloped them on the port side in a dense hemi-sphere of yellow-red explosions from the shrapnel shells, and the shredded projectiles contributed to the shield. Nicholas eyed their shell stocks with concern. Going into battle with less than thirty percent was not a scenario a Titan commander liked to face, and Silly's expression confirmed that.

"A destroyer is lining up to fire," Feugers reported, but they had already seen it in the holoscreen's tactical simula-tion. Fortunately for them, the ship was very close to the other three and didn't require any flak screen adjustments.

"They ought to see us saving their alien butts," the commander growled, zooming in with both hands on the target interception indicator. It was at ninety-six percent. A respectable value.

Come on, Jason, report back! he thought impatiently. This was the second time they had disobeyed an order that would be considered treason, and punishable by death, by a military tribunal.

"If this goes wrong, we're toast," Daussel commented in a rare deviation from the normal flow of communication. It was a clear expression of nerves.

"Jason knows what he's doing," Nicholas insisted. *You do, brother, don't you?*

The flak shield held, except for a few unpowered kinetic projectiles that were foiled quite gracefully by the *Oberon*'s freshly repaired, though still battered, carbine armor. Except for tentative protests from the molecular bond generators, the damage indicator showed no significant data spikes.

"Time is against us, anyway," Silly stated in an I-knew-it-all-along tone. She pointed to more red symbols with preliminary internal ship identifiers for the Click cruisers. Increasing numbers of them were awakening from their temporary blindness and joining the beating the *Oberon* was beginning to take.

"We need to increase density of the flak field," Nicholas advised her.

"Depending on how many more of them want to come to the party, we'll be pretty much finished in a few minutes. That's a *hell of a lot* of missiles and mass catapults."

"Unless Jason does something in a few minutes that makes sense of this madness, it won't matter anyway."

"That's right. Feugers, full flak coverage!" she shouted without breaking away from his gaze. "Two minutes, then, unless something happens that I want to see, we return fire."

"Silly—"

She interrupted him and raised a finger. "No. What I'm doing now is absolute madness, you said so yourself. I don't know how much more trust I could possibly show than risking the *Oberon*, and my own neck, against every single one of my instincts. That should tell you enough about how much I trust you. But I am the commander of this ship and the armed remnant of our species."

"You're right," he admitted, nodding, which caused a fleeting cloud of surprise to pass over her face. "What he said sounds crazy, but what if it's true? Could we afford to not try?"

"Either way, we should hope the Clicks will look favorably on our efforts," Daussel said, pointing to the strategic map between them that they had criminally disregarded during their conversation.

Two alien ships, each nearly 20,000 kilometers from the *Oberon*, were starting to move again when they were hit by hypersonic missiles. The nuclear warheads fissioned, resulting in massive fireballs that tore open their hulls like sheet metal and hurled their molten remnants into space. One of the two ships perished in a secondary explosion, presumably in its magazine, the other was still maneuverable, but immediately extended its radiators, which had already begun to glow cherry red while giving no certain indication of the heat inside.

"Now would be a good time for Jason to get his act together," Silly remarked, then shouted, "Realign the railguns. Commence targeting, fire on my command! Priority on the frigates! And get our Barracudas back. There's about to be a lot of work for them!"

Come on Jason, you crazy son of a bitch, Nicholas caught himself in a burst of adrenaline-fueled excitement. After all, it wasn't just the *Oberon* that was at stake after this stunt of theirs. Once again, the entire Earth was at risk should the aliens decide to finally finish it off. *Now or never!*

24

Problem.

The strange sensation was incomprehensible at first. Then Jason adjusted his perception. It was almost like before in the tank.

"Mother!"

Agreement. Problem.

Something about the connection was different. Weaker —No, less. It lacked the overwhelming volume and scope of emotions and complex thoughts that still made his head ache. Communication with the Click female was just as immediate as before, but what had been a rainbow was now focused into a laser beam. Clear, simple, and also strangely disappointing. It was as if something important was missing, which now confronted him as a void, a place where he had not even known that something could exist.

"What kind of problem?" he asked, denied the possibility to feel and know what she meant.

Complex. Simple explanation. Ship explodes even

earlier, rescue forces have turned away. Must use escape pods.

"Go ahead."

Not ready yet. Other problem. No communication with water people of warm depths.

"Clicks? You have no connection with the Clicks?"

Agreement. Destroyed components. Other problem.

"What?" He demanded impatiently.

Water people of warm depths attack ship of Coldhearts.

"What kind of ship? We have no more ships."

Great monster of unfortunate shame.

"What?"

Must abandon ship. Now. Send yours to the right hemisphere, Mother instructed him.

"Baker. Everyone to starboard. We've got to get to the escape pods. Quick!" he shouted. The mutant pulled his cigar from the corner of his mouth with two fingers and pointed at Rochshaz.

"Round up the boys and get the wounded to starboard with us. Chop-chop!"

Mother was busy quietly operating the controls of the console Jason had used to springboard into the tank. Her long fingers, three times as thick as the spidery appendages he had seen in the tank, flew nimbly and yet quickly over the buttons and knobs, operating something he could not see by gesturing in the air. Some kind of augmented reality, perhaps.

"What about the little bugger?" Baker smirked. "Be a

shame to lose him to an exploding shuttle when I could wrap his guts around his neck instead."

"He'll be fine. Someone like him always manages."

"He has that code you care so much about," the mutant reminded him as the shuttle was rocked by a violent tremor.

Departure, Mother transmitted, and a wave of excitement washed over him through their invisible bond. It was so strong that he felt dizzy.

"Evacuate. Now!" he shouted breathlessly as he followed the Click. She used her four legs to step over the corpses and run into the right outer corridor. Before, it had been dark and the walls had formed a dull, strangely iridescent barrier. Now it was brighter, making it easy to see several passageways had opened up. There had to be close to a dozen. From the left, Baker's mutants ran and limped in, then vanished into the escape pods as if they were being swallowed by them.

Mother pointed, almost humanlike, to an opening farther to the right.

"I'm not going anywhere with that critter," Baker said, patting Jason on the shoulder as another tremor nearly knocked them off their feet.

"Go with your boys."

"You betcha, kid. See you on the other side."

"Keep your transponder on." Jason pointed to the mutant's improvised radio. Baker nodded and walked into the first opening, where two others had just squeezed in.

Jason took off after Mother and slipped through the oval passageway into an astonishingly spacious cuboid. Despite its size, it contained neither seats nor anything one could interact with. Opposite, a picture window spanned the wall and acted like a magnifying glass. To Jason, everything behind it looked slightly blurry, yet he made out a small hemisphere of explosions in the darkness next to the blue glow of the Earth that filled half the window.

"Can you control this thing?" he asked, shaking his head when the Click female showed no reaction and sat on the floor.

He intensified his thoughts. *"Can you control this escape pod?"*

Two-fold answer: Minimal for drop mechanism catapult sequence.

"We need to get right into that flak fire out there!" He stretched out a hand and pointed to the *Oberon*'s flak screen, which he would have recognized anytime, anywhere, since there was only one ship left in the entire Federation that had the capability for it.

Self-death. Not possible.

"Perhaps it is the only chance before they destroy each other," he objected.

Hope for rescue by water people of warm depths, came the telepathic response with images of spaceships gathering a cube of metal from the vacuum, followed by feelings of relief.

"I understand that, but that is my home there," he thought, holding back nothing of the mixture of sadness and amazement that filled his statement as he became aware of that fact. He had never had a home other than the *Oberon*, no matter how much he had convinced himself to despise it. *"And we need a truce."*

Reluctant agreement.

A jolt shook the escape pod, and they were hurled into

space at a brutal acceleration. Since they were sitting on the correct side of the wall, the brief, violent change in momentum was bearable. Except for a groan and possibly some bruises, nothing worse than what he had experienced in the last few days happened. Outside the window, the background grew rapidly before the acceleration forces subsided and their progress became calmer. He guessed these were not escape pods for use in a vacuum, but on planets. After all, this was an atmospheric shuttle. His forearm display, at least, suggested that the atmospheric composition inside had not changed significantly, except for a touch more ozone. The temperature also remained stable.

"Mother," he thought, as he looked at the Click sitting across from him. Her legs were folded under her in a very uncomfortable-looking contortion, as if she were meditating. *"Why didn't you blow yourselves up?"*

Specify?

"Why didn't you destroy the shuttle when we came aboard? You usually do. We thought we were embarking on a suicide mission because we lacked a better alternative, but you did nothing."

Not possible. I am in phase of fecundity-pregnancy-fertilization.

Jason felt an unpleasant warmth suffuse his cheeks.

"Pardon?"

Incomprehension.

"You are... pregnant?"

Ready for fertilization, followed by delivery of eggs. Important. Rare.

"You're a VIP. I understand. But why were you in the Pacific?"

Large toxic water on poison-homeworld-Cold-hearts. Target for egg delivery, she answered. It was strange to sit silently across from her while receiving so much of her inner life, even now that it was a mere reflection of their prior connection.

"You wanted to lay eggs in the Pacific?"

Jason gulped. He had wondered why the Clicks hadn't bombed Terra and solved the problem of humankind once and for all. Now he knew why, and he didn't like it at all. Instead of an invasion, they planned to colonize Earth. The oceans were not in dispute, and with the force in orbit, they had no trouble whatsoever making sure that any attempt at interference was choked off with orbital laser fire. *Choke off* would literally describe what would happen in the years and decades to come—people slowly asphyxiating in the arcologies if they didn't kill each other off first.

"You wanted to take possession of Terra, not destroy it."

Agreement. Something that felt like an oscillation between shame and pride seeped through their bond. **Water worlds extremely rare in big nothingness. Eggs need space or die before conception of light.**

"Before they are born, they die if they are not deposited in an ocean?" He tried to sort out the confusingly complex images and feelings.

Agreement. Limitation: time horizon.

"What does that mean?"

Oceans acid-toxin-hot. Changes required. Preparing to lay eggs, Mother explained patiently and openly. **Water colony of warm depths makes preparations. Optimistic broodmother, egg-laying impor-**

tance, beautiful brightness ray supervises cleanup of birthing grounds. Then big-Coldhearts attack.

The accompanying images and sensations of the mutants who butchered her fellow species like machines, flashed through him like a lightning bolt, followed by disgust and fear. Not for himself, but for his potential offspring, for which a deep sense of duty prevailed in him. It was Mother's feelings he was experiencing, and yet they were so haunting that he shuddered. They had been infinitely lucky to have intercepted the right shuttle—he was only starting to realize just how lucky. He hoped that it was a twist of fate and that such a once-in-a-century coincidence was cause for optimism, that things would change for the better.

Coldhearts did not want to take optimistic brood-mother, egg-laying importance, beautiful brightness ray hostage?

"No. We wanted to get off Terra because there was no way for us to get to the nearest arcology. Our alternative was an ugly death in the open. We were very lucky," he explained. He cleared his throat. *"I just wish so many deaths had not been necessary for us to communicate with each other."*

Many sunken on both sides, Mother agreed with him. **Prevent more sunken.**

"Yes. Prevent." Outside the window, the battle was much closer by now. They were about to plunge into the flak screen that filled half the horizon with flickering explosions that continued unabated. *"Why can't you talk to your people? You are a leader."*

Communication in big nothingness difficult. No medium available.

"Would have been too good if you could have just whistled them back." He sighed. He had never seen the *Oberon*'s flak screen in real life, only on recordings or optical sensor images. The sheer force and extent of the explosions was overwhelming. *If there was a hell,* he thought, *its burning gates would probably look exactly like this.*

"*How tight is your suit?*" he asked as an idea came to him.

Oh, he translated her mental reaction to his inner images. **Great danger. Suit not made for big nothingness. Tight, but no long heat production. Liquid becomes cold-water-solidity.**

"*Ice, you mean?*"

Agreement.

How long?

One-twelfth. Possible. Certain? No.

"*I don't know what that means, but mine won't last long either. Apparently, our people don't yet understand the signal that an escape pod from the shuttle is flying directly into their fire.*"

Through the window, Jason saw the *Oberon* returning fire on several Clicks ships that were hammering the Titan from the right. More and more missile drives bloomed, sending whole swarms toward the flak shield in hopes of overwhelming it. But before long, the first railgun shells slammed into the hulls of the alien ships, awakening blossoms of flame. From a distance, it was beautiful, but for an officer like him, it was merely an indication of heightened adrenaline and mortal fear. Every member of the Fleet knew the feeling all too well when the first shudders of combat were felt on board. In those days, there were no crew members who didn't have combat experience, only those who had survived and those who could no longer tell of it. The same was probably true for the Clicks.

Signal, Mother repeated. **Can operate emergency opening. Hope for recovery.**

"Yes, I also hope for recovery. If it does not work, at least we have tried."

Yes.

Mother rose onto her four powerful legs. Their servo motors made every movement something mechanical-technical. She walked to the large window, outside which half the universe seemed to be caught in a permanent explosion.

Sad-Angry-Motherless, must get closer, she instructed him. The feelings and images reflected back to him, where she equated him as a person with his telepathic name, made him wince. A spoken name was just air expelled from his mouth, enriched with the vibrations of vocal cords. It was merely an act of verbal reduction of numerous first-person thoughts that constituted how he saw himself and had nothing to do with how others saw him. Hearing how Mother perceived and understood him made tears roll down his cheeks. Everything about it was right, unfiltered, and almost too close to what was going on inside him and entirely embodied him. That another sentient being could ever comprehend what could not be put into words was touching and a little disturbing at the same time, although he never wanted it to be any other way again.

Pain of the heart? Mother asked, and a cautious feeler of sympathy reached him.

"No, it's all right," he responded and went to her.

Hold fast to optimistic broodmother, egg-laying importance, beautiful brightness ray.

He did so. Almost simultaneously, the window flew away as if it had been removed by an invisible black hole. It disappeared into the raging inferno so rapidly that he perceived only a brief reflection before everything spun around him. They had been blown out by what little atmosphere there had been inside the escape pod and were whirling around each other. Fortunately, their arms were intertwined. He had grabbed her forearms as tightly as he could, and their legs had probably instinctively knotted together to keep from being pulled into nothingness on their own.

When he eventually got used to the unsteady horizon, to the fact that the earth kept appearing and disappearing, he concentrated on Mother's face—or rather her helmet—and following an impulse, lowered his head. He started to get cold, which was not a good sign because it meant the icy vacuum had already found a way into his suit. Mother did the same until their helmets touched.

Sad-Angry-Motherless, she transmitted. The connection was weak, but he could feel it like the tickle of the weak morning sun on his skin, a tender embrace against the loneliness that enfolded him like a soft bed.

"You hear me!" he thought with relief.

Destruction ended.

At first, he didn't understand what she was trying to tell him, but then he noticed there was no fire around her anymore, no explosions or exhaust flares. He didn't see the *Oberon* or any Click ships because the world around them was spinning too fast, but there was no flickering or flashing. There was only a fleeting blue ball that kept returning, and the infinite darkness.

"It worked," he realized, exultant.

Yes. In case of end of this life cycle, great satisfaction.

"Yes," Jason agreed with her. Then it was worth it. *"I'm cold."*

I also freeze.

"Maybe we do have a lot in common." He hoped his fatalistic sarcasm was a concept she could understand, but she merely sent a wave of earnest agreement, which was also fine with him. *"Mother, this enemy who attacked us here, you have fought them before. Above your homeworld."*

Yes. Lost battle but further invasion prevented. Nightmare elementals gone since then, but never gone, she explained, without him understanding very much of what reached him.

"Why are they coming out of the gates?"

Unclear. Stable connection to mirror world required. Reality assessors disagree on origin and function, no access possible, but no jump possibility for nightmare elementals.

"Nightmare elementals," he repeated. *"Are those the invaders? These images, they remind me of nightmare creatures. I understand that. But what are they?"*

Unclear. Reality assessors disagree.

Jason heard a distant roar that reminded him of the waves on Lagunia crashing against Atlantis's flog. It was a familiar sound that gave him a twinge of melancholy and reminded him again that there was more at stake than his emotional baggage and all the things he had taken too seriously all his life by thinking they were important. It was the little things that carried so much weight that their mere existence became something precious. At least in hindsight.

"... Localization..."

A verbal fragment penetrated his weakening power of reasoning. What had happened? Why was his hearing so bad? Where was he at?

"... you that..."

"Uh-huh," he commented languidly.

"Jason." His name pierced through the veil of his approaching unconsciousness like a harpoon through water, striking him deep into his mind.

"Who's there?" he asked, but already knew there was something familiar in the echo that passed through his helmet.

Radio! That's a radio signal!

"Jason, it's Nicholas! It's really you, by Omega!" His brother sounded excited. Why so excited?

"We'll get you, don't worry! Meyer himself is piloting the shuttle that's coming to bring you home!" Nicholas shouted. He was usually so cool and composed that Jason wondered if his brother's pain over the loss of their mother was even greater than his own, and if he had barred himself from showing any emotion to protect himself. Now, in light of what he had shared with Mother, the term Cold-hearts seemed extremely fitting for humans, especially Nicholas, though he loved him.

"*Us,*" he whispered. "You have to come for *us.*"

"We will, don't worry. Your job is to keep breathing, you hear? Don't lose consciousness. Your vitals are okay, but you have to make sure you stay awake."

"I've seen things, Nicholas."

"Tell me about them." Somewhere in the blurry darkness clouding Jason's sight, something began to glow. He wanted so much to feel Mother's presence again, the bond between them. He felt like a drug addict craving his next fix, and yet he couldn't stop thinking about it.

"The Clicks," he murmured weakly. "They're so much more than we think... *thought* they are..." He chuckled, knowing it sounded insane but was too exhausted to care. "We must not fight. No more fighting. Stop fighting."

"We'll get you back, Jason. *Both* of you."

"They're not shooting at Mother. She's a leader."

Something inside him admonished him that it hadn't been a good idea to say that, but it didn't matter anymore as the dark cloak of unconsciousness slowly but surely wrapped itself around his mind, and eyes, and the world receded into the background, far away and yet so close that he found it hard to breathe.

"Mother?" he thought, but he couldn't find the bond. He desperately searched for it, tugging at it even though it was invisible, a memory fading to a trickle of something he had once tasted in the distant past. He received no answer, as much as he longed for it, only to find there was no longer any world at all in which he could long for anything. He was alone and at the same time he was not. There was still a presence that, like him, was growing cold, so close that he had mistaken it for himself, yet he no longer possessed a presence of his own as he slipped away into the darkness.

25

"Good morning, sleepyhead."

Jason opened his eyes and saw Nicholas's grinning face. When had he last seen his brother grin? His own lips twisted into a smile in reply. He knew something was wrong, that he hadn't just awakened after going to bed the night before. Something had happened, but his memories wouldn't fall into place. At least not yet.

"Where am I?" he asked, but instead of answering, Nicholas fell upon him and smothered him with arms and clothes. He squeezed him so tightly that Jason's breath caught. "Hey, it's okay, little brother. It's okay."

Nicholas immediately didn't let go of him. He continued his intimate embrace and released half-suppressed sobs. Jason returned the embrace and wrapped his arms around his brother's strong back. While others characterized him as controlled and over precise, Jason knew that it was how Nicholas suppressed what had once defined him as a child. Social insecurity, yes, but also optimism and a desire for emotional closeness to experience what he had long lacked. Nicholas was a researcher—no an autist—and the brutal loss of his lover, Laura, did not leave him unaffected any more than the loss of the father whom he had so adored.

"It's all right, little brother," he repeated, not without emotion. "I haven't seen you this real in a long time."

Nicholas slowly broke away from Jason and wiped his eyes and cheeks with the backs of his hands to rid himself of what were surely burning tears.

"I'm just glad you're alive. For a while there, I worried you had abandoned me, left me alone in this damned universe." His brother sniffed and put on a smile.

Jason nodded appreciatively. "Cynical fatalism. You may yet become a normal member of our abysmal society after all." A thought flashed through him like lightning. No, not a thought, a memory that suddenly popped into his head and made his fingertips tingle. He sat up so fast that Nicholas backed away. *"Mother!"*

"You haven't forgotten that she—"

"No, no!" he interrupted him, shaking his head. "Not *our* mother. *Mother*—the Click who was with me. Where is she?"

"Ah, we recovered her. She's still alive. She is clearly better able to survive a vacuum than you are."

"Where is she?" Jason repeated with narrowed eyes.

"In the brig, of course. We—"

"We can't!"

"What?"

"You have to release her."

"I think that's an unnecessary risk. Since we got... *her* on board, the Clicks have ceased firing. Obviously, she's important enough to finally make the aliens come to their senses." Nicholas smiled proudly and patted him on the shoulder. "I don't know how you did it, but it worked!"

"I told you they're not our enemies! We—*What*?" He faltered when he saw the worried look on his brother's face. "I'm not crazy!"

"How about you tell me and Silly everything right now? Calmly. Then we'll go from there, okay?"

"I have to see her *now*. I'm sure she's scared."

Nicholas looked even more confused than before.

"I know this sounds crazy, but you didn't feel what I felt. The whole first contact—it's all been a huge misunderstanding, just like the attack on Harbingen and the destruction of our homeworld. They communicate very differently than we do, and—" He stopped when his brother put a hand on his chest and pushed him back into bed. Only now did he realize he was in a bed and that he was in the *Oberon*'s infirmary, identifiable by the white-paneled walls, reminiscent of a padded cell, and the many tubes and apparatuses hanging from the ceiling that were connected to his cot. Computer displays beeped and hummed away next to him.

At least I'm still alive, he thought, knowing he must have sounded crazy with his tumbling words and feverish eyes. The urge to rush to Mother's aid was almost overwhelming. But why? Was it closeness to her that the bond of telepathy had established after only a short time, as if they had known each other forever, sharing their sensations and thoughts in ways Jason had never thought possible? Or was it the idea of being in her shoes, locked up with the human enemy without the only person who could save her because he could vouch for her?

Probably both.

"I have to see her," he repeated more sedately, but no less emphatically.

"As soon as you're released. I promise," Nicholas assured him.

"And when will I be released?"

"Right after we talk."

"All right, then. Is there anything else—"

"You were exposed to a vacuum for eight minutes," his brother explained, and all the joy and relief on his face gradually gave way to his old, stony countenance, which made Jason tense intuitively.

"Why are you looking like I have Dunkelheimer lice?"

"Your suit made sure you didn't die after two minutes, but it wasn't designed for the vacuum of space. Not that I know what the thing was supposed to be for exactly, but you suffered some serious physical damage—"

"Out with it!" he urged Nicholas. His brother took a deep breath and nodded.

"The capillaries in your lungs have burst and an aneurysm in your brain has formed and detached. In addition, there is severe arterial damage in both arms and—"

"Stop right there." Jason swallowed and took it all in, but it didn't shock him as much as it should have judging by the look on his brother's face. He needed to end this war, and he needed to end it as soon as possible. "I feel great, I don't know how you did it, but I'm still alive and can move everything"—he wiggled his fingers and toes—"and we're talking. So, what's the problem? I guess the old girl's infirmary isn't so badly equipped after all."

"Yes, it is," Nicholas objected, waving to a Marine in a black uniform standing by the door that Jason noticed for the first time. The door opened and Baker walked in. His height and width barely fit through the steel frame. In the right corner of the mutant's mouth hung his signature cigar butt.

"I told you it's against regulations—" Nicholas began disapprovingly, but Baker dismissed him with a gesture of his right paw and grinned at Jason.

"Looking rosy-cheeked again, kid," the giant boomed in a deep bass. "You were as pale as a cold schnitzel yesterday."

"Baker." Jason smiled delightedly and held out a fist to him, as was customary among mutants. When their fingers touched, he felt like a toddler, his hand was so tiny. "Took a time out."

"'Took a break from dying, you might say," Baker mumbled, taking a drag on his cigar, which lit up like the red alarm light in Jason's old cabin.

"How did you guys do it?"

"Your Fleet guys here were nice enough to bring us aboard instead of blasting us. You Harbinger bastards aren't as bad as they always say in the Sol system." Baker winked at Nicholas, who sat in emphatic silence on the edge of Jason's bed and nodded gravely, with a hint of gratitude.

Why is he grateful? The idea confused Jason.

"Thank you for visiting. I'm obviously much better now." Jason smiled at the mutant and then looked at his brother. "So, now we could—"

"Not so fast, kid. I already told these children that our

prisoner isn't so bad, and she'll be fine. After all, she's survived the last thirty-six hours without you."

"Wait a minute, thirty-six hours?" Jason asked in horror and looked reproachfully at his brother.

"Yes. You didn't miss very much, though, except for von Solheim completely freaking out and assuring Silly that she'll definitely swing for it now. The Clicks are still there, but they're not blockading Terra as tightly as they were before, although it doesn't make any difference since we don't have anything left that can fly. Now they're all in our immediate vicinity, nearly one thousand ships, all bearing down on us and able to melt us into hot gas compounds at any moment. But they haven't. They're doing absolutely nothing except sending us their clicking jamming signals for all they're worth."

"I'll make this short and sweet," Baker's rumbling voice interjected. "They were able to keep you in a coma here, but they couldn't save some of your organs, so my guys had to step forward. You've got a new set of lungs—ones with a triple air filter and hyperosmotic membranes, so at least you can breathe almost any shit as long as there's oxygen and nitrogen in any appreciable quantity. We also had to install stimulus reflex lines and cortical stimulators, or you'd be a pile of drooling yogurt right now. Is that still how you say it?"

Nicholas shook his head. Baker shrugged his mighty shoulders.

"What? You put implants in me?" Jason asked in horror. "But that's illegal!"

"Oh, what difference does it make now?" The mutant waved dismissively. "Your people have been getting them for a long time! The best shit we have is Harbinger-made. You should be glad that you're not such a weakling anymore. Well, still pretty weak, but not as weak as before. Sort of like an Egyptian army ant that's no longer a Southern California leaf cutter—"

"Okay, okay, got it." Jason wasn't sure what to think about this. Something in his body was no longer himself. The reflex to complain about blatantly breaking civilian and Fleet laws bothered him because he had been trained at the Academy. But he figured he could deal with it since there might be no going back to the regular fleet now, if it even existed anymore. The feeling of alienation from his own body, however, was something else entirely. Aloud, he said hesitantly, "Thanks anyway."

He looked not only at Baker, but at Nicholas, who must not have found it difficult to make the decision for him.

"It was the right thing to do," he assured him, and his brother nodded gratefully with relief. "I'll get used to it somehow. Anyway, I don't feel particularly different than before."

"That's the spirit," Baker said with a grin.

"I'd like to go see Mother now," Jason said.

"First we have to talk to Silly."

"But I don't want to talk to—"

"Yes, you do," Nicholas interrupted him seriously. "You have your differences, I know that, but she's still the commander of this ship and doing a damned fine job so far considering the circumstances. Whether you like each other or not, it's primarily thanks to *her* that you're still alive and not getting shot at right now. You can imagine how difficult it was for her to trust your short radio message and bet everything on one card. On *your* card. For your sake, she committed the *Oberon*, violated the battle plan, and risked her own neck by throwing away her only chance at a pardon from the admiral and the Fleet for her Silly Maneuver."

"Surely, she did that because you begged her to," Jason growled.

"I talked her into it, yes," Nicholas admitted, his gaze unyielding. "But does that make a difference?"

"No," he finally admitted and sighed. He didn't know if he would have done the same for Silly, no matter who was trying to persuade him. "I guess not." He expelled a long breath. "All right, then, let's go see her. I'll tell you all about what happened. Then we'll go to Mother. Promise?"

"Promise." Nicholas nodded and looked at Baker. "Thank you again for your *surgical help*."

When Jason had finished, Silly silently looked at him for a while, chewing pensively on her lower lip. He was beginning to wonder whether she had suffered a short circuit in her brain when she took a deep breath and slowly nodded.

"I'll be honest with you, Jason. Part of me hates you for trying to ruin your father's life and cause him grief." Her eyes grew moist. "I loved him like the father I never had. Some people don't really appreciate their closest relatives, and it made me angry the way you just slapped away a gift fate handed to you while it constantly slapped me around until I met Konrad." He was about to say something, but she raised a hand and shook her head. "I am fully aware that

336

this is a projection and you are not to blame. Konrad once said to me: 'Silly, a family is the coziest straitjacket in the world.' Today, I understand what he meant by that. I don't hate you—I never have. In my eyes you were a disrespectful, ungrateful lout, and probably still are today, but there's one thing you're not, although I always accused you of it, and that's selfish. I realized that when I observed how you took care of the refugees and recruits we didn't have enough time for and not enough heart. The fact that you stayed behind on Earth for these mutants because you couldn't keep your word was merely the final proof that I've been wrong about you."

"I don't hate you either, Silly. I just think you're a worrying, impulsive ascetic who doesn't enjoy life." Jason grinned to soften the angry red blush suffusing her cheeks before adding, "But I'll say this: you're a damn good commander, even if it's hard for me to admit it." He swallowed and took a deep breath. "My father would be proud of you, I'm sure."

To his surprise, Silly did something he hadn't even known she was capable of, she began to cry. She didn't sob or convulse. Her eyes merely filled with tears that ran down her cheek.

"Thank you," she said, and there was more meaning in that one word than he would have thought possible. It hit him like a blow.

Silly cleared her throat and nodded. "I believe you. That's what I was going to say. I won't hide the fact that this all sounds completely absurd and crazy, but I believe you. I do. I have no idea what to do with this fact, but I believe you. The fleet admiral is sending me angry radio messages every half hour for me to turn myself in so he can put a noose around my neck, and he's starting to get on my nerves so much that I'm tempted to do it myself."

"Did she just make a joke?" Jason asked Nicholas. His brother merely raised his hands as if to say "I'm as amazed as you are."

The commander didn't seem to notice their exchange or else deliberately ignored it.

"The Clicks have us in a headlock but they're not squeezing yet. That's another sign you must be telling the truth, and also that you were not under any hallucination or alien influence. We have been discussing this for some time now, I must admit, but the Clicks have everything in hand, and we have nothing. Yet none of us could think of a single reason why they shouldn't put an end to us once and for all, now that they can."

"I'm not crazy!" Jason objected before he realized that she hadn't claimed that at all. "Although I have to admit that it felt that way, and I'm a little afraid that it might be crazy after all."

"What if it's a ruse?" Nicholas wondered.

They were in Silly's cabin. She still hadn't moved into Konrad's empty captain's quarters, and probably never would.

"A ruse? What kind of ruse?"

"The way you told it, that 'Mother' was the last of her kind on the shuttle, alone with you, the mutants, and that..." Nicholas's gaze hardened, *"murderer."*

"I know, I've thought of that, too," Jason admitted candidly. "But I know that's not the case."

"Why? Because of that connection you told me about?" Silly wanted to know.

"Yes. It sounds crazy, but I *know* what she thinks—or thought. I know what she *felt*. Nothing can be concealed in that connection. In fact, I would assume the Clicks don't even know the concept of a lie. It should be completely foreign to them because, in the telepathic bond I experienced, everything is out in the open. Your entire inner network of thoughts and emotions is completely exposed, free for anyone to explore." Jason saw Nicholas's eyes widen in shock, and Silly looked as if he had told them about the sixth circle of hell. He felt compelled to clarify what he was saying. "This may sound horrible to you because you're afraid of sharing your inner demons, I understand that. But it's not like that. Not at all. Don't think of it as voyeurism, think of it as an accepting embrace. Once you see the totality of what a being thinks and feels, the *why* becomes self-evident, and what remains are no longer mere fragments of actions that we interpret through the lens of our character, experiences, and upbringing, brutally reducing and twisting them in the process. No, what remains is compassion and understanding, an unprecedented closeness."

"That sounds as scary as it does desirable," Silly mused. "And I really hope you're right that the Clicks may not know how to lie. If you can always read your counterpart's intentions like an open book, that would even make sense. Then there would only be one species among two parties that could maintain a social system based on lies and deception for their own advantage. A better basis for communication, after all."

"Very misanthropic," Nicholas said but nodded. "Now all we need is a bright idea about how to deal with a thousand alien ships that have their guns trained on us."

"No, we need much more than that, we need an idea about how to end this war," Jason said firmly. "It's based on a misunderstanding. They fired first, yes, but only because they thought we were about to make a colossal blunder that was going to cost all of us a lot."

"I don't know how we were going to convince humanity of *that* after seventy years of war and millions of deaths."

Silly sighed and leaned back in her chair.

"Well, one step at a time."

26

Jason inhaled deeply and tried to suppress the nausea that had risen into his throat and formed a dense lump. The unarmed shuttle, formerly his father's ceremonial vessel, was a sharpened torus with four massive high-performance engines that would have been the 20th-century equivalent of a muscle car with tinted windows. His father had almost never used it unless ceremony required it and tolerated no deviation, however much he had enjoyed liberties with his rank. Now the *Diligence* had become the only choice they had since it was unarmed. It didn't even have a communications laser that could be overloaded enough to burn through a tin can.

Next to him, in the copilot's lavish, sprawling armchair, sat Mother. Her legs were intricately crossed, forming a tangled knot. It was easy to see that the seat had not been built for Click anatomy, and yet she somehow managed to sit gracefully and rest her arms, imperious and relaxed, on the backrests. Her long fingers moved lightly up and down as if in rhythm with a silent melody.

Behind them sat twelve senior officers, carefully selected according to their branch of service. They were trusted representatives of their respective service badges, and their words carried weight among their comrades. It had been difficult for Silly to agree to his proposal and determine the emissaries by a brief democratic procedure, one that could set a dangerous precedent on a ship, and yet it was the only way to sway the crew ranks to go along with an outcome that went against everything they had ever learned and believed. Should they succeed in this venture, they needed to ensure that no one believed it to be a hoax, like cake that somehow tasted stale because "those people up there" had baked it. Silly and Nicholas had known him since childhood, and even for them to believe half of what he had reported had amounted to crossing a line.

Humans and aliens knew nothing but war. Mutual hatred developed naturally, beginning with their kindergarten play and continuing through school curricula that left no doubt about what their common goal was as a society: to survive. And that was only possible if they united to destroy the external threat. It was an attitude that had always made sense to Jason, and he had never questioned it. All too vivid were memories of the fragments of the moon Kor that had turned his world, his home, into a devastated wasteland where superstorms and radiation anomalies alternated, transforming a once-beautiful blue planet into a hostile hell and a mass grave. Jason had to admit to himself that he also found it difficult to see past this.

"Mother," he thought, and compassion reached for him like an invisible hand.

Outside the sleekly shaped window, the flagship of the

Click fleet grew ever closer. It was a long flight, nearly an hour. Although they had only a few thousand kilometers to cover, they wanted to make sure they were not perceived as a danger, so they did not take any chances. The enemy—no, the *Clicks*—had enough time to scan their vessel from every angle and confirm that they were unarmed. So far. After all, they had been on the move for thirty minutes and the weapons remained silent, which he took as a good sign.

Jason, she replied in a mental image of his sense of self that loomed over him like a bell and felt as if it embodied his essential being. **You are distressed.**

"I had to think of my homeworld. Almost a billion people died that day. Most of them burned to death. Only twenty million survived because my father made a momentous decision."

Blue technology world of Coldhearts. Mother's image of Harbingen reminded him of something beautiful that had been locked in a macabre cage. **The goal of our fleet was destruction of research on gates in mirror world. Our reconnaissance reported identification of several centers on the moon Kor. Its destruction was not the desired result of the plan. It surprised reality assessors. Contrary to planning.**

"Reality assessors. Their scientists," Jason translated to himself. The exchange grew steadily easier as he got used to it and incorporated the alien communication into his own symbolic interactionism, an increasingly smooth process, though it still made his head spin.

Scientists. Knowledge collector. Yes. Accurate. Identify reality, assess it for connections and laws, create continuity. Expel mysticism.

"Your scientists did not expect the moon to break up."

Correct assumption. Agreement. Yes. Water folk of warm depths fight for survival against Coldhearts. But water folk of warm depths do not destroy breeding places.

"Kor was hollowed out, riddled with industrial plants and heat pumps," Jason explained. *"Some hits damaged the antimatter containment chambers in the depths and ensured its destruction."*

Antimatter.

"A dangerous technology."

Agreement. Yes.

"You said that breeding places are precious. Can you explain that to me? Attacking a population center is considered unethical, even by us. Civilian casualties are to be avoided, current doctrine, and humans of past centuries after World War II on Terra have all affirmed that only military targets are to be attacked. Nevertheless, it has happened time and time again, as morality has often taken a back seat to strategic goals."

Inconsistent.

"Yes," he thought and sighed. *"That seems to be one of the things about our species. Contradictions."*

Breeding places are destroyed, Mother replied to his surprise, and Jason had to swallow as he received the images of boiling oceans and submarines using microwave emitters to burst whole colonies of eggs that lay like a rash on the ocean floor. His human self was disgusted by it and perceived it as a danger, but in Mother's transmission, he saw only the future, something worth protecting... for someone else. **After taking over a breeding place, the**

breeding world is claimed, and all unhatched offspring are destroyed to banish their DNA from the world's cycle and allow new broodmothers to pass on their evolutionary heritage. Perceiving his sense of horror, she added with some puzzlement, **No moral problem.**

"We call that genocide." Jason felt like someone who had just learned that the new dog he had been given would bite after petting it for a while and thinking it good-natured. *"The eradication of a people."*

No eradication, she objected, and only now did he notice that her complex sensations and thought constructs were becoming more practiced and automatic in his mind. They formed into sentences that his mind created as if he were grasping the rules of a newly learned game without having to think about them. **Inferior brood loses its offspring, already hatched young are integrated into the swarm and welcomed.**

"Is there no rebellion then? No civil war?"

Mother took a while to digest the concept behind civil war and grasp it, which effectively answered his questions.

No, she transmitted anyway. **Normal process. New broodmothers responsible for totality of the swarm and its welfare.**

An idea occurred to Jason. *"How many swarms are there?"*

Two and a half twelve-units.

"Thirty. As many as there are planets inhabited by you." He nodded his understanding. There were clearly fewer worlds with extensive oceans than rocky planets with ice, which still served the Federation as acceptable marginal

worlds on which the construction of habitats was worth-while. *"So, always one swarm per planet."*

Agreement. Brood needs space. Fewer conflicts. Swarms accept this.

"And how do conflicts arise?"

Finding new colony world. Swarms decide which of them is the strongest and has the greatest probability of survival.

"War," he translated. *"You wage war and the swarm, the brood that wins, gets the new world and creates a new swarm?"*

Yes. Agreement. New swarm emerges after colonization.

"But what does the old one get out of it?" he asked, curious. The concept seemed extremely foreign to him, although he felt it through her perspective. On second thought, it did not surprise him that they were at war, otherwise they would not have had warships. Was the fight for survival and advantages for their own survival a law of nature? A kind of framework for evolution, in which war *had* to take place?

Passing on DNA, enabling life for unhatched eggs. Great importance and meaningfulness. Fulfillment for broodmothers.

"I don't sense any hatred in you for the other swarms. Why not?"

Incomprehension.

"When we wage war it is for survival. We hate our enemy and do everything to destroy them. They are the enemy." Putting it that way, with complete candor, had a shocking effect on Jason because he could not hide

346

anything he thought. He therefore remembered war, devoid of the euphemisms he surely used in conversation with other people., because that's what one did.

No hatred, Mother responded. **Conflict serves the water people of warm depths. Eradication of warrior males in this consciousness necessary. No feelings of hatred or rejection.**

"But you are familiar with the feeling of hate," he remarked. *"So, you must know it, must have felt it and experienced it."*

Agreement. Yes. Hatred of predators that eat or steal eggs. Frustration, anger over natural disasters. Volcanoes, earthquakes, landslides that kill unhatched brood.

"Do you also hate us humans?" Jason asked the question that most concerned him. So far, he had received no such sentiments from their side, and yet he wondered how they viewed this war. A Federation fleet, despite any doctrine or ethical protestations, surely could not have resisted bombarding the Clicks' homeworld and wiping them all out.

Coldhearts have destroyed Brood-Moon-Bright-Silver-Streak Under-Stars. Unhatched brood over two million of young broodmother who won colony battle. Great defeat. Grief-disappointment. But Coldhearts don't use Bright-Silver-Streak Under-Stars for own brood rearing. Leave world again after their bombs contaminate waters. Mother paused briefly, and their connection subsided to mere bodily sensations. Jason always perceived these as so alien that it made him feel vaguely seasick.

I wonder if it's the same for her, the other way around, he thought to himself.

Optimistic broodmother, egg-laying importance, beautiful brightness ray felt hatred for Coldhearts at that time.

"That's very specific," he remarked, trying to understand how it was possible to hate situationally and then let the feeling drift away like a passing cloud.

To him, it looked like the Clicks were fighting this war out of necessity, ironically, just like the Federation. So, the reason was the same, but the way of thinking about the conflict seemed to be fundamentally different. While the necessity had stimulated hatred and distrust among humans, which increased the longer the conflict lasted, the fundamental motivation for the Clicks had not changed at all. War was waged against humans in order to not be wiped out, that was just the way it was. It was primarily to protect the swarms and not to destroy humanity, at least not beyond eliminating the threat, especially since the Federation worlds were largely uninteresting to them because they contained too few oceans.

Of course. Reason for hatred. I sense that you have other feelings. Hate for your inseminator, love and fear at the same time. But inseminator gone into next consciousness. No longer here.

Jason tensed up inside.

Distance too short. Excuse.

"No, that's all right," he thought. She saw and witnessed everything in him as it arose and revealed itself in him. *"Yes, he is dead, but he is still alive in me."*

Coldhearts can hate those who are no longer in this cycle?

"If you mean this life, yes. We can even hate fictional characters in a film."

Persons that do not exist?

"Actors."

Explain. Images are confusing.

Jason tried to remember the last holo-movie he had seen. It was *Zarathustra*, a psychological thriller starring William Balthar, about a killer who brutally murdered several prostitutes on Dunkelheim in pursuit of his sick fascination with Jack the Ripper. Quite an entertaining flick, if somewhat predictable.

At the time, he and his comrades had been given a full day off after the ship had docked for maintenance. If his memories were not romanticized, it had been one of the most relaxing evenings in a long time.

Incomprehension. Film. The characters in the film are untruths.

"You mean liars."

Agreement. Concept of lies... Mother seemed to move this concept and knowledge back and forth within herself and her own thoughts stiffened. The result was fright and disbelief. **These actors are paid to... *lie?***

"Well, not exactly..."

But they are not who they pretend to be. Suddenly, Jason wasn't so happy that his brain was translating their transmissions more and more precisely. Discomfort spread through him. **They pretend to be other Coldheart.**

"Yes, basically they are professional liars," he finally admitted, now confused himself.

349

And in these films, they torture and kill others of your kind and you and your brood brothers and sisters watch them do it and call it *Entertainment***? To reduce tension?** Now Mother seemed fully confused and repulsed at the same time, and her feelings became his own.

"When you put it that way, it seems rather absurd," he thought, unable to separate her disgust from his own.

Confusing. My thoughts would not calm down if I had to watch others of the water people of warm depths being murdered by mine. I would be frightened or angry.

"So are we. We are afraid of the killer. Well, at least something like that. We are afraid of what else he might do, and we worry about his victims. We hope that they will somehow survive. Not knowing is the reason for the tension."

Incomprehension. Films are not for relaxation?

"Yes, they are, but..."

But you felt tension.

"Yes, but... I don't know either. It confuses me when I think about it like that. I honestly never gave it much thought. It's probably an archaic evolutionary drive for us to fear, to worry, to empathize. There are other films, too. Love stories, for example."

Comprehend. That is about fertilization? Oh. Mating. Common mode of reproduction in mammals.

Jason managed not to blush as his thoughts of sex automatically flowed through their bond and Mother absorbed and processed them as if she were reading an encyclopedia. No feeling of shame came back to him.

Discomfort?

"No, it's okay. Yes, love films are about mating, but not

merely in the sense of procreation. They are about love."

Love. Something like brood protection.

Jason processed what she felt when she thought of her brood. It was an impersonal feeling, yet just as encompassing and fulfilling as what he understood love to be for another person, like his brother Nicholas. Or his mother.

"Yes, we have the same concept."

And in the love films, the liars are looking for love. Is that also an untruth?

"Sometimes. Often it is about the fact that one of the lovers thinks the other is cheating on him or that his feelings are not real."

That is painful. Emotional pain. Mother thought of her hatched young not recognizing her specific gill vibrations and becoming estranged from her, a thought that caused deep sadness in her.

"Yes, very much. That's why we hope the truth will come out in the end, and they'll come together after all. Well, at least women, who are more likely to watch such films, compared to us men."

But you do not want to see how all is well.

"No, we do. In the end, everything is usually fine, they have found each other and get married."

Marriage. Mating covenant. Your thoughts are confusing.

"It is a contract to stay together to reaffirm one's love."

As a bureaucratic act.

"Yes. Spouses want security, I guess. I've never been married. But they promise each other to stay together and be there for each other. That's generally considered romantic."

Romance. Now Mother seemed to reach the limit of

her power of imagination. **This is like sharing beauty. Of a brightness ray at the end of a planetary rotation period. With subsequent mating.**

"That might have been my own definition," he thought and swallowed. Now his cheeks were certainly red.

Comprehension. If this is the desired state of the two lying lovers, why does the film not begin with them entering into the bond-covenant for legally guaranteed romance? That would cause joy, would it? Not Relaxation? Mother wanted to know.

"No, that would be boring."

Incomprehension.

"We want it to be uncertain whether it will end well. He has to fight for her and she for him."

Fight. I thought love? Where is the connection between love and fighting?

"I think we only really value things when we have fought for them," Jason replied and sighed. Their conversation was not going at all as he had hoped. If their flight lasted any longer, he would surely doubt himself and all humanity. *"We are a strange species, I admit."*

Strange, she agreed with him. **Fascinating. Fighting is important for you.**

"Actually, we want peace. Everyone longs for it."

But I saw 'divorce' in your thoughts. The *dissolution* of a bond-covenant. Grief, loss.

"Yes, we tend not to value things for a long time."

Drama. You long for drama.

"Not exactly. Actually, we would like to have peace."

But the love films in your memory all end with the couple finding each other and getting married. Why

do these movies not go further and show the happiness shared by the paid liars? Incomprehension.

"No one cares about that because we like to believe that they live happily ever after. This is even a common closing phrase of love stories: 'They lived happily ever after.'"

But that is improbable.

"Yes, they usually come into conflict at some point, or fall in love again because someone is younger, has more money, is better looking, or doesn't get on his or her nerves with his or her idiosyncrasies." At least Jason knew a little bit about that, because he knew exactly why he had never gotten married.

Addiction to conflict.

"More or less, I think."

The bond-covenant is also made in a *church*. What is that? Your thoughts on this are fleeting, the concept is not consistent.

"Religion? Oh, Jesus..."

Discomfort?

"Yes. No. I mean, it probably won't be any easier." Jason stared at the displays in front of him and almost begged the chronometer to make the minutes go by faster.

Can you explain this to me? Mother's sincere request was difficult to refuse because her curiosity was honest and imbued with deep fascination.

"I can explain mine to you. Well, at least the one I officially belong to. My homeworld, which you destroyed, was equal parts Catholic and Protestant."

Where is the distinction?

"At Omega," thought Jason.

Omega?

27

So, this *Jesus* was the son of a fictitious omnipotent being who had no wife? Then how did he mate and father a son?

"He did not directly conceive him, but an earthly woman carried him to term. 'Immaculate conception' is what we call this."

'Mary.'

"Yes."

And she gave birth to this Jesus but did not perform a mating act. How is that possible?

"Well..."

And why has the omnipotent being never given birth to another son? And why not a daughter? Why is an omnipotent being reduced to one sex?

"He is not. God is everything, including you and me. At least we believe that."

But you are thinking of a male being.

"Yes, that occurs automatically because 'God' as a word in

its original languages has the masculine article and we call him the 'Father.'"

Wouldn't 'it' have to be sexless, like the cosmos it supposedly created?

"I guess so, but..." Jason rubbed his face. *"I'm really not a theologian. This was all written almost three millennia ago."*

By males, Mother repeated his thoughts. **Fascination. I would like to know more about it.**

"Sir?" one of the officers behind him called. Until then he had been standing there in tense silence.

"Yes?" Jason asked immediately, grateful for the interruption.

"Something's happening."

He saw it himself. The radar screen showed several objects that had broken away from a single Click warship and were flying toward them in a looping semicircle. Flying toward them *fast*.

"We've got company," he said and was about to activate the sensor sweep as if on automatic before he stopped and forced himself to keep his feet still. If the aliens wanted to blast them away, they would have done it long ago and could do it now at any time, should they feel like it. An active sensor sweep, on the other hand, could be seen as an aggressive act in this tense situation.

"Mother," he thought. *"Can you send your sounds?"*

Spatial orientation sounds. Mine will know I'm on board, but it is not meaningful communication, she reminded him.

"I know, but at least they'll know for sure you're on board. Anything that can help us is useful."

Your radio waves should be sufficient, but the

signal will be weak. Our ships use sufficient signal boosters.

Jason set the radio to the frequencies she had specified and then signaled to her. Mother leaned forward slightly in her seat and made the typical clicking sounds that gave the Clicks their name.

He shuddered, thinking back to the many nights in his bunk as a junior lieutenant when he had been unable to sleep and had heard recordings of the Click signals as if they could tell him why he was going to war. Back then, the fear of flying through space in a tin can filled with air and being attacked and perhaps destroyed at any moment, losing everything in a matter of minutes, had all been new. The alien sounds were so strange and, at the same time, scary that they had hardly let him fall asleep, and that was precisely why he listened to them. With sleep had come the nightmares, the fears of young men going to war who had not yet experienced what it really meant. Then, when the dying began, everything was very different, purer, rawer, more horrible, yet in a strange way also more grounded than all the bad things his imagination had conjured.

He wondered if it would be the same this time. Mother's sounds were still strange, but no longer as eerie because he knew who created them. She was not the unknown entity hidden behind dark armor he had taken her for, a being identifiable only by blurry and distorted images, an entity he was convinced was malevolent and had caused this war by destroying a peaceful Federation prospector ship for no reason. She was no heartless robot.

Now, behind the armor, he saw the filigree water creature whose limbs seemed almost ethereal with colors that shimmered behind its translucent scalp and flashed in fire-works of lightning. He saw the emotions and complex sensations and thoughts that composed it and gave Mother a "face" that was so much more than any conventional interpersonal relationship. The closest thing to compare with a telepathic exchange triggered by closeness was the bond between family members, mother and child.

Jason thought he could still hear Mother's transmission, only to find that the clicking sounds were coming from the speaker above the consoles and sounded different. More varied, intense and somehow *demanding*.

"Mother?" he asked in his thoughts.

They explore us, measure distance and texture.

"Do you mean they are scanning us?"

Yes.

"Is that good or bad?"

It is normal.

"At least they're not shooting at us."

They will not. Broodmother is too important.

"Your swarm, it is part of this force, isn't it?"

Largest part of the force is my swarm.

"Then why did they let you fly unprotected into the Pacific Ocean?"

My decision. 'Terra' safe, has no offensive capacities. I had to supervise transformation activities myself, as I have the mental capacities for this far-reaching task. Warrior males do not.

"Conversion," he repeated thoughtfully, to distract himself from the flurry of clicks booming from the speakers, which had a driving and sinister feel about them that

pushed his already high adrenaline levels even higher. *"You mean, cleaning the toxic water?"*

Yes. Raising pH—Jason was happy to know the equivalent of what she thought—**creating habitat for transform algae. Oxygen producers. Reducing CO_2 in the atmosphere, favoring settlement of base builders and building a basic ecosystem. The process is complex.**

"Oh," Jason responded as he saw changes in her thoughts that were so complex with their confusing processes in the ocean. She seemed to comprehend them simultaneously side by side with all their sensory impressions and chemical processes, a whole cosmos of tiny processes, contributing to the big picture. *"A shuttle and several fighters."*

Yes. They circle us to make sure it's not a trap.

~

It soon turned out that the Clicks were apparently convinced they were not walking into a trap because after ten minutes the enemy shuttle docked at their rear airlock.

Not 'enemy,' he admonished himself, but the habit of over three decades was hard to put aside. *Hopefully no longer enemies.*

It took the aliens another ten minutes to adjust the connector rings so the airlocks worked and sealed in both directions. The senior officers in the cabin of the *Diligence* became visibly tense, nervously straightening their uniforms like cadets on their first day at the Academy. They were relieved when Jason and Mother moved aft to stand directly in front of the hatch. Their gazes were fixed on the Click, following her as if they were glued to her armor. He saw they were uncomfortable, uncertain, and perhaps there was a glimmer of suppressed fear in their eyes. But next to all the confusion and emotional turmoil that must be going on inside them, there was apparently no room for hatred. Perhaps it was because the aliens had so far been perceived more as a natural disaster in the minds of the military, a faceless problem that caused deaths and injuries, against which one fought as best one could. Wars among humans worked differently. One hated the enemy's ideology, their looks, their political views, and maybe the cultural differences that just made them *different*. People were amazingly creative in rejecting differences and going to war because of it.

But they hadn't known anything about the Clicks. They were simply there and had to be destroyed in order not to die themselves.

Maybe, he thought, *this really has a chance.*

You worry, Mother remarked, sending a wave of goodwill and inner strength through their telepathic bond that wrapped around him like a warm cloak.

"Yes," he admitted. There was nothing to hide in this connection anyway, and he slowly got used to feeling like an open book that could be leafed through at will. There was something reassuring in that. *"This is important. It's big. It is confusing."*

It is unfamiliar.

"Yes, unfamiliar. Part of me still thinks it's wrong not to have a gun in my hand."

We will need to learn.

"You are the most important leader of this fleet, aren't you? Because your swarm provides the most ships in it?"

Yes. My brood has claimed Terra after winning an elimination battle.

"Then this should be easy, right?"

No, not easy. Other broodmothers are gathered and several highest-ranking pollinators. They will not be pleased to possibly give up an ocean world that is badly damaged but can be saved. Habitat is very precious to us.

"That doesn't sound very optimistic."

I am optimistic broodmother, egg-laying importance, beautiful brightness ray. She sent the complex meaning pattern of her sense of self and outshone his worries.

"We'll do it," he thought. He turned to his people. "When this hatch opens, I want you to have your breathing masks ready. Double-check your oxygen supplies and vitals monitors. What we're about to do here could mean the end of an endless war, but it will require discipline and foresight. Question each of your inner stirrings to see if they arise out of habit and which of your intentions might have an unintended consequence. We are here for *peace*. Remember that at every second and suborn your thoughts and feelings to that one concept. Understood?"

The senior officers nodded silently.

The airlock opened and opposite them stood two heavily armored Clicks. Their unusually beefy suits were like those worn by the drop troopers who had engaged in a fierce skirmish with Baker's mutants. The fact that the mutants had not been able to reduce them to mincemeat without some effort strongly suggested that they should not be underestimated.

As soon as the alien soldiers recognized the broodmother, they quickly lowered their laser rifles and imperceptibly adjusted the position of their feet. Jason believed it meant something, perhaps a nuance in their body language. Maybe it was a big deal, he simply didn't know. Even Mother's appearance and body language was so alien to him that without their telepathic bond he would have felt as if he were trapped in a xenologist's nightmare.

Clicking sounds were audible once the hatch opened, and they became more intense. He dared not move until Mother restored their bond. How she did it was a mystery to him, after all, he did not know how to speak to, or rather, *think* to, her. Possibly, he lacked a corresponding organ or simply the practice, the intuitive knowledge.

We will follow these warrior males. They are subject to me.

"That's good," he replied with relief. That would make things much easier.

Not necessarily, she said, immediately quelling his timid optimism. **In this matter, the other broodmothers have agreed with their commanding inseminators to exercise caution. My authority is not null and void, but it is limited until it is ensured that I am not subject to any foreign chemical or telepathic influence.**

Jason nodded, proud of his ability to translate her complex thoughts fluently into approximate human explanations he could understand. She interpreted the gesture correctly.

There are forms of telepathic corruption that we greatly fear. The great darkness of the mind is the worst fate in the imagination of the water people of warm depths. It drove many of us mad when we made the first jumps through the mirror world.

"Transit sleep." He thought of the pictures of coma patients from history class that made him shudder every time. Their faces were always distorted as if they were caught in a nightmare, and their eyes were as empty as the darkness between the stars, except that something still seemed to gleam out of them.

Disturbing. Fear. Fright. Mother's emotional reactions were so numerous and impressive that they threatened to overwhelm him, and his temples began to throb in protest. **The mirror world. It annihilates consciousness. Cruel.**

"Yes."

Now we follow the males. They will lead us to a secured facility where you and yours will be immersed in wellbeing tanks. Possibility of communication and analysis of your bodies.

Jason became uncomfortable at the thought, even though what she perceived as a wellbeing tank—warm, breathable for her, and as normal an environment as a nitrogen-rich oxygen atmosphere was for humans—was something he knew himself. The sensation of floating naked and feeling defenseless had been hard to bear, but he had still been in control because he had known Baker and the mutants were there, not hundreds of Clicks analyzing him.

No danger for you, Mother assured him. **If you are in danger, then only if I am too.**

"You could be in danger?" Jason saw their only lifeline already swimming away.

Yes. But unlikely. Quiet now, our connection is monitored.

The Click guards searched each of them for weapons, which his people grudgingly endured. He couldn't blame them. After all, he was already demanding a lot from them by their mere, unarmed, presence. When the guards were certain no one was carrying a weapon, they were herded through the airlock like a bunch of geese and then led through the dark, turquoise-green-illuminated corridors, which still looked strange, a little lower than usual, but also a little wider. Strangely, the walls lacked contours, although he could see welding joints and hatches here and there.

"Sir?" asked an older lieutenant commander next to him.

"I'm not your superior, Holmfeld," he replied, after reading the name on the uniform of the officer looking sidelong at him. The man looked extremely controlled.

"Bradley," the other tried again, even though he appeared to have a hard time using that name. "I'm having my doubts right now about whether what we're doing here is such a good idea."

That's occurred to you just now? Jason wanted to growl, followed shortly by *You don't say, Sherlock!* But since he didn't feel like making jokes or being cynical in this environment, he said instead, "What's on your mind?"

"Soldiers."

Jason raised a brow.

"If all goes well," Holmfeld explained in a low voice, which the Clicks didn't seem to mind, if they noticed at all, "we will enter into a dialogue. One that you said will take place telepathically, and we can't hide anything. Aside from the fact that that prospect gives me the heebie-jeebies, it could lead to unforeseen problems."

"But we're looking at those problems right now, aren't we?"

The lieutenant commander screwed up his face. "All I'm saying is that we're all warriors, trained for the sole purpose of killing Clicks in the best way we can. That might be a bad basis for talking—*thinking*—about peace. We should have brought civilians whose memories aren't crammed with loss, anger, grief, and aggression."

"That's a good point," Jason murmured back, "but the Clicks we'll be talking to are also likely to be warriors, except for the broodmothers. There are a thousand warships around us. I think that, to the contrary, communication between soldiers of both species could lead to better understanding because they have experienced things similar to what we have. Their anger is our anger, their loss is our loss. A civilian will never fully understand what we feel, what it's like to be trapped on a ship and not know if the deck is going to explode in front of you and you're going to be sucked into a vacuum to die an agonizing death if you haven't been cooked by plasma first."

"Hmm," Holmfeld said and remained silent.

The Clicks led them through a huge room filled with strange contraptions that reminded Jason of oversized plastic toys. Alien soldiers stood shoulder-to-shoulder on either side of them as they went from one door to the next. Their trained laser weapons and slatted helmets followed the dozen humans, their archenemies, every step of the way. He could imagine all too well how they must feel. What would he think and feel if he hadn't met Mother and was ordered to come to the ship's hangar to keep an eye on a detachment of Clicks? The analogy was not precise, he was sure, after all, he *had* experienced Mother's feelings and thoughts as extremely different from his own. Yet they were fundamentally comparable with positive and negative memories, stimuli of pain and wellbeing, sadness and joy, and many more that always seemed similar for all conscious beings. He would have given a lot to be able to look behind their helmets and sense their thoughts. If he was honest with himself, he longed for it, longed for the warmth of the bond with Mother. Without it, he felt strangely alone in the universe, like a drop of water separated from the ocean, when he should be part of something much larger, more encompassing.

Their short journey through the alien ship ended in a fascinating room, a perfect sphere at least twenty meters in diameter. There was a bridge in the center with a bulkhead on each side. On the inner side of the sphere were many dozens of green *wellbeing* tanks that were currently empty. Unlike on Mother's shuttle, the robotic grappling arms that had stripped her of her armor were on a short railing to the right and left of the bridge, with boxlike chests set into them. Channels ran along the smooth floor like drains of a gutter, as Jason knew them from Harbingen's cities, which had always been at the mercy of abundant rains.

In the middle of the bridge, they were clearly ordered to

stop—raised laser rifles were an easily learned vocabulary in any language.

This is the habitat of our flagship. Mother reopened her link, and Jason breathed a sigh of relief as the enfolding feeling returned. **This is where the inseminators and broodmothers spend most of their time. There are two dozen wellbeing tanks.**

"That is why you insisted on twelve emissaries."

Yes. It is the logical number.

"The metric system has prevailed where I live, but I am not a mathematician."

Four of the present broodmothers—she pointed in a very human manner to four larger Clicks whose shells shimmered a similar pearlescent color to her own—**and eight commanding inseminators**—her long, outstretched finger wandered to eight smaller aliens in black tanks, which Jason could not visually distinguish from the other warriors —**will go to their respective tanks and after an intensive quantum diffusion analysis will make contact.**

"Quantum diffusion? Isn't that only possible at extremely low temperatures?" he thought, but Mother didn't seem willing to go into this.

This process may require a little more time.

"Can we wait here in the meantime and talk more with each other?" Jason felt shame rising within him at his child-like longing for closeness and sharing that were stirring within him. But a wave of understanding and self-interested fascination quickly drove the negative feeling away.

Exchange, she agreed, and her V-shaped helmet tilted slightly.

Jason's eyes grew wide as he watched the robotic arms

rapidly disrobe the twelve Click leaders. Water and nutrient fluids poured out of the suits as soon as the first seals hissed open, and flowed toward the floor gutters. The slender bodies that emerged crawled onto the railing like a combination of octopuses and insects and nimbly pushed themselves off. Then they began to float and fly toward the tanks.

"Weightlessness. There is a zero-G field here!" He blurted the thoughts with a surge of amazement.

Yes.

After an urgent wave from him, his comrades disrobed, at first reluctantly and visibly filled with shame and discomfort, before climbing unsteadily onto the railing and flying toward their tanks.

Now we wait.

"Wait for an end to the war?"

So, we hope. This could be a first step.

28

"I don't have a good feeling about this," Nicholas muttered as their shuttle made a long sweeping turn along the approach vector marked in the HUD toward the docking bay of the sky fortress. The space station's mighty starscrapers poked out of its massive hull like the spines of a particularly invulnerable hedgehog. Defense domes with their sleek railgun barrels and dark launch pads formed an ugly rash on the underside. There, the Earth-facing portion of the orbital elevator stretched like a fishing line through the bands of clouds below.

Jason was fascinated by the sight, and he tried to memorize every little detail to share with Mother later. Her optosensory perception was so distinctly different from his that his visual perception fascinated her every time as much as hers fascinated him. Her eyes were more color sensitive, probably due to their origin in deep water, and shaped to compensate for the lensing effect of water. This meant that without the filter systems in her helmet, everything she perceived was far too bright and intense with a fisheye effect that greatly distorted things.

Now, she was sitting behind him in the passenger compartment, together with "mighty warrior, octopus-devourer, wise authority," one of the most important inseminators in the Click fleet, one who enjoyed great respect among the broodmothers. He had already impregnated two of them, ensuring a multitude of offspring for their species with a favorable gene profile. Jason had connected with him only briefly, but the half hour had been enough to surprise him. He had expected a fierce spirit, which, corresponding to a warrior, was darker, more determined, and also more aggressive than that of Mother. But what had come to him from the mind of Inseminator—he had shortened the Click's name to avoid always having the image in his head of how he had killed one of the strange giant squids; he could not think of a better comparison to the strange, tentacled monster—resembled more the emotions of a sober-minded samurai.

Inseminator was extremely deliberate, concerned about the welfare of his subordinate warrior males, and quick-witted. In his spare time, he was interested in the polyphonic bubbling sounds of small rainbow fish—what Jason called the sticklebacks the Click was always thinking about. Jason recognized their complex melodies of life and found them fascinating. To hear and *feel* them through the mind of such a boundless, conscious aquatic being was an experience Inseminator was happy to share with him. He did not know whether it was because Inseminator sensed how touched Jason was by the Click's hobby, or because they were two warriors who had not wasted their boundless exchange of ideas on boasts or signs of strength. Whatever the reason, Inseminator eventually agreed to the plan Jason and Mother had come up with and to the twelve senior officers selected from the *Oberon*.

He was sitting at the very back of the shuttle next to Mother and Jason. Silly and Nicholas were in the cockpit, accompanied by ten Black Legion Marines and ten alien honor guards, sitting across from each other as if they were stalking one other. Nevertheless, the atmosphere was not as tense as it could have been, probably because neither detachment carried weapons. In military terms, it was pretty outrageous, but he and Mother had come up with the idea as an important sign. What could be a better symbol for beginning peace negotiations than escorts unarmed on both sides? A fact that might even unite the legionnaires and the alien soldiers when they faced the armed guards waiting in the sky fortress. For Jason, at any rate, it had been clear that no weapons in the world would have been sufficient to overpower von Solheim's men, if he were so foolish as to fire upon them. Their mutual demonstration for peace was probably more effective than a useless show of strength.

This day could become a turning point in time, and that meant they had to do things differently from what they had done so far. After all, what was the value of such a turning point if nothing changed?

"Jason?"

"Huh?" He was startled from his thoughts and then sighed, "I'm sorry. You said..."

"... that I didn't have a good feeling about this." Nicholas pointed at Silly, who was busy flying the shuttle manually. Any time a high-ranking officer had the chance to pilot a ship again with analog controls, he usually didn't pass it up.

"He'll understand," Jason assured his brother, as the sky fortress rapidly grew in the cockpit window, about to fill it completely with its gigantic dimensions. It would certainly have appeared considerably more threatening had he not known that its ammunition supplies were all but depleted and that the many thousands of soldiers inside were trapped there.

"He was pretty angry," Nicholas said.

"I've never known you to be so brooding."

"And I don't think of you as so naively optimistic."

"Hmm. I admit I got a little carried away by our conversations on the *Dark Current*," Jason said as he watched Silly steer them with surprising precision and smoothness toward the final phase of the approach vector, directly toward the circular mouth of one of the docking bays at the base of the starscraper. "It was really impressive. The zero-G chamber on their ship, the way our officers floated into the tanks. They looked like preserved corpses, but when they came back, I hardly recognized them."

"They were quite... enthusiastic."

"Yes. That's because of the bond." Jason leaned closer to his brother over the armrest. "Nicholas, it's indescribable. It's like for the first time you're experiencing real closeness with another living being, the first time you're not ashamed of what's going on in your head because someone sees you in your entirety."

"Let's hope the fleet admiral doesn't think you sound like some lunatic or drug addict," Nicholas said, doubtful.

"I'll take your word for it that Click communication is impressive, but remember, Hannibal von Solheim is considered a pragmatist, an old-school hard-ass and out-and-out ascetic, not exactly an empathic aesthete."

"But he's also considered very correct and principled. I've always imagined him as unpretentious."

"Then I hope you're right. We'll know a lot more in a moment." Nicholas pointed to the circular docking bulge they were approaching before Silly swung the shuttle 180 degrees and finally handed control over to the pilot software.

"So, here we are," the *Oberon*'s CO said lightly, though there was a hint of tension evident on her face.

"You shouldn't have come along," Nicholas said anxiously.

"A commander takes responsibility for her decisions," she replied firmly. "That's what your father taught me, and he lived by it and made the *Oberon* what it is today. I don't intend to throw those principles out the window. My choices were my choices and I stand by them. I will not hide behind my crew."

"Von Solheim has no leverage whatsoever against the *Oberon*. She's one of the few remaining warships in the system and by far the most powerful. He'll know that."

"If this is going to work," she said, gesturing with a thumb over her shoulder without looking toward the aliens, "we need to send every sign we can to make it clear that we mean business and believe in an outcome. And could there be a better one than my personal presence here?"

Nicholas didn't answer, just contorted his face as if he were in physical pain.

"Daussel has everything under control," she assured him as a jolt went through the shuttle and several lights on the console jumped from yellow to green. "And if anything should happen, you'll do fine."

Nicholas remained silent.

"Thank you," Jason said, and Silly seemed surprised. "Thank you for believing in it and committing to this plan."

"It's the only plan possible."

"That makes your commitment to its success all the more important."

Silly nodded curtly, then rose and walked along the cordon formed by legionnaires and Clicks. As she passed, she nodded to Mother and Inseminator before stopping in front of the ramp bulkhead just as it began to open.

Excitement, Mother transmitted, and Jason sensed turmoil surging within her. He could hardly blame her. He only had to recall how he had boarded her flagship with his delegation. Into an absolutely alien environment and into the hands of what had been their archenemy, not knowing what result he would bring back, if he ever came out again.

"We guarantee your safety. And if we can't, we will go down with you. But the fleet admiral is not a barbarian and not blinded."

Confidence. I hope for a solution.

"It will not be easy, but it is possible," he thought, unable to hide his concern that the Clicks' minimal demands might be extremely difficult for the Admiralty to swallow.

As the bulkhead opened with a hydraulic hiss and the

ramp descended, condensing gases from the vent valves blocked their view. The steam dissipated slowly, giving them time to catch their breath before they had a clear view of their reception committee.

In a large hall built for diplomatic ceremonial, when important personalities such as the leaders of core worlds or great trade magnates came to visit, an impressive display met them. Star-spangled banners with the eagle-and-sword crest of the Terran Federation hung from the lavishly high ceilings, and on the walls were ten-meter-high standards of the various strike groups with their own symbols and badges of honor.

Several hundred heavily armored Marines with angled Gauss rifles formed two tapering formations. At their narrow ends stood three individuals who had to be at least fifty meters from where Jason was standing. He recognized Fleet Admiral von Solheim by his tall, slender figure. Behind him were a half dozen cadets holding the flags of the admiralty aloft, which fluttered in the light breeze of the air conditioning.

A young sergeant stepped forward, held a small pipe to his lips, and played an ascending triad.

"Permission to come aboard?" Silly asked following protocol since space stations were treated as ships in the fleet. Her voice carried far on invisible microphones and echoed throughout the hall.

"*This reception is honorable,*" Jason explained over his bond to Mother.

I comprehend. Her slight apprehension at the sight of so many warriors and insignia dissolved somewhat under his admiration and the pride that such a sight would involuntarily inspire in any soldier.

"Permission granted," rang the Fleet Admiral's reply, and they walked down the ramp to the deck of the sky fortress and made their way to their host. Mother and Inseminator followed behind them, between the two files of legionnaires and Click soldiers. Out of the corner of his eye, Jason saw that the space station Marines remained motionless as clay figures, though they were certainly anything but still behind their featureless armor.

Five paces from the admiral and his two companions were Admirals Legutke and Saunders, who flanked von Solheim. Silly raised a hand and the two honor guards stopped. At two paces in front of the three, she stopped and snapped a salute.

"Captain Silvea Thurnau reporting as ordered, accompanied by Commander Nicholas Bradley and Lieutenant Commander Jason Bradley." They both saluted before stepping to the side. "We bring with us the negotiators from the other side, optimistic broodmother, egg-laying importance, beautiful brightness ray and mighty warrior, octopus-devourer, wise authority," Silly declared, and if the admirals found these names, strangely comical in pronounced form, or even amusing, they didn't let on. Instead, they nodded seriously to the aliens and with undisguised tension.

"Thank you. Captain Silvea Thurnau, you are under arrest until further notice for multiple counts of insubordination," Fleet Admiral von Solheim said sternly. He waved and two Marines stepped forward and handcuffed her with taser cuffs.

"Wait a minute!" Jason blurted, but Nicholas put a hand on his arm. Silly shook her head.

"Do you have something to say, Lieutenant Commander?" Admiral Saunders asked with open belligerence. "There are still rules that apply to everyone and that we abide by at Fleet, believe it or not."

Jason looked at von Solheim, whose expression was as featureless as a smoothly polished stone. Legutke, on the other hand, even more slender and bonier than his superior, showed a trace of disapproval. Apparently, he disagreed with the way the *Oberon*'s commander was being treated. Or maybe Jason was imagining it out of pure wishful thinking.

He addressed the fleet admiral and pointedly ignored Saunders. "Admiral, if it weren't for Captain Thurnau, we wouldn't be here now. Punishing her for that is—"

"Careful, young man," Saunders growled at him like a dog.

"What?" he asked sharply. He knew he was on thin ice, but the injustice of the moment, together with Saunders's condescending arrogance, enraged him so much that he didn't care about the possible consequences. After all, they could hardly conduct negotiations without him, and that should have been clear, even to that blowhard. "Do you want to negotiate with the broodmother yourself? Based on your *extensive experience*?"

"That—" the admiral started. His face had visibly reddened, but von Solheim signed him to be silent with a very discreet gesture.

"That's enough now, Lieutenant Commander. I understand your frustration, but we don't know what these nego-

377

tiations will result in, nor what fate will befall Terra. Based on the current facts, Captain Thurnau has violated direct orders several times, and at crucial moments in the battle. We are not a band of pirates, but the Terran Federation Fleet." The tall admiral possessed an aura of authority that seemed to fill the entire room. "And we abide by rules as long as they are valid and can be applied. That's more than I should have to explain to a Fleet officer, and it's the last time I'll do it. Do you understand?"

"Yes, sir," Nicholas replied quickly, nudging Jason. Silly remained stoic as she was led away, though Jason imagined she had nodded ever so slightly at him.

"Understood, sir," he reluctantly relented.

"Good, then we will now begin our discussions." Von Solheim took a step forward and bowed his head slightly to the two Clicks, a balanced diplomatic gesture, well-measured, not too much but not too little either, Jason had to acknowledge, at least from a human point of view. "I welcome optimistic broodmother, beautiful brightness ray of warm layers and mighty warrior, octopus-devourer, wise authority to the home base of the Terran Fleet."

Jason translated by keeping his bond open with Mother, who had assured him she would share everything unfiltered with the supreme inseminator. It was easy for him, after all, he didn't have to do anything but listen. His inner reactions to what he heard came by themselves and flowed to her. So did his assessment of the admiral's formalities and gestures, as well as his astonishment at hearing the words that came closest to the names of the two aliens, though they represented an almost criminal assault of the complexity that really lay behind them. It struck him how great his responsibility was, but also his importance to this meeting, since everything that emanated from von Solheim and the two aliens passed through him, as if through a filter.

For the first time, the power and obligation made him nervous.

Sad-Angry-Motherless has a high moral standard, he felt Mother think and had to smile at the Click version of his name, that sense of self that came from someone else. It was still as confusing as the first time.

"Lieutenant Commander?" Von Solheim looked at him questioningly. The two Clicks mimicked the fleet admiral's implied bow.

"Mother and Inseminator—those are their titles, for simplicity—thank you for the invitation."

"They told you that telepathically?"

"'Told' is the wrong word. When the bond is open, everything is open, their entire inner life. They amplify and weaken certain aspects to make something clear, but otherwise it's like seeing an open book, except the contents as a whole are always completely apparent. They don't have to sort it or think about it," Jason explained.

"Fascinating," von Solheim said. "Really fascinating. If I hadn't read your senior officers' reports and if the two emissaries weren't standing in front of me, which would have been unthinkable just hours ago, I would say you were crazy."

"It's hard for me. After an hour, I won't be able to maintain contact because the headache will be too bad," Jason said to encourage haste. Besides, it was the painful truth. "Our brains seem capable of their kind of telepathic connection but are not entirely adapted to it."

It could also result in brain damage, the thought flashed through his mind, but future scientists and reality assessors would have to figure that out, as well as ways to make communication more bearable.

"Tell Mother and Inseminator that they are under my protection here and no harm will come to them. If you need anything or are disturbed about anything, you are to let me know. I am aware of the explosive nature of this meeting, as well as the many pitfalls that an exchange between two alien species inevitably involves in every word and gesture. I'm sure we can work around them if we are honest with each other."

"They agree and feel gratitude. I mean, they express their gratitude."

"That fast?"

"The moment you speak a word, they feel my interpretation and the concept behind it. There's no delay."

Von Solheim raised a brow and nodded slowly. "Please follow me."

The fleet admiral stepped aside and gestured to the door, where two Marines briskly moved into guard positions. He led them down a long corridor—their parade almost absurdly pompous under the circumstances—to an elevator that carried only the three admirals, himself with Nicholas, and the two Clicks. They ordered their guards to stay behind, who accepted the instruction without hesitation.

The silence in the cabin grew uncomfortably thick until at last the elevator's relieving *pling!* sounded, and the door opened onto a short hallway. At its end was a conference room adorned on one side with the three flags of the Terran

Federation, the Fleet, and the fleet admiral's personal seal in the center, and on the other side were three more, apparently printed in short order, that showed the Clicks' homeworld, the one at Attila, as they had assumed it to be.

The gesture has a well-intentioned motive, Mother thought, dispelling his brief sense of shame. **Aquamarine is our most important industrial and military center. I am relieved that you could not attack and destroy it.**

"Your brood is growing there," he noted with fright.

Yes. Cause for relief.

The two Clicks positioned themselves on one side of the room and the three admirals at the other. Clearly, they had thought that normal chairs might pose an anatomical problem for the aliens, so it was reverent and courteous that von Solheim had decided to stand as well. Now the negotiations began, and Jason's temples were already protesting with a quiet throbbing.

29

"You want *what*?" Admiral Saunders blurted.

"Admiral," Jason explained. "You have been engaged in a massive effort to save, or rather rebuild, our oceans for over a week."

"They brought a colonization fleet!"

"No, they brought the necessary chemicals and microbes to make the oceans habitable for them. Oceans, I would note, that we have turned into toxic broths more like diluted lye than what was once Earth's greatest habitat."

"It's the same thing!"

All along, Saunders had been talking loudest and most, while Legutke merely listened with his fingertips placed together. Von Solheim merely asked a question now and then.

I wonder if they colluded. A conversational strategy in which Saunders played the blustering, demanding one and von Solheim would interject from time to time and pretend to concede a little. Good cop, bad cop?

"It's not the same. They could have bombed us, but

that's not in the Clicks' interest," Jason said. "That's because they dislike eradicating habitats. In their moral sense, it's not their place to be destructive to ecosystems. They even destroy their own eggs if too many are fertilized and calculations show that the respective biosphere cannot feed them, or that other species would be wiped out. We have been their enemies, so far, and they have made sure that we are incapable of fighting, but—"

"No buts. They crippled us, and the people of Terra would have starved or suffocated over time. They must have known that."

"Yes, and may I remind you that this is war, and our plan with Iron Hammer, was to reduce their suspected homeworld to rubble?" Jason looked from the two Clicks standing motionless on his left to the three admirals on his right and then across to Nicholas, who was conspicuously restrained. He was probably still pondering Silly's fate and what it might mean for him, the *Oberon*, and their future. Saunders's face flushed, whether because of Jason's lecturing tone or the fact that he was talking so freely about the most secret operation in the history of the Fleet in the presence of the enemy. Perhaps the admiral didn't yet understand that there really were no secrets in the telepathic band over which the aliens communicated.

"We are not giving up Terra," von Solheim said resolutely. "It is the cradle of humanity, our cultural and evolutionary heritage. We could never just abandon it to an alien species. The societal implications would be tantamount to suicide."

Jason turned to Mother and Inseminator.

384

Incomprehension, she transmitted. **Water habitat is not inhabited by people. Why do they feel offended?**

"Pride, I think."

Mother tried to understand the concept, looking for correspondences in her own experience, and came up with the feelings she felt toward her hatched offspring, who were healthy and strong, a product of her DNA, and her care as a broodmother. She had trouble applying the concept to other things, though, like her home planet.

"Admiral," he tried to explain, "the Clicks left their homeworld a century ago because it was devastated by Species X. They were afraid to return. In that respect, I think they have a much more pragmatic attitude when it comes to the survival of their society. They've never tried to recapture Lagunia in all this time only because we've been occupying their legacy. They have taken no offense at that."

"I guess what you're saying, Lieutenant Commander," Admiral Legutke said, speaking up for the first time, "is that we shouldn't merely apply our standards to these negotiations, but theirs as well. An exchange of the... *glasses* we look through, if you will."

Jason understood that the man with the Francophone accent was speaking primarily to his two colleagues and not to him, but he nodded politely to keep up appearances.

"We inhabit their former homeworld, all they ask is that they be allowed to claim the oceans of Terra, which we don't inhabit or use anyway."

"That's going to be a tough sell, kid," Saunders grumbled.

Coldhearts see habitable celestial bodies as posses-

sions, Inseminator noted with astonishment. **How is that possible?**

"The water people of warm depths see no offense in this demand, as they do not consider planets as something that can be possessed. To them, complex ecosystems are their natural habitat and cannot be owned."

"But they do claim their worlds."

"No. They protect their descendants. They see each world they defend as a breeding ground, a place where their offspring can hatch and mature before traveling to the stars or spending their lives in the depths where there are hot geysers. Their claim is always to their breeding regions and the protection of their brood, not to the entire ecosystem or even an entire solar system," Jason said, explaining what he was receiving from Mother and Inseminator.

"It's the same thing!" Saunders said.

"Like the Native Americans," Legutke said, though it seemed his colleague had something else to add.

"Now, what's that supposed to mean?"

"As white settlers moved westward from the American east coast, serious differences in attitudes toward land and property became apparent. Our ancestors occupied the regions where they roamed and hunted buffalo and issued them letters transferring 'ownership' of those areas to the United States. In exchange for signing, the tribes usually received money, alcohol, and weapons, yet they could not even understand what they were signing. It was often argued that they had not been forced to agree, and that may be true in some cases, but the whites could not imagine that the Native Americans did not have a recorded legal system and saw themselves as part of the land, a brushstroke in the overall painting. To them, nature was not something that could be owned because *they* belonged to nature. So how could you sell what you were?" Legutke pointed to the two aliens in their pearlescent armor. "At that time, a fundamental difference in viewpoints became apparent and the very possibility of comprehension was still lacking. Whites simply considered the natives uneducated and uncivilized. Conceptual thinking is not a constant. It is dependent on culture. I think that here we are also dealing with such a difference, one even more fundamental but quite analogous. We should keep that in mind."

Von Solheim looked to his subordinate and appeared thoughtful. Saunders's expression hardened even more.

You feel like your species is the evil in this conflict and ours are the misunderstood 'good guys,'" Mother translated his feelings, seeming confused.

"*Yes,*" Jason admitted. "*We are stubborn, violent, and mendacious, and you are nature-oriented, honest, and pragmatic.*"

That is a misperception. We started this war, not you. Our first contact ship crews acted too rashly when they detected an activating ring structure on space sonar. We killed a peaceful research vessel and all its reality assessors on board, which you hold in high regard and associate with peace, because we did not question ourselves. We reacted with violence at first contact with another intelligent conscious species out of concern for our broods. This was a selfish mistake, and we now realize that you understandably viewed us as a great aggressive threat to your civilization. In addition, there are ongoing wars between our broods

over fertilization rights, resulting in the death of many eggs, while your species strives to create peace among yourselves, despite great cultural differences that have the potential to divide you.

Jason thought about what he felt and could see the sense in it. Nevertheless, it was difficult not to feel like a dull animal in front of the telepathic greatness of these two beings.

Without your attempts at peaceful communication on my shuttle, I would not now be at this stage of the cycle and would have become a painful loss to my people. Your commander gave up her future to make these negotiations possible, Inseminator added. Your self-assessment seems unrealistically harsh to me.

"Lieutenant Commander?" von Solheim broke in.

"Yes, sir?"

"Perhaps there is a compromise. There are several worlds of the Clicks that we know harbor large land masses. How would Mother and Inseminator feel if we decided on some kind of exchange as a basis for continued peace? They colonize the Terran seas, and we colonize resource-rich, habitable continents on one of their worlds."

"Sir," Saunders objected, "we cannot give aliens permanent, free access to our economic and cultural center! The impact on the economy and morale of our forces would be devastating."

"Sol's economy is virtually nonexistent," Legutke reminded him casually. "As is most of the Fleet. As paradoxical as it sounds, now may be the only opportunity to usher in a paradigm shift and peace, because the Fleet will have to be fundamentally rebuilt."

"What is a fleet worth in peacetime?"

"Human life. I'm aware that our influence may wane and our funds minimized, but there's still Species X out there, an unknown enemy that even the Clicks are fighting, or have fought. So, you won't have to worry about lack of work, Michael. Basically," the lanky admiral continued, "the fleet admiral's proposal is a classic one: The establishment of diplomatic missions on each other's shores, except that the respective embassies, with extraterritorial rights, are continents or oceans, as the case may be."

Jason was taken aback by the cogency of Legutke's remarks and the calmness with which he delivered them. Von Solheim seemed to agree and nodded curtly.

"That's my proposal."

"That said, we are not conducting these negotiations from a position of strength," Legutke added.

"Which is due to the intervention of Captain Thurnau," Saunders indicated. "Otherwise, our position would look significantly different."

"No," Jason contradicted the stout admiral. "In that case, these talks wouldn't have happened at all because Mother and I would be dead. The war would have gone on and we would have lost."

"You may think that, *Lieutenant Commander*, but the way I see it, you're a logistics officer who—"

"Enough," the fleet admiral intervened and turned to Mother and Inseminator. "Do you agree with this proposal?"

Agreement, both transmitted.

It wasn't much of a concession for them because they didn't have to fear a powerful human fleet, most of which might have been destroyed by Species X, and they had no interest in land masses. But Jason kept that thought to himself. After all, he sensed no ulterior motives or hidden strategies through the bond, only the joy at the prospect of having found a new breeding ground for their offspring.

EPILOGUE
WAR AND PEACE

Nicholas stood in his father's cabin and gazed at the pictures that hung beside the bed. One was of their family on their last picnic in the park outside Harbinger Palace. The war had still been a distant affair, real but relegated to places less fortified than their core world, which was poised to eclipse Terra thanks to Omega's ever-faster rate of technological progression. But destiny was not a river that followed a well-worn course, a constant stream that inevitably flowed into the sea. It was more like an avalanche, unpredictable and subject to its righteous power.

Next to it hung the photo of that strange woman his father had never spoken about, except to say that she reminded him of an important lesson he had learned from one of his biggest mistakes. There were three other photos. One showed his and Jason's mother in her uniform as a captain in the Harbinger fleet, bearing the dark bird of prey and the Terran crest next to it. She was barely smiling, which was probably because it was her official file photo. Someone who did not know Konrad Bradley would probably not have noticed that the choice of this particular picture did not justify the suspicion he was an emotionally cold man. On the contrary, Nicholas recognized in the slightly raised corners of her mouth what made her tick: an unshakable optimism, coupled with an undeniable rebelliousness which was concealed in the hint of a smile, one which, if it had been any more obvious, would have exceeded the parameters for biometric file photos. Below it, he saw a picture of himself on his first promotion to lieutenant and one of Jason at his graduation from the Academy on Eden. How their father had obtained the photo remained his secret.

"I still want to hate him," Jason said just after he stepped up beside him. Nicholas hadn't even heard him enter. "But now that he's dead, I miss him. Back at the Academy, I was able to mask that feeling with my anger, but now that I know I'll never be able to see him again, I'm ashamed."

"We usually don't appreciate what we have until we lose it."

"We will avenge him, brother dear." Jason put an arm around his shoulders. It felt light. Nicholas looked down at the hand next to his chin and then back at their family photo.

"We will," he breathed. "Where do you think we go from here?"

"Negotiating the details won't be easy because the underlying concepts are so different. The most important thing is the unconditional will for peace. We have that of necessity and the Clicks from a lack of interest in our subjugation or annihilation. They are not interested in our worlds."

"Our soldiers, the ones on the *Oberon* I mean, will not find it easy to accept that. They all lost their families and friends to the Clicks' attack."

"That was never their intention."

"Explain that to our officers and crewmen," Nicholas said. "They hate no one more than the Clicks for what they did to us. Your twelve emissaries have done little to change that, and now they're pleading like addicts to reconnect with the aliens. The crew believes they've lost their minds, and I'm beginning to believe it, too."

He saw an alien gleam in Jason's eyes and sighed. *He longs for it himself. Of course.*

"The exiles hate them even more. One of them killed our father, and they hated Omega, while the Clicks were mere faceless enemies."

"Are," he corrected his brother. "For most of us, they still are, and the Exiles are far away, or long since history."

"Maybe," Jason muttered.

Nicholas abruptly changed the subject. "The Clicks aren't going to help us liberate the core worlds, are they?"

"No. They will not sacrifice their fleets to recapture the spirits we summoned. They're afraid of the 'nightmare elementals,' as they call them."

"Hellcat claims to have seen 'demons' according to his report." He sighed. "I can't blame them. To think that after a tentative first peace they'd use their own ships to bail us out because our plan to destroy their homeland went awry would be too much of a good thing, I guess; just too good to be true."

"As far as that goes, I guess we're on our own. But at least Terra is liberated again and we're alive. That's the best situation for making a difference. The *Oberon* is still flying and it's the superstar in the brand-new Trans-Luna space dock."

Nicholas smiled faintly. "Since you're already here, I guess the official peace treaty will be signed today?"

Jason nodded but seemed less free than he should, considering that he had been working toward it for several days.

"What is it?"

"There's something else that's very important and will determine our next step—*your* next step as captain of this ship."

"Acting captain," he corrected his brother grimly, trying not to think about the fact that Silly had always insisted on that distinction, too, until his father had been killed and she couldn't hide behind that anymore.

Jason didn't elaborate. "There is a way to contact Omega's data store."

"No, there isn't." Nicholas shook his head. What was wrong with his brother? Omega was dead, destroyed, its planet-spanning artificial neurons cut off and burned in the hellfire of lunar fragments. The memory core was worthless even if they could get access to it, which was absolutely impossible without the access codes. And those had died with their father, erased from this universe.

"Yes, there is," Jason insisted. "But for you to understand why, I have to ask you to stay very calm right now, the rational, controlled Nicholas."

Nicholas turned away from the pictures and looked at

his brother, only to see a shadow standing next to them out of the corner of his eye. Startled, he wheeled around and saw a nondescript figure in black combat fatigues just stripping off a chameleon cloak that flickered with his movements, reflecting the surroundings like shattered glass.

"YOU!" he shouted when he recognized the cold look on the narrow face. He had drawn his pistol before he even thought about it, but Sirion had already disarmed him, broken the weapon into its component parts, and dropped it before Nicholas even realized what the swirling shadow in front of him was doing.

"I just want to talk," the killer said tonelessly, and Nicholas noticed the cold eyes slide to where the photos hung. Something in the dark pupils changed.

"And I want to kill you, murderer!" He literally spat out the words as he was overcome by rage fueled by grief, grief that this inhuman had robbed him of his beloved father. A cold-blooded and calculating machine who was concerned only with achieving his goal: to kill his father.

"Wait!" Jason shouted, shaking his head as if trying to figure out for himself what had just happened and why a gun's components were lying on the floor. "You have to listen to him!"

"I don't have to do anything! That monster killed Laura and tried to kill Father!"

"Yes," Sirion admitted freely, dodging the blow Nicholas threw directly at his nose. As his knuckles flew through air and he stumbled, Jason caught him and held him back while the killer calmly appraised him and stared again at the photos.

"Just take a good look!" Nicholas snarled hatefully. The

feeling was so overwhelming that he hadn't grasped it fully before the words crossed his quivering lips.

"He wasn't lying," Sirion said softly, and his cold aura lingered, lowering the temperature of the room by a few degrees. Yet the emptiness in his eyes flickered with a hint of confusion and something Nicholas knew all too well about himself and would never have expected in this man, uncertainty.

"What are you talking about?" Jason grunted, groaning under the effort of holding him back.

"He told me there was a picture of my mother hanging next to his bed," the killer explained. "I detected no deceit in his voice, and yet I had doubts." He reached out a hand and almost touched the picture of the woman in ship's overalls looking belligerently at the camera. Just before his fingers met the plasma glass, he jerked back as if burned.

"What are you doing?" Nicholas grumbled at his brother, ceasing his attempt to break free now that the initial rush of anger was subsiding, and the hatred was cooling to something harsher. Jason's grip loosened a little.

"He was trying to save Dad."

"Bullshit!"

"It's true," Sirion said, so emotionlessly that any suggestion of a lie evaporated. Nicholas wondered if this killer even needed to lie. "I wanted to kill him more than anything." His gaze wandered into the distance. "But he changed something in me. I don't apologize for it. He killed my mother and destroyed her heritage, made me an orphan in the industrial stations around Artros. Still, I respect the wishes of a dead man who taught me something important by entrusting to me, his worst enemy, with what he should not have entrusted to anyone."

"The codes to Omega's data storage," Nicholas breathed, and all his hatred was now shrouded in a cloud of disbelief. His thoughts raced. Was this even possible? His father had not given those codes to anyone, not even to him. His most solemn oath to their commander-in-chief, the AI that was destroyed, had kept him from doing so. That he had betrayed this most sacred commitment to this hired assassin, of all people, could only mean a few things. What had happened to that woman in the photo had imposed some great burden on him and he'd extricated himself from it in his final moments with a show of trust that transferred the burden to this killer. This had flattered Sirion, and yet also compelled him to undertake a mission, provided he was as principled as his father believed him to be. *This* mission. A brilliant move, or a desperate one. And now this man stood before him.

"I have decided to give the codes only to you two, his descendants. You shall decide what to do with them," Sirion said. "And with that, I free myself from it. He gave them to me verbally and I'm giving them to you verbally so no one can find them on any data storage device. So, listen carefully because you will never see me again."

"I won't thank you for it." Nicholas looked somberly at him.

"Your anger won't help you," the killer replied, and Nicholas sensed there was more to that statement than his words suggested, much more that came from some unfathomable depth. "Should my death bring you relief, rest assured that he who lives by the sword will die by the sword.

Now listen if you ever wish to have access to Omega's data store."

～

Sirion disappeared, and they were silent for a while. Nicholas tried to figure out what their new knowledge meant, what doors it opened, and whether those doors should be opened at all.

"I want him to die," he whispered more to himself, but Jason heard.

"He has one last score to settle, I think, and someone like him doesn't walk off the stage until he succeeds. I've been observing him, and I don't see what power in this universe could stop him."

An intrusive whine from the telephone receiver beside the bed snapped them out of their somber mood. They both reached for the receiver. Nicholas wanted to let Jason go first, a kind of Pavlovian reflex as a younger brother, but he pulled back and shook his head.

"Captain?"

Nicholas grimaced and picked up the phone.

"Yes? Thank you. Put it right through." He hung up and pointed to the large display behind the desk that now showed the image of a female news announcer from the prime feed. She was wearing a high-collar jacket with a Terra badge on one lapel. Receiving a clear image, any at all, felt strange, though the Click blockade hadn't lasted that long.

"Breaking news" ran from right to left on an intrusive ticker tape at the bottom of the screen.

"... Fleet Admiral Hannibal von Solheim went before

the press," the announcer said just as her image was replaced by live film footage in the sky fortress press room. Any Federation citizen would recognize its unfurled banners and the deliberately rough steel wall behind them.

"Dear comrades, dear Federation citizens," intoned von Solheim, the eagle-faced image of a Prussian aristocrat. "Before we brief you today on the progress of peace negotiations with the Water People of the Warm Deeps, I wish to announce a decision that is both personal and professional. Effective immediately, I am resigning my position as fleet admiral."

Off-camera, a murmur went through the assembled members of the press. The fleet admiral waited patiently behind his desk, without showing the slightest emotion, then continued.

"A series of misjudgments and false assessments of the overall situation has reaffirmed my resolve to abide by a maxim that I have always wanted to exemplify and do so now: to act always for the good of the Federation and the women, men, and children who live in it. It is not the office that should define me, but my ability to follow that maxim to the best of my ability. This I can no longer do to my satisfaction. I will be honest with you, I am not a man of politics, but a man of war, and I was chosen for this post as such. Now, however, a time of politics and peace is dawning, and for this we need someone else. A calm, diplomatic person who can think outside previous doctrines and has the foresight to free himself from old prejudices that held me when they should not have. As my last official acts, therefore, I have ordered that Captain Silvea Thurnau be reinstated and that the *Oberon* be named flagship of the Sol

Fleet. As my successor, I have appointed Admiral Legutke on a provisional basis and hope that the parliamentary defense commission will permanently agree to my recommendation. He is the right man for the job, and I will actively support him. We need peace, and for that, we need Legutke, along with all of you out there. Don't give up, look ahead to a new future. It will require some sacrifices from each of us, but it also promises light at the end of our long darkness. Thank you."

The voices of the journalists rose like a storm as von Solheim first took a step back and then turned on his heel. Legutke came into the picture, and the two men gave each other textbook salutes and shook hands.

"Silly is free," Jason said in surprise. "The *Oberon*! The flagship?"

"A smart move." Nicholas nodded, yet his relief at Silly's release and reinstatement ebbed as he saw through von Solheim's last official act. "Our flagship status is a superficial promotion, an honor, and a political achievement that vividly signals change. But it also forces us under the direct and close supervision of the new fleet admiral and puts us in charge of the Fleet remnants still in Sol."

Jason's glee faded. "A golden bit in our mouth."

"Yes. But Legutke seems like a good man. Let's wait and see."

"We have to get to Harbingen with the codes, you know that."

"Yes," Nicholas said, sighing before turning off the screen with a gesture. "That's the life of an officer. One damned thing after another."

As if to punctuate his statement, the phone rang again and he yanked the receiver to his ear.

"Yes?" He listened to what Lieutenant Jung was telling him and frowned

"What is it?" Jason asked as Nicholas hung up.

"A ship from Lagunia has arrived and their captain, a certain Devlin Myers, wants to talk to Dad. He says he has secret information about Harbingen and Lagunia and the Clicks. It was quite confusing." Nicholas tasted the name on his tongue like a wine he hadn't tasted in a very long time. "I know that name. Ah... the *Quantum Bitch*. I did a routine check on that ship a few weeks ago when Dad sent me along to see what our Marines were doing on those missions."

"Secret information about Harbingen," Jason repeated, and they exchanged looks that left no doubt as to what the other was thinking.

Harbingen.

They would have to go back to Harbingen, and that realization was as electrifying as it was terrifying.

But not today. Not yet.

AFTERWORD

Dear Reader,

The journey of the *Oberon* will continue with the last, fourth volume, *Oberon Unleashed*.

If you enjoyed this book, I would be very happy if you could give it a star rating at the end of this e-book or write a short review on Amazon. That's the best way to help authors like me keep writing exciting books in the future. If you want to get in touch with me directly, you can do that. Just write to: Joshua@joshuatcalvert.com. I answer every email!

If you subscribe to my newsletter, I'll regularly tell you a bit about myself and my writing, and discuss the great themes of science fiction. Plus, as a thank you, you'll receive my e-book *Rift: The Transition* exclusively and for free: www.joshuatcalvert.com.

Warm regards,
   Joshua T. Calvert

Made in United States
North Haven, CT
23 May 2024

52752705R00243